1985

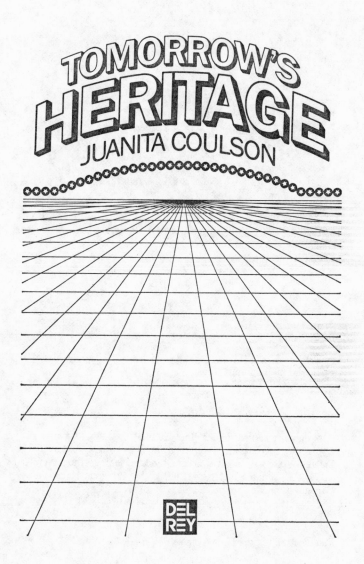

TOMORROW'S HERITAGE

JUANITA COULSON

DEL REY

With sincere gratitude for their help,
encouragement, and expertise to:
Terry Adamski, Harry J. N. Andruschak, and
Kay and Gary Anderson

TABLE OF CONTENTS

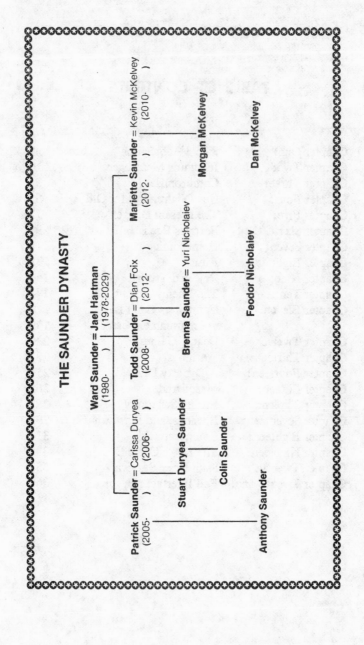

THE SAUNDER DYNASTY

Ward Saunder = Jael Hartman
(1980-   ) (1978-2029)

Patrick Saunder = Carissa Duryea
(2005-   )   (2006-   )

Todd Saunder = Dian Foix
(2008-   )   (2012-   )

Mariette Saunder = Kevin McKelvey
(2010-   )

Stuart Duryea Saunder

Brenna Saunder = Yuri Nicholaiev
(2012-   )

Morgan McKelvey

Colin Saunder

Feodor Nicholaiev

Dan McKelvey

Anthony Saunder

CHAPTER ONE

SIGNAL ACQUISITION

THE message terminal paged Todd very politely, and a dulcet-voiced Kenyan apologized for intruding. "Mr. Saunder, we have a confirm on your reservations aboard the orbital shuttle. Three ComLink executive passenger accommodations. Departure time 1815 hours today. Will that be satisfactory, sir?"

"That's fine. Thank you," Todd said. In fact, it was not fine. It was cutting very close the connections for the other two people who were going to ride the shuttle with Todd. The Alamshah Corporation PR man on the terminal knew that very well. A bit of sly underhanded dealing between economic rivals. Nairobi was Alamshah's territory, not ComLink's. And they weren't going to let ComLink's president forget that. The courtesy was a pleasant smoke screen. In the same carefully correct tone the PR man had used, Todd asked, "Have Dr. Foix and Chief Tech Isaacs checked in yet?"

There was a pause. Then, with thinly veiled regret, the man replied. "They have just arrived, sir." Todd suppressed a grin. So, despite the tricky scheduling, they would all make the shuttle flight without any trouble. The smooth voice continued. "They are debarking from the Central North American Union gate and should be up directly. Will there be anything else, Mr. Saunder?"

"No. All is in order. Please convey my appreciation to Haddad."

"We are always happy to cooperate, sir," the anonymous rival purred. "Have a pleasant journey." Ritual completed, he cleared the circuit.

Todd glanced impatiently at the elevator. It would take Dian and Beth a while to cross the spaceport's gigantic concourse and ride up to ComLink's executive suite. Nothing to do but wait. They would have two hours to spare before liftoff, anyway. Time to enjoy the view, and the view offered by a towering structure in a mile-high city was spectacular. The designer had installed a 360-degree outlook, so that Todd could see both Mount Kenya, prodding the clouds 120 kilometers to the north, and the rugged green hills on the west, where the Rift slashed through the continent. Planet-building in progress. And Nairobi sat at an altitude that was, figuratively, already partway up to an orbit that could girdle that world. Down range, to the southeast, Todd thought he could make out the distant haze that might be Mombasa and the ocean. Probably an illusion. They wouldn't be able to eyeball the port city until they took off.

When the elevator sighed open, Todd hurried to embrace Dian. Beth Isaacs grinned fondly at them and Dian finally broke free, pretending to gulp for breath. "You do make me feel missed." She laughed. "Absence makes the heart grow passionate, huh?"

Unrepentant, Todd smirked at her. Every time he touched her velvety skin and saw the mischievous sparkle in those dark eyes, he felt renewed. The feelings hadn't waned over the months. They had deepened, grown into something very much worth cherishing.

"How's the family, boss?" Beth asked with sincere interest. Like a great many people, she shared the Saunders' lives vicariously, fascinated by the famous clan.

Todd shrugged. "Great, at least the planetside bunch are. Pat's election campaign is racking up astronomical successes. Carissa's playing the part of the perfect candidate's wife. And Mother figures her boy has the whole thing sewed up." Dian peered up at him, feeling Todd's edginess. Finally he told them what was nagging at him. "Jael badgered me to bring Mariette home for the annual reunion. Dad's memorial ceremonies, the holidays, all that. Mari wouldn't come last year," he finished sorrowfully.

Jael Saunder's little chickens, leaving the roost, scattering and going their separate ways. That was normal. What wasn't normal were the widening philosophical differences among them, the fraying affections, old ties coming to pieces.

"Mari's just miffed because Protectors of Earth cut the Colony's funds again." Beth sounded patronizing as she said that. There were times when the chief Tech's loyalty bordered on chauvinism, embarrassing Todd. Beth's steadfastness was classic. For all the publicity Pat and Mariette gathered in their special careers and interests, for Beth telecommunications made Earth and its satellites go around—and her boss was the top man in that field. Argument concluded.

"Miffed hardly describes Mari," Todd said, smiling. "But . . . I guess I'll make the trip, if Mari takes my hint and extends the invitation. Haven't been up to Goddard for a while. Besides, I'd like baby sister to come home for Dad's anniversary myself. The reunion could be an excuse to mend some fences between her and Pat and Mother. Jael's right about that, at least."

Dian and Beth exchanged a look. "There's another reason for getting Mariette planetside at this particular time," Dian said.

Todd didn't dare believe. His gaze shifted from the lovely black woman in his arms to the tall tech and back again. "You've got an update?"

Dian nodded to Beth. His top translator and his top tech, friends and co-workers. Beth opened the case she was carrying and Todd watched closely, his heartbeat quickening. Beth set out a self-powered mini-viewer and inserted a data wafer. She was going to bypass the suite's fancy built-in monitors. This show was going to be strictly private, for an audience of three. Beth's bony face tightened with concentration as she cued the system. A series of printouts and images flashed on the small screen. Beth froze the image for Todd. The top part of the frame—the signal Dian and the others had sent out. The bottom part—response. The same binary pattern. But now it was rearranged in key areas to give the correct answer to a posed mathematical question. Todd wasn't in the women's league in decryption, but even he could see the startling proof in the results.

Stunned, he sank down, sitting on the edge of a desk, gawking at the screen. They had passed the test. More importantly, the other end of this communications linkage had passed *its* test. "It's there," he said shakily. "And it's intelligent."

Dian cradled her head on his shoulder, sharing his victory.
Beth's eyes glowed. She was a proud mother displaying her brainchild. Dian looked up at Todd. "You wanted us to keep at it until
we were absolutely, positively sure. We're sure. This last stuff we
broke down . . . no doubts. We shook it every possible way. And
we can prove everything."

Beth cued the monitor again. Another frame appeared. Todd
puzzled over the figures, and Beth took pity and explained.
"Those are course corrections, boss. It's fine-tuning and coming
about to bring itself right into the dock." Then she laughed at her
own nautical phrasing. Beth had received her earliest language
training working at Sea-Search Rescue, which used human and
dolphin teams. "It's funny; there's a lot of similarity in the way
this vehicle's correcting itself to the way the dolphins home in on
the human team members' signals. Interesting."

"Very," Todd agreed.

More than interesting. Phenomenal! Like being present at the
discovery of fire. Or, in his case, being the sponsor of the discov-
erers.

An alien messenger vehicle from the stars. Incoming. The implications were staggering. The vehicle was nearing Neptune's
orbit, moving steadily closer. And the traveler wasn't silent. Even
when they had first detected it, weeks earlier, the alien had been
broadcasting on a frequency to which no one else was listening.

Dian and Beth and Project Search had listened, and they had
captured fire and carried it home to Todd from the realm of the
stars. At first they had been cautious, hoarding the data, not
publishing. Not yet. Nobody wanted to jump to conclusions.
There had been so many disappointments, not only for Project
Search but for all its predecessors during the decades since
telecommunications had given mankind a way to talk to space.

Another intelligent species—or its machine! And history would
note that Todd Saunder, a scientific dabbler, a "mere" corporation president, was responsible for this first contact with a species
from a distant world. He had had the dream, and he had paid the
bills.

And what bills they had been! Robbing his own pockets to support the project. He hadn't beggared himself, as Mari was doing
to keep Goddard Colony viable. But he had had to do some fancy

juggling. He hadn't taken in outsiders. This was going to be his, all the way. There had been a lot of long, dry months. Funds going out of Todd Saunder's personal fortune, none coming back. None might *ever* return a profit. That didn't matter. What was on that little screen mattered.

His father's dream, and his, come true. Ward Saunder hadn't lived to see it fulfilled. But the continuity of family, of a family quest—that gave the triumph to father and son both. Todd shivered. His mouth had gone dry and he felt giddy, his heart beating like launch thrusters on full. The exhilaration was very much like being drunk. He almost laughed at the sensations.

"When are you going to release the data?" Dian asked.

Todd woke from the dream, seeing reality. Delivering the news. The world wasn't going to react to this wonder the way he had. Some would share his sense of awe and achievement. But a great many humans would panic. Inevitably, there would be cries of alien invasion.

Even Project Search had dealt with that possibility at the beginning. They all would have been fools not to recognize the atavistic fears that lurked in the human species. The very word brought on instinctual ripples of self-defense. Alien.

Hostile? Or friendly? The mood of Project Search's members matched Todd's. If any alien life form they contacted *were* hostile, there wasn't much they could do about it. And, as it turned out, the vehicle they were communicating with had been broadcasting before Project Search ever turned its ears that way. The only chance element had been *which* humans first spotted the signals coming in from some four billion kilometers out from the Sun. *Somebody,* eventually, was bound to hear the message and talk back to the vehicle. But because Todd's people had taken the risk and searched the right frequencies, the glory—and the terror, if they had guessed wrong—would be his.

He made up his mind. This had been thrashed out three years ago, at the start. He had mentally rehearsed the subsequent steps many times, not allowing himself to believe he would ever carry them out. Until now. "The year-end Global Science Council meeting. I'm a member. I'll put in a request to be included on the agenda. They'll think I'm going to read a paper on a new telecommunications breakthrough. They're right."

"We have to wait that long?" Beth squeaked in dismay. "That's weeks." She wanted to deliver their brainchild to the world right now.

Dian agreed with her. But she also saw Todd's point. "The data are solid. Next comes selling it."

He nodded. "I know how you both feel. I feel the same. But this isn't going to go down easy. We knew that. We've got to prepare ourselves to cope with the public. Just maybe I can get us the best salesman on Earth to trumpet the cause."

The women eyed him hopefully. Dian silently mouthed. "Patrick." Todd grinned an acknowledgment. His brother would be able to charm the paranoiacs out of their holes—if he could be convinced. Not all the scientists would likely take the data without an argument, either. There was a storm of backlash waiting ahead. Beth complained that the time of the big announcement was too far off. Suddenly, to Todd, it seemed much too close.

Dian rolled her eyes. "We've bottled this up so long already. All the other techs up on the sat network wonder why Beth and I and Wu Min and Anatole and the others spend so much time out on inspection shuttle runs."

"Just a little bit longer," Todd said with sympathy. "The hiding is almost over."

Data leaks. Critics could destroy Project Search if they had let loose unconfirmed data or announced too soon. A year ago, they had gone to security status, intensified it tenfold when the alien messenger's response started coming a few months later. No electronic relays from ComLink's satellites. None. It meant Dian and Todd and the others did a lot of tedious eyeball checks, riding out on long swings to Project Search's little orbiter to pick up the fresh data. And it meant frustrating delays between collection and decryption on safe terminals and comps. Lid on tight. No outsiders allowed. Not until the proofs were in. Checked. Double-checked. Redundancy and yet more redundancy.

And now they had confirmed it.

"Get me more," Todd insisted. "Everything you can. Pile it on. I don't care if it duplicates. I want it so convincing it'll cross the critics' eyes at that conference. We *can't* be solid enough." In the back of his mind was a horror—standing on the podium, an amateur getting in on his father's credentials, and world-famous scientists ripping his presentation to shreds. That possibility set his teeth on edge far more than the risk of the alien's hostility could. He looked searchingly at Dian. "Come to the family reunion with me this year? Please? It'll only be a day before the conference. I want you there. I . . . I'm going to tell them first. All of them together, the first ones to hear the news. It's important to me. Please?" he repeated.

Dian countered with another question. "What about Mariette? When you go up to Goddard, are you going to tell her then? She's a Spacer, too. She knows just what this means to all humanity."

"No." Todd didn't hesitate. "It wouldn't be fair. She has to learn when Pat and Mother do. Maybe, just maybe, this will pull us all together again. I hope to hell it does. Will you come with me?"

The brown eyes were veiled against him. For a moment Todd thought Dian would refuse. Then, to his great relief, she acquiesced. "Okay. We'll do it your way."

"Great! Thank you. Beth?"

"You're the boss," the chief tech said. "What's the schedule?"

"We go up to orbit on our regular tour. You and Dian and the others make one last pickup from Search's orbiter. Tie it tight. Every detail. I'll go fetch Mariette—or try to," he amended. Convincing his hot-tempered sister might be the toughest part of the whole plan. "With luck, I'll bring her back with me and we'll ride planetside together in a couple of weeks. Everyone. I want all of you up there on the platform with me at that Science Council conference. We share. Just as we have for so long."

Beth rubbed her eyes hard, looking acutely embarrassed. Dian covered for the older woman. "Teamwork. Big wrap-up. Okay. So we hoard it just a little bit longer. Personally, I think you ought to thumb your nose at the conference and tell the world yourself, now. ComLink's able to reach the whole planet and Goddard and the Moon. Simultaneous broadcast." She met Todd's steady look and smiled. "No, huh? Well, I'm outvoted. You're still paying, lover."

They decided to celebrate, now that the decisions were made. Two hours till launch. Time enough to dip into the suite's bar. The three of them toasted one another in a good vintage wine, left from the times before the Chaos, years when it seemed mankind might become extinct. They had survived that, made it through to better days. By the time they reached the dregs, they were mellow and sure the better times had just barely started. Project Search was on top of the world, and heading up and out. The sky was *not* the limit.

Neither was the Solar System.

The shuttle's attendants gave them a disapproving glare when they boarded. Beth was giggly, and Dian's sassy cracks were coming thick and fast. Todd greeted the crew jovially, then laughed at their expressions. He read the scorn there: "Foolish white man. Getting drunk before launch."

Drunk in more ways than one, Todd admitted, settling into his couch. Dian's dark fingers curled around his. Shared secrets. He was soaring, in free fall before the thrusters fired. He wanted to tell the attendants they were wrong. The old divisions among nationalities and colors and languages were vanishing. Soon they would be gone forever. They would be *Homo sapiens*. One genetic group, ready to meet a far different genetic product. It wouldn't matter then that Todd Saunder's paternal great-grandmother had traced her ancestry to the slave days. It would make no difference that his own genes were linked, distantly, to other Africans from the far side of this continent. The lines would dissolve.

He sobered, wishing no new lines to be drawn.

They couldn't let that happen.

So much to do. Go through the forms of a normal work routine. The data were still under wraps, and, like Dian and Beth, he would have to pretend nothing out of the ordinary was happening. See if Mariette would balk at his inviting himself to the habitat. Convince her. Get the presentation organized. Take Mari and Dian to Saunderhome. The conference . . .

So very much.

The deep roar of dynamic stress was building, pressing him down while the ship thundered upward, piercing the clouds. Arcing, slowly, slowly, ever rising. Views coming up on the individual passenger screens. Mombasa, fading to a dot. The immensity of the Indian Ocean, a sparkling pool. Dwindling below them.

And from this altitude, the perspective changed. He would eventually be able to see all of it.

And ahead, in the blackness above the atmosphere, the satellites of *Homo sapiens* waited.

Beyond it all, also waiting, there were stars.

CHAPTER TWO

✩✩✩✩✩✩✩✩✩

INCOMING MESSENGER

TODD realized he had read the same row of figures three times. His thoughts kept drifting away from his supervisors' year-end predictions. Giving up on the reports, he looked at the other screens lining the bulkheads around him. Their displays tapped his own ComLink Corporation and rival telecom networks, plus the offerings of the entertainment companies leasing those outlets. Fiction and fact, frivolous to grimly serious, the monitors showed humanity laughing at itself, weeping over its agonies, struggling to survive. Dramas, comedies, news from Earth and space . . . a documentary on the Trans-Pacific war, on medicine's fight against the neo-anthrax mutation and the rat invasions in the cities, on the damage wrought by the African volcanoes, on the "sports" tally of dead and injured in the controlled-violence arenas in South America and the Middle East.

And, of course, there was always politics. Campaigns like his brother's were heating up in the races for seats on Protectors of Earth's global council.

Todd cued the monitors, asking for a readout from the science satellites. ERS orbiters coordinated with ground and sea stations, painting Earth in a startling variety of colors and viewpoints. Some lenses showed red vegetation and yellow soil. Others traced foliage blight in angry blues or mapped pollution with brilliant greens and black. Civilian access to declassified military scanners

converted the globe into bright orange danger areas and safe purple and white ones, where plague and radiation had abated
enough to let life exist there once more. Other systems corrected
to human vision norms. On those monitors, a beautiful, cloud-
chased sphere floated in infinite blackness. Todd stared at those
views a long time.

Ident numbers in the corners of the screens noted the sources
for each scene. The science network borrowed from ComLink
and other commercial chains, continually updating, checking,
cross-filing. Twenty years ago, that hadn't been the case. When
the wars were at their worst, the monetary bases collapsing, national boundaries vanishing, new ones forming, the Death Years
and the Chaos reached out into space, destroying man's orbiting
eyes. A saner policy had risen out of the ruins. Now treaties guaranteed neutrality, at least in orbit. The satellite networks maintained a friendly, peaceful rivalry. Still, Todd noted with approval
that Saunder Enterprises' ComLink net was reading ninety percent optimal. His competitors' equipment and governmental
tie-ins needed tune-ups or replacement as often as not. Com
Link's output was unquestionably the best. After the space wars,
when he and his father had built ComLink, they had improved
greatly on the systems the missiles had wrecked. The readouts
showed the results.

Todd leaned back in his chair, smug, assessing. Vignetting and
sidelap on the ERS terminals—quite acceptable. High and low
orbiters and planetary stations working fine in tandem. Tireless
and patient, his corporation kept watch over the world and over
man, helping Earth communicate, educate itself, entertain itself,
and take its own pulse. Navstar GPS and ground-based tracking
systems regulated Earth's business and pleasure transportation.
Only military craft were masked against that guidance, their
jammers confusing the scans. ERS inventoried oceans and fresh
waters; crops; forests; animal and fish migration and harvest; the
fossil, nuclear, tidal, wind, and geothermal fuel supplies and output. With methodical disinterest, satellites counted the catch in
the Antarctic krill fisheries, syntha-food production, mining operations, blight, toxic dump seepage. Man-made changes on the
maps entered the records beside avalanches and tsunamis and
other events over which humanity had no control.

Thermal scans traced the extent of the Canadian, Siberian, and Scandian glacial breakouts. Drought regions, lands parched and needing the moisture bound up in that new ice, were marked. Floods, winds, missile strikes. On Earth's night side, lenses penetrated the darkness, cataloging the glowing dots that were population centers. The Tangshan quake, like the Upper Baltic conflicts and some plague areas, left vast sections of Earth lightless. On the day side, the enlarged Guinea Basin, a war aftermath, and the mid-continent engorgement of the Mississippi-Missouri Rivers caused by the New Madrid quake graphically demonstrated that man and nature could be equally cruel.

Looking at the immense, shallow lake on the face of old America, Todd felt a memory resurfacing. The family, together on a summer evening. One of the pleasant times, when Ward and Jael weren't quarreling, for once, and when her parents weren't picking at them all, increasing the friction. 2019—that was when they were living in the industrial towns rising out of the craters west of Chicago. Jael was holding seven-year-old Mariette on her lap, Todd remembered, and he remembered leaning on the chair, squeezing close to his mother, jealous of his sister's privileges as the youngest. Pat, fourteen years old and almost grown up, was looking over Jael's shoulder. Dad was sitting nearby, fussing over a design for one of his inventions. Jael's velvety soft voice read to them from a recently published book, describing how the world she'd known as a girl had just been torn apart and reshaped.

"You know what an earthquake is, don't you, Mari?" Mariette, drowsy and resisting sleep, nodded, trying not to suck her thumb.

Jael turned a page, and photos leaped at Todd. They were crude tri-di pictures, needing the still-to-be-created refinement of Ward Saunder's holo-mode patent to make them fully realistic. Yet they had tremendous impact on an eleven-year-old's imagination. Todd had gazed in morbid fascination at the camera's portrait of the catastrophe. The Earth's crust had shifted massively. Whole cities had been flattened into rubble, populations wiped out, fissures opened, highways ripped to pieces. The very land sank, forming an incredible depression across the continent's heart. St. Louis and many other cities simply ceased to exist. Water lines rose thirty meters at Louisville and Cincinnati and other river cities as the mighty Mississippi-Missouri system reversed and rushed to fill the newly formed lake bed. The dammed waters continued to spread, creating a shallow lake hundreds of kilometers long, altering the map beyond recognition. The book Jael held had been issued to bring the intelligent reader up to date on this change.

"Geologists said it was lots worse than the 1811 quake," Ward commented absently. "Tangshan's probably going to cut loose sooner or later, too, over in China. Plenty of shaky areas around the world due for surprises. Wonder who gets it next?" he speculated, aware of the grief natural phenomena caused, but insatiably curious. Todd remembered looking at his father, absorbing the words, sharing his father's inquisitive nature.

"Don't frighten the children," Jael said primly, cuddling Mariette closer.

Twenty-one years ago, yet the moment was vivid. Todd saw Pat's face as they both grimaced over Jael's protective remark. They weren't children, and they weren't scared. As if it were happening now, Todd felt the paper pages between his fingers, relived the amazement of years still earlier, when he had discovered that truth and fiction could be expressed in this form as well as on a vid screen. His mother's silky shirt brushed his arm as she reached to turn those pages. Her perfume tickled his nose. Pat's dark hair was close to Todd's as they looked at the pictures. Pat pointed out the text under one photo. The voice that was destined to become one of the world's most recognizable said, "They weren't ready for it, were they? If they'd been prepared, more might have survived."

"That's right, Patrick." Jael took the opportunity to point out a moral lesson. "You should always be ready for surprises, then you can handle them better."

Todd had wondered then how one got ready for an earthquake. But his mother sincerely believed the theory, and she taught Pat to believe it, too. How were they going to handle the surprise Todd was about to hand them? Nothing in their experience—in human experience—would prepare them for the event.

His attention returned to the present. The ERS scans were showing Earth's polar regions. The Arctic glaciers seemed smaller than last winter's, so maybe that problem was finally easing. The Antarctic was nearing midsummer, its weather as mild as it ever

got. Alone of Earth's continents, Antarctica had escaped the
heavy missile strikes and toxic dumps and radiation during the
Death Years and the Chaos. The renewed treaties of '91 and '21
had kept the bottom of the world neutral, just barely, a common
ground preserved from destruction. Navstar tracked a supply
plane crossing the glaciers, heading for the plateau's Pole of Inaccessibility. Incoming for Saunder Enterprises Antarctic Enclave,
maintaining that cryogenics facility's contact with the world. The
Enclave was a sub-glacial construction; there was little to see at
its location, little to mark the place where thousands of lives were
locked away in frozen sleep.

If only we'd had it operational before Dad . . .

Todd pushed the wish away. "Give me a view spaceward," he
cued the scans. "Pick up Goddard Colony and Lunar Base
Copernicus." Screens blinked. The huge lens carried by the sat
platform ComLink supplied to the Global Science Council
reached out and framed the Moon. Small detail was visible.
Comp arrows locked in on the military base and the research center nearby. Goddard, though, was too distant to define well. Todd
regarded the screens a moment, then canceled the comps' effort to
nail down the view precisely. He knew where Goddard was and
didn't need the arrows and grids to bracket it. Goddard Colony—
that faint, glowing speck, proof of human courage and faith, even
if most of its inhabitants scorned the wave of new mysticism
preoccupying much of Earth's population. "Beautiful," Todd
whispered. "I wish Pat could see things this way and know how it
is. *Really* see it." He didn't bother hoping the same for Jael. She
had made her attitude clear. She wasn't going to change. Pat,
though, could be persuaded. He *had* to be persuaded.

"Give me Earthward view, eastern CNAU and oceanic en-
virons." The screen blinked again and drew from the scans of
Geosynch Orbiter HQ. Lower satellites in ComLink supple-
mented to provide a complete picture.

The Atlantic was dark and peaceful, a blue-black canyon divid-
ing the continents. ERS deep-sea probes showed the mid-line
trench and seabed geothermal and mining activities. A could-be
hurricane was brewing off the Azores but didn't look troublesome
yet. Mapper scans drew lines, and idents marked the waters and
landmasses, adding appropriate tags to everything. At a distance,

the globe looked serene. Closer views showed irreparable scars. Atlantic Inlet was twice the size of old Chesapeake Bay. Monitors, relentlessly searching for data, showed the ruins under the waters. In the Caribbean, a scar left from the two-day conflict fifty years ago had separated Yucatan from the mainland. Todd was grateful that had happened before he was born. If it happened now, it would probably destroy the planetside haven he loved.

"Let's see Saunderhome." Zoom lenses took him in low over the Caribbean states of Central North American Union. The viewpoint narrowed to a cluster of natural and artificial islands, then tightened still more. The smoky haze which had obscured the area a week ago was dissipating. Apparently the minor volcanic eruption in the Windwards was over. Saunderhome was washed clean by tropical rain, a jewel-like tropical paradise of green vegetation and reefs and white sands connected by dainty bridges and underwater tunnels. Extreme close-up carried Todd in to twenty meters' elevation. He could see striations on the reefs, tell deep from shallow waters, follow groundskeepers and security guards riding or walking along the paths or bridges. Security guards. They hadn't needed them when they first lived at Saunderhome. They hadn't needed that many servants, either. They had been content to rough it.

"Shift north. Eastern continent view." Another collective blink from the monitors. Snow was falling through the Great Lakes, good for next spring's crops. Humanity was long overdue for a favorable climate shift back to "normal," whatever that was. None of the changes in this century had benefited mankind at all. Fog lay over CNAU from the Maritimes to the United Ghetto States enclaves in Michigan and Ohio and south below Atlantic Inlet. No problem. Like the infrared ERS satellites, ComLink could penetrate these weather conditions. In theory, Todd knew fog had caused telecom problems years ago. But thanks to Ward Saunder's genius, all that was history.

"You wouldn't believe all we've done with your inventions, Dad," Todd said. The monitors waited patiently for an order they could translate. "No, you probably *would* believe. In fact, you'd be enthralled. You were never afraid of the future. You'd think it was funny that they dreamed up a special name for family corporations like us. They call us quasi-nations. How's that? Monitor bank two, show Saunder holdings planetside."

There were enough displays to push the screens' capacity. The system gauged the in-flow and split signals, faceting the screens to accept a series of shrunken views. Saunder Enterprises rarely bought or leased dwellings or offices or vacation estates; it traded Ward Saunder's patents for financial power. As a result, Saunder enclaves dotted the globe. Offices, factories, syntha-food plants, fisheries, seabed mines, transit lines, telecom, energy . . . expanding every year. There were science-oriented SE enclaves, most of them churning out pure profit. SE Enclave was largely altruistic, operating at a loss. But it had gained favors from the contributing world governments for supplying that cryogenic storehouse: Saunderhome in the Caribbean; an Alpine mini-country of their own; a former billionaire's office building and bombproof underground apartment complex in New York–Philadelphia; branch offices in New Washington, Yokohama, and twenty other locations around the planet.

"Monarch?" Todd hadn't heard Dian come into the office. But he nodded and smiled, welcoming her now as she slid her tether line along the rail beside his chair. Her slender brown arm went around his shoulders.

"You mean, monarch of all I survey?" Todd returned her embrace. "Cancel and return to general ComLink net overview," he said in a toneless programmer's voice. The screens obeyed, once more displaying the standard fare. Todd looked up at Dian. "I'm just big brother's eyes and ears in the sky, so he can pull Earth's strings. No monarchs here."

"Huh! And good thing. Hey, ComLink *is* the strings. Without you, all those politicians, including your own brother, would be talking to themselves, not the voters. Might be a lot quieter down there if they did." Dian laughed softly at the idea.

"Ah, but it pays. 'You say it, we'll replay it, worldwide and all the way out to Goddard and the Moon. We'll translate it, and pretty you up, and make you sound like the savior of mankind. For a fat fee.' " Dian's dark stare forced Todd to ease off from the bitter tirade. "Ignore me. As a matter of fact, earlier I was trying to see Earth as if it were brand-new to me, wondering what I'd make of the view."

"Starting with the family's impressive properties?" Obviously, Dian hadn't missed the display of Saunder Enterprises' holdings.

Todd smiled sheepishly. "I'm a chauvinist, telling myself that the Saunders aren't such a bad example of what's been going on with *Homo sapiens* these past few years. It's odd that we never acquired a permanent property where things all started to take off for us . . ."

"In my territory, up by the Chicago United Ghetto States enclave," Dian said. "From a rickatick lab out in the '95 war craters to Saunder Enterprises. Pretty impressive." She was teasing again, but Todd didn't respond.

"Saunderhome's the earliest photo record Jael kept for us. She must have thrown away the other pictures. She kept some of Dad and us kids, but not of the places we lived. And so many of those I associate with Dad, with the five of us, trying to stay alive . . ."

Grief cut at him. Dian began kneading his neck and shoulders gently, working at the tension gathering there. She shifted with his body's reactions, coping expertly with the zero gravity. After a lengthy silence while she soothed his nerves, Dian asked, "You still planning to save the announcement?"

"Yes." Dian didn't stop the massage, but he could feel her impatience. He tried to crane his neck to look at her, but she pushed his head around face forward again, concentrating on a stubborn knot of muscles near his spine. "We've been through this," Todd reminded her.

"Okay. Risky. You sit on it too long, and it's somebody else's baby, not yours. You found it. You ought to have the credit for dropping it in the Science Council's lap first . . ."

"*We* found it."

"Ar-gue! Project Search *team,* huh?" Dian spit out the words with capital letters and sarcastic underlinings. "You paid."

"Don't bring that up. I'm still hurting from the tradeoffs it's costing me. It was worth it, though." Todd grunted as Dian popped loose a particularly nasty kink in his back. His voice was distorted by the pummeling she was delivering. "This isn't going to be simple. Never is. But now that we've got it, it's my job to untangle it. It's not enough just to put out a press release and then spell out the details for the Science Council in a couple of weeks. This reaches to Goddard and beyond. When the theocracies and

politicians get hold of it . . ." Dian made an obscene comment
and Todd chuckled. "Yes, but they will. It's going to be general
knowledge. The timing's the thing. I've got to try and get Pat's
help. So we wait." He hesitated for a moment. "Will Beth and the
others last until after the reunion?"

Dian's hands dug in painfully along his neck for a moment.
Then she resumed the massage, softening it to a caress. "They'll
wait. Trust."

"I do. But I know how it feels. Hell, the urge to blab the news
right now to the world is almost irresistible. I want to do it myself, and never mind waiting to share it with the family first."

"So?" Dian patted his shoulders, finishing her ministrations.
She floated around him and perched on the edge of the monitor
console. Her expression was wry.

"Just how do you suggest I make that announcement, Dr.
Foix?" Todd asked. "Just break in on their favorite entertainment
system or local news outlet? Our news is going to change everything radically, no matter how it's done. Our species is a masterpiece of contradictory reactions, anyway. Never more than right
now." He stared at the ERS views of Earth in space and chuckled
bitterly. "Look at it, so peaceful. The epitome of the new Spirit
of Humanity movement, cutting across religions, uniting the
believers down there. And the same beings still wage war against
each other, kill one another, even organize arenas where per-
formers and spectators both can be maimed and killed, just so the
excess violence gets boiled off from human society. How to break
the news? 'Hey, humanity, there's an alien vehicle headed this
way, a messenger from another intelligent species, one more powerful and advanced than we are. But I don't want you to get excited about this. Stay calm. Everything's going to work out
okay.' "

Dian cocked her head, her dark brown eyes glittering with the
joy and wonder of the discovery they had made. "You could do
it . . ."

"No, I'm no orator. And that's what it'll take—someone to
make them accept, keep down the fear, convince them the alien
will bring the wonderful future. I'm not that person. Most of
them have never heard of me. But if *Pat* . . ." Todd wondered if

he was making the decision on a superstitious base: If he pretended the scheme would work, maybe it would come true.

"No worries about converting little sis to the cause, huh?" Dian said slyly. "You know, this just might throw those wild-eyed secessionists at Goddard back on the tracks."

"Why not, as long as we're wishing."

Dian's pert features hardened. So did her voice. "Wishing. That's what it is and we know it. We can't hide what we've found, and we're going to trigger off a massive reaction. Hope against hope, some of them—a lot of them—are going to panic. They'll blow up the news and dress it in alien invasion stuff." She touched his face, communicating her willingness to share despite her cynicism. "But a first contact is going to take place. No stopping it, or you. You detected it, and you deserve the credit. If we're lucky, and there's someone in the future to write a history about this era, your name is going to get remembered. I want that."

"Take the long view," Todd said, reciting a phrase they had bandied back and forth for many months.

"Affirmative . . ."

The fear was there, deep within his mind, the way it had been ever since they had conclusively confirmed the data three weeks ago. It was wonderful, a dream of ages, Ward's dream, his, come true. Yet the excitement and the anticipation were being tainted by his fear of the consequences. He hadn't looked that far ahead, at the beginning, hadn't allowed himself to contemplate the impossible—that Project Search would succeed. Now he would have to live with the inevitable reactions. If he hadn't detected the signal, someone else would have, eventually. But that didn't change the fact that he would be the first to announce the existence of the extraterrestrial signal to mankind. That responsibility was going to remain with him the rest of his life.

An *interrupt* beeped on Todd's personal monitor, one of his secretary techs reminding him that Pat's speech was coming up. Todd acknowledged, releasing his seat webbing and clicking his tether line onto the safety rail.

"We could watch it from in here," Dian suggested softly. "Privacy."

"We could, but rank hath responsibilities as well as privileges. The troops will expect me to put in an appearance."

"Huh! I know you. Responsibility! Reason you space up here to Geosynch so much is to get away from all that responsibility down at the planetside ComLink offices. You hide up here and let Mikhail and Elaine and your other execs handle all the tough stuff while you loaf."

Todd grinned, admitting it. "That's a major advantage in owning the company. Nobody can fire me for playing Spacer games on company time. Well, I can't be a coward and hide out *all* the time. Besides, I'd rather watch Pat on the main screen . . ."

Dian's tether made a whistling sound as it scooted along the rail behind Todd's. They swam out of the office and into the corridor. "Safer to be a coward, my grandma said. She sure patched up a lot of people who played at bein' brave and got themselves shot and shrapneled and missile-concussed. She told me never to be too dumb to run for cover."

Todd smiled grimly, not commenting. Wyoma Lee Foix was a legend. No one could count the heroic stories about her work among the shattered populations that were to become the Midwestern United Ghetto States. Dian quoted her beloved grandmother frequently, but Todd was never quite sure how much was truth and how much myth in the making. Dian talked the coward's way out, but she wasn't the type, any more than Wyoma Lee had been.

They hand-over-handed, their tethers sliding on the guide rails as they moved toward Main Com Display. Todd's orientation remained with the office monitors' view of Earth. He felt as if he were climbing "up" toward Main Com.

Actually, he was moving parallel to Geosynch HQ's orbit. Earth was "down there," and the satellite and all its occupants and attendant mini-satellites were racing west to east, keeping pace with Earth's rotation. This distortion in his usual thought patterns annoyed Todd. If he kept up, he would arrive at Main Com Display flailing and dizzy, like a newcomer from planetside.

Main Com Display was abnormally noisy. Conversation vied with the muted audio of hundreds of monitor screens. Apparently Geosynch's staff had decided to use Pat's speech as an excuse for general socializing. Todd raised an eyebrow, but said nothing. All work and no goofing off made for personnel problems. He had always had better results holding the presidential reins loosely and letting his subordinates in the corporation put on the pressure when necessary. The work output proved the tactic was a good one.

Techs, on and off duty, maintenance personnel, and a bunch of civilian and military pilots laying over temporarily at the satellite crowded the island below the supervisor's cage. Nothing of interest showed on the huge main screen yet, so they were floating around or anchored in their seats, talking and swapping gossip. Todd and Dian made their way the length of the cylindrical chamber. Questions and opinions assaulted them as they did.

"Think it's about the Trans-Pacific war, boss?"

"Has to be, huh, Dian? Or maybe it's about the appeal for glacier relief funds."

"Bigger than that. Must be peace news. The P.O.E. arbitration committee's been wrangling with them for weeks."

"Your brother . . . uh . . . Mr. Saunder wouldn't ask us for a global and lunar feed unless it was really important, would he, boss?"

Todd smiled cryptically, confirming nothing, but he shared the sentiments. They all hoped a peace announcement was in the offing. Twelve years' madness in the Pacific had cost millions of lives, countless lost resources, and desperately needed production. It was the only current on-going major war afflicting a planet already bled anemic by war and natural disaster. Whether an old nation or one of the many new ones rising out of the earlier catastrophes, they had all been hurt; everyone wanted an end to it.

When they reached the supervisor's cage, Todd scaled the webbing. He pivoted and untangled his tether, then inserted his length through the cage door. Beth Isaacs patted the empty command chair at her side. "Saved a seat for you, boss."

"Thanks. Any trouble?"

"None whatsoever. Ground stations and ComLink Central assure it'll rip right through." Beth shifted her position as if to offer her chair to Dian. But the black woman refused with a smile. She settled herself against the cage's outer webbing while Beth fine-tuned the booth's axes. Servos rotated them until the suspended cage gave the three of them a straight-line view of the large main screen.

Gib Owens left the other pilots on the island and floated up toward the cage. Todd hooked his thumbs in his jumper's thigh pockets, waiting. Owens steadied at eye level, bobbing slightly, clinging to the outer webbing. The pilots peered up at him, trying to eavesdrop. "This broadcast won't delay our launch, will it, sir?" Owens asked.

His question wasn't subtle, but then he was young. Goddard pilots and their counterparts posted at Lunar Base Copernicus and patrolling the military sats always assumed there must be things going on that Todd could tell them. He was a Saunder and, therefore, would know where the secrets were hidden. Todd wondered why his noncommittal response to the earlier questions hadn't satisfied Owens. "You want to scrub and launch later?" he asked. "It's a good window, but if you think . . ."

"Oh, no, sir! Comps read fine." Owens hung there, his boyish, freckled face hopeful. He hardly looked old enough to qualify for a pilot's regs. A lot of pilots didn't. The plague mutations had put huge gaps in Earth's population, and some age groups had been hit especially hard. There were many pilots in their teens and early twenties, doing the jobs that used to be assigned to men and women in their late twenties and early thirties. The kids piled up expertise fast. They had to, if the shuttles needed them.

Todd gave Owens a thumbs-up. "I'll be suited and geared on time, Captain. Rely on it." Defeated, the pilot returned him a sloppy salute and propelled himself back down to the island.

"You could have thrown him a bone," Dian said. She and Beth Isaacs snickered conspiratorially. The black woman and the tall chief tech indeed held a secret Owens and his fellow pilots would have liked to know in advance of the rest of the world. But they weren't telling.

Todd grumbled. "Why does everyone think I know Pat's brains inside out? He doesn't tip me off about his speeches. I don't know if this damned announcement of his will delay the launch. His campaign manager or Jael calls me and says the candidate will make a speech and is buying this much air time. I plug them through and collect my fee. I work here just like the rest of you . . ."

"Except you have a bigger office," Beth muttered.

Todd glowered at her. ". . . and I'm always the last one to get the word."

"No, Goddard will be. I wonder how bad *this* speech is going to hurt them." Dian's face showed that she was sorry the moment she had spoken. Beth lost her grin and became absorbed in the master readout boards. Todd couldn't slump effectively in zero gravity, but he wanted to—the posture would have expressed his current emotions.

On the three-meters-square main screen, a world renowned newscaster was introducing the Protectors of Earth Trans-Pacific Conflict arbitration committee. Inserts framing the central image showed scenes from around the world. Nightside inhabitants were waking up, registering their presence on the instant-feedback response boards. Reporters conducted quickie interviews with national leaders or common citizens around the globe, adding local color commentary. In villages and controlled-violence arenas, in isolated country areas and megalopolises, the Earth's activities slowed down, attention turning to ComLink and Todd's rival network outlets. Anyone who wanted to close-view an insert program could cue it and have it replayed later. Most of Todd's staff didn't bother. Like Todd, they were capable of absorbing multiple inputs and automatically sifting the chaff from the material they wanted to retain. Four generations of media-reared humans had done that, each generation improving on the efficiency of the one before. By now, print media were becoming rare, and telecom handled the bulk of human information.

"When did they sign *him* on?" Dian wondered, indicating the newsman on the main screen. "I thought Dmitri Kirshon was a member of World Advancement Party."

"He was," Beth said. "Rumor has it that the man switched over to Earth First a couple of days ago, and they put Kirshon right to work. It's all the same reactionary coalition, anyway."

"Huh! The anti-Spacer, back-to-the-good-old-days coalition. I was there, and the good old days were hell."

Beth agreed fully. "Probably World Advancement and President Galbraith's Social Traditionalists will claim Patrick Saunder bought Kirshon off. Oh, well. Maybe he did."

"Not personally," Todd corrected her. "Pat wouldn't bother. Jael handles that kind of stuff. She enjoys the dirty work."

Beth's long fingers skipped over the console, guiding her eyes as she studied the boards. She spoke toward the chief duty tech's monitor screen and the signal relayed to the job stations on the island below. "We're into the red a bit, Noelle, on forty-five dee ess. If they need it planetside, be prepared to boost the South Sino sat feed." Dian tapped another readout, drawing Beth's attention silently. The taller woman nodded. "Sava, stretch the Greater Mediterranean translator-splits, please."

"I thought Maintenance had that orbiter locked," Dian complained.

"Compared to Worldwide TeleCom's and Incorporated Network's, it's gorgeous. For ComLink, it's merely adequate. We have standards to keep up," Beth stated with pride. "I've put it on the top of Maintenance's list. They'll have it in A-One shape for the next global compaign speech."

"Acceptable. Bet that's a rebuttal from the Third Millennium Movement or the United Theocracies at the other end of the scale." Dian made jokes out of the political parties' names, speaking with mocking awe. "No matter what Patrick says, they'll scream and demand equal time under P.O.E.'s campaign rules . . ."

The women's conversation, other murmuring voices, and the audio confusion lapped at the fringes of Todd's awareness. Dian's earlier comment drummed in his mind: *"Goddard will be the last to know."* True, if only by a second and a fraction. And it was likely this would be one more blow to the shaky situation existing between the space station and Earth. Pat's speeches had hurt Goddard Colony—and Mariette Saunder—often this past year. Saunder Enterprises was a family quasi-nation. But Pat and Mariette were heading in opposite directions fast, philosophically and literally.

And who's in the middle? Me, as usual.

The famous newscaster's image was crisp. Color phasing good. The modified holo-mode gave his face and form three dimensions. Pat's treasurer ought to be pleased with the product. Numbers would move from Pat's accounts over to Todd's ledgers. Mariette would contribute a small sum also, buying the broadcast

for Goddard Colony in order to keep up to the minute re the anti-
Spacer campaign. Three ledgers, three siblings—separate, scrupu-
lously maintained and audited. Jael hired only the best, whether it
was a cook for Saunderhome, a sharpshooter security guard, or a
bookkeeper. In places where they didn't own an enclave, the
Saunders cheerfully paid taxes to the government in charge. But
whenever possible, the input and outgo of the family corporation
went from one sibling's pocket to another. Jael called it intra-
family courtesy. Their rivals, particularly the other family-owned
quasi-nations, like the Nakamuras, Alamshahs, and LeFevre
Société, called them a power-grabbing monopoly threatening to
consume the entire world.

Click-click status on the ComLink signal. Jael leased Todd's
best techs to handle their political broadcasts.

The newsman's voice was mellifluous, almost as persuasive as
Pat's. Kirshon's Slavic accent didn't matter. ComLink's translator-splitter instantly converted his words into a thousand tongues
and dialects. One world, one language, with a little help from
Ward Saunder's patents and ComLink's satellites.

*Alien messenger, listening to us out there at thirty A.U., what
will you make of Pat's speech, once the signal crosses the gulf
and reaches you? And what will your response be?*

Maybe the next response would include that all-important key
that would help them break down the remaining mysteries in the
alien's signal. Convert it all to real language, not blips and patterned static, testing each other's ability to riddle out spectra or
numerical sequences.

Todd glanced at the satellite's watchdog monitors. Little orbiting cameras provided an exterior view of Geosynch HQ, Todd's
home in space. The satellite was a silly-looking structure, by
planetside standards. Gravity didn't matter here, nor did neatly
rounded corners or roofs over warehouses. The orbiter's offices,
shuttleport, living quarters, and maintenance facilities bulged with
knobby extensions, spindly girders, and connecting tunnels sticking out at odd angles. Robot teleoperators crept over the satellite's skin, repairing or adding onto the original massive structure.
Annexes held clusters of com and power sats, ready for place-
ment in various orbits. Old sats, brought in for repair or recy-
cling, rode in the collection shack "ahead" of the main body of

Geosynch HQ. Five spacecraft rode in parking orbit. Access tunnels and electronic umbilici tethered them to docking. Todd's private ship, an interorbital shuttle he share-leased with Mariette, waited first in line to depart.

In a couple of hours, Gib Owens and I will ride her up to Goddard. And if Pat kicks Mari with this speech, I'll walk into a million-megaton explosion.

Thirty-two thousand kilometers away, close-up techs wearing miniaturized chest pack cameras doubled as crowd control around the podium, focusing on various guests and committee members. The screen divided, showing an assortment of group and individual portraits to Earth and space. The media theater of Protectors of Earth had been designed to showcase the organization's triumphs in just this way. Three decades of wars and disasters had stimulated P.O.E.'s rise to near-absolute global authority. World leaders scrambled to join its ranks, and many of them had gathered in the theater for this occasion. CNAU President Galbraith was there, even though the aging politician was a puppet without much real power. His nation provided the land for P.O.E.'s facilities and he showed up at all its functions, reliving the days when his office had genuine clout. P.O.E. Chairman Li Chu presided over the famous guests and committeemen. She was retiring after her present term and had already named Patrick her political heir. Cynically, Todd wondered if Jael had bought the woman off to gain that favor. The Chairmanship of Protectors of Earth was now, in effect, the command post for Earth, and in a few months that post would belong to Patrick Saunder.

All the power-wielders and would-be rulers who hoped to bask in Pat's reflected glory were there. So were the military, the P.O.E. enforcement officers. Todd stared at the uniformed group, wishing he could read their minds. Were these men and women going to go along with whatever the committee had worked out at the secret conferences? That was crucial, if there was ever to be peace. Dawes, Ubaldi, Chen Chang . . . the old generals, covered with medals, warriors who had survived the worst the Death Years could throw at them. The only public comments anyone heard from them were totally predictable. "Defense posture." "A strong protective force is the best peace treaty." They weren't likely to be conciliatory. It was the young officers who would carry out the terms—if they were willing to cooperate. Todd looked along the row, assessing. His eyes were drawn to one particular black face. General Ames, Dawes's second in command. Todd sought his memories but didn't recall ever reading or hearing any statement from the man, not for the public. Yet the analysts pictured Ames as a potential power behind the throne, thanks to his rapport with the troops. He had come up from the same sort of hell on Earth many of the soldiers had. What was he thinking? Right now, Ames was watching Pat narrowly, his stare never wavering. The intensity of the young general's gaze unsettled Todd, but he couldn't read the emotions behind that stare. Ames wore a ghetto mask, hiding his true feelings.

His fellow committeemen crowded around Pat, hoping his glamour would rub off on their own election campaigns. Despite seeming modesty, Pat was aware of his assets. His dark good looks and dominating height and voice he had inherited from his father. The political talent was his own. He had used the combination to climb very high, very fast, but was wise enough not to flaunt those gifts. The Earth First Party candidate ran his hand through his hair in a seemingly absentminded gesture which was pure calculation. Todd smiled, remembering how often he and Mariette had watched Pat rehearse that trick when they were kids, calling Pat a vid ham. Pat had laughed as loudly as they. And he kept on practicing. He found he could call attention to his unusual wavy black hair with its red glints. He found out, too, how to use his sharp, strong features, tall body, and theatrical flair. Most of all, he discovered his voice, honing and polishing it to perfection.

But he wasn't a kid any more. The tricks were second nature now. The adolescent who had once postured for his siblings could now command billions with his stage presence. Crises and wounds in humanity's collective psyche had created a demand for answers, and Patrick Saunder promised he would find them. Attractive, likable, and rich, he gave the audience what they wanted and became someone they trusted to show them the way out of the mess.

Techs panned the V.I.P. guests in the theater audience. Carissa gazed adoringly at Pat, on stage as much as he was. Not even Todd's staff was immune to Carissa's sweet, blond prettiness. He heard several sighs from the duty stations. Dian cocked her curly head, studying Carissa's picture. "Is she okay? She looks terribly thin and bleached out."

"I didn't notice anything wrong the last time I saw her, a week ago. She's always seemed kind of delicate. I'm sure Pat wouldn't let her continue this campaign tour if she were ill." Guilt nagged at Todd. Carissa *did* look exceptionally pale and shaky. Had he been so callous he hadn't noticed those changes last week?

Jael sat almost out of camera frame, next to Carissa. She didn't edge in or try to hog the lens. Jael preferred the shadows. She was eyeing Carissa sidelong. The lenses caught the distinctive white streaks in Jael's auburn hair, drawing the eye. Todd watched his mother while Jael looked at Carissa. Jael's expression was strangely possessive, making Todd squirm, unsure why he felt so uneasy.

Behind his mother and sister-in-law, rival candidates Fairchild and Dabrowski did everything but wave flags and make faces to attract attention. Pat's competitors wanted to piggyback on Carissa's photogenic beauty. They knew ComLink would feature her for color shots and must have taken the chairs behind her with exactly that purpose in mind. Even though Fairchild's Third Millennium Movement and Dabrowski's World Expansionists were Spacers, Todd was disgusted by their behavior. If only the Spacers had someone as popular as Pat . . . !

Someone who could defeat his anti-Spacer brother in the campaign.

Family treason. No wonder Jael had given him a tongue-lashing a week ago when he dared suggest that maybe Pat's campaign platform wasn't in the best interests of Earth, the Saunders, or humanity in general.

Beth Isaacs sensed a windup in the intro. "Ready in case of trouble. Let's go." On-duty techs notched their chairs forward, guaranteeing clear-voice countermands if they had to talk to the systems. A sensible precaution, but one that had never been needed. ComLink was over-loaded with redundancies and safe-guards.

A storm of applause greeted the committee as the newsman recited the last member's name. The loudest cheers were for Pat, but he graciously included his co-members in the acknowledgment. The others formed a semi-circle behind him on the stage, smiling triumphantly. When the clapping abated, Pat began quietly. "Listeners, Citizens of Earth . . ."

Sound choked off throughout the theater at that key phrase, Patrick Saunder's trademark speech opener. The hush seemed startling after the tumult.

"Listeners," Patrick repeated, "we know you have been waiting a long time for the results of our arbitration. We appreciate your patience. Protectors of Earth is very happy to tell you we have succeeded. After intense negotiations, the Nippon-Malaysia Alliance and the Maui-Andean Populist Democracies have agreed to a total and unconditional armistice, effective immediately."

One of the military pilots, a Malaysian, whooped in joy. Techs and other pilots joined his celebration. Then they turned quiet, eager to hear more good news.

". . . terrible conflict has hurt us all," Pat was saying, "not merely those in the war zones. The neo-smallpox mutation, the loss of the Galapagos Geothermal Seabed Installation, the crop failures caused by blockades along the iceberg tow routes, extinction of marine and land animal life, pollution from toxic fallout and nuclear strikes—these affect every man, woman, and child on Earth. Those in the Trans-Pacific have suffered most of all."

Pat paused for dramatic effect while ComLink's campaign programmers inserted corroborating images, framing the main screen. Blood, plague, ravaged cities, and lifeless croplands and ocean beds. The viewers had seen it all before, but somehow the ugliness gained fresh impact if they watched while Pat described it. His words flowed, each syllable and hesitation planned. SE's patented translator carried him into cosmopolitan towers and primitive villages. Instant interpretation. They were hearing him, not a machine voice. In their own languages, Pat came across warm and sincere, all his personality intact. ComLink's competitors hadn't yet fully mastered Ward Saunder's technique. It would be years before they could duplicate that global voice power.

"The killing is over, Listeners. The Trans-Pacific region is at peace. After twelve years, no missiles are being launched, no viral pestilence released from the labs, no wholesale executions. P.O.E. truce teams are stationed now throughout Nippon-Malaysia and the Maui-Andean Democracies to enforce the armistice. The truce *is* being honored faithfully. Hostilities are over, at last."

That mesmerizing voice shook with emotion. Pat's eyes looked teary, and he communicated a profound sense of weary pride and thanksgiving to an entire world. Beth Isaacs sniffled and bowed her head, murmuring prayerfully. "Thank you . . ." Neither Dian nor Todd was a convert to the new mysticism, but they knew what the woman was feeling. Dian pressed Beth's arm. The black woman was fighting her own flood of tears. Todd's throat felt thick. He wished he were on Earth at this moment, facing Pat directly, not through a vid signal. He wanted to clasp Pat in a bearhug and share the triumph of peace.

Let it be true. No political fast ones this time, big brother. No deals behind the scenes.

Peace! An ocean, a billion people, exhausted lands and countries—accepting peace, accepting the committee's arbitration, under Pat's guidance.

Todd stared at Pat's image, emotions overwhelming him. He had never loved that face, that person, so much. Nothing thus far compared. Pat helping Jael pull them out of potential financial disaster when Ward died so suddenly and tragically. Pat rescuing Todd from drowning. Pat sweeping Mari up and running like hell ahead of a rioting mob near the crater towns west of Chicago, saving himself and her through superhuman effort.

Now he had saved not only the war zone but the rest of the planet that could have, would have, been destroyed if the war had spread, as it had threatened to do. There were no words. Todd sat helplessly, too moved to weep, the happy shouts and fervent prayers ringing around him throughout the great orbiting viewing room.

CHAPTER THREE

☆☆☆☆☆☆☆☆☆

COMPROMISES

AGAINST his will, the moment was escaping. Apprehension over-rode hope. The tenseness in his shoulders crept back as Todd looked at the screen. Pat's pale-eyed stare never wavered. His eyes were so like Ward's and Mari's, an unusual, very light blue that could reach out, grab the person seeing them, and hold their fascinated victim. Pat used no prompter, not even an out-of-frame holo-mode cue that could easily be hidden from both the global audience and the V.I.P.s assembled in the theater. But Todd knew Pat was taking in the instant feedback response from the techs' monitor directly in front of the podium. If the response from the voters was steady, Pat would plow ahead. If it wavered, he would cut and trim his words without telltale hesitation, suiting his speech to the audience's mood. He made it work, making their viewpoint his own, convincing them he was leading them, not the opposite.

He began spelling out the peace treaty's terms. Mostly standard form. P.O.E. was accumulating a good arbitration record. By now its committees had the science of truce-making worked out. Opposing rulers would usually concede this and argue about that. Give here, compromise there . . .

". . . no further missile launches. All missiles on site have been disarmed by P.O.E. enforcement teams. Five: Full stop on all chemico-viral experiments. Total destruction of all lethal materials currently on hand. Total ban on any further stockpiling."

The world shuddered on hearing that. Mutations stimulated by man's scientific experiments had already escaped the labs and outrun their creators' intentions. The viruses had mutated numerous times and the planned protective measures proved useless against the new strains. Pandemics swept the Earth. Mankind had conquered smallpox, once. The Trans-Pacific conflict and earlier wars and their experimentations had let loose a similar but more ruthless killer to fill smallpox's vacant niche in the biological chain. Millions died in those plagues and the ones caused by the neo-anthrax virus.

"Six: All military units will disarm. They will place themselves under the command of P.O.E. enforcement troops and be dispersed to their respective home countries."

Fairchild and Dabrowski began squirming as the audience-reaction lenses panned the theater. How could they or any of Patrick's rivals rebut this speech? Who could take a stand against peace? Even the combatants were glad to be out of it. The arbitration team had given the region's rulers a way out of disaster and helped them save face. Todd sympathized with the Spacer candidates' dilemma. Yet his own doubts grew. What would be the price of this wonderful news? He read Pat's face. Something unpleasant was coming. Pat was leading up to it very skillfully. Some of the peace terms must be hard to swallow. There was a giveaway look in those eyes. Todd leaned forward, intent on the screen.

"Both groups have signed a mutual confinement pact. To facilitate the move toward peace, all convicted war criminals and rebellious factors on either side will be taken into custody at once by P.O.E. forces. These will be transported and confined in Saunder Enterprises Antarctic Enclave Cryogenic Preservement chambers."

Patrick made no mention of trials. The "convictions" were a foregone conclusion. Guilty, guilty, guilty. Nippon-Malaysia and the Maui-Andeans each had expendable "war criminals" and would-be usurpers in their ranks. The arbitration committee had given them a chance to swap and get rid of the human problems, under the guise of a peace treaty. The P.O.E. not only had

brought order to their war-ravaged countries but provided them
with a convenient hole in which to drop genuine military mass
murderers, political embarrassments, and all future rivals for the
surviving generals and premiers. Peace accomplished through
merciless amputation and a Saunder Enterprises enclave.

A print crawl had started up the sides of the screen while Pat
explained the details of the confinement. The lettering moved rapidly, faster than normal scan speed. The names of the war criminals and rebels zipped upward and disappeared. Since most of the
global audience was functionally illiterate, they would never be
able to read that crawl. The highly trained ComLink techs and
the pilots watching in Geosynch HQ *could* read the names, however. Elation turned to fury. The Malaysian pilot who had been
so gleeful moments before pointed to a name being sucked off the
top of the screen. "Djailolo?" he cried out. "He's no war criminal! Halmahera and Takeda just want him out of the way. They'll
starve off the rest of Djailolo's people and crush the outer islands!
Damn them! Damn those fucking Earth Firsters!" His companions tried to calm him, even though they, too, were bitter. Protests were futile. The peace pact had already been agreed to. By
now the condemned were probably in their icy coffins in Antarctica, beyond hope of rescue by their adherents or relatives. The
world desperately wanted peace, enough to sacrifice these victims
to cryogenic sleep.

"We wish to stress that the transportees accepted their sentences voluntarily," Pat explained. Most of the world would believe him, because it wanted to, and because doing so was easier
than thinking about the dark implications behind this aspect of
the truce.

Todd swallowed nausea. Voluntary? What choice did the condemned have? None. Such things had happened before, were happening more and more frequently as Earth's governments became
used to the convenience of the polar Enclave. They had learned it
wasn't wise to make martyrs out of their enemies, so they didn't
execute them nowadays; instead they ran through mock trials and
shipped the convicts off to limbo. In the past ten years, ever since
the initial successful revival of a volunteer Cryogenic Preservement, the facility had become the world's most popular prison
as well as a refuge for the wealthy and beloved of every nation.

Ward Saunder had planned the Antarctic enclave as a hedge against death for artists, religious leaders, altruistic scientists, and public servants who would otherwise be lost to disease, age, or accident. Of course, there were also the wealthy ill and elderly, who could pay handsomely for their cubicles in the Enclave.

Furthermore, since the Death Years, Earth's genetic pool had been carefully tended in the Enclave as well; sperm and ova and tissue samples collected from millions of people were stored and filed against a global disaster. Sterility had followed some of the plagues and the nuclear and toxic catastrophes. Protectors of Earth had accepted Saunder Enterprises' offer to make the Enclave a neutral storehouse for the human race's future inheritance. The new mysticism preached that life was infinitely precious and must be protected. The Saunders had been praised as selfless saviors of people who would have died without their aid, and as preservers of Earth's population yet to be born. The costs were kept minimal, more proof of Saunder generosity.

Pat had launched his political career on the wave of that gratitude. He was still riding the wave. He made it sound so right. No messy executions. No expensive long-term imprisonments. Just frozen sleep, and the would-be martyrs lost all chance to die nobly for their causes. They disappeared, along with the interred wealthy and the geniuses and the criminals. They were all visible on relay vid images from the pole. P.O.E.'s Human Rights Committee monitored the steadily growing suspended population via twice-annual tours, reassuring the world that all was in order. The willing and unwilling confinees weren't dead. They weren't exactly alive, either, and all too soon the political dissidents' followers lost hope and gave up their fights for freedom or rebellion.

". . . will live into the future, Listeners, that marvelous, peaceful future we are all working for, a future where war and hunger and disease do not exist." Then Pat said, as if as an afterthought, "The people of the Trans-Pacific area need all their resources to bind their wounds and rebuild their ruined cities and lands. Therefore, as executive in charge of Saunder Enterprises Antarctic Enclave, I hereby cancel all debts involved in this confinement pact. We will donate the use of the cryogenic cubicles involved in perpetuity. This is our contribution to a lasting peace."

As he spoke, the last of the long list of "confinees" rolled up off the screen and was gone. Too many of those names had been supporters of Pat's political rivals. His contribution must have sounded very generous. In fact, he could well afford it, financially and, especially, politically. The gesture would buy him millions of votes in the war zone and elsewhere, and his opponents had nothing to equal the tactic. There was only one P.O.E. chartered cryogenic facility on Earth, and it belonged to Saunder Enterprises.

But Pat still wasn't finished. Todd hunched his shoulders, afraid to hear what other deals his brother had made. "To replace the loss of the Galapagos Geothermal Seabed Installation, we are providing, at basic cost, labor, material, and supportive funding from CNAU Western Power Corporation . . ."

Todd slammed a fist down hard on the supervisor's console. Inertial reaction slung him into the webbing, and he had to grab for an anchor to keep from being rebounded painfully. Dian and Beth jumped with surprise as Todd growled, "That's your company, Pat. Damn you. Ground-based fusion and fossil energy. You're using this to squeeze out Goddard Power Sats throughout the Pacific!"

The techs and pilots heard him, but Todd didn't care. Seething, he wished he could travel with the feedback signal, down to Earth, and confront his brother. Maybe he would pay attention after a good physical shaking-up. But SE employees were barred from responding on the instant feedback circuits. That was only for paying clients—voters. And from Pat's expression, it was obvious the favorable poll was far outweighing the negative vote. The audience was accepting the peace, convictions, financial fast shuffling, and all. Pat soothed that small, restless remaining portion of his listeners with another sweeping humanitarian donation. "The P.O.E. is taking immediate steps to relieve the breakdown of vital services in the war zone. We will supply food, shelter, and transportation . . ."

"Let me guess," Todd said. His tone made Beth Isaacs edge away from him warily. "You're going to 'donate' those services from SE Consolidated Industries—your subsidiary, again. And I'll bet you get a juicy rakeback from Premier Takeda and President Halmahera and Ybarra and the rest."

Pat wouldn't admit that in public, of course. He called no attention to his financial involvements. He made the petty details seem logical and right, selling the truce and himself. "He heads the P.O.E. Transport Committee," Dian said. "Huh! *And* the Shelter Agency Council *and* the one regulating the fisheries, grain suppliers, and hydro energy outfits. Li'l interest in every one of those humanitarian efforts P.O.E. is providing."

"Rely on it," Todd said bitterly. "Technically, if there's profit to be made out of the Antarctic Enclave, he gets *that,* too. Talk about grave robbing!"

"Hey!" Dian cut through his tirade, drawing his attention. She scowled and defended the polar installation. "Bad points, yes. But it stopped the killing, in its own way. Don't rip it down. I know some people who would have been executed if the facility hadn't been there for them as an out. And I know some people on the Human Rights Committee, which checks up on the Enclave, too. Good people. Honest."

"Okay, but the system, the political confinements . . . damn," Todd said without force. "And all the rest of this. Pat's grabbing right and left, mostly at Goddard's expense. He'll take a loss for a while, but it'll eventually print out black. Kevin McKelvey and some of the Colony Planning Group have been trying to hold down the secessionist talk. Pat's practically driving them over the brink. He's not helping *me*, either, financially or with this visit to Mariette. Damn you," he repeated, glowering impotently at the main screen.

"A little victory. It won't last," Dian said softly. Only the three of them in the booth could hear her words amid the uproar from below. Dian glanced at Beth Isaacs, then at Todd. "News conferences. Surprises. They go lots of ways." Todd smiled, nodding to the women. The alien messenger. A *real* surprise for Pat's political campaign! He wasn't going to be able to trade on the side with *that* element. For once, everything would have to be out in the open. Though he hoped for Pat's understanding and assistance in explaining the messenger's significance to the world, Todd began to relish the prospect of dumping the news on his brother's handsome head.

". . . thank the Spirit of Humanity, which led us to peace." Pat was leaving his audience on a prayerful, mystical note. Shrewdly, he planted references to the Earth First Party. The listeners must be reminded that there was a hard-working human agency helping out the spiritual guidance. Todd tried to read the man behind those platitudes, but that was becoming more and more difficult to do as time went on. He wanted to shut off that magnificent voice or pretend it wasn't Pat spouting this hypocrisy. Did winning the Chairmanship mean so much to Pat that he would throw away his own sister and the Goddard Colony in order to rule Protectors of Earth?

Todd pitied Fairchild and Pat's other opponents. By the time they prepared their answering speeches, initial sour reactions to the peace treaty details would have faded. Nobody would want to hear an oration reminding them of the disturbing side of that pact.

Just the right pacing, just the right emotional tone. "Listeners, Earth is always first in our hearts. We must cherish her as she has nourished us. We must keep her safe and make Earth and her people once more beautiful, productive, and happy. Let us go together into that future, led by the Spirit of Humanity. Good day and good night, everywhere, Listeners." Pat signed off with a smile.

He ought to patent that smile, just as Jael patented Ward's inventions and made us all rich. We Saunders patent everything, even hypocrisy.

Dmitri Kirshon was back on the main screen now, summing up what had been announced. He behaved as if he thought someone might actually listen to him. Most of the cameras remained with Pat and the committee, showing a variety of scenes in the miniviews framing Kirshon's image. Todd saw well-wishers crowding the platform, offering congratulations. Other cameras followed Jael and Carissa as the Saunder women made their way past the stage toward the V.I.P. lounge. Inevitably, there would be after-the-event up-close interviews with Pat, the ranking members of P.O.E., and representatives from the former combatants. Everybody would say predictable things, but the public wanted to enjoy the news at length and wouldn't care about content. Todd's ComLink reporters would ask only the right questions, and they would do their best to shut out the rival nets' digging inquiries. That was what ComLink got paid for.

Todd took a deep breath, getting his anger in hand. Then he

released his safety straps and pushed up out of the chair. He clambered down the outside webbing at a reckless speed, stretching his tether, hurrying through the Main Com Display area toward the living quarters access.

"Boss, what did you—"

The tech who had started to ask a question broke off abruptly as Todd swam past her. He saw his stormcloud mood mirrored in the woman's shocked face. Gib Owens and the pilots and techs watched him move past the duty stations. No one else tried to detain him. Todd hovered impatiently beside the access, then dived through as it sighed open.

Sometimes this tunnel was busy with two-way traffic. Now he was alone. Everyone else on Geosynch HQ was back in Main Com. The tether made a whispering noise, sliding along the anchor rail. It tugged at his waist, forcibly reminding Todd where he was. Other places and situations intruded on his senses, his orientation still awry. He resisted the temptations. He wasn't swimming in the warm waters off Saunderhome. He was orbiting Earth. There should be no sensation of "up" or "down." Yet there was. Moving toward the tunnel's end, he was a swimmer, rising to the surface. Bright sunlit waters seemed to surround him. No, not water, but a fragile, shimmering, metallic tube. He was breathing recycled air, and beyond the tunnel walls lay high vacuum, not a reef.

Todd arrived at the outer lock and voice-cued it. As he did, he felt air pressure shifting and heard the lock opening at the far end of the tunnel. He glanced that way and saw Dian leaving Main Com. She was following him, but making no effort to overtake him.

He planted his feet against the open door and shoved off hard, pulling his safety tether to its limits, sailing out into the branch corridor which led to his quarters. The small tunnels were too warm, again. He made a mental note to speak to the life-support programmer tech. Things at ComLink ought to run smoothly. Usually, they did, which made glitches that much more irritating. His sweat wouldn't evaporate properly. When he reached his quarters, he was sticky as well as mad.

Todd jerked loose his tether and floated free along the curve of the spheroid room. He guided his course reflexively, using action

and reaction. Steering past the web-shrouded bed, he caught the
stanchions and drew himself down into the seat in front of the
monitor terminals. Then he snapped the belt in place, glowering
at the miniversion of the Main Com Display, on which an ex-
cited-sounding reporter was addressing the worldwide audience.
"We're in P.O.E.'s reserved lounge with Jael Hartman Saunder,
co-founder of Saunder Enterprises, mother of the candidate. Jael,
could we have a moment . . . ?"

Todd's gaze flicked away from the screen, up to an array of tri-
di family photos covering the metal and plasticene bulkheads.
Jael and Ward's wedding picture, side by side with Pat and
Carissa's. Childhood candids, showing Mari and Pat knobby
kneed and gawky, yet already growing into that pale-eyed, dark-
haired physical beauty they possessed now. Even the uninformed
viewer, seeing those pictures, would realize they were brother and
sister. Todd Saunder was the oddball, too normal, neither ugly
nor handsome, a lost-in-the-crowd kid and adult. His siblings got
the good looks, he used to admit, then had teased them by claim-
ing that he got the brains in the second generation—Ward's
brains. There was a shot of Mari and Kevin McKelvey, a photo
Todd himself had taken last year that captured their vitality and
reckless natures. Kevin's curly mane rested against Mari's black
hair, his heavy, rugged face close to her vid-star one. *Mari and
Pat go for blondes. I'm still the oddball, latching onto Dian.* There
were no recent photos of Jael. She had never liked the camera,
and hated it now that her once-solid face and body were softening
with age.

". . . must be a very proud event for you. Carissa, how do you
feel? Holding up under the campaigning? Today's kind of a break
in the schedule, isn't it?"

The on-going interviews drew Todd's eyes. Jael was gracious,
doing her best to live down her reputation as a cutthroat busi-
nesswoman. She put Carissa stage front, and Carissa smiled.
That ought to be good for a few million extra votes. Carissa's
ash-blond hair was slightly disheveled, but not messy. Her green
eyes were wide with innocent delight. She looked lovely and vul-
nerable. "Oh, it's just wonderful," she said in that husky voice,
one that was becoming almost as famous as her husband's. Her
voice had a poignant little crack in it, an endearing, childlike

note. "What? I can't hear you. It's so loud in here! Everybody's so happy! I just know everything will work out perfectly!" She jumped as the milling crowd jostled her. Jael's burly security guards eased back the crush, not discouraging the Saunders' admirers, but keeping their charges safe from mauling. Carissa grabbed at her stylish hat and scarf and laughed. She looked like a beautiful adolescent at a carnival.

"ComLink Tele network, top priority, Todd Saunder. I want a personal channel," Todd ordered the systems. "Put me through to the location on screen one."

"Whom did you wish to speak to, sir?"

Dian floated in while Todd set up the call. She hooked her feet around the bed webbing and sat in the air, her arms crossed under her breasts. Todd told the terminal, "Jael or Patrick Saunder. Either one. I've got plenty to say to both of them. Hurry it up."

"Give the poor comp a chance," Dian said.

The terminal acknowledged. "Thank you, sir. Your party will be on the line in just a few minutes." The comp had a female voice today, one with a slight French accent, very sexy. Some people forgot there was no living presence behind a voice like that and reacted accordingly. Todd hadn't done so since he was a boy.

"Better to take it out on the equipment than on someone who can feel it. Maybe this way I'll be calm enough to be coherent when they complete the call."

Dian's brown face was a mask. She was inside her United Ghetto States guise, presenting an unruffled, unreadable exterior to the world. Todd sensed the reason. In her own way, she was as upset as he was. But Dian wasn't a screamer. Her anger took a different form.

". . . isn't it true that your son controls the housing industries and krill fisheries in Antarctica, the ones supplying the war zones? Doesn't he have the controlling interest in SE Trans Co, too? Isn't that profit-taking . . . ?"

A crack reporter from Worldwide TeleCom had managed to break through the security cordon. Guards edged toward him, but Jael stopped them with a pitying smile. "That's a false assumption. If you examine the evidence, you'll find there's no basis for such an accusation. In fact, I resent it."

Her plump face quivered with righteous indignation on her son's behalf. It was a good performance. This stylish matron on the edge of tears surely couldn't be the same corporation president who had ruined kings and brought nations to their knees. Jael didn't look the part, not at all. The rival network reporter seemed to be picking on a gentle, innocent victim.

Nuñez wasn't fooled, however. He knew his target and bored in. "But what about that energy-funding clause in the treaty? Isn't that also Patrick Saunder's company? Won't he . . . ?"

"I know nothing whatever about such matters, young man."

Todd groaned. "They're not going to believe that, Mother. What's the matter with you? Quit putting on the fluttery-dowager role. A year ago, you would have thrown Nuñez to the sharks."

"A year ago your brother hadn't announced he was a candidate for the Chairmanship," Dian put in. Todd met her penetrating stare. "She'll shuffle the cretins around a while, then dump them," she added. "Works every time."

"Did your grandmother tell you that?" Todd asked sourly. He shook his head, seeing the screen, but thinking how the language changed to suit recent history. Before one of the BW pandemics, "cretin" had been a word in a medical textbook. After whole populations were afflicted with viral-caused thyroid anomalies, the word moved into general usage as an epithet, hurled with malice aforethought. Todd concentrated on Jael's corny routine, disgusted. "This is as phony as Pat's speeches. They've both changed, for the worse, since he got into politics."

"Carissa hasn't changed," Dian commented. "She's still a high-fashion doll."

Todd wasn't sure how to respond to that barb. He drummed his fingers on the console, muttering, "Hurry up. What's taking so long on this damned call?"

Still on screen, Jael put her arm around Carissa, drawing the delicate younger woman out of the reporter's reach. The guards cut him off and pressured him to the outside of the cordon, thereby effectively silencing him. "That does it for Nuñez," Dian said. "He's not bad. Maybe ComLink should hire him."

"Maybe he's got too much integrity to switch sides." Dian blinked at him, and Todd backed down, shrugging off the suggestion. "You stalling me, Tele network?"

Before he could say anything further, the private channel screen went black. Then it came up with a picture of Jael and Carissa, huddled close to a terminal in the lounge. Background noise assaulted the speakers despite the override filters. "Is that you, Todd?" Jael asked ingenuously.

"The signal's not that bad. It's me. I want to say a few words about that marvelous stunt you and Pat pulled on me. What happened to those heartrending pleas that we had to keep the family together and your begging me to coax Mari into coming to Dad's birthday memorial? Remember? You said you'd make any concession, any promise, so I could pull it off. You promised me you wouldn't do anything else to Goddard's pipeline. Right?"

Geosynch HQ wasn't that far from Earth. There was no discernible time lapse. Todd didn't have to wait for Jael's reaction. The teary matron was gone. "Keep your voice down," her soft, ominous voice warned. "You're blasting all over the lounge."

Undaunted, Todd pushed on sarcastically. "Oh, am I? Maybe I ought to borrow my techs back from you and go global. I want you to understand that I'm mad and in no mood for cute answers. I want to know why the hell you set me up for this. It's a damned dirty trick."

Carissa's green eyes widened more than normal. Startled, she watched Jael and Todd's image, a spectator at a controlled-violence arena match, expecting to see blood spilled.

"Todd, shut up," Jael said savagely in an even lower tone. "You haven't the faintest idea what we've been up against. I'd expect that from Mariette, but not from you. I thought you had more sense, realized what's involved in this campaign . . ."

"I realize, all too well. That's the trouble. Don't delude yourself, Mother. Mari understands what's going on, too. You're killing her, *that's* what's involved. It's not easy to overlook."

The computer voice broke in. "Here is your second call, sir."

The screen split vertically, Jael and Carissa on the left, a confusing tangle of faces and bodies on the right. Pat was coming out of the melee, still talking to his aides and colleagues. A big-breasted, revealingly clad honey blonde hung on his arm. Todd wondered scornfully if she was the latest spare-time playmate for the candidate. Since Carissa didn't seem to mind her husband's notorious extracurricular flings, it was no one else's business. His attitude probably made him more fascinating to a lot of the voters, too.

"What? Yeah, you're right, Jake. Just wait until nobody's watching, then boot him out. Arrange a mix-up with his press ident so P.O.E. won't get edgy." Pat shrugged out of the blonde's grasp and loomed over the terminal. He was obviously somewhere else in the huge lounge, visible to Jael and Carissa only via their screen. Strongmen guards elbowed the crowd back, giving Pat space. "Todd? That you, kid? How did the speech come through up there in orbit?"

"Smelling like a boatload of month-old dead krill."

A crease deepened between Pat's dark eyebrows. "Hey! What are you . . . ?"

"What am I supposed to say? That it was wonderful? That I love being stabbed in the back? That Mari's going to love it, too? You'd better understand me . . ."

"Shut *up!*" Jael roared at them.

There was a time when that would have chastened both men. Now they went on without any sign of repentance. "I can handle my own arguments," Pat said heavily. "And as for you—"

"She's in on this," Todd cut in. "I'm paying for the call, anyway, so what's your complaint? I thought I was due some answers, and it didn't look like you'd have the grace to call *me.*"

"We can straighten this out, kid," Pat said, the faintest hint of apology in his tone.

"Can we? How? You don't hear me. I don't think you've really listened to me for months, years. I'm the one you take for granted, isn't that so? I'm not even talking the same language you are." Todd's anger was faltering, becoming weary frustration. He closed his eyes a moment, then said, "How long do you think you can keep on juggling all these lies? You're lying to me now, along with everyone else. I thought I was part of the family, a trusted member of the firm, not just a flunky. You keep wanting me to come planetside more often, you say. Is that so it'll look good for the campaign? *Candidate's brother supports him in drive for the Chairmanship.* Going to set up a session on all the satellite nets, interviewers catching us together, me nodding and yes-manning?

Why bother with all this family unity nonsense if you were going
to pull—"

Pat sliced through Todd's bitterness; he appeared concerned.
"Has Mariette canceled on you?"

Todd didn't know whether to laugh or rage at his brother. He
wanted to hit him. Impossible. Telecom was a handy tool, but it
made direct contact wishful thinking. "I do admire your ability to
trim away the fat. You get right down to what's important—important to *you*. No! Mari hasn't canceled. I'm not sure why she
hasn't. Maybe I'll get the word halfway there and have to turn
around and come back. Wouldn't that be interesting?" Todd considered the matter more calmly, resignation setting in. "No," he
said quietly, "no cancellation. And if she were going to, she
would have by now."

"You're going ahead with the trip to the Colony, then?" Jael
dug at him from the second part of the Earth-based conversation.

"What if I said no?" Todd heard Dian suck in her breath.

Jael's face crumpled. "You wouldn't do that, Todd. Please!
You promised!"

"So did you and Pat. Promises don't seem to mean a lot between us any more. Promises go two ways. I *told* you I didn't
have a prayer of persuading Mari to come to Saunderhome if you
didn't lay off Goddard for a while."

"Todd . . ." Jael's eyes were misty. She wasn't faking it this
time. Those tears were angry tears. She didn't cry for any other
reason.

Jael, standing on the shore, watching the rescue crews returning
from the flier's wreckage, knowing they hadn't found Ward's
body. Pat embracing her, and Todd and Mariette crowding close,
forming a tight, mourning circle. They had wept, but Jael hadn't
then. Only later, sobbing with fury, she had cursed the weather
and the sloppy flight traffic control, blaming those for the tragedy,
and crying as she hadn't while the agony of Ward's death raked at
her. In pain or grief, she was stoic, enduring both without tears.

"Mother, let me explain," Pat said. Todd heaved a sigh, loving
and hating them, outflanked, helpless. They were light-years
apart, and the distance was increasing every week.

"Never mind," he muttered.

"I *have* to explain it to you, kid," Pat insisted. He was in so

tight on the screen he blocked all view of the crowds and the
heavily armed bodyguards surrounding him. Lowering that world-
famous voice, he whispered, "I had to deal. It was a last-minute
maneuver by Ybarra and the others. They were ready to wipe everything out and go back to killing one another. Dammit, kid!
Do you think I *want* to drown you or Mari? I wanted to tip you
off, but I couldn't." A subtle warning crept into his words. "We
may have to go to scramblers when we call each other in the future, Todd. The campaign's getting really ugly. The Spacers
would love to sabotage me. One word of the final details before
this public broadcast, and the whole truce would have collapsed."

Grim speculations whirled in Todd's mind. Secret deals. Why?
The answer was all too plain—so that the Trans-Pacific leaders
would have ample opportunity to round up all those "war criminals" and political rivals and ship them off to the pole before
anyone could stop them. Now, what was done was done.

I had to deal.

"You wouldn't have dealt with those warlord bastards five
years ago, Pat, or even one year ago," Todd said with great sorrow.

Jael opened her mouth, thought better of whatever she had
been about to say, and fell silent. She watched her sons, waiting,
as she had when they were kids squabbling over toys. She had let
them blacken eyes and bloody noses, then would pick up the
mess and punish them both. Lesson five in Jael Hartman
Saunder's theories on child rearing. It had worked, then. But in
those days, there had been three Saunder siblings fighting and
spitting childish epithets. This time, a crucial factor in the argument centered around that third sibling and the space station to
which she was devoting her life and fortune.

Pat raked both hands through his dark hair. The lenses recorded a dancing curtain of reddish highlights in the black waves.
Those pale eyes were haunted, not seeing Todd or Jael or
Carissa. Seeing nightmares come to life. "The children . . . it was
. . . my God, the children. The little bodies, all stick-bones and
distended bellies, looking at you, past hoping. Plague sores covering them, and the one little girl . . ." Pat leaned on the terminal
frame, getting out the memory, a man forced to describe the horror to free his soul. "Dying, bleeding . . . I . . . I was holding

her, trying to make the doctors . . . they wouldn't bother. Triage, they said. No chance for her, for any of those thousands of victims. I was there. I had to . . . had to do *something*. It stinks. The damned fucking war, it . . . well, it's over! It's over! I don't care what I had to deal to pull it off, kid. Do you hear me? I *had* to." Visibly, he came back to the present, pleading in his manner. "You think I enjoy compromising, lying? It's the goal that counts. I can make it up to you, and to Mari, once I get where I'm going."

"I've heard that one before, somewhere," Todd said, hurting for himself and Pat and the victims. He reached for the key, intending to use manual cutoff to avoid further heartache. "I'll believe it when it happens. If I'm going to catch my window for Goddard, I'll have to leave—"

"Todd! Wait!" Jael broke in, staying his hand. "You're mad because we couldn't tell you. Forgive us. We apologize. We truly do." A muscle twitched along Pat's jawline, but he didn't contradict her. "Whatever we have to do to make it up, we will. To you and Mari. Bring her home. I'm begging you." Her voice shook. Todd wanted to touch her, console her, as she said, "I couldn't bear it if she missed yet another of Ward's birthday memorials. We didn't time things this way. It wasn't deliberate. It just happened. Please! Believe us!"

"I'll . . . I'll try."

"Promise!"

"Mother, it's not that simple. I said I'll try. What happens depends on Mari's reaction to Pat's speech. It's not exactly the sort of send-off I wanted." Again he wanted to reach out to them, regretting the life styles and the distances that separated them. There were some things he couldn't express with a word or even a look. "I've really got to go now. And Pat, Mother—don't call Mariette. Let me smooth her feathers. If you call her, you'll probably make things worse. Just trust me on this."

Pat raised his hand in an oath. "Okay, kid. No calls. Just tell her . . . tell her I miss the brat. Will you do that?"

"Yes. I'll tell her." Todd broke the connections before they could say anything more. He wanted to hold onto the moment of affection they had shared toward the end of the three-way conversation. The screen returned to the media channels. He saw Pat moving away from the terminal, the busty blonde closing in and taking his arm again, squirming close as Pat shook hands with P.O.E. officers and the others gathered in the lounge. Jael was doing the same, on a lesser scale. She and Carissa, bodyguards in tow, guarded as Pat was, circulated through the happy crowd.

"Your mother is something impressive," Dian said softly. "She's a fighter. Special. Like . . ." She didn't finish. Her grand-mother had meant a great deal to the language tech. Her loving memories were mingled with an almost worshipful awe.

"Pat's looking haggard. He's not sleeping well. He looks worse than any time I can remember since Dad's funeral," Todd said. "His makeup experts must be frantic. He's making it tough for them to pretty him up for the cameras."

"He's older than he was when your dad died, by eleven years, and under lots more stress."

Todd sighed again and looked at his already-assembled luggage, wishing he hadn't been so efficient. If he hadn't packed during the night-rotation duty period, he would have some mindless activity to occupy him now. "Jael knew," he said bitterly. "She knew. Pat told her, but not me. I doubt he even told 'Rissa. So much for pil-low talk. Jael's his political bedfellow, not little Carissa. He owes Jael, and she won't let him forget it. I see he's starting to yank at the bit, though. I thought he owed me, too, but obviously not. I haven't bought him a hundredth of the votes Jael has." He paused, then remarked with wonder, "He's really going to make it. The Chairmanship of Protectors of Earth. My brother. It doesn't seem possible. Jael's going to make him uncrowned king of the world or die trying . . ."

He flinched at his own words. No. Jael wasn't going to die. It wouldn't happen again. They wouldn't let it. There was a pre-servement chamber waiting for her in SE Antarctic Enclave if she fell ill or was hurt. They had never had a chance with Ward, but Jael would survive. All of them would.

Aware of Dian's scrutiny, Todd forced a smile. "We've come a long way since the days when we had to correct reporters who insisted on putting a final 's' on 'Saunder.' "

"Cancel," Dian said.

"I can't." She left the webbing and floated into his lap, kissing him gently. Todd was pleasantly surprised, then understood the strategy. "It's not that I wouldn't enjoy it, but there isn't time. I hate to rush things."

"I know." She kissed him again, lingeringly. "I could go with you." They weighed the options silently, then she shook her head. "No, I'd better stay and finish the messenger data for the Science Council. Besides, Kevin can be a big blond bear when he's mad. And I like your sis plenty, but when she's takin' off, she's a terror —you and your brother and mama all rolled up in one!"

"The best and the worst. We all got a share of temper." Todd grinned at her. "Okay, my cute coward, I'll do the dirty work. Maybe that's because I take after Jael. You tidy up that presentation on the alien signals."

"Yes, sir! Full-range holo-mode, grid corrections, split feeds and shifts, the whole arsenal. Did you pack your grav medications?" Dian asked suddenly, shifting topics. "Coriolis countereffects? CV stimulants? Going from null to one can be . . ."

Todd pushed her off his lap, feigning annoyance. "Nag. Yes, I've got all the meds, and my clothes, and the tape files to update in case I get any spare time while I'm up there." He forgot the rest, drifting up beside Dian as he released the safety belt. They rationed themselves to a few intense kisses. Then he washed up, put on a fresh, non-sweaty jumper, and collected his baggage.

At Suitup, Dian chatted with Gib Owens while Todd wriggled into his gear. The young captain was space-dressed, except for his helmet. "No side trips now, Gib," Dian teased him. "We heard about you and that redhead over on the Pacific side Geosynch station. You gonna ditch the Colony and come down and play free-fall lover with the rest of us?"

Blushing, Owens said, "Nah! I don't detour. She's, well, she's all right. Thing is, I've got to convert her to habitat living. You better plan on filling a vacancy on the ComLink roster."

"Huh! Don't bother us. We've got a waiting list of eager Spacers just shoving and scratching to get on board."

"Goddard has, too," Owens boasted. The banter didn't hide his sincerity. His pride was typical of Goddard's citizens. Not even Todd's ComLink personnel were counted as "true" Spacers, because they rotated planetside too frequently for the Colonists' taste.

Dian had slipped into her thickest United Ghetto States dialect, winking slyly at the pilot. "Tol' him not to read you poetry, this time up. I remember what you said, gripin' 'bout that."

Owens blushed deeper, looking worriedly at Todd, who smirked at him, then put on his helmet. Owens followed suit, and they glided on their tethers into the air lock. Dian pressed close to the side viewport as they proceeded along the tunnel. She waved and Todd returned her good-bye, holding her image in his mind's eye as the ship's door closed between them.

He and Owens went through the final checks rapidly. "You want me to take her out, sir?" Owens asked.

"No, I'd better stay in practice or my pilot's regs will lapse. You ride backup."

"You're the boss, Mr. Saunder."

They went through this ritual every flight. The shuttle's owner-ship papers were complicated. Licensing said a Goddard pilot had to ride with Todd or Todd's designated substitute whenever the ship was traveling inter-orbit. In actuality, the entire upkeep of the vehicle fell to Todd's accounts. Mariette couldn't afford it, not with the other demands on her funds from Goddard Colony.

All the readouts were green. Hisses and clicks came through the earphones. Umbilicals and tunnels retracted, setting them free. Owens's voice droned along on the final reports, confirming the data showing on Todd's boards. They made a last check of their seat restraints and Todd cued the navs and propulsion systems. Just as the clocks hit 1430, the vernier thrusters fired.

"Good timing, sir," Owens complimented him. That, too, was ritual.

Thrusters pushed them away gently from the massive satellite. They went from centimeter increments to halfmeters to meters. There was almost no sense of motion. Todd gauged progress by the readouts and by the way Geosynch HQ was shrinking in apparent size on his screens. They were outside the perimeter patrolled by the little orbiter maintenance watchdogs now, and he could see the whole asymmetrical crazy quilt of his office-warehouse in space. Twinkling miniature stars danced here and there—busy robot space spiders, spinning more metallic fabric over HQ's skin.

Far away, in a lower orbit, Todd saw a shining sail kilometers in length—a solar collecting wall, part of Goddard Power Sats' network. Much lower, beyond visual range, there were other sails, drinking up longwave infrared for Patrick Saunder's competing energy corporation. Everywhere you went in space or on Earth, there was a Saunder waiting to power your vehicle or supply your communications or entertainment needs.

Sunlight bounced off Geosynch HQ. The screens filtered the glare, but Todd winced just the same. Then the shuttle swung on its vertical axis, lining up the vector. Tracking said they were standing off well enough. Navs confirmed. Main propulsion came up, the ion thrusters beginning to kick them into the climb toward one-quarter gravity acceleration. That acceleration was very gradual and muted the stresses. Yet Geosynch HQ dwindled quickly on the screens, proof of the shuttle's building speed. Todd watched his satellite fall behind with mixed anachronistic emotions. Leaving port. The small ship, sailing away from the docks. And he was on the ship, excited at the journey awaiting him, but sorry to be leaving Dian and his people on the floating city in space. Fear, even after many such beginnings and safe voyages. Strong awareness of death waiting a short reach away, outside the hull. Most of all, he felt a tremendous, childlike wonder, reveling in the countless sounds and sights enveloping his being.

On the view screens, Earth floated, achingly beautiful. The Moon was a glowing pearl, a second planetfall, but not his destination. An arrow on the nav monitors marked Goddard Colony's location, too tiny yet to see, with the naked eye.

Geosynch HQ was gone now, lost over the visibility horizon, noted only by sensor blips. The blackness closed in. Their ship seemed motionless, suspended between Earth and Moon.

He and Gib Owens were alone, setting forth across a sea far wider than any planetary waters, soaring up into eternal night, a night in which the Sun never set.

CHAPTER FOUR

☆☆☆☆☆☆☆☆☆

NEW NIGHTMARES FOR OLD

The call had come in from CNAU Caribbean Rescue. Todd couldn't remember who had taken it, could barely remember their climbing into the boat, bucketing through gale warnings to reach that lonely jumble of rocks off the Florida Keys. Rescue warned them not to fly. All air traffic was grounded. They tried to stop them from setting out by boat, in fact. No chance of that. The Saunders never hesitated. They went together, as a family, not daring to speak except to exhort the captain to hurry.

The tropical disturbance had passed by the time they reached the site. It made the emotional devastation that much worse. Todd teetered on a rocky perch, staring in horror at the wreckage smeared down the cliffs and into the surf below. Rescue officers tried to lead him away, telling him and Pat to take their mother back to the boat and wait.

It was too late. He had seen—so had Jael and Pat and Mariette. The Rescue crew was carrying a litter up from the storm-battered seaside cliffs. The man on the stretcher wasn't Ward Saunder, though. A black man, terribly hurt. Roy Paige, Ward's co-pilot and second in command at the lab. Jael stopped the stretcher bearers, touched Paige's bloody forehead, whispered something to him. Something private, personal. The two of them had been together so long, had known Ward an equal length of

time. Paige's tortured reply was a cold blade in Todd's gut, twist-
ing.

"Couldn't . . . went down so fast. Knocked us right outa . . .
outa the sky. Couldn't . . . oh, God, Jael! Tried to hol' onto him.
The water! Tide hit me. Couldn't . . . I blacked out. He's . . . he
wasn't there any more. He was already dead, even then, even . . .
even then . . ."

Nightmare, a recurring one. It had returned, unbidden, unwel-
come, again and again throughout these eleven years. Roy Paige,
reaching out, pleading for forgiveness when he had no need, when
he had struggled past all human comprehension to save his
friend's dead body. Jael, dry-eyed, clasping that hand—the only
whole limb Paige had left. His legs and right arm were bloody
pulp, his head swollen and gory as well. Pat, holding Mari close,
weeping with her, his free arm around his brother as Todd's tears
began to fall.

"He wasn't there any more . . ."

Todd jolted to wakefulness, useless alarms jangling along his
nerves. He was in the shuttle. All that had happened a long while
ago. Old grief. The wound hadn't healed, and sometimes the
memory came back full strength. He forced himself to calm
down, stretching and yawning.

"Rough day, sir?" Owens asked politely.

Todd bit off a retort. "Something like that."

"Eyeball status in about an hour, docking in two."

"Good. Right on schedule, then." Todd rubbed his eyes. For
all the exhilaration he had felt when they launched, this had been
a nominal, very boring flight. He and Owens had tended chores,
confirmed their ETA with Goddard Traffic Control, and fine-
tuned the course. After the initial stress period, they had ditched
their helmets and opened some suit seals, getting comfortable.
They had taken turns overseeing the comps and screens. They
had read, updated the logs, and talked. Todd had steered the conversation onto safe topics. To his relief, Owens didn't dig for private info. They stuck to flight shoptalk, sports, speculations on
which faction would have the most survivors when the controlled-
violence arena season was over in Brazil, and gossip about mu-

tual acquaintances along the ComLink, Goddard, and Lunar Base circuits.

There had been the regular interruptions. Nav sensors pinpointed space junk and lower orbiting objects. Ship idents and sats were already in the comps. There wasn't a remote danger of collision. Nevertheless, the rules set up during spaceflight's infancy required that Todd acknowledge each contact and reconfirm his own position.

Up at L5, duty watch changed at 1800 hours, and the pleasant soprano voice on the com was replaced by a baritone with an Israeli accent. That gave Todd and the young pilot several minutes' worth of ribald jokes.

Time had begun to wear, and Todd had dozed off. The nap hadn't refreshed him, thanks to the nightmare. He stretched again, debating whether or not to take another grav medication. The first dose hadn't quite overcome acceleration's demands on his circulatory system. Anyway, when he reached Goddard, he would be due for another gel capsule. He muffled a yawn and compared his watch with the ship's clocks. ETA 2500, Atlantic Time. Nocturnal watch. He hoped Mari and Kevin were on that rotation currently and wouldn't have to miss sleep because of his arrival. They had promised they would meet him at docking . . .

Todd leaned forward against his safety webbing, staring. Shock gave way to disbelief. He tumbled the data using keys, not trusting his voice to be steady. His fingers flew as he demanded a recompute. The monitors had to be wrong, a glitch somewhere. Scans and multiple backups ran checks in split fractions of seconds. Range numbers—and the blip—took over the screens once more. No mistake.

Not possible. Todd gaped, bewildered, wanting the evidence to go away. That configuration couldn't be there. Nobody had seen anything like that since . . . He shoved panic away, breathing evenly. "Gib?" His mouth had suddenly become very dry. He gulped hard and spoke again, loud enough to be heard this time. "Gib? We've got problems."

"What?" The pilot had a music tape on his private channel, had been tapping his knee in rhythm. Now he darted a glance at Todd's monitors and gasped. Hastily, he threw the display on his own screens.

The comps fed continually, and each new datum made matters worse. There was no way to argue the blip out of existence. Something was there, and closing with them frighteningly fast.

"ASAT?" Todd wondered, then answered himself. "No. That's more than an anti-satellite device. Lots heavier. Missile? Hasn't been one of those in orbit since the Space Neutrality Treaty was signed. We're through with that crazy stuff, knocking each other's satellites to bits. We *have* to be. Damn."

Todd had a wild urge to laugh hysterically. The situation couldn't be real. But it was. He had been spacing since his teens. He knew the risks. A few times it had been scary, but he had come through. This particular risk had never come up before, however. Freak equipment failure, maintenance mistakes— explainable problems, part of the package. That blip wasn't ex- plainable in those terms. Not at all. Whatever it was wouldn't identify itself, wouldn't acknowledge anything their nav comps were throwing at it. All the careful programming designed to eliminate collisions in space was useless. The green mark was coming on steadily, uncaring that it was bringing sudden death to the two men riding in the shuttle.

Owens was on the com. The pilot didn't seem so young any more. Todd recognized the crisp tone and manner—military. Owens was acting like a combat-trained pilot from a planetside war zone, or like one of the Lunar Base fighters. He boosted the uplink gain to maximum. "GC Traffic, this is SE Shuttle One- Five. Copy Feed. Urgent. Data going to you now." Owens com- pressed the signal, giving coordinates and tracking states to Goddard as fast as possible, straining the systems. "Hostile on intercept. Classified A Priority One. ETA impact twenty minutes. Sensors read DE armed. Immediate countereffort needed."

"What the hell is going on?" Todd yelled. "Where did you get that classification?"

"Better suit up full, sir," Owens said absently, treating Todd as supercargo. "Things may get a bit rough."

"Captain, I want to know what you're doing, and I want to know now."

Todd's adrenaline-charged demand made Owens give him a second look. "Yes, sir," he said with considerably more deference. "I'll explain as soon as I can. Help's on the way. Right now we've got to raise orbit and dodge, if possible."

They locked stares. Todd wondered where this help was supposed to come from. Goddard? They were much too far out for the Colony's regular craft to reach them in time.

"Okay," Todd said finally. "Go. But we *will* talk about this, Captain. Rely on it."

Todd grabbed his helmet and jammed it on, snapping the seals shut. Owens was already reprogramming. Orbital maneuvering systems whined up to full power as the corrections sped in. Todd secured his throat and sleeve openings. Inside his protective gear, he began to sweat, then shivered as a chilly wetness snaked along his spine. Owens was trying to complete his resuiting with one hand while he cued the comps manually with the other. Todd reached over to help him and earned a twisted smile in thanks.

"Brace."

The burn smashed Todd into the couch. Pacing himself, he let air out of his lungs as gradually as he could, counting his pulse, attempting to be detached. A long burn. But he wasn't going to give Owens lectures about fuel expense.

When the correction was completed, alarm lights flashed, protesting the drain on the reserves. Together, Todd and the pilot peered at the readouts. New figures came up on their position and the bogey's.

"My God," Todd growled, aghast. "It's altering vector, too. Following us."

"Have to try another orbit change."

"There isn't time." Even as he argued, Todd was working with Owens, frantically pushing another burn into the OMS. There weren't many options, not if they hoped to evade. "If we could just jam its guidance frequencies . . ."

"I already tried that," Owens said.

"You're saying we've got military counterjam gear on this ship? Who gave you the authority to install it? That makes us fair target! The Neutrality Treaty . . ."

"Screw the Treaty. Wouldn't make any difference," Owens said with tired contempt. "That hostile's on full FET and DSCS override plus, bombing right through everything we can throw. Come on, come on . . ."

He was no longer talking to Todd. To whom *was* he talking? Owens was much too familiar with military hardware for Todd's taste. He searched his mind for declassified write-ups of satellite killers and counterdeterrents. Leftovers from the Twenties, all of those, when the space wars had nearly wiped out Earth's communications systems and resource-monitoring satellites as well as every spy orbiter. Old stuff, part of history. Todd had been in his teens. Owens had been in diapers. Ward had coached Todd and taught him as they built ComLink to replace the ruins of that madness in space . . .

Except a new war in space was rushing at him, and he was about to be one of its victims.

Why?

He hated his ignorance and Owens's secrecy. A modern, directed energy weapon or something even worse was homing in on them.

He was going to die, and he wouldn't even know the reason why. That seemed the worst thing about it—not knowing why. They had done everything they could, yet the damned thing was overtaking them, closing fast. In fifteen minutes, he and Gib Owens would be minuscule pieces of flesh and bone, if that much of them survived. They would be strewn along the shuttle's orbital path, drifting to Goddard and beyond.

"It's not after us," Owens said, glaring at the screens. The bogey was coming up on visual. "We just got in the way. They'll get here in time, though," the young pilot added cryptically.

"Who?"

Todd hadn't expected an answer, and he didn't get one. The scans methodically plotted collision courses. Minutes to kill-distance. The thing didn't need to impact to wipe them out. If it got near enough, it would kill them when it disintegrated.

Todd felt a strange, remote sadness. He wished he had Beth Isaacs' faith in the new mysticism. There was so much he wanted to say and do and learn, a lifetime's worth and more. The alien messenger. How was it going to be received? What would the alien species be like? Would Dian and the team be able to break down the language and speak directly to the unknown beings out there? The discovery of the ages . . .

His discovery. And he would never live to see its outcome.

*I'm glad you didn't come along on this trip, Dian. Finish the
job for us, will you . . . ?*

He cued the tracking monitors, perversely seeking the latest
data, wanting to be informed up to the last second. To Todd's
stunned amazement, new blips appeared and a swarm of new
numbers.

Ships! Coming in on a different vector! Six of them!

"Right on track!" Owens pounded enthusiastically on the console. The little blips brightened and grew, visuals shaping and
defining the fast incoming craft. "Get it! Go! *Go!*"

Todd tried to cope. Help. On the way. Gib's happy yelps
confirmed that. But the newcomers bore no idents, didn't match
any configuration in the comps. Sensors read heavy armament, a
lot of top-level military hardware, probably classified. The ships
hurtled in on a bypassing vector, avoiding the shuttle and heading
on intercept with the hostile.

Then coherent light laced dazzling ribbons across the exterior
scans. Todd's momentary surge of fear faded as he realized the
salvo wasn't targeted for him and Gib, not when they could see
the burst edge-on.

What was it? Something very sophisticated, he was sure. The
shuttle's view screens overloaded and shut down to save the systems. Images solarized as a returning blast of light surged from
impact point. Giving up, all the screens went dark.

Todd counted down from the numbers frozen on the kill-range
estimate. Could the ship's radiation-counter gear handle the
wave? The civilian shuttle hadn't been built with hostilities in
mind, but he had no way of knowing how much forbidden military shielding Owens might have installed.

Useless to worry. The wave would hit them just about . . .
now.

He clutched the restraints, his head bouncing inside the cushioned helmet. The shuttle yawed violently to the right, pitched
up, and every alarm went off. Battered by noise and movement,
his middle ears rebelled against the tumbling horizon.

Emergency systems took over, fighting for attitude control. Very
gradually, Todd fell back into the couch. His stomach heaved and
his ears rang as if echoing the warning claxons. But the sickening
motion was steadying out, bit by bit. He willed his internal sys-

tems to quiet down, too, glad he had a tough stomach. Todd swallowed hard, trying to relieve the throbbing pressure in his ears.

The screens were recuperating, also. Rearward visuals revealed a shimmering cloud of metallic substances continuing on the bogey's vector. Sensors warned that the stuff was nasty, but it was widely scattered. The shields ought to be able to take it.

Either the unknowns' weapons had detonated the hostile, or it had been triggered to self-destruct. In any case, it had touched off while it was still out of killing range, thankfully.

Gingerly, Todd swiveled his head, testing his equilibrium. The shuttle was still a trifle unsteady, but not enough to bring back his nausea. "Gib?" He looked anxiously at Owens when the pilot didn't respond. Todd wriggled out of his seat harness and hooked a tether to his belt and the overhead anchor as a precaution. He crawled close to Owens's couch. "Gib? You hurt?"

The pilot mumbled and stirred slightly. That was reassuring, but Todd warned the man to take it slow, nevertheless. With the systems coming up to capacity, he could plug in the med monitors to assess Owens's condition. As he waited for the display, he peered closely at the other man, noting a trickle of blood running down the side of Gib's face. Despite the inner padding, Owens must have cracked his scalp open during that wild tumble from the shock wave.

The med monitors reported Owens's vitals were good, but the possibility of head injury and muscle strain existed. Gib fumbled with his helmet, and Todd repeated his earlier warning, pressing the man back in his couch. He opened the helmet faceplace for a closer look at the wound, fearing the pilot would pull his helmet off, anyway, if he didn't give him some open air. He was making the younger man as comfortable as he could when the com cut in.

"Shuttle One-Five, do you read?"

On the exterior views, Todd saw the newcomers breaking formation. Some headed for the impact point, tracking the hostile's debris. Others were setting up parallel orbits to the shuttle's. Todd waited a long minute, then called deliberately, "I read you. Identity?"

There was a noticeable pause. Then a woman's voice replied, "GC Defense Unit Three. Do you need assistance, One-Five?"

Owens grunted and tried to sit up. ". . . 'm okay . . ."

"You are not okay." Owens sighed and submitted with remarkably little fuss. Todd let the mysterious friendlies stew for a while as he checked the readouts. When he went back on com, he made his voice as impersonal as the woman's. "Unit Three, we can make Goddard without assistance. Ship's integrity is go. My co-pilot is injured. I want to dock without delay. Request medical personnel meet us. Also notify Mariette Saunder what happened, or put me through . . ."

"We are under personal com restriction, Shuttle One-Five. We will relay your message."

Todd wasn't surprised. He said with a bit of heat. "Recomputing course-adjust and fuel reserves. Stand by for update."

"Affirm. We will escort, One-Five."

They didn't ask if he wanted an escort. They told him. Todd picked up some of their background chatter as they traded info first with each other and then with Goddard Control. The audio shorthand resembled Owens's earlier military in-group slang.

Todd finished reprogramming, then strapped Gib and himself in securely for the course correction. They had altered orbit considerably and he didn't want to waste time, so the burn was very expensive. He grimaced as the fuel readings dropped sharply. Well, Saunder Enterprises could afford it. At least his branch of the family corporation could. If Mari refused to foot her share of the bill, he would—

Todd halted his runaway irritation. Why had he been ready to retaliate before he had been hit? Whatever disagreements they had had, he knew Mari wasn't petty. If she could scrape up the funds, she would pay him back without hesitation. There would be plenty else for them to squabble about when he saw her, but not that.

When he saw her . . . ETA update to Goddard now read 2430. Sooner than he and Gib had planned. Better sooner than never.

Todd realized he was shuddering. Delayed reaction. He noted his tremors as if it were someone else's body. He had been remarkably calm during the last minutes as the hostile homed in on them. He hadn't known he could be that collected in such a situation. Now that the immediate danger was over, jitters racked him. Odd. The physical sensations were quite similar to those he had felt when he had a definite confirm on the alien messenger's existence, when it first returned the signal they had sent it. The stimulus had been quite different—giddy elation rather than icy terror. Yet his body treated both emotional shocks identically.

Owens barely spoke throughout the trip, even though he seemed to be conscious. When Todd talked to him, the pilot, if he responded at all, mumbled unintelligibly. The med readouts continued low nominal, not serious enough, it seemed to Todd, to produce this result. Was it a genuine injury aftereffect? Or had Owens found a handy excuse to avoid answering Todd's questions? Todd eyed the young pilot suspiciously. Perhaps he was being unfair, just as he had been anticipating Mari to bitch about fuel expenses. Such uncharitable doubts were new to him. So was being menaced by a satellite and shuttle killer.

The habitat came up on visuals. Scanners picked out the wheel against the blackness long before Todd could eyeball it. He watched as the speck grew and took on distinct form. The screens showed the original construction-shack sections of the banded torus and various outliers and other work stations orbiting close by. Todd had made this approach often, but he never tired of the view. Even now, his ragged nerves couldn't spoil his enjoyment of that massive beauty.

Goddard Colony *was* beautiful. Pat and the anti-Spacers couldn't see it that way. Ward Saunder would have. Todd longed to share the view with his father. The station had been a dream almost off the drawing boards, but not quite, when Ward had been killed. They would have ridden up here together, searching for bits of poetic description from old books they had read, a friendly rivalry in praising the great space wheel with words.

Goddard's space spiders were busy, weaving fresh hide for the station. Little commuter craft plied the vacuum between Goddard and the nearby orbiting factories and mass driver terminal stations. A tow vessel should be arriving soon from the major lunar mining collection point, bring a fresh cargo of precious compacted Moon soil for breakdown and manufacture.

At first, everything seemed normal. Then anomalies crept into the familiar scene. Todd cued zoom scan to port, studying the orbiting spacecraft factory. Usually the open-sided drydock held an assortment of mini-shuttles and a cargo hauler. Now the regular output was parked outside the structure, as if to make room for more important work. Todd saw several sleek, military-type craft resembling the Unit Three fighters. And there was another ship, larger and built to handle—eventually—a planetary gravity stress. Todd had seen the design proposed three years before, when he had been a guest during the Colony's monthly Planning Group meeting. The discussion had been heated, fired by the pioneering spirit so prevalent on the habitat. In the end, as much as the Group wanted to go ahead, they had tabled the blueprint, admitting they couldn't swing the funds from P.O.E.'s supplementary credits or from their own profit picture. The Mars Base Colony ship would have to go on indefinite standby, for at least ten years.

Yet there it was, half built.

Goddard Traffic Control took over the shuttle's guidance. From this point on, Todd and Gib would be passengers. Retros and vernier thrusters aligned the ship delicately onto Tracking's preplotted course. Todd adjusted his orientation again as the shuttle decelerated and began to match the habitat's rotation. They were dropping from one-quarter to null gravity, speed and motion shifting confusingly.

Resolution was sharp and stark. Objects stood out brilliantly or were hidden in deepest shadow. Docking brought arriving ships in on a track that avoided the Colony's solar collectors' glare. As a result, he could gaze at the station without squinting. His curiosity aroused by the shipbuilding in the spacecraft factory, Todd studied the torus, not sure what he was looking for.

Suddenly, he wanted to slow the shuttle. He was in too close and moving closer. Too close to see what had happened to Section Four of the immense wheel. Something was very wrong. What *had* happened? A gap was torn out of the station, penetrating the outer radiation shield. The interior was ripped open and shattered. It was a massive wound in the space station's integrity.

Alert now, he saw another wound. Not as big as the one that had destroyed Section Four, but bad. Section Two was also hurt, and it was residential. Day or night, the disaster was bound to have caught many people in their homes. Had they had time to get to adjacent areas and secure life-support? Todd fervently hoped so, badly shaken by what he had seen.

Unexpectedly he saw the catastrophe through alien eyes. What would they—the species which had built the alien messenger vehicle—think of this? They must have had space stations, might still have some. Had their stations ever suffered this kind of damage? Why? And how?

Todd knew the how, here. He didn't want to look at it squarely, but the likelihood was unavoidable. Missile strike.

"Shuttle One-Five, prepare for docking in five minutes."

He woke out of his speculations, making final safety checks. They drifted in toward Goddard's hub. By now the Colony was too huge for the scanners to take in, no matter how much they reduced the view. He could pick up remotes from Goddard's own orbiting watchdog cameras. That was the only way he could get the full picture from this close in.

Coming into port. Our ship survived a pirate attack . . .

The brightly lit docking bay was straight ahead. A bright green cross flashed on the nav screens. Todd's escort had dropped back. Were they waiting their turns to dock, or getting ready to take off on another rescue mission? They had delivered their charges and were now free to get back to work. What *was* their work? How much defense and rescue did they have to do? And whom were they defending Goddard from?

The shuttle coasted slowly inside the docking bay. Relative forward motion ceased. The ship's OMS thrusters shut down, and the station's low-field magnetic grapnels reached for them. The craft shivered at the contact. By centimeters, they were pulled into berth. Connecting tunnels and umbilicals locked in place. All the external sounds Todd had left at Geosynch HQ were back. The shuttle was on Goddard Colony's life-support systems.

While pressure came up, Todd put a final entry in the trip log and cut off the internal systems. Owens peered at him through slitted eyelids and groaned. He didn't seem interested when Todd told him they were docked. Interior screens scanned the shuttle's air lock as it opened. A med team floated through the connecting tunnel and into the ship. Other station personnel followed. Cargo supervisors? They didn't look the type, even though a couple of them started running inventory as soon as they arrived inside the craft. Two of them took up positions by the air lock. Guards? That had never happened on any of Todd's previous trips to Goddard.

The cockpit hatch opened, and medics rushed in. Despite the pressurization, they remained fully suited. Todd was reassured by that. Whatever was going on at the Colony, they weren't letting safety standards slide. A couple of medics began checking out Owens while another scanned Todd. He okayed him re residual radiation or obvious injuries, then started upshipping his heavier equipment.

"That's not necessary. I'm not hurt," Todd said quickly.

No argument. Not even a suggestion he go to Sickbay for a thorough look-see. Instead, the medic nodded and shoved the heavy examining gear across the cockpit to his co-workers.

"Is Gib . . . ?"

"Too early to tell, sir." The tone told Todd to mind his own business.

The space was becoming crowded. The medics wouldn't let Todd help, and he was in their way. They angled a stretcher awkwardly over his head and the consoles and positioned it to carry the pilot. Todd didn't need any stronger hint. He pushed off and left.

At the air lock, other Goddard personnel were still checking inventory, or pretending to. Normally Todd took no interest in unloading, beyond signing the forms when Goddard's accounting department asked him to. This time he eyed the people thoughtfully and asked several questions. He got no more satisfaction than he had from the medics. Disgusted, he reached for his personal luggage on the rack by the air lock. A guard came between him and the bag. "That'll be taken care of, sir. You'll be staying in your sister's housing unit? Then we'll deliver it there."

Todd tried to edge around the human barricade. Another guard joined the first. They politely but firmly fended off Todd's efforts. "What is this? Are you confiscating my luggage?"

"No, sir. Regulations, sir. Your luggage is quite safe. If you need anything from it immediately, you can requisition it from Security . . ."

"I will! I'll just talk to Kevin McKelvey. *He's* in charge of Se-

curity, in case you've forgotten, and he just happens to be living
with my sister." Todd hadn't used a name for clout in a long time.
Previously, the magic name "Saunder" had been enough to get results. Here it seemed as if McKelvey's should do it. The only result was a peculiar, patronizing attitude, as if the guards knew
something Todd didn't, something funny. "You're going to keep
the luggage? You want to see my ID, too?"

"No, sir. We know who you are."

"Really? I was beginning to wonder." Todd dived out the air
lock, leaving his luggage behind. Two more guards were waiting
beyond the exit tunnel. They swam up alongside him, hemming
Todd in, although they didn't touch or restrain him in any way.
"And what are *you?*" Todd asked acidly. "My honor guard?"

"Just making sure you get to Port of Entry okay, sir," one of
the unrequested escorts explained. "There's been a lot of new
construction since you were here last, Mr. Saunder. Some of it's
kind of dangerous. You're not properly suited up for those areas."

Visions of the damaged torus sections flashed in Todd's mind.
Was that the construction they referred to? But here they were at
the Hub, not out on the wheel, where the wrecked sections were.
An escort didn't make any sense here. An *armed* escort. Both
men wore military side arms. One of them was a civilian. The
other was part of Kevin McKelvey's liaison detachment posted at
Goddard from Lunar Base Copernicus. They worked expertly together. Playing escort efficiently and being ready to disable an invader. It was plain this sort of duty wasn't new to either of them.

Did they think *he* was an invader?

Sobered, Todd made his way through the Hub from docking.
The areas around Traffic Control seemed abnormally crowded.
Perhaps the extra personnel were needed to handle the Defense
Units' comings and goings. Obviously they had been tracking that
missile by the time Gib called them. Rescue must have already
been on its way when the shuttle sent a Mayday. But in spite of
the claims of Todd's escort, he saw no new construction. He *did*
see large numbers of sealed hatches marked "No Admittance
Without Planning Group Authorization." Another change since
his last trip. Something very much out of the way was taking
place here.

Defensive measures? The next step would be offensive. Was

that what was going on in the sealed-off rooms? Installing cannons and counterstrike equipment? He recoiled from the idea and its implications.

There were more armed guards, more mingling of the military and civilians. Some of the civilians acted green, but the same combat-ready manner marked them all. The regular staff wouldn't speak to Todd. He knew many of them, and they knew him. He had been a loyal supporter of Goddard Colony since its inception and was no stranger here. Not only did his attempted greetings bring no response, but occasionally he received a glare of naked hatred, shocking him.

At Suit Storage, the guards removed their helmets but kept on their pressure suits while the guest stripped to his jumper. Like Defense Unit Three, they waited to get him off their hands so they could return to regular chores. Todd was about to ask them what those regular chores were when the outer door opened and a group of Colonists drifted in, heading for the suit lockers. Mariette came in right behind them, scooting her anchoring tether hurriedly along the rail until she reached Todd. She flung her arms about him and together they bobbed about, held only by her safety line.

Todd grunted in the enthusiasm of her embrace, grinning. She pressed her close-cropped dark hair against his cheek and he felt her tremble. When they came up for air, he tweaked her chin. "Are you crying, Mari?"

She *was* sniffling. But she was also beaming, that smile, like Pat's, which made sunlight dim. "Not any more. Not now that you're here! Oh, it's so good to see you!" She hugged him again as Todd yelped in sham protest and clung to the rail for balance.

Kevin McKelvey remained by the outer door, talking to a couple of soldiers and several civilians. He wore his commander's uniform, but the Lunar Base patches had been removed. McKelvey's strong face showed fresh worry lines. "Check the circuits and let me know. Don't let them get that close again," he said. The soldiers and civilians rushed away. No chatter. No joking. Very serious and intent. Todd was used to the special zeal of Goddard citizens, but usually that dedication was leavened with laughter. Now there was none. Those who had been suiting up were gone, too. The three of them were alone in the locker room.

Keeping one arm about his waist, Mariette steered Todd toward the outer hall. He didn't bother hooking up his own tether. She was his anchor. Kevin followed them through the door and shut it. His oversized paw engulfed Todd's hand, and Kevin underlined Mariette's welcome with a hearty, "Damned glad you made it, Todd."

"It's nice to know I'm appreciated. It would have been a lot nicer if I'd had some warning about the fireworks you were going to stage for me."

"That's not fair," Mariette protested.

"No outraged innocence, Mari. I'm not in the mood."

"Neither are we," Kevin's basso growl broke in. His ruddy complexion darkened threateningly. "This isn't a game. And we're not putting on a show."

"But you *are* keeping secrets, from me and from Earth," Todd said. "And I'm tired of it. I think I'm overdue for explanations. Gib promised me some, then dodged by getting himself concussed, or a reasonable facsimile thereof."

Kevin's annoyed look told Todd he had scored a hit with that guess. But the officer offered no apologies.

"Is Gib hurt badly?" Mariette asked, concerned.

"I don't think it's serious," Todd said. "The medics weren't very worried. How about it, Kevin? Are they taking him to Sickbay, or to Debriefing?"

"Maybe a little of both, depending on the doctors' verdict."

Todd's patience snapped. "All right. We've said hello. The amenities have been satisfied. Your medics wanted me out of their hair before Gib said anything incriminating. And your escort took me through this armed camp to make sure I didn't butt in on any superspy stuff. What's this all about? I'm not an enemy. I came riding up here, peacefully planning a visit to my sister, and some missile almost makes it a case of like father, like son . . ."

Mariette's face turned deathly white. "Don't!"

"Well, dammit, that's what happened. Are you going to tell me why I'm being shot at and treated like an invader? Or do I draw my own conclusions?"

"We'll tell you as much as we can," Mariette promised. Kevin started to argue, and she rounded on him as quickly as action and reaction allowed. He steadied her, holding her by the shoulders, meeting her eyes. Todd was embarrassed to be present, an intruder on an intimate scene. They did nothing but look at each other, yet everything was obvious. The relationship had always been intense. Now it was a conflagration.

Kevin broke the stillness at last. "Let's grab some gravity. Then we can talk." He led the way to the nearby elevator.

As they crowded into the aluminum cage, Todd said, "I assume your apartment wasn't damaged when Section Two got mangled." Their reactions were so fierce he was taken aback. Lamely, he mumbled an apology. "Uh, were there many casualties?"

"Yes." Kevin didn't elaborate, and Todd wished he could disappear for a while.

They traveled out along the immense spoke. Elevator view panels showed them their progress toward the torus. Other spokes, containing similar elevators, were radiating arms reaching from the Hub to the wheel. At each level, the angle of view of those spokes widened, and above them the incredible bulk of the torus loomed larger and larger.

Any trip to Goddard or a return to Earth from Todd's satellite chain exacted a price. Todd's cardiovascular system, bones, and muscles complained. He hadn't noticed the sinus congestion so much at ComLink. Now, rising toward one gravity, he did. He could make the adjustment rapidly compared with some, but there were always a few upsetting minutes when he first arrived. On schedule, his viscera roiled. He endured the inner confusion while the cage moved twenty meters farther up the spoke. He marveled that Goddard's citizens could make this trip so frequently, going to their jobs elsewhere on the torus, out to the lunar mining collection net, or to the various adjacent stations.

A few years earlier, Mari had hired Todd's media people to produce a recruitment documentary about Goddard. They had made a few converts. But most of the Earth audience rejected the euphoric picture of habitat living. No matter how bad problems were on Earth, space dwelling seemed far worse, an alien, "unnatural" world. To the Goddard citizen, life in the habitat was "clean," and many looked back on their former existence on Earth with revulsion.

Had the species which built the alien vehicle faced this same division in its ranks? Had one faction adopted space and another turned its back on it? And had a third sought to hold those two opposing factions together?

Was it even possible to hold them together? Or was Todd Saunder fighting a hopeless battle? He wished he could hear the opinion of his counterpart out of the aliens' past, if there had been such. If they had survived this war of living choices, there might be a chance for humanity to do so, too.

The view panels displayed scenes from Goddard's outer watchdog cameras. They showed the blasted sections of the wheel. The devastation was, in its way, as severe as that dealt Earth by manmade catastrophes and the Tangshan and New Madrid quakes. Yet there had been no exodus from Goddard. The surviving sections of the torus were lit and bustling with activity under the protection of the lunar soil radiation shields covering the wheel. Reconstruction was already underway. They weren't leaving.

Planetsiders had moved back into Earth's ravaged lands and rebuilt, too.

Homo sapiens, the defiant species.

Would the species which sent the alien messenger understand these nuances in human behavior? There were so many questions he wanted to ask—of the messenger, and of Mari and Kevin.

Todd's ComLink personnel were space-oriented and sympathetic to Goddard. But they spaced for mere four- or six-week stints, then were rotated planetside. More and more Goddard Colonists signed on for indefinite periods, and some were turning down leaves to Earth altogether. There were children being born in the habitat. What would those children be like in ten or twenty years? Todd doubted they would adapt to an Earthside existence any better than most present Earthmen could adapt to space. The environments were too different. Goddard citizens were leaving planetary origins behind. Their world was artificial and fully satisfying. Eventually, they would never want to go "home" to Earth.

The elevator cage sighed to a stop, finally. They stepped out onto a platform surrounded by a mini-park. Lush grass, young shade trees, and flowers scented the air and pleased the eye. Mari looked over at Todd. "Did you remember to take your med gravs? You look queasy."

"My God! You're as bad as Dian . . ."

"Good for her, then."

"What is this, a conspiracy? Yes, I took the damned medications, a whole pharmacy full." He was a trifle weak, just the same. As they started through the park, to Todd's chagrin, he stumbled and nearly fell. Kevin gripped his elbow, helping him toward the pedestrian walkway. "I'm not that feeble," Todd said. The big man paid him no attention, so Todd decided to go gracefully.

More guards, marching on patrol even here, in a residential section. They appeared to be drilling, the military people instructing the civilians in how to follow orders and handle their side arms. The ranking guard in the nearest group saluted Kevin smartly. "Good afternoon, Governor."

"Good afternoon, Ma Jiang. It's okay. I'll vouch for him." Again Todd sensed hostility toward him where there had never been any before. Why must McKelvey vouch for him? And what would happen if he didn't?

Belatedly, another surprising thing hit Todd. "Governor?" he asked, bewildered. That Sino expatriate guard hadn't sounded as if he were reverting to quaint British slang. He had addressed McKelvey with much respect, setting "Governor" with an initial capital letter.

"We'll talk about that, too," Kevin promised. He and Mariette paused in the shopping area near the park, as if giving Todd time to get used to a lot of new things—of which there were plenty. The convenience shops weren't new, but their goods and displays were. Ordinarily, the stores featured foods and fashions imported from Earth, entertainment tapes and so forth. Luxury and leisure items for the people in this torus section. Now the luxury items were crowded into the corners. Locally produced propaganda tapes, and even a few microfiche printouts and a couple of real books, filled the display shelves. Hard-sell tape presentations blared from the stores' monitor screens. Images of Goddard's planetside political allies and Colony orators ranted, blaming Patrick Saunder and Earth First Party for Goddard's slow economic strangulation this past year. There was not a moderate voice among them, no one pleading for understanding and patience.

Slowly, Mari and Kevin edged out onto the walkway, Todd following along like a puppet. They might be setting this snail's pace out of consideration for his recent arrival from null gravity. Or was there another reason? McKelvey was stony-faced. Mariette was a drama tape, as she usually was. Todd had no problem reading volumes in her expression. She was wearing her teeth-of-the-hurricane face. She had always gone to that mode whenever Jael or one of her brothers was about to stomp her for some whim or mischief. What was Mari expecting him to blow up about this time?

Todd studied his surroundings carefully. Section One was the oldest residential area of Goddard. After five years' growth, the saplings brought from Earth were almost full-sized, adorning the lawns, the park, and overhanging the pathway here and there. Decorative shrubs and flower beds bordered the little grassy plots separating each apartment unit. There was some new construction here, and that was most unusual. There was nothing in the Planning Group's growth projection about this, not for another five years. Yet mini beam-builders and workmen swarmed over the roofs of each tri-story dwelling. The changes threatened more than orderly aesthetics. A fourth story added to every unit would severely strain the ecosystem's precisely planned balance. There would have to be a lot of adjustment.

But they *had* to have new housing, to accommodate those dispossessed when Section Two was destroyed. Even these extra stories wouldn't be enough. A fourth floor atop every residential dwelling throughout the torus still couldn't handle the overflow. Where were the rest going to live?

Maybe they had no need for housing, ever again.

The shocks continued coming. The horizon was wrong. A gently upcurving perspective was a normal part of the torus environment. The lofty ceiling imitated the sky. Reflected solar light made the landscape almost Earth "normal." The warm, humid air was sub-tropical and very soft.

Abruptly, a quarter of a kilometer away, the curving horizon stopped. So did the sunlight, the open ceiling effect, and there was no air beyond that point. Things hadn't looked like this since Section Two had been completed and joined to One. A transparent buffer, rimmed by heavily reinforced metal, blocked all access between the sections once more. A vacuum barrier. They had never expected to use them, once the torus sections were joined and the wheel finished. Odds were a million to one that a really large piece of space junk would impact and damage the station.

A million to one odds.

Todd was seeing, from the inside out, the destruction he had observed while he was approaching Goddard Colony. As bad as it had looked from a distance, the damage was much worse from this angle. He was frighteningly aware that he wore no spacesuit, had no protection, should that buffer give way. That was instant death up there, just on the other side of that wall. Somehow, the trees and flowers and grass and people hurrying past him, continuing their daily lives, made the realization more awful.

Section Two had been hit, not by a random meteor, but by the tremendous killing force of a modern anti-satellite missile.

CHAPTER FIVE

THE PRESENT DANGER

It must have happened with terrifying suddenness. The shields had held. Section One's and Section Three's life-support hadn't bled away into space. But the planetlike illusion of Goddard's extended horizon was ruined. Through the transparent part of the buffer, Todd saw space spiders rebuilding. The robots and the human riggers could rebuild bulkheads, radiation shields, and dwellings. The station's horticulturists could replant trees and grass. But what of the people who had been inside when the missile struck?

Todd had attended a celebration at Mariette's apartment, not much over three years ago. He had congratulated them on the completion of Section Two and wished them continued success and prosperity.

Good wishes weren't worth much against missiles.

His thoughts a jumble, Todd walked on toward that gigantic wall. Kevin had let go of his arm, presumably deciding the smaller man wasn't going to fall on his face if he did. Before Todd could cross the empty zone that led from the last grassy plot to the buffer, Mari and Kevin guided him into Apartment Twelve's courtyard. More guards. Again they saluted Kevin and addressed him as "Governor." One of the soldiers cued the service monitors for them, hailing three single-lifters down to ground level for their convenience.

Todd stepped onto one of the little elevators. The safety casing slid shut around him as Mariette got on the carrier next to his. Kevin caught one at the far end of the wall. The miniature platform squeaked loudly when Kevin boarded. Fortunately, Goddard's metallurgists had allowed for cargo as heavy as McKelvey. The lifter didn't collapse.

They rode up the side of the building. The smooth ascent gave Todd a widening overview of Section One. He could look across to other apartments and down on the mini-parks and stores. To his right, that ugly barrier soared to the torus' "sky." Its top edge was lost in the glow of sunlight filtered in from Goddard's outer solar collectors.

They alighted at the third-story terrace, where noise assaulted them. Workmen cursed and equipment whined and hammered. The lower stories were solidly faced in lunar clay brick, all doors, windows, and brick terraces fully complete, had been for nearly five years. Up top, there were piles of steel and aluminum and silicate insulation, and a great deal of confusion. It looked as if it would be weeks, if not months, before the apartments would be ready for occupancy.

Another guard was on duty outside the apartment. Kevin returned his salute. "I've notified the Planning Group. I'm not on call for the next couple of hours, except for emergencies. I mean that. Let Legislator Mikhail handle things. But if you have to, go Priority Red and grab me, and don't waste time."

McKelvey often appeared easy-going, even phlegmatic. But Todd had seen that relaxed amiability disappear in a moment. The guard had, too. He snapped to attention. "Will do, sir. You won't be interrupted."

Todd relished the soundproofing inside the apartment. Construction clamor dampened to a distant murmur. His sister and Kevin walked by him as he stood just beyond the door, looking around. After so many changes, the apartment was a haven of stability. Kevin and Mariette had changed almost nothing since he had moved in with her a year and a half ago. The place was typical of Goddard, compact but open enough not to feel cramped. The glass, metal, and fabrics were all of local manufacture, produced from lunar raw products shipped to the Colony *via* the mass driver. Two holo-mode murals divided the sleeping alcove from the living areas, refresher, and food dispenser. The photos reminded a visitor of the occupants' origins. The picture opposite the entryway was Mari's favorite aerial view of Saunderhome, drenched in tropical sunlight. At right angles to that was a large scene of a brooding, rain-lashed Scottish mountain.

Todd dropped into the nearest chair. The upholstery rustled against his jumper and the fiberglass chair frame. The cloth felt like velvet, but its distinctive underlying texture proved it was Goddard silica fabric. "I hope you don't mind sleeping on the couch," Mari was saying. She prowled about fluffing sofa pillows, playing hostess. "We're a trifle crowded. No guest units available right now."

"No, not at all." Todd glanced out the window, remembering how many people had been on the pathways and in the shops, far more than normal. "I was expecting you to be sharing with a family or two, after I saw what happened to Section Two."

"We volunteered to share," Kevin said, "but they didn't assign anyone to our apartment." That fact bothered the big man, as if he felt guilty but was helpless to rectify the situation. Todd thought of the guards' saluting Kevin and everyone's treating him with deference. Maybe rank had its privileges, and that's why the housing programmers hadn't taken up Kevin's offer. A governor, after all, must have some dignity and not be forced to double up his housing like an ordinary citizen. If that was the way it was, Kevin was uncomfortable with those privileges.

"I invited myself," Todd said lightly. "The couch will be a lot softer than sleeping on the lab floor."

"You *did* used to go to sleep there, didn't you?" Mariette laughed. "After you tried to stay awake until all hours watching Dad's experiments. You were crazy. Still are."

"Something to eat, drink?" Kevin asked, waving at the dispenser alcove.

"Talk."

"Well, *I* want something," Mariette announced. She marched into the little room and cued her selections loudly.

Kevin seemed amused by her behavior. He dragged a chair up alongside Todd's and sat down, waiting, not putting forward any information. Todd sighed in exasperation. This was going to be hard work. "Questions: What's this about your being governor?

And since when does Goddard have combat-equipped 'Defense Units,' or civilians wearing side arms? Those were practically drill teams I saw outside. What happened to the Colony Planning Group? Did you get rid of your elected representatives, or what?"

"The Planning Group is still running things. It's still a democracy," Kevin said a bit testily. "But things have changed since you were here in September."

"That's obvious! Pat would love to know how you got promoted from liaison officer to governor in a mere two months. At that rate, he should have won the P.O.E. Chairmanship a week after he started to campaign."

Todd's sarcasm brought angry curses from the dispenser alcove. Mariette took out her spleen on the equipment rather than on her brother. Then she came back to the living area and slapped tumblers of amaranth liquor down on the serving tables, splashing some of the contents. Kevin grinned and picked up the glass nearest him, sipping the dark liquid. "Mari, he has no way of knowing. Let me tell him, since you promised him some answers."

Grudgingly, Mariette nodded. She sat on the edge of the fiberglass bench beneath the holo-mode mural of Saunderhome. The backdrop of waving palms and white sand highlighted her beauty, but she was unaware of the effect. She watched Kevin intently.

The big man stared into nothing for a while. "Todd," he finally began, "it's not a military coup. I can tell that's what you've been thinking. I didn't want the job. The Planning Group and Goddard's citizens insisted I take it. I agreed, as long as they understood that it's temporary. I'll hold office only during the present danger."

"The present danger," Todd muttered, considering the term.

"The Colony needs defense coordination, and it needs it fast. The station was never set up to cope with hostile assaults. My people are helping train the citizens to protect themselves, and to protect the Colony, if worse comes to worst. I repeat, the position is strictly temporary," Kevin said firmly.

"Forgive me if I harbor a doubt regarding that. Temporary governorships or kingships have a way of becoming permanent." Kevin looked sour, but he didn't argue the point further. Todd's mouth was dry. He took a swig of the amaranth and grimaced. The Colony's home-brewed alcohol was a taste he had never acquired. It left a raw streak down his gullet. He pushed the tumbler out of easy reach, lest he absentmindedly drink more. "Okay. I'll accept a beefed-up security force and a citizen army, some sort of civil defense. But the way they're training . . . are you expecting a boarding party? I'll agree, after what happened to me out in orbit, you need *something*."

Kevin's bright blue eyes shone with a fighter's anger. "We had to act first and discuss whether it was overreaction later. We'll show you why. Defense posture had to go into high gear."

Mariette had been lacing and unlacing her long fingers. Now she reached for a nearby view monitor, swiveling the screen so that Todd and Kevin could see it easily. "Computer, this is Mariette Saunder, Torus Section One, Unit A-Three, Apartment Twelve. Code Clearance Zero Zero Eighteen Dash Six. Replay October nine missile attack. Exterior scans. Final five minutes. Put on scrambler lock, for viewing at this monitor only. Run."

Todd saw a missile approaching Goddard's long-range cameras, coming at incredible speed. Collision systems going to full alert. Tracking, plotting and following and trying desperately to outguess the hostile's changing vector. Claxons rang while numbers flickered across the techs' screens. Hair prickled on Todd's neck as, in the center of the monitor, a fast-moving dot grew rapidly into a cylindrical shape.

Shining, inexorable, bringing death and destruction.

"We weren't prepared," Kevin said with surprising calm. "We *thought* we were. We had had advance warnings. Our planetside allies have their spies, and they told us something nasty was likely to happen. We figured it would be another attempt to sabotage our shuttles or sats. We thought if they fired anything at us, it'd be small enough for us to handle. Nobody expected the warheads to be that effective or their jammer overrides so good."

Todd was hypnotized by the playback. He wanted to look away, but he couldn't. There were silvery darts at the edges of the screen now. Ships from Goddard. Not the superfast military craft which had come to his and Gib's rescue. He could tell without reading the dancing figures that the little ships would never be able to reach the missile in time to do any good.

"That first attack taught us some lessons." Mariette's voice shook. "We did confuse their guidance frequencies a trifle, though."

"Yes," Kevin said. "A slight diversion, enough to put it off target." He had forgotten his drink. "We got lucky, or the outcome would have been much worse."

The playback wasn't holo-mode, but it was far too realistic, anyway. Todd gripped the chair arms, his knuckles whitening. It was difficult to convince himself this was merely an image. His heart was starting to race just as it had when the missile had homed in on *him.*

"It dodged our outlying detectors," Kevin said. "Terrific masking devices they've got, Todd. The best military developments. They've made some modern improvements on your father's original telecom patents, the ones the brass bought up during the Satellite Wars. We had to catch up fast, so we borrowed."

"From Lunar Base Copernicus."

"You named it. I *am* a liaison officer. Thank God the base is on our side. The next hostile didn't get through so easily."

Todd tried to pry his fingers loose from the chair arm. *Our side.* He had warned Pat. The lunar science and military bases had suffered fund cuts in much the same way Goddard had. The results had been predictable. Starving economically, united by their common space environments, Goddard and the military base on the Moon had joined forces. The base was giving Goddard classified weapons and ships, probably lending trained pilots and other personnel to boot. Allies, against their enemies on Earth.

On the monitor, the hostile loomed in the exterior scans. Man's electronic servants showed him the last seconds before impact. The missile hurtled in, its apparent size exploding awesomely until it filled the entire screen.

No zoom focus. Real-size factor.

Involuntarily, Todd flinched. Pointless. This had taken place nearly two months ago. It was all over. If he had been in Section Two of the station . . .

"Explosive decompression," Todd whispered.

"Not quite," Kevin corrected him. "Close, though. The sheer size of the torus, and the meteor strike buffers, helped. And if it hadn't been for our outer radiation shield of lunar soil, that damned thing would have ripped the whole section to bits and fried us all. It was bad enough as it was." He sighed tiredly and went on. "The bastards programmed the strike during Section Two's nocturnal hours. Some people never had a chance to get moving. I mean, that missile came in on burn mode all the way, Todd. They wanted us dead. And they used a hell of a propulsion system to do the job—top-quality military hardware. Killed fifty-eight people outright and put another one hundred and six in Sickbay. Some of them are still there. Four Planning Group members were killed or hurt. That's when we woke up. The Group ordered a total Colony meeting and an election to fill the vacant offices temporarily. That's when they slapped this governorship on me. I barely got us organized when the second missile came in a few weeks later."

The screen went blank. Todd massaged his temples. He was dizzy, and not from Coriolis effect.

"Second missile? My God. Slow down and give me a chance to take all this in. For starters, why haven't you broadcast this? Earth has to know. They'd be as horrified and angry as I am. And why haven't you taken the injured planetside? Surely Goddard's Sickbay isn't equipped to handle injuries of this nature . . ."

"They refused," Mari said simply, sounding surprised that Todd had asked the question.

"What? And you went along with their decision? Todd gasped in outrage. "Critically wounded people! How in the hell could they make rational judgments about their treatment? Mari, what's the matter with you and Kevin? You know they could get better medical care on Earth!"

"We don't agree."

"And for terminal cases, you could have arranged for cryo preservation in our own Antarctic Enclave—"

"*No!*" Mari's color was very high, her sharp features taut with defiance. "No! If they're going to die, they want to go clean, the way *we'd* want to. We're fellow Colonists. We're damned if we'll send any of our people to the pole. They'd just love to get a few more of us into that frozen limbo and dispose of us, just like they're picking off our planetside allies."

Invisible hammers were pounding Todd's skull. "You're not making any sense. What's that supposed to mean?"

"It means our allies go to SE Antarctic Enclave and disappear —that is, if their enemies don't simply assassinate them instead."

"Disappear? Confinees are cryogenically preserved, for God's sake! You know that. Get off this paranoia track!"

"They're *dead!* Not figuratively, not cryogenic sleep—dead! Killed in their own countries, or sent to the Enclave and conveniently allowed to die."

Todd looked from one to the other, stunned. "How can you believe that? Dad set up the Enclave, remember? Its purpose is to save lives, not take them. The P.O.E.'s Human Rights Committee watchdogs tour there twice a year—you can see *anyone,* criminal or would-be saint, who's preserved there, any time, via holo-mode relay. The Enclave's neutral territory, strictly protected by the P.O.E. There's no 'enemy agent' involved, dammit. It's an altruistic gift from the family, and it costs Saunder Enterprises plenty to maintain, too."

"It's a sham," Kevin said quietly. As Todd started to argue, the young governor softened the accusation. "Maybe not the whole Enclave. We're not sure. Probably it does fine by the famous artists and musicians and philosophers, the non-political confinees. But *our* people, dissidents and rebels, like those Pat's arbitration committee just shipped off from the Trans-Pacific, they're getting a one-way ticket. I don't care how glorious a future the Earth Firsters deliver if they live up to their promises—those people aren't going to be revived, ever. They're gone."

Todd rubbed his temples harder, his head throbbing. "Look, you seem to forget I helped set up the Enclave, too. I worked with Dad. I was on the board of directors. Okay, I was a kid, getting in on a courtesy pass because I was Dad's 'aide.' But I was there. I know how it operates. It's a genuine, workable facility. We proved that with a successful revival of that criminal volunteer before we ever started building—"

"And you haven't been on the board of directors for what—eight years?" Mari cut in. Todd had to think back, realizing she spoke the truth. "You don't know what's going on there, do you? How long since you've been to the Enclave?"

"It's restricted territory, P.O.E. franchise; only Enclave person-nel and the Human Rights Committee are permitted access. Not even the P.O.E. Chairman can go there if he isn't also a member of the Human Rights Committee . . ."

"And who's on the Committee? Anyone you ever heard of? Do you know if they're trustworthy? Or do you just take P.O.E.'s word for it?" Mari demanded. She added with a vicious snarl, "Or Earth First Party's word for it, that is."

"Mari . . ."

"Don't tell us any lies about the Human Rights Committee," Kevin said, stopping Todd. "We don't trust it. The truth is, there are damned few planetsiders we *do* trust any more."

"Does that mean you don't trust me, either?"

Todd waited a painfully long time for a reply. His shock deepened as the moments passed. Kevin and Mari were silently swapping opinions, and he was locked out. He hadn't realized this wall had come between them. When the missile shattered the torus sections, buffers had gone up to protect the survivors. There was a buffer between him and his sister now, too, and Todd had no weapons to break it down except words and a lifetime of love.

Then, just as he had begun to despair, Mariette stretched her hand to him. He seized it as he would a lifeline. She was still angry, but there was love in her pale eyes, too. The wall *could* be breached!

"We trust you, Todd," she said very softly. Her fingers tight-ened about his, her short nails digging into his flesh. He endured that, feeling the high-strung nature of her emotions. Even a hurt-ful touch was better than no touch at all.

Todd struggled to collect his thoughts. "This tape was made October ninth? Just a week after I was here. My God," he breathed. "Today's December fifteenth. How . . . how many at-tacks in all?"

"Four, counting today's." Todd's jaw dropped at McKelvey's response. Kevin shrugged. Perhaps he could accept the horror with such courage because of his background and training. "Mari wanted to call you today, while we were scrambling. I couldn't let her. We were on full scrambler. Nothing to help the missile track us, no personal messages. We didn't have any time to spare. It's damned fortunate Unit Three was on patrol out where they were. Do you understand what I'm saying, Todd?"

"Not really. Gib said our shuttle wasn't the target, that we just got in the way . . ."

"That's right." Mariette explained as she would to a child. "They shadowed you, using the shuttle's systems output as a screen. They must have figured, after Pat's little speech, that the Colony would be in too much of an uproar to stay on top of the defense scans."

Todd laughed weakly. "This . . . this is impossible. This whole mess. You put classified military equipment in my shuttle. Okay, after today, I appreciate the fact that I'm still alive partially because of that equipment. But the stuff also makes me fair game for whoever's . . . who *is* launching these attacks?"

He couldn't imagine why he hadn't asked that earlier. The grav medications and stresses must be heavier than he had realized; either that, or he was getting old.

They were maddeningly quiet for so long he wanted to yell at them.

"When we're sure, we'll tell you," Kevin said at last. "They're obviously putting the missiles together in orbit, covering their activities with jammers, maybe with holo-modes to pass the missiles off as empty space or orbiting junk, until they're ready to launch. They're not amateurs. It's either bootleg materiel or captured war booty. Damned good stuff, too," he added, admiring the enemy's ingenuity and cunning. Kevin locked his large hands behind his golden head and tilted far back in his chair, threatening to overturn it. "The birds disintegrate both what they impact and themselves. The launchers don't want to leave us any leftovers to trace back to them, obviously. What they apparently hadn't thought out is—we can sweep up the dust in our net and sift through the pieces until we pin down their identities."

"Net?" Todd brightened. "Of course! The mass driver package collection station. It must work just as well on missile pieces as it does on lunar soil being lobbed up from the Moon."

Kevin grinned, a predatory leer. "You named it. But *you're* a Spacer. Even though they're building in orbit, they're not. Eventually, we'll have it all analyzed."

"Good! Rely on it, that's what you need," Todd said. "While you do that, let me handle the groundwork. I can spread this news worldwide on ComLink. When we haul the hard evidence into P.O.E.'s court, we can slap sanctions on your attackers and cut them off at the ankles. Listen, don't wait. Go with what you've got right now. I don't know why you're sitting on it. We have to stop this before anyone else gets hurt. The Space Neutrality Treaty—"

Their response was less obscene than Gib Owens's, but equally contemptuous. "Don't quote that farce," Mari retorted. "The Earth Firsters have ignored any treaty that gets in their way, especially anything pertaining to Goddard. And now that they have the Chairmanship practically in their pockets, they'll bury us."

"Are you implying Pat's responsible for these attacks?" Fists clenched, Todd half rose from his chair, anger overcoming common sense. Kevin's own chair came down with a thump, and the man was ready to fight back if Todd crossed over the line. It wouldn't be a contest.

Mari caught Todd's arm, urging him to sit down. "No! Not Pat!" she cried. "Not . . . personally."

The fact that she qualified her retraction shook Todd more than anything else she or Kevin had said. He wrenched out of her grasp, walking away from them both, thinking hard.

What was happening to them? How could Mari doubt Pat, even for an instant? Yet . . . how could Pat so ruthlessly cut out Goddard's planetside allies economically when he knew he was also destroying Goddard in the process? Pat had voted against every funding measure for Goddard for the past year. Earth First Party's platform was adamantly against Goddard's continuance. A frivolous waste of Earth's irreplaceable resources, they called it, shouting down counterarguments, their majority ruling. And Pat was their star, following the party line, swaying global opinion more and more to their side.

Todd came back to the mural of Saunderhome, to Mari. Pat's dreams and Mari's were 400,000 kilometers apart. Tentatively, Todd caressed Mariette's high cheekbone, wanting to recapture the old closeness. Danger was fraying their lifelong affection, trying to pull them apart.

"Mari, Pat can't see things your way. He's planetbound. He al-

ways will be, both he and Jael. Space makes them, literally, sick.
But that doesn't mean Pat hates you. Sure, he wants that Chairmanship, wants it more than he ever wanted anything. But even
to win votes, do you think he'd order missile attacks against Goddard? Against anyone? Not after what we all lived through in
California and outside Chicago during the Death Years, Mari.
Life is precious to him, *all* life. He spouts a lot of garbage, I
know, in those speeches. But what happened to us, and especially
what happened to Dad, shaped his ideas forever."

His throat ached with suppressed anguish. Marietta cradled her
head in his hand, sighing. Kevin didn't interfere for several long
moments. But then he said, "Maybe your brother didn't sign the
orders, Todd. But the Earth First Party has a big interest in
wrecking Goddard. You can't deny that. And Patrick Saunder
leads the party. By my definition, that *does* make him responsible
for this, even if only indirectly. Ah!" He looked away, gazing out
the window at the vacuum barrier that safely shut them off from
Section Two's wreckage. "It doesn't matter, anyway. Earth wants
to get rid of us, and it goes both ways. Only our technique is a
trifle different."

Mari glanced at Kevin searchingly, and he turned toward her.
Again they conferred in that private, silent language. This time,
though, Todd understood them. "Secession? You can't pull it off.
Not yet."

"They're cutting our throats, Todd," Mari said, chewing her
lip. "Too many of our planetside supporters are quitting or
bailing out. And plenty are disappearing into Antarctica. No
wonder those who are left are scared or becoming too weak to
fight back. Dummy corporations and undercover stuff! Somebody's trying to make the power sat sabotages look like the work
of the Ganz-Heil League or the Nakamuras. But we don't think it
is. Whoever they are, they want to destroy Goddard, not just shut
us off as an energy source. We won't play games with Earth First,
and Earth First has to rule it all. If they can't enslave us, they'll
wipe us out!"

"You still haven't got the clout or the funds to swing total independence. Section Four was an agriculture area, wasn't it? I
thought so. You're on short rations, have a severe housing crisis,
funds drying up, power sats being sabotaged or boycotted . . .

you just can't do it. Not yet. This is the wrong route. I keep telling you, broadcast this. You're, what, clamping the lid on everything? No leaves? Full censorship? That's stupid. How long can you hope to hold the blackout? Look, go to Earth with it. I'll donate all the air time you need. You can have ComLink's entertainment and docudrama departments, full propaganda push. You don't have to limp along with just a few staunch planetside allies. Turn Earth's attitude around. Mari shouldn't have to bankroll you singlehandedly any more, and I know she's exhausted her trusts."

"If Jael would—"

Todd cut his sister off. "You know she won't. She can't. She's plowing everything into Pat's campaign. You had a third of the inheritance from Dad, Mari. The division was fair, admit it." He rushed back to the basic topic. "Spread the news. I'll get you Frank Chabot and Miguel Falco, my best media people. Lay it on. Goddard will be swamped with sympathy and support—and funds! People always root for the underdog."

"We don't need their help," Mariette said pettishly, pulling away from him.

Todd snorted in derision. "Don't you? Who's buying Goddard Power Sats' output if not planetsiders? Where are your new recruits going to come from?"

"We'll stand by our allies. And when we pinpoint the missile launchers, we'll handle that. Then we can think about more recruitment." Mari stood up and began pacing. "Sooner or later, we're going independent, Todd. There's no stopping us. So just quit telling us we can't do it. As for telling Earth about the missile strikes, we'll probably have to let Fairchild go to Protectors of Earth with the news, whether we like it or not. But not for the reasons you cite."

Kevin frowned, and Mari continued on in support of their Third Millennium Movement ally. "What else can she do? Pat's killing Fairchild with the voters, her and Dabrowski and every other Chairmanship candidate. She's fighting for her political life. We've *got* to crack the barriers, for the Spacers' sake. That speech of Pat's! 'For the good of humanity . . . !' For the good of Pat Saunder, he would have said if he'd been honest."

Todd stepped into Mari's path, holding her. "It *is* for the good of humanity. Or do you want mankind to head back into the Chaos and the Death Years? Pat and those arbitrators swung some juicy deals for themselves, granted. But they ended the war. It's called compromise, Mari. Remember? Jael taught the Saunders how to be experts at that. It's the only way we got out of some mighty tight places. Come *on!* Pat's not your enemy. You know that."

"Do I?" For a fraction of a second, Todd wasn't in the station. He was hanging in space, his protective suit crumbling away, leaving him naked to high vacuum. Mari sensed his fear, and her arms closed about him. "Oh, Todd! I didn't really mean that. I wish . . . I wish . . . we're drifting apart, aren't we? And I don't want that to happen."

He held her tightly. "We won't *let* it happen." Above Mari's head he saw McKelvey and read warnings in the big man's face. Jealousy. Not sexual jealousy, but a fierce possessiveness that didn't grant much space even to a brother. Todd sensed he was on thin ice. "We won't let it," he repeated insistently. He looked from Mari to Kevin and back again. "It's not too late to mend fences, unless you're planning to take off for Mars tomorrow."

Todd had the rare pleasure of seeing Kevin McKelvey at a loss. "How did you . . . ? You saw her, when you were coming in? But . . ." For a moment, the cool soldier's demeanor cracked. Kevin was ingenuously startled.

"Give me credit for some brains. I read your propaganda. I keep up on *all* the family's projects." Todd grinned and tapped a finger to his forehead. "It goes with the telecom business. Anything you want to know, I've got the resources to dig it out. I don't make a bad intermediary for family squabbles, either." Mariette hugged him roughly, pretending to be annoyed. Todd savored the lightness as long as he dared. Then he sobered. "You can't afford a Mars colony. I can show you the stats, if you're ignoring them yourselves. You must know you're not ready . . ."

"Mankind's never ready for the new and daring, the exploration. If we waited until all the problems were solved, enough funds piled up, we'd never go anywhere. We'd die out as a species. That's why we're going now, ready or not, while we've got the courage and the will." Kevin spoke with calm confidence. Mari nodded, fire in her eyes, excited by the prospect. "We know what the difficulties are, yes," Kevin went on. "But those won't hold us back. We're going to Mars, and beyond. There's a Solar System, a universe . . . waiting for us. The planetsiders can crawl in their holes and stagnate. Our destiny's tied to the stars."

He made Todd believe, suspended his doubts, for the moment. There was no logical argument against such idealism. Kevin was right, in some respects; it took just that kind of daring to get this job done. Yet throughout human history, such ventures triumphed at a high price—explorers' lives and the aftereffects of opening those new frontiers. Inevitably, what the Colonists meant to do would affect all mankind.

Todd shook his head. "The fact remains, you can't really afford it, any more than Earth could afford the Trans-Pacific war. There's going to be a heavy bill to pay, for Mars and for Earth. Earth isn't going to recuperate for decades. Mari, you know Pat won't get the payoff right away. He'll hurt, for now. So will I. But it's worth it, to stop the killing. Isn't it worth it to you?" The situation wasn't equal. He and Pat had diversified. Mari had plowed her fortune into Goddard and borrowed against her future inheritance from Jael as well. Unless the Colony made it, Mariette would be bankrupt.

"Peace at a price," Mariette said sadly. "And somehow I always pay the biggest portion. Why doesn't it go both ways? Why isn't someone willing to pay a price to bring Goddard peace and stop killing our people?"

"They will be—"

Kevin broke in, his deep voice hard. "Even if Fairchild breaks the news about the missile attacks, they won't stop. You're naive if you think they will, Todd. Oh, they'll probably form an investigative committee and make a lot of horrified noises. But our enemies aren't going to pay much attention to that. There's too much at stake. They're not going to give up until we stop them ourselves."

The ominous tone turned Todd's gut to ice. "Wipe them out, whoever they are? Then what? You abandon Earth, turn your back on it and head out to Mars? Forget the rest of us. We're dinosaurs, already extinct. Is that your feeling?"

Kevin seemed a bit uncomfortable. "No, not exactly. But the future means an inevitable separation between the Spacers and the Earth-bound. There's no other course. For now, well, we have friends down there. We'll stick by them as long as we can. We don't want anything to happen to them."

Todd feared this was a prelude to more paranoiac talk about SE Antarctic Enclave. "Tell Pat what you think and how you feel. Tell him to his face. Give him a chance to defend himself against your accusations. Anybody deserves that, Mari, even your own brother."

"That's not fair," she protested.

"Yes, it is. You accused him. Maybe he's accusing you, on other counts. Hell, I don't know. We hardly ever get together as we used to." It was so. Time passing too quickly, people he loved slipping away from one another and from him. And there was a time when they had mattered more to each other than anything else in the world.

"Jael put you up to this, didn't she? She wants you to drag me to Dad's birthday anniversary." There was less rancor in Mariette's manner than Todd had feared.

"I want you to come, too. So does Pat. He said to tell you he misses you. Yes, he did, don't shake your head. You two always were too bullheaded. Jael figured I might be able to coax you into kissing and making up, despite everything." Such teasing had worked when they were kids. Now he felt stubborn resistance. Maybe he had said too much, too little, or said it in the wrong way. He gazed at Mariette, seeing the reckless little girl. Impatient, she had skinned knees and elbows countless times rather than wait or use caution. He knew what it felt like, wanting to own, to possess something unique and precious.

The stars.

I want the stars, too, Mari. And I've already touched them, through the alien messenger. Wait. Just a little while longer. Don't hurt yourself with your impatience this time. I want to tell you. But I can't. It has to be equal—all of us together, sharing. I resented Pat's holding back information from me. Now I realize I'm doing the same thing to you and Pat and Mother. But please . . . wait. It will be worth it. You'll see . . .

"Jael." Mariette spoke so softly Todd strained to hear her. "She looked so old on that broadcast today. I hadn't realized how much she was aging recently. Why doesn't she retire?"

"Mother? Retire? Unthinkable! you know that." Todd hesitated, then said, "I don't want to be morbid, but you know how much Dad's birthday anniversary means to her."

"Yes, I know," Mari replied wistfully.

"It can be like old times, if we try. Jael wants it so much. It gives Dad back to us, even for a little while. All us chickens, back home under Mama's wings. Okay, hell, she was maternal off and on, depending on whether her business cutthroating gave enough time for us. But we're family. We came through plenty together because we *were* together. When you consider how many people have no family continuity at all . . ."

"Like Dian," Mari said suddenly.

Mari, caring, fiercely protective of "her people" on the Colony. Empathizing with Dian Foix, orphaned during the Death Years, living through the Chaos while her heroine grandmother patched up the wounded and rescued the damned. And Pat, caring, holding a dying baby, begging doctors to save her, forgetting he was supposed to be a cold-blooded politician, interested only in votes.

They could care so much; the capacity was tremendous.

Mari moved over to Kevin's chair and leaned over the back, clasping her slender hands across his chest. After a long minute's consideration, she nodded. "All right. I'll come to Saunderhome." Her announcement took both men by surprise. Kevin squirmed around to look at her. Mariette laid a finger on his lips. "I've decided I will. That's that. I'll go, Todd, if you promise me something in return." Kevin relaxed, as if he had guessed what she had in mind.

"Conditions?"

"Compromises," Mari replied slyly.

Defeated, cornered by his own words, Todd smiled. "What?"

"Information. You bragged you could tap in on anybody." Todd didn't know whether to keep fighting or submit gracefully. He was more than cornered; he was trapped. "Information we can't get. Maybe only a Saunder can get it, a Saunder with inside connections and a global telecom network to dip into. It can't be Pat. He couldn't step off that campaign platform, even if he believed the way we did. And it certainly can't be Carissa. Jael's as wrapped up in the campaign as Pat is. Besides, we can't count on her being impartial."

"Don't be overconfident about me, either," Todd said sourly. "Impartiality about what?"

"Survival, of our allies and our private funding on Earth." Kevin drew her arms about his neck, holding her hands in his.

"You're talking espionage."

"No." Mari was emphatic. Why didn't Todd trust her denial? "Saunder Enterprises is a quasi-nation, duly chartered by P.O.E. We're not asking you to hunt out anything that shouldn't be available to any member of the family, or to the president of ComLink Corporation." Her manner became wheedling. "Todd, you must. You're the only one who knows how to bypass all those accountants' data locks and the rest of that comp technicalese. You say you took up where Dad left off. You understand his patents better than anyone, right?"

"A few SE top techs might disagree with you about that." Todd enjoyed the flattery but knew he was hemmed in all around the circle.

Did he *want* to say no? It wasn't paranoia to think they were being threatened here at Goddard. If the missiles were real, could any of the rest of it be real, too? Against his will, Todd felt a growing curiosity. He was being sucked into a whirlpool, not knowing where it would take him.

"Just what am I supposed to find if I push through the accountants' comp locks?"

"Fund juggling. Account clipping. Rigged trials . . ."

"Mari," Todd said wearily, "I can't do anything to reverse court decisions. Those are people who were convicted in dozens of nations. Whether or not you and I agree with the judgments, the trials are over and done with. Surely there are appeals court, legal means . . ."

"If the victims are still alive. Find out for us, Todd." She paused, and Kevin gently stroked her hands, encouraging her. "If they're frozen but okay, well, we hate it—it's against their will—but there's a future for them. And we'll see that future gets here as fast as possible, and their governments will eventually revoke their sentences. I don't care if you and I and Pat are all grayheaded and doddering by then. I'll personally go to Antarctica and escort them home to their families, to their grandchildren."

Todd rubbed his chin, thinking over the technicalities involved.

Kevin nudged him. "We're mostly worried about the Antarctic confinees, it's true. But our finances are in serious shape, too. We've tried to get the data, demand audits. Our people planetside keep getting snarled in red tape. They won't be looking for you to come in on the flank. Just get us some proof so we can tell the world and make them turn loose those funds."

"Any other little miracles you'd like me to perform while I'm at it?"

Mariette lit up. "You'll do it?"

Todd spread his hands in surrender. He didn't mention his own growing suspicions on the same matters which concerned them. He had to save himself *some* bargaining power for later. "Do I have a choice? It's blackmail, you know. You set this up, Mari. You were planning to do this all along, weren't you? Okay. And in exchange, you'll come to Saunderhome for Dad's anniversary. Agreed?" Mariette left Kevin and rushed to him, wrapping him in one of her exuberant embraces. *"Oof!* Hey! It won't be so bad. Dian's going with me. She and Kevin and Carissa can play peacemakers if we start getting out of hand with family togetherness."

"Sweet little Carissa," Mari said cattily. Todd had never quite understood her dislike of Pat's wife. "Is she bothering to keep track of that blond bitch with the over-developed mammaries, or does she just let Pat run out to the end of his leash now and then?"

This wasn't the time or the place to let her explore that animosity. Todd grabbed what he had won before things could go wrong. "If my shuttle's ready after the maintenance checks, we could catch a window on the next turn-around vector. I'm going to pick up Dian and Beth Isaacs and a few of my rotation personnel at Geosynch HQ for a ride to Orleans Port."

Dian and Beth and the others on Project Search's team were going to be his guests at the Science Council conference, when he would read the paper regarding the alien messenger vehicle. They had worked very hard, and they deserved to be there with him when the spotlights turned his way.

"I'll set it up for the two of you with Traffic Control," Kevin said. Mariette's face fell, but she didn't seem too surprised. Kevin heaved himself up out of his chair and stood in front of the picture of the mountain. "I won't be accompanying you planetside. I'm needed here. Please make my apologies."

"Jael's hoping you'll join us," Todd said. "She asked about you specifically."

"Sorry. I can't. Maybe there'll be another time, when things aren't so tense. I admired your father tremendously. I'd be honored to be included in a family commemoration for him. But not at this time." There was a note of finality Todd couldn't miss. Unlike Mari, Kevin wasn't nursing a possible "yes" in his mind.

Kevin McKelvey wasn't boasting. He *was* needed. It wasn't merely his expertise in military matters and the fact that the liaison troops were loyal to him and able to share their training with Goddard's civilians. Kevin had served on the Colony's Planning Group for two years. He had been good at it, and the Group had turned to him often for leadership. In some form or another, he had been bound to rise to the top. He didn't seem to yearn for political power the way Pat did. But he had a gift of command, as did Pat. People recognized it and sought him out.

The Saunder women were drawn to men of action and vision, out-of-the-ordinary men. Ward Saunder, the fey, eccentric scientist. Jael Hartman's old-money family hadn't seen his potential, but Jael had turned her back on a world of tradition, elegance, and wealth in order to marry the penniless inventor. Now Mariette was turning her back on Earth and risking everything because of her belief in Kevin McKelvey and the Colony he led. With McKelvey at Goddard, Mariette's presence at Saunderhome would be a mere token appearance. No matter how many quarrels Todd patched up, Mariette would head back to the Colony, and to Kevin, as soon as she could. A foregone conclusion.

Kevin stood at parade rest. "You take care of her," he said heavily.

"Of course I will," Todd returned, bristling. "What kind of order is that? She's my sister."

"That's the only reason she's going planetside."

Suddenly, Todd realized that wasn't a quaint male-superiority statement. Kevin was merely stating the, to him, obvious. Mariette wouldn't have agreed to this trip to Earth for anyone *but* Todd. And Kevin wouldn't have felt she was safe with anyone less personally interested in her welfare. In his own way, McKelvey was expressing a great deal of confidence in Todd.

Then Kevin slapped his hands together loudly, making Todd start. "How about some food, since everything's settled?"

"Look, if you're on short rations . . ."

"We've got storehouses. We're dispersing and decentralizing. We're doing fine. No problem. We've got some nice cottonseed derivatives for you to try out. You'll like them better than our amaranth moonshine, I'll bet," Kevin said with a wink, noting Todd's barely touched glass. "And the usual fish and rice and yams—oh, and there're some green vegetables and plump little chickens. Why don't I just plug through your diet card and whip us up something?" Kevin went into the dispenser alcove. His bulk nearly filled the mini-room. Todd wondered where they had got a diet card file on him. He hadn't given it to them.

They have files on everything, probably. They're fully computerized and comfortable with technology, racing to meet the future. Bright, well informed, and brave to the point of fanaticism.

But they need me to probe SE's files planetside. That's a tie with Earth they can't afford to cut yet.

Kevin waited for the dispenser monitor to okay his selections. "I imagine you'll want some sack time, too, after running through that shooting gallery."

"I'd like to check in on Gib, see if he's doing okay . . ."

"Sure! I'll arrange it. He'll appreciate the thought. What can we do to entertain you until a launch window clears? That'll probably be thirty-six hours away, or so. Maybe a run out to the docks? Would you like to see how we're coming on the Mars colonizer? We'll trust you to keep that under your hat."

Irrepressible. Fund shortages and missile attacks be damned. They were going to try for Mars. They might even make it. And twenty years hence, the Goddard Colonists who stayed with the first station would undoubtedly be worrying about a growing independence movement among their children on another planet.

A ride out to the docks would probably give Todd a close-up view of the damage to the torus as well. The threat of extinction, and the hope of an endless series of tomorrows on Mars.

"Yes, I'd enjoy seeing the Mars ship. Very much," Todd said, smiling.

"We thought you would." Kevin grinned back at him, letting down the barriers. No pomp, suitable to a space colony governor. This was the big bear of a man Todd had met on numerous other visits to Goddard, a slow-talking giant with a wry sense of humor, very likable, someone Todd was glad Mariette had fallen in love with. She had picked some bad ones in the past. This time she had shown some sense.

Mari relayed the trays as Kevin passed them out, and they gathered around the table to eat. Todd was relieved to discover they had programmed some wine for him rather than more amaranth liquor. The wine, too, was locally produced. But it had vigor, waking his tongue. Nothing subtle about it, though the flavor was good. Kevin raised his glass and clinked it against Todd's and Mariette's. "To us. Good fortune attend us." They drank to that, and Kevin licked drops of amaranth off his lips. "And just as soon as we clear away the petty details, we'll get started. Mars it is!"

CHAPTER SIX

☆☆☆☆☆☆☆☆☆

FORTRESS EDEN

TODD felt as if he had been tiptoeing across a thin hull for the past several days. The tension was getting to him. At Goddard, once Mari had agreed to come to the family reunion, she and McKelvey had been in good spirits. They had taken Todd on the tour of the facilities, and he had given them his promise not to reveal the missile attacks or their planned Mars expedition. They wanted both of those to be Fairchild's ammunition in her campaign against the Earth First Party. That promise had seemed a cheap price for Todd to pay—keep his mouth shut in exchange for a harmonious trip to Earth and Saunderhome.

True to her word, Mari *had* been easy to get along with on the flight down to Geosynch HQ. Their pilot, Gib Owens's temporary replacement, was a fellow habitat citizen, of course. That made Mari comfortable. It was safety in numbers, with Todd the outsider.

Matters changed, though, as soon as they arrived at Geosynch. While they waited for the heavy orbital ship and a good re-entry window, Mari went on the defensive. She began making cryptic remarks, being sarcastic in the middle of commonplace conversations, until Todd's staff scratched their heads in confusion. Todd seethed every time Mari capped one of her stunts by glaring a warning at *him* to keep the cat in the bag. Dian wasn't fooled for long. Eventually, in private, she demanded to know what was

going on. There was a brief yelling match between the siblings before Mari grumpily acknowledged she had caused the confrontation herself. She liked Dian, trusted her. So Dian was let in on
the news. Part of it. Todd held back some of the details about the
most recent missile attack, but Dian was horrified enough by what
they told her. He didn't like to think how she would react if she
knew how hair-raising things had been there for a while.

Even after Dian joined their little conspiracy, Mari didn't shut
up. Some devil nagged at her. It always had, Todd admitted with
resignation. Perhaps it was part of his sister's lifelong fascination
with danger. She desperately wanted to bottle up the information
so that Fairchild could use it as a surprise against the anti-
Spacers. At the same time, Mari was like a little girl figuratively
cupping her hands, hiding a treasure, and gloating, "I'll bet you
can't guess what I've got!"

By the time the Earth shuttle docked at Geosynch HQ to pick
them up, Todd wanted to shake Mari until her teeth rattled—not
an easy trick in free fall.

Secrets. On all sides. And he was in the middle of them. He
had to concoct convincing reasons to explain why Beth Isaacs
and Anatole and Wu Min were riding down to Earth with him
and Dian and Mari. The other passengers on the heavy orbital vehicle knew the work schedules of everyone along the satellite net.
Project Search wasn't exactly a secret, but it wasn't everyday
knowledge, either, not even among those highly trained techs
sharing the trip with them. More lies. Todd told anyone who
asked that Beth and her colleagues were going to New Washington to update some new improvements on ComLink's translator-
splitter. To his relief, the cover story was accepted without question. Mari, too, took it at face value. Dian and the others stayed
away from any talk about the Global Science Council as well, despite their mutual eagerness regarding the upcoming event.

The process frayed Todd's patience. He was becoming sick of it
all, was almost sorry he had decided to sit on the revelation about
the alien messenger this long. But it wouldn't be much longer before he could tell *someone* . . .

To top off his edgy mood, the landing at Orleans Spaceport was
particularly sloppy. They touched down and jounced for kilometers, Mari bitching most of the way, comparing this shoddy pilot-

ing to the crack techniques of *her* Goddardites. Disembarking, too, was inefficient and seemed to take forever. Todd had planned to be at Saunderhome by noon, and he began to wonder if they would make it by sunset at this rate. At last the gate checks were complete and they and the other shuttle passengers stepped onto the ride strip for another too-slow trip over to the global terminal.

The handle of the little case Todd was carrying grew slippery with his sweat. He glanced down at it in annoyance, taking a better grip. Such a small container to hold such momentous news: holo-mode data cubes, crammed with vital information about the alien messenger. Dian smiled at him, reading his mind. Then she turned back to Mariette. Beth and Anatole and Wu Min were listening with interest as Mari described Goddard's speed language-learning experiments, its attempt to bridge the gaps in the multinational Colony.

Todd's sweaty palms itched, and his jumper was sticking to his back. The air-recycling mechanism inside the travel tube must have failed. Pat's SE Trans Company share-leased part of Orleans' facilities, and big brother deserved a complaint.

Mariette had arrived at the same conclusion. She mopped her high forehead with her sleeve. "Pat's not paying his rent? It must be forty degrees centigrade in here." Dian and Beth Isaacs seconded her opinion. The other two techs who had ridden down with Todd, and a group of passengers from one of Riccardi's Incorporated Network's satellites, grumbled, too. Some of them glowered up at the arching polarized plexi window-roof covering the ride strip. It was still more than a kilometer to the global terminal, too far to carry luggage in this heat. Normally, if Todd had been in a hurry and alone, he would have toted his baggage and walked ahead, adding his own pace to that of the rolling conveyor. Condensation dripped from the plexi, now and then splattering one of the passengers underneath. Todd wished there were some way to get over to the private hangars quickly. He was anxious to climb into an air-conditioned flier and get airborne.

The ride strip was bumpy, needing repair. Several times it had shifted under his feet, nearly tipping over his luggage. A few people took extra steps and nudged their bags along with their knees. Most just endured the discomfort.

Then Todd saw something move at the edge of his vision, to

his left, beyond the dark plexi. A lot of confusion out there. Vast crowds were surging this way and that across the terminal's domestic runways, taxi lanes, and maintenance areas. They were milling about the ground traffic near the hangars, also. The normal view out there showed nothing more interesting than baggage trams or a mechanic heading for work. Today the hectares of pavement resembled an insects' nest. People swarmed, running, waving objects Todd couldn't identify, their mouths moving, though no sound reached him inside the insulated plexi.

"What's going on out there?" a Riccardi tech asked of no one in particular.

He was a competitor, but Dian answered him in a friendly tone. "It's just a run-of-the-mill civil insurrection." She wasn't joking. The sparkle was gone from her eyes. It was as if a door were slamming inside her, to guard against a hostile outside world.

"They're coming this way!" Beth Isaacs shouted.

Part of the crowd split off and rushed toward the transfer tube, a sea of humanity, soundlessly howling. In the middle of that sea, several men and women rode a commandeered baggage tram. The power was on full, and some of the mob couldn't get out of its way. The tram squashed them under its treads and rumbled on. Blood spattered; the motorized tram careened wildly, aiming for the plexi window-roof.

"Gonna hit us," Dian warned, slipping into her old accent. "Gotta make a barricade. Luggage."

Todd grasped her idea and shouted. "This way, everybody over to this side of the ride strip! Pile the luggage Up! Get down! Hurry!" He couldn't play general for everyone. Riccardi's employees were leaderless and refused his orders. Dian helped Todd push Beth Isaacs, Mariette, and the rest of their group flat on the moving strip, despite Mariette's wanting to stand up and see what was coming.

Todd peeked over the heap of baggage as the tram smashed into the plexi wall. The entire tube roof shuddered, though it didn't break. The sound penetrated, however, dinning at the trapped passengers. Stalled, nose up and treads spinning futilely, the tram perched against the transparent wall. The mob overran it and began beating with fists and clubs on the polarized barrier.

Riccardi's personnel grew panicky, screaming. Those who were still standing staggered into one another and into their luggage. Normally they rode this strip without conscious thought. Now they lost all sense of balance, as helpless as babies.

Alarms went off, lances of noise stabbing Todd's ears. How many times was he going to be hit with that terrifying sound in one week? he wondered bitterly. He craned his neck, looking toward the far end of the ride strip, still a half-kilometer distant. Uniformed security troops, running, trying to get at the point of attack.

How many? Were they CNAU Civil Order Enforcement or some of the terminal staff? Todd had more faith in the national troops. But right now he would welcome any kind of assistance.

Most of the security guards were probably already busy fighting that army of rioters out on the tarmac beyond the plexi.

"We'd better try to make it to the terminal," Todd decided. Dian was on her hands and knees, laboriously dragging a suitcase, edging forward in the ride strip's direction of travel.

Mari crouched beside Beth and the two techs. "If I only had a . . ."

What had Mariette been about to say? "If I only had a gun?" Goddard Colonists didn't like playing sitting duck. Mari had been through too much of that recently. She wanted to fight back.

"Forget it," Todd told his sister. "There're too many of them. Come on. Get moving that way, toward the guards." He unfastened his jumper and slid the little case with the holo-mode masters inside. The stretched cloth held the case snugly against his chest. He couldn't risk having the case knocked about or taken out of his hand. But if they broke through and killed him, they would get the case, anyway.

As that thought struck him, he heard cracking plexi and an animal roar exploding from dozens of throats, even above the tortured whine of an abused tram engine. The mob had picked up the tram and hurled it against the window-roof until they had broken it!

"Get 'em! Get the damn Spacers!"

"Kill 'em! Kill 'em all!"

"Spacers! Spacers!"

The murderous crowd spilled through the narrow opening, running along the ride strip, chasing the passengers. Todd saw them in slow motion, time and space distorted. The women struggled to move, crawling or stumbling forward and trying to keep the baggage with them as protection. Their pursuers were stumbling, too, almost comically. But they kept coming, still yelling, promising what they were going to do when they reached the unarmed Spacers.

Todd dropped back, letting the women and the two male techs move ahead of him. Parallel to him, outside the plexi windowroof, the rioters who hadn't broken through continued to scream silently and pound on the wall between them. No threat from them, so far.

Inside the tube, it was a different story. The leader of the tram commandeers outraced his companions. He was tall, taller than Pat, but thin. Eyes burned in a dark, plague-ravaged face. Gaunt hollows showed when his puffing cheeks sucked in as he gulped for breath. He knocked down a Riccardi tech, stomping the woman mercilessly, then rushed on, heading toward Todd's group.

Filthy, clawlike hands reached out for Todd's throat.

Todd avoided the clumsy charge, tripping the man. They both swayed awkwardly for a second as the mob leader clutched at Todd's jumper, trying to stay on his feet. Todd felt the holo-mode case shifting against his skin. Fearing he would lose it, he brought his knee up sharply, then kicked the man's skinny legs out from under him.

His attacker toppled backward, falling half on and half off the ride strip, writhing and screaming. The tall man was unable to get a solid purchase on the strip or the narrow stationary curbing at its edge. His long legs dragged forward along the strip while he hung onto the curb, or tried to.

In another few seconds, some of his followers had caught up. They tripped over his legs, still extended out into the strip, blocking their way. A few jumped over him and approached, yelling obscenely. Others were busy beating and kicking the trapped Riccardi techs. Todd saw a club raise and come down on a tech's head, splattering blood.

"Spacers! Kill the bastards and bitches!"

"Wipe 'em out!"

Hate for the humans who had escaped an Earth-bound, miserable existence. The mob was in rags, haggard-looking. Todd didn't
know if they were starving or drugged or simply searching for
loot and victims. He didn't care. Rational thought ceased as more
of the rioters loped directly for him and the women behind him.

He picked up a suitcase and threw it, hard. The bulky makeshift missile bowled into the charging forerunners, stopping two
of them instantly and knocking the rest off their strides. Shrieks
of outrage and pain echoed off the roof and curving walls.

"Hey, lover, that's it!" Dian imitated Todd, throwing several
small pieces of luggage. She lacked the strength to knock anyone
down, but the unexpected barrage kept the rioters dancing and
ducking.

"Steady me, Beth!" Mari yelled. She swung a case around her
head as the taller woman bent double, holding Mari by the waist
to prevent her from falling. Mari let go of the case as if it were a
discus and roared in triumph as a woman rioter went down.

The techs added their throwing arms to Todd's as he yelled
warnings. "Take your time! We've only got so many!"

"Let me get a clear shot at the damn Spacers!" Someone in the
mob had a gun. He was pushing people out of the way and pointing the pistol at Todd's group.

Instinctively, Todd dived at Dian and Mari, and the techs tried
to shield Beth Isaacs. Mari attempted to squirm away, reaching
for another suitcase to throw.

"Dammit, Mari, get your head down!" Todd couldn't grab at
her. He had his hands full with Dian. She was thrashing, whispering incoherently. There were nightmares in her expression. He
didn't know what she was reliving but feared it was something
very much like what was happening now. The world in slow motion. Would he see the bullet leave the muzzle in slow motion,
close in on them slowly, race slowly to kill one of them?

A shot cracked and he flinched, then realized the sound came
from the other direction. The rioter wasn't pointing a gun at them
any more. He was gawking in disbelief at a spreading bloodstain
high on his chest. Then he was falling like a tree sheared off in a
hurricane.

More shots followed, bullets ripping into the mob, the rever-
berations hitting Todd's ears again and again. The screams

changed. No more cries of hate or demands to kill the Spacers. The rioters fled in terror, forgetting their prey. Again and again the shots came, picking out targets at random. The would-be killers left a trail of blood and bodies as they tried to get to the opening they had smashed with the tram. It was very far off now, from Todd's position.

Outside the transfer tube, other rioters who had been keeping pace with the ride strip halted, realizing the danger. They scattered, running back across the tarmac toward the hangars and the fields beyond.

Uniformed guards loped past Todd's party, firing as they came, driving the panic-stricken mob before them. Not all of the mob *could* run. Some lay motionless on the strip, being carried along as was Todd. Others were wounded and crawling. The guards finished them off casually, like men and women in a factory with a boring job to complete.

Some guards checked the injured Riccardi techs, then called for medics. Another officer and a uniformed man and woman helped Beth Isaacs and Mari to their feet. Todd picked Dian up, holding her close until her reactions cooled.

"Sorry about this, sir," the officer was saying. Todd's eyes were drawn to the side arm the man was holding. If Mari had had one of those, maybe the Riccardi techs wouldn't have been hurt. "Mr. Saunder? And you're Mariette Saunder, aren't you? Really sorry this happened," he said, as if enough apologies would remove their lingering shock. "We thought this bunch of cretins was heading for the syntha-food plants west of here. Didn't expect them to hit the terminal. Don't worry about your luggage, folks. We'll deliver it to your gate. You're going to the SE private hangars, sir?" Todd nodded. "Fine, we'll take care of it. And if there's any damage, Orleans Terminal will replace everything at no charge."

"Just an everyday riot, huh?" Mari said sarcastically.

The officer's bland smile never wavered. "Anyone hurt here? The terminal's doctors will—"

"They're not hurt. They're *Saunders*." Two guards were helping a limping Riccardi tech along the moving ride strip. The tech glared daggers at Todd and Mariette. "They probably staged this. My people are . . . God! Susan's dead! Those . . . those animals killed her. Do you care about that, Saunder? Do you? You're going to get a lesson one of these days . . ."

"I know you're Todd's competitor," Mari began.

"Don't." Todd pinched her arm lightly. "Can't you see he's out of his head? Sure, it's a rival company. There's a little friction . . ."

"Spacers. You're the damned Spacer they should have killed," the man ranted, focusing on Mariette especially. "Damned Goddard bitch."

The officer spoke loudly to drown him out. "Eckard, take care of Mr. Saunder and his group, will you? Make sure they get V.I.P. courtesy. And retrieve their baggage." He saluted Todd, then he and his guards hurried on, cutting in between the Saunder group and the raving Riccardi tech, separating the two more widely. In a moment, Todd couldn't hear the tech's curses at all.

"That officious—"

Dian stopped Mariette this time. "It won't do any good. It never does, with that kind." More nightmares. Wyoma Lee and a big-eyed little girl, caught in the anarchy of the Death Years and the Chaos. The United Ghetto States had been born out of that miniature dark age. Dian had seen too much, and she remembered too much, unable to forget it, ever.

The ride strip finally ended. Because everyone was weak-kneed, Todd decided they would spend some time in the terminal lounge to wind down. A couple of drinks and some talk to release the tension helped considerably. Beth Isaacs and the techs had to reschedule their flight to New Washington as a result of the delay, but Todd promised them he didn't mind the extra expense as long as no one was hurt. They carefully avoided mentioning the injuries and death among the Riccardi techs. Todd, Dian, and Mari saw the others off to their jet, then took a courtesy tram to the SE hangars.

"I'll bet Beth puts through an inquiry to the terminal hospital to check up on them," Dian said. Mari and Todd glanced at each other over her head, saying nothing. "Beth's like that," Dian went on, "no matter how many dirty tricks Riccardi plays on ComLink."

"Yes, Beth *is* like that," Todd agreed with a gentle smile. "We could use a few billion more like her. That would solve nearly every problem Earth's got."

The seacraft was primed and ready when they arrived at the SE hangars. Todd chatted with the mechanics while Dian and Mari fussed over the luggage, making sure the guards hadn't overlooked anything. The one case that really concerned Todd still rode safely inside his jumper. He didn't remove it until they were aboard and rolling out on the taxi strip.

The wind was right. He made a good takeoff and banked, peering down at the air terminal and shuttleport and the land around. Orleans Port extended in a narrow strip nearly to the western horizon. The incoming shuttles required a long glide strip; some of the craft using it were military, but mostly they were owned by the three telecommunications corporations or scientific groups. Protectors of Earth subsidized the extremely expensive upkeep of the shuttleport and the domestic terminal's operation. Despite some of the flaws, such as faulty air-conditioning and a bumpy ride strip on the three-kilometer transfer from shuttleport to global terminal, the overview was one of tidy, well-maintained group transportation facilities.

Beyond the pavement, hangars, and passenger and shipping terminals, things changed drastically. The old cities had reached out to follow the construction while the combined port was building. For a while, there had been a boom along the Gulf, an economic surge the area had needed badly. Agriculture had suffered when the river patterns shifted after the New Madrid quake, and the ripple effect from that catastrophe had crippled industry and tourism. The region had needed the income port construction brought. But the boom was over, and it showed. Decayed and burned-out suburbs surrounded the luxuries and conveniences of the port. Empty factories and constructions barns, crumbling highways, ill-kept rapid-transit tracks—the whole area from the dried-up swamps to the Sabine was a vast blot on the land. Off to the west, fires raged, oily black smoke boiling up into the cloudless sky. The syntha-food plant the officer had mentioned? Or was something else being torched? It didn't seem to matter, in that patch of misery down there.

Unfortunately, the scene was too typical. Todd had flown over other ruins and rotting slums. They seemed to girdle every major population center throughout the world, though some were worse than others. Every time he saw this sort of human dungheap, he felt lucky, and very depressed. His reaction didn't lessen his impotent anger with the rioters. Yet he shrank away from a sense of guilt, knowing he could never see life from their point of view, never know hunger and frustration so awful it made a man strike out in blind rage, uncaring if he hurt the innocent.

Humanity had a long history of seeking scapegoats. In this era, it was the rich, the Spacers, and anyone who was in one's way when the agony of deprivation and fear became too much.

And I'm going to turn that fear into stark horror, for some of them. Unless Pat helps me, makes it seem like salvation, not one more, overwhelming enemy from outer space, something that's going to hurt them and make their hellish lives still worse—if that's possible.

"The air's filthy, even without that smoke," Mariette observed.

"Not too bad. You can get upwind and breathe," Dian said tonelessly. "In some clear air, you don't dare do that. The other side's fillin' it up with toxins you can't see, smell, or taste."

Todd banked again, turning away from the land, heading out over the Gulf, setting a course east by southeast. Dian grabbed at the safety bar and eyed him with worry. As the craft leveled out and picked up speed and altitude, she smiled a bit, settling back in the second seat.

The water was a blue-green carpet flowing back beneath them. It made depth perception tricky. Todd kept close track of the scanners to be sure of his position. There weren't any tall obstructions on his flight path, and it was easy enough to wink at regulations over this comparatively peaceful section of the Central North American Union. He would have ignored those laws years ago. He and Pat and Mariette had skimmed the low waves and practically scooped up whitecaps, on many a flight out to Saunderhome. By now, though, he ought to have outgrown such reckless stunts.

"Is that one of the cargo blimps?" Dian asked, staring out the side window at a bulbous shape off to their right.

"Probably." Mariette leaned over the seat to look. "Yes, that's one. Some of the island groups make fairly steady use of them in good weather. Very fuel-efficient. They can certainly use the money elsewhere. Look! Off there! That's one of the Sea-Search Rescue Stations. Drop down a little, Todd, so Dian can see the dolphins . . ."

Dian's smile widened tolerantly. "I know about the dolphin-human Rescue teams. And Beth received her initial language translation background in one of the island universities, where she did a couple of semesters of good work with the Rescue people."

"Did she? They do a great job. Don't know how we ever managed without the cross-species teams . . ."

Todd was encouraged by Mariette's chatty, cheerful manner. She had insisted Dian ride in the front seat, saying she had seen everything along the route. But now she played tour guide, constantly leaning forward between the seats and pointing out scenes of interest. Todd turned and grinned at her. Mariette rapped her knuckles lightly on his head. "Pay attention to your piloting."

"This isn't exactly a heavy traffic route," Todd defended himself. But he faced forward, all the same.

"You wanted to play air jockey and override the auto-program," Mariette said. "It's your job to get us there in one piece. Correction, three pieces."

Dian's brown face broke into her sunshine grin, lifting Todd's spirits. He forgot the ugly riot, the grimy slums around Orleans Port, enjoying the flight. They talked and took in the scenery. Occasionally Todd detoured, on request, to give them a good view of something below. Both Todd and Mari vicariously enjoyed Dian's fresh viewpoint of what she was seeing. She had been on numerous commercial flights around the globe and on many small-craft trips with Todd, but never on a flight to Saunderhome.

Todd checked in at scheduled times, getting the weather, setting up an ETA with Saunderhome's automated control system. As scanners started picking up their destination after an hour's flight, Mariette squeezed Dian's shoulder and pointed once more. "Up ahead. About one o'clock. There! That's Saunderhome."

"We're still a good slice out, and it's visible already. Big place. You didn't tell me it was that big," Dian teased Todd.

His mouth quirked and he steadied the craft, aligning the vector. "You never asked for specifics. It's just the little old place we call home."

Mari crossed her arms on the back of Dian's seat, pillowing her cheek on her hands, looking at Todd. "Remember?"

He was momentarily startled to realize how closely their thoughts had run. "I remember," he said. "Especially the first time Dad let me handle the Swift all the way."

Dian was amazed. "A Swift? A model '97 Swift? A prop plane? Were they still operating when you could fly?"

"They certainly were." Mari tugged at the curling hair on the back of Todd's neck until he shivered away. "He was fourteen, all legs and arms and impossible curiosity. He'd been practically chewing on the Swift's wings and whining until Dad let him take the controls. 'How come Pat can fly it and I can't?'" she mimicked in a boy's cracking voice. Todd laughed at the reminiscence.

"It was in the Twenties then," Dian said, counting time backward from Todd's present age. The darkness was in her expression again.

Todd sobered. "Yeah, bad times. For you, your grandmother, us—everybody. Somehow Dad and Jael managed to dodge the worst of it. Ward's inventions were really starting to earn us some clout. He and Mother began building Saunderhome in 2015, after Jael swung some sort of deal with a Caribbean ruler who was trying to hang onto his island empire. Dad picked up that old Swift somewhere, restored it, and made flights back and forth from Saunderhome to Florida." Nostalgia made him sigh. "The damned thing bucketed like a dolphin chasing a rescue hoverboat in a high surf. Sure was fun to fly, though. Nothing like it around today. No more seat-of-the-pants stuff . . ."

"Teach 'em young, huh?" Dian spoke lightly. She offered no comments on what she and Wyoma Lee Foix had been doing while the Saunder fortunes were accumulating, buying them dream palaces and private aircraft as toys.

"We've all been handling fliers and boats since we were kids," Mariette said. "Cars, too, when there was some place to drive them. Never made a mistake yet on land, sea, or air . . ."

"It only takes one." Todd saw Mari's reflection in the console plexi. Her bright smile vanished at that veiled reference to Ward's fatal crash. Dian sensed the instant shift in mood, but she didn't pry.

Finally, Mariette perked up, forcing away the memories. "Dian? Over there—the lee islands. There's some incredible fishing there, and great boating waters. We lease it now and then as sort of an extra playground. There's a botanical museum there, too. You might enjoy a side trip over from Saunderhome while we're here."

"Sounds interesting," Dian replied politely.

Todd took an update call from Saunderhome Control, adjusting his approach slightly. The flier responded beautifully. It wasn't the same thrill handling the Swift had been, so many years ago. But he was still very much in control of a fine machine, making it move with him. As much as he loved life in Geosynch HQ style, there were times, spacing, when he missed this, missed all of it. Contact with the planet, with weather, with unregulated air currents, oceans of water, land, wild growing things—*everything*. That was his youth, before he had discovered space travel, before he had looked down on Earth from an exalted distance and seen it reduced to a floating ball of brown and white and deepest blue.

Youth! He chuckled to himself, arousing the women's wonder. He didn't explain his amusement. He had been thinking like an old man in his dotage, looking back over six or seven decades, not less than four. He wasn't ready to be stored in the Enclave *yet!* He had many vigorous years left, years in which to fly and love Dian and touch the Earth and surround himself with space . . .

Years in which to learn what the alien messenger would teach them.

"SE Three TS, you are cleared to land VFR. Welcome back, sir."

"Thank you," Todd told the unseen controller. "That you, Jessups?"

"Yes, sir."

"How's the wife and kids?"

"Got a new one, sir—a boy."

Todd twisted in his seat and winked at Mariette. She remembered the man, too. He had been in the family's employ for years. "Is that so? We'll have to bring him a present next trip, maybe a free-fall balloon." Mari clapped a hand over her mouth, muffling a guffaw. Dian just looked pained at the very tired Spacer's joke.

"Uh . . . yes, sir. That'd be nice; he'd enjoy it, I know. See you in a little while, Mr. Saunder."

Todd followed the track, idly cueing the weather pick-ups and navstar corrections. The would-be hurricane in the eastern Atlantic which he spotted a week ago had dissipated, but another was coming up from farther south and west in the ocean and looked as if it might turn into something nasty in a few days. Saunderhome would have to button down. Navstar confirmed that the flier was dead on course, not a second's deviation. Todd felt smug. He could still match the autoprogramming for everything but really tiring, long-distance flying.

There was a natural line of outer reefs which Jael's climate engineers had strengthened and extended into a massive seawall after the hurricane of '33. Todd cut speed drastically and dropped down so Dian could get a good look at the wall and the tidal energy generators outside. Then he noticed new construction activity along the reefs. The seawall had been raised at least three meters in some places, more in others. There were gaps around the perimeter, where sunken constructs bridged the space. Todd recognized the heavy metal under the water. Defense gates. If needed, they could lift up and block all the gaps, forming a solid barrier against seacraft. He wondered what that was all about. Was Jael expecting trouble from Saunderhome's island neighbors? Or was she just getting neurotic and expecting an invasion? Nobody had tried a sea attack since the last century, not unless it was to coordinate with aerial strikes. Maybe that was it. But what did Jael plan to do about the "enemy in the air"?

He banked, following the perimeter reefs in a swooping arc, and saw the answer. The inner walls were bunkers. Most of them were camouflaged with jungle greenery and similar disguises to trick the pilot's eye, but one or two were still under construction. How could he have missed all this the last time he flew in? Then Todd remembered. He had been reading some files and had the ship on auto. He must have flown right over the new defense line and not even noticed it.

How far down did the bunkers go? Saunderhome was built on an extensive and deep reef. An artificial bedrock could be created in the shallower waters, thanks to modern technology. He had an uneasy feeling that the bunkers were occupied by some of Saunderhome's now-ubiquitous security force, perhaps armed with anti-aerial weapons and missiles.

Not here, too! Was Geosynch HQ the only place where he needn't feel as if he were in a fortress?

Neither Pat nor Jael had told him a damned thing about this, or why any of it was necessary. But then Mari and Kevin hadn't warned him about the possibility of a missile attack on Goddard, either.

Mariette had been very quiet while he made the circle of the perimeter. Dian, too, remained silent. Todd knew they must be thinking the same things he was, worrying about it. Mari tried to distract them. "Make a wide swing and come buzzing, like we used to. Give Dian the whole thing from a skid-ride angle."

"Okay, but be sure you're strapped in snug."

He took them down another notch and swerved northwest, cutting power still further with a little climb. Then he fell over on the wing and rushed across the island complex, barely clearing the palms and the miniature mountain topping the main isle. They almost hovered as Todd balanced the ship skillfully. Dian sucked in her breath, hanging onto the safety bar.

The inner perimeter hadn't altered noticeably. The boat passages through the secondary reefs and under the connecting bridges were busy with servants' craft bustling from the main delivery docks out to the maintenance reefs and storage islands. People looked up from tending lawns, piloting boats, or working in the gardens, recognized the flier, and waved greetings. Mariette waved back enthusiastically, and Todd dipped the wings.

"Fruit and vegetable gardens," Mariette said, nodding to the left. Dian stretched her neck, trying to see, and Todd banked for her convenience. "Ward and Jael always loved fresh tropical food. And that's the old heliport. They wore that one out before Earth opened Orleans Terminal. Now it's easier to transfer there to our hangars and fly out from the coast, wherever we're coming planetside from." Todd dived very low over the helipad on the eastern shore, then pulled up hard to miss the line of tall trees on the slopes leading up to the main house.

Mariette looked behind them, still describing the heliport. "V.I.P.s flew in here day and night when CNAU was negotiating to take in the Caribbean." Grass was encroaching on the asphalt, evidence of how little the old landing spot was used nowadays. "Jael turned this place into a summit for the big shots while they figured out how to carve up a hemisphere . . ."

"Mari," Todd said. "Truce. You promised."

"Oh, all right." She stabbed a long finger below them. "The family castle. Complete with moat. We've got bridges, too, but no drawbridge. Jael's the dragon. Okay, okay, Todd. No more!"

The mansion had never stopped growing. A new terrace had just been added to one of the guest wings. Much of the huge house was sunken in the island's natural hills. Top stories and extensions seemed to grow out of the lush slopes. Glass, polished metal, volcanic facing—all made Saunderhome unique. There was no other national or quasi-national retreat like this in the world. It lay in the hollow of the island's hand, paths snaking between swaying trees and jungle growth, surrounded by clean beaches and visitors' bungalows, each with its private dock. Shallow, brilliantly clear waters ringed the main island. In the midday Sun, the submerged tunnels connecting Saunderhome with the outer reefs seemed to shift with the gently rippling water.

"Rain or shine, you can go anywhere you want to here," Mariette said of the tunnels and small bridges. "Anywhere as long as you aren't afraid of heights or underwater passageways."

"It's all very impressive," Dian said diplomatically. Todd wondered if she was bitter. She must be thinking of the tremendous cost; Saunderhome, rising like a jewel from the waters while pandemic and war racked the world she had grown up in. If Dian was angry, she didn't show it.

Todd completed the flyby and banked on the opposite end of the run, coming about toward the beach landing strip on the westernmost outer island. He came in fast. Maintenance kept the strip in superb shape. Dian tried not to tense up. She knew they were coming in low for a regulation landing, no longer daredevil sightseeing. Mariette fidgeted while they rolled toward the hangars, anxious for them to be there.

He cut down to taxi and rolled up close to the waiting group of staffers. Jael's flier was out on the strip, being washed and tuned up. Two more Saunder aircraft sat on the auxiliary strips, apparently being readied for trips to the mainland or to other islands. Dark shapes inside the hangar were surrounded by large piles of tools and equipment. Todd wondered what sort of repairs would necessitate that much hardware.

He closed the comp log and cued the door. Softly, the ports swung open wide like unfolding wings, and steps with safety handrails untelescoped from the flier's side. Staffers were already back by the cargo bay, ready to start unloading when Todd released the seal. A maintenance tram was maneuvering at the ship's nose, hooking up to tow her in close to the hangars for checking over and refueling. A couple of fringed-canopy trav-carts waited nearby. Staff were already loading the second one with the baggage.

Despite the handrails, eager hands reached up to steady Dian and Mari and Todd as they climbed down the steps. Todd politely shrugged off an attempt to take the holo-mode case from him. He arched his back, stretching, drawing a deep breath. The atmosphere at Saunderhome always seemed cleaner and more invigorating than air anywhere else on the planet. Perhaps it was boyhood impression, deeply ingrained. Whenever they had flown to Saunderhome during those bad years, it was an escape from pandemic, conflagration, the rat population explosion, and all variety of disasters. The landings here on the island brought freedom, a sense of having been let loose from prison—or from a death sentence.

A stocky black man separated himself from the other bustling staffers and hurried toward them. Todd noticed a slight hesitation in his gait. The man's face was whole, a masterpiece of electro-stimulus healing and surgical reconstruction, a lot of that. He was smiling at them, his broad dark face split in a wide grin.

Roy Paige. Alive. And yet Todd saw him half dead, memories ruthlessly thrusting him eleven years into the past. Reminders, appropriate to the reason for this family reunion. Roy Paige was the last person to see Ward Saunder alive, before the waves had closed over him forever.

CHAPTER SEVEN

HOMECOMING

"HI, there!" Paige called to them. "Good flight?"

"Fine! Smooth as—" Todd broke off, realizing the older man wasn't listening. He was looking past Todd, at Mariette. Todd moved aside as the two of them moved toward each other, embracing warmly. When the emotional moment eased up, he said, "Dian, this is Roy Paige, an old friend, a very good friend. Roy, Dian Foix."

Paige let go of Mariette and offered his hand. "I'm very proud to meet you, Dr. Foix. I mean that sincerely."

Dian didn't look down at the myoelectrically operated fingers gripping hers. She reacted to the warm yet lifeless touch very nicely. Todd had seen people recoil involuntarily from contact with Roy's prosthesis, even though the limb was a superb copy of a human arm and hand.

"I'm honored to meet you, too, Mr. Paige. Read about your work with Ward Saunder. One article said you taught him everything he knew." A lilt was creeping into Dian's voice. She was beginning to drop certain sounds and slur others, recognizing a fellow United Ghetto States expatriate.

Paige, too, slipped into former inflections. "That'd be a brother's article. Didn't hardly happen that way. The boss taught *me*. Wish I'd been smart enough to take it all in. Heard 'bout you. I 'member your grandmother. Immortal lady. *Im-mort-al*.

You take after her. I see you been workin' on this one," he said
slyly, jerking a thumb in Todd's direction. "Long overdue for
shapin' up. You'll make him straighten out and fly level. Glad
he's finally gettin' some taste in his women . . ."

"You say that 'bout all the ComLink women you meet?" Dian
said, enjoying the flattery but not swallowing it. Mariette was
smirking at them both. So was Todd.

"Huh! I would if he'd bring 'em to Saunderhome. First chance
I've had to look you over." Paige waved at the lead trav-cart.
"Got orders to hustle you on over to the main island before it
gets too hot. Shall we go?"

Mari and Roy Paige led the way, Todd and Dian a few paces
behind. Todd watched his sister and Roy, countless similar scenes
replaying in his mind. Mariette was taller than the black man
now. But there was a time when she had skipped along by his
knee, her tiny hand hidden in his big brown one. After the accident, Mari was the one who made the quickest adjustment to
Roy's prostheses. Then, as now, she would slow her long stride to
allow for his occasionally hesitant steps. He barely limped at all,
but there were limits to what medicine could do. The teasing, un-
cle-and-niece relationship remained as warm as ever.

Dian slid across the narrow trav-cart seat to make room, and
Todd climbed in beside her. Mariette sat up front with Roy. The
canopy fringe waved in a warm breeze as they rolled away from
the airstrip, taking the paved path leading toward the mansion.
Glass and metal reflected sunlight dazzlingly, and the sea and the
waters inside the reefs shimmered and sparkled. Todd was forced
to squint against the glare despite the tinted lenses he was wearing. The trav-cart rode silently over a little rise, snaking between
a row of tall palms. Ahead, beyond the bridge, Saunderhome
loomed like a fairy castle transported to the tropics.

Dian snuggled close to him. "It's beautiful. And the air's so
clean!" Todd smiled contentedly, his arm about her, the precious
case riding securely at his feet. "That's a lot of sunlight," Dian
added thoughtfully. "With the eroded ozone and this heavy solar
input . . ."

"Saunderhome has its own medical facility," Todd said,
amused by her concern. "It passes out sunscreen with breakfast
every day. No problems."

"Well, that's good. I mean, Roy and us other properly skinned folks are okay, but I wouldn't want you to get UV-scorched, lover."

Dian made it sound like a joke, but Todd wished she hadn't brought the matter up. Ozone erosion. Another marvelous goody left over from some of the turn-of-the-century wars. It was one of the details Goddard Colony's planetside political supporters kept bringing up in their orations—hammering home how mankind had nearly wrecked its planet and made it unsafe for life. Earth First countered by promising to salvage Earth and not repeat past mistakes. After all, humanity had coped with the ozone depletion with human ingenuity and modern pharmaceuticals.

And the debate went on.

Todd noticed several men walking along the inner reef near the bridge. Not regular staffers, but they didn't look like Saunderhome's sort of outside visitors, either. They weren't in uniform and he saw no guns. Yet he knew they were security guards. They displayed the ever-on-the-alert manner and posture that went with the breed. Saunderhome hadn't needed armed security guards on patrol like this since the early Thirties, when the Chaos started easing off. Why was it necessary now?

The trav-cart rolled out onto a gridded metal span, rising up over the pellucid waters girdling the main island. The bridge looked fragile, but Todd had read the design specs and knew the structure could last out a hurricane. Indeed, it already had survived several such and countless tropical storms. Dian leaned over and peered at the fish darting among the water plants below. "I can count the pebbles down there," she marveled. "I didn't think planetside water could be this pure any more."

"Most of it isn't," Todd said. "This wouldn't be, either, but it's a small area, and we've got a good filtration barrier on the outer reefs. Self-contained throughout, that's the family's humble home."

"Your daddy built a hell of a place. And no patent fees to pay," Dian baited him. Todd, too busy enjoying the familiar scenery, wouldn't rise to the lure.

The house and hill bulked too large to see fully now. The trav-cart drove off the bridge onto the beltway path at the water's edge and turned left. Roy followed the curving pavement north for fifty meters, then angled sharply, starting up the hill toward the mansion. Foliage grew close to the pavement. Bamboo canes waved in the easterlies. A riot of tropical flowers filled the air with fragrance. Palms cast welcome shade. Fronds and trailing vines had been trimmed back so that the lane was free. Yet the effect was one of riding through a jungle. The air became heavy with the smells of damp earth and bark. Todd showed Dian that the mossy, vine-laced rocky hillside directly ahead of them was only partly natural. A large door was cleverly designed to blend in with the existing landscape. As Dian admired it, Todd noted that sections on the main house which had formerly been open to view were now also hidden behind rocky camouflage. Again he wondered why. Had these changes been taking place for months and he had simply overlooked them, or were the alterations new, like the security guards?

The door opened at their approach and Roy Paige drove inside. Artificial lighting replaced the Sun's radiance, and Todd's lenses adjusted rapidly to accommodate the shift. Dian looked up at the massive door as they passed underneath. Todd explained, before she could ask, that the reinforced door was part of Saunderhome's elaborate hurricane protection system. The place could be buttoned up tightly in a matter of minutes, shutters and doors locking into place against the terrible winds and rains. In fact, from the appearance of the main house, Todd judged Saunderhome could be sealed even more thoroughly than it ever had been, sufficient to bury the place until a hurricane passed . . . or till it rode out a hostile aerial assault?

The lowest level of the house was a combination receivables warehouse, storage facility, and parking garage for trav-carts. Paige didn't go far into the cavernous stone-walled expanse. He parked in one of several slots beside a bank of elevators. The other trav-cart was nearby, already empty. By now the luggage had probably been delivered to the travelers' suites.

They took the elevator up two levels and exited into an expensively decorated foyer. Two doors opened off that. Staffers, having finished putting the luggage in the rooms, were returning to the garage level. Roy made them wait until he could double-check the suites to be sure the job had been done right, then dismissed them. As they disappeared into one of the elevators,

Roy also checked the service monitors in the hall. Apparently satisfied, he gave Mariette a parting embrace. "I'll tell Jael you're here. It's good to have you back, little Mari. Good to meet you, Dr. Foix. And you, behave yourself," he warned Todd, his grin spoiling the lecture. He backed into the waiting elevator and left them alone.

Mari tapped her toe. "As if Jael hasn't had a running progress report on us all the way down from orbit." She looked at her feet and scuffed the edge of her boot across the carpeting. "This is new, isn't it? Lovely. Silicate. At least she doesn't refuse to buy an occasional Goddard product."

"Don't start," Todd pleaded.

"Not if I don't have to. Not if she and Pat don't make me. Oh, why couldn't they have left things the way they were?" Mariette cried suddenly. She swung around and trotted across the foyer to her suite. The door wasn't built for slamming, but somehow she cued it with enough firmness to communicate her irritation.

"I'm not sure I'm ready for more of her moods," Todd said wearily.

"What set her off this time?"

"It's safer not to ask. Maybe it was the long ride down from Goddard. Come on." He touched Dian's elbow lightly and escorted her into his own suite.

The luggage was sitting on courtesy racks, awaiting their convenience. Closets, elegant furnishings, well-stocked dispenser, spanking clean refresher units—everything polished, neat, and the very best. The drapes at the outside window-wall had been opened partway. Dian strolled over and looked out. "Fancy view, to put it mildly."

Todd set the holo-mode case on the bed and thrust his hands deep in his pockets. "Yes. Beautiful. Everything at Saunderhome's beautiful, more so than it used to be. That's one good thing about this new wing—the view. I used to have to climb up top to the weather tower to get this kind of panorama. Dad and I spent a lot of hours up there, making com test runs and playing with his new scanners. He perfected at least twenty patents in that tower. The view from there looks different—in clear, as you might say."

The window-wall was tinted according to the latest medical

recommendations to protect eyesight and skin. The suite overlooked a steep slope blanketed with vegetation. Below, a cabana
opened onto a private, fenced beach. Absently, Todd explained
that there was a direct-access elevator off the refresher, should
Dian want to swim. Beyond the sand and the inner waterways
and reefs, the Caribbean stretched to a misty, cloudless horizon.
Surf chopped at the rocks bordering the perimeter. Todd couldn't
quite make out the camouflaged bunkers on that defense line.
Gulls wheeled above the little supply boats heading for the outer
islands. In the far distance to the north, a blackness past the blue-
green waters marked the beginnings of the Puerto Rican Trench.

"That's almost the bottom of the Atlantic," Todd said, indicating the area.

"I know. Deep waters. Very deep. As you said, it's a big drop
down from Goddard and Geosynch." Dian cocked her head.
"The haunts of the very rich. I used to dream about things like
this. Saw it on vid dramas, but never believed anyone really lived
this way. All this posh. All this money. And a view a vid
producer would kill for to get in his next romantic production.
All this . . . and you don't like it."

"Not the way it is now. I guess I don't, no. Mari was griping
for both of us. Jael's changing things, maybe to keep up with the
enlarging Saunder image and Pat's advancing career. But this isn't
what Mari and I think of when we remember Saunderhome.
That's gone. The original house was where that garage is now. A
roomy place, protected from hurricanes, safe and cozy. Jael always hated it, though. Said it made her feel like a mole. What she
really meant was, it wasn't grand and sprawling and impressive.
She started adding on even before Dad died, so the V.I.P.s would
be impressed. But, dammit, we were a real family when Saunderhome was less pretentious. When *we* were less pretentious."

Dian let him ramble, holding him, staring out at the
magnificent land and seascape.

"I've been coming back here less and less often of late," Todd
said wistfully. "Especially since Jael built these new wings. This
suite's been here five years. You'd think I'd be used to it by now.
But I'm not. I never felt comfortable. Maybe it lacked something.
You, I realize now. This time maybe things will feel right, just as
they do at my place in New Washington or North L.A. or Bonn

or Bangkok. Well, we won't have much to spend in any one place, for a while. Lots of things about to happen . . ."

The alien messenger. He held back, not saying that, not sure why. He had almost whispered his last sentence, hinting at the revelation, as if he were afraid of eavesdroppers.

Idiocy. It wasn't going to be a secret any more, not after tonight. Ward's birthday anniversary—the perfect time to tell them, especially if one believed in the survival of the soul, of Ward's soul. If he were watching tonight, he would be proud of them.

And yet . . .

Todd wanted to hurry the clock forward. And he wanted to stop it, turn it backward through the years. The once-in-a-lifetime announcement *could* only happen once. Once in his lifetime, and once in humanity's lifetime. Part of Todd wanted to be a kid again, able to ask Ward's advice, taking that strong guidance, letting Ward drop bombshells on the world consciousness with his inventive breakthroughs in a dozen scientific fields. But Ward was dead. It was up to his son to carry on the tradition.

One hell of a bombshell, Dad. Like nothing we've encountered, ever.

The page monitor chimed pleasantly, followed by Jael's filtered voice. "May I come in, Todd?"

"Of course, Mother!" Todd fought an aberrant impulse to move away from Dian. Foolish. He wasn't a kid, smuggling a girl up to his room. What had made him react that way? Jael had never been one of those reactionary neo-moralists, even if her own life style had been rigidly monogamous.

Nonetheless, he put his hands elsewhere, and Dian stepped back on her own volition. Jael didn't hurry into the room. There were times when it was necessary for her to rush, but even then she created the impression she was strolling elegantly. Old-money upbringing and upper-class manners. She had never let go of those. Surplus kilos hadn't diminished the former society belle's grace. Todd bent his head and met her kiss, her small, plump hands touching his face and shoulders.

"Let me see you," she said, looking him over maternally.

"Mother, it's only been a few weeks, for God's sake. You act as if I've been in prison for twenty years."

Jael ignored his embarrassed protests. "You're too pale. Don't you use med lamps in those space stations of yours? There's such a thing as too little ultraviolet."

"Satellites, not space stations."

"He says he gets busy and forgets his turn at the health and fitness rooms." Dian aided and abetted Jael's nagging.

"It's all her fault," Todd accused Dian. "I can never tan up as well as she does, so why bother?"

A blush didn't show well on Dian's creamy brown skin, but Todd detected a bit of reddening and chuckled. He realized that Jael had been somewhat tense when she entered the suite. Now she was relaxing.

"And you, Mother, you look great." Todd brushed aside her ritual complaints. Jael specialized in modest self-denigration. She was getting too fat. Her hair needed a specialist. Her hands were a mess. Her clothes were dowdy. The new doctor wasn't prescribing enough nutri-supplements to keep her energy levels up. He had heard it all for years and sympathized for years and reassured her none of it made any difference. It didn't. Her energy was awesome. Her clothes were the ultimate in fashion. Her hands were soft and beautiful. Her lustrous hair, stylishly middle-length, displayed that attractive white streak that was Jael's trademark. She covered her excess weight with loose, long-sleeved tunics over pants or half saris. The outfits flattered her busty figure. She was really doing fine, and she knew it. She just wanted to hear her devoted family tell her so.

Mari had been right, though. Age lines were encroaching on that full face. The white streak was a trifle wider than it had been a year ago. Jael's eyes seemed duller, fatigue of the hard-fought political campaign starting to show.

Unconsciously, Todd was comparing himself with Jael. Most of his features and his body structure came from Jael's side of the family. Was he going to have increasing weight problems, as did Jael, when he grew older? He hoped his nondescript brown hair would gray as attractively as Jael's had, but that was probably a vain wish. She was the only one of the Hartmans with that particular physical attribute. Pat and Mari stayed handsomely lean, and it was likely they would still be trim and good-looking into their eighties. It didn't seem fair. They rarely bothered with real exercise and ate and drank as they pleased. Already Todd had to watch his caloric intake and increase his exercise regimen just to maintain his weight and figure. As time wore on, he sympathized more and more sincerely with Jael's familiar complaints about her health.

"I'm so glad you've come to Saunderhome, Dian," Jael said, offering her hand. She didn't rush things. That wasn't Jael's style.

"The schedules just wouldn't work out before now," Dian replied tactfully. The missed connections had been deliberate on her part. Todd wasn't entirely sure why. He had coaxed Dian to come with him when he flew to the island, ever since they realized, months ago, that what they felt for each other was a lot stronger than an employer and trained specialist relationship. Dian never gave him an answer that *was* an answer. He suspected the problem lay in the cultural gap. Dian was repressing her U.G.S. accent now, very much in her expert translator's telecom voice—the tone guaranteed to reveal no trace of her origins.

"Well, I'm happy the schedules meshed this time—very happy. It's long overdue." Jael shook her head and laughed. Todd saw himself in her once more. That head shake was the same thing he did when he was uncertain of his ground, socially. But why was Jael uncertain? She and Dian had met before, though not often. The major difference this time was *where* they were meeting, at Saunderhome, Jael's home territory. It was almost as if she looked at Dian in an entirely new light, as a woman who might be a rival, an invader.

"Thank you, Mrs. Saun—"

"No titles! I hate them. I'll put up with them in public, but not here among my family and friends."

Dian resisted for a moment, then said softly, "Very well—Jael."

"Good! After all, you're a prospective member of the family yourself, aren't you?" Jael smiled at them both fondly. Dian raised a slim black eyebrow, but said nothing. Jael wandered around the room, visually assessing the servants' work. "And Mariette's young man, did he come?" She tried to make the question sound offhanded. It didn't work. Todd and Dian both understood that Jael was fully informed on everything that happened here. She already must know that Kevin McKelvey wasn't among the current guests.

"Uh . . . I'm afraid not. He couldn't get away." Todd felt defensive of the man.

"Oh, yes. Of course. He's been elected governor up there, hasn't he?" Word traveled fast. How had she known? Todd reviewed his words and actions since he had left Goddard. He said nothing about Kevin's elevation in rank, but Mariette had, to some techs at Geosynch. Todd didn't like to think he had spies in his organization. That must be the case, though.

"What's he like? I mean, is he a good person? I wouldn't want Mariette to . . . she's had some very unhappy experiences with men in the past, you know."

"Very well," Todd replied with a sigh. "He's no airboat daredevil or vid-drama type. Not at all like the others."

"Good. Time she settled down. I wish he were going to be here. I'd so wanted to meet him. You know, I never have. Haven't even spoken to him on the com. The opportunity never arose. I'd like to meet him in person. You can tell so much more about someone face to face. Don't you agree, Dian?" Jael asked softly.

Dian nodded mutely, flicking a glance toward Todd. She reminded him of a spooky wild creature, ready to run if danger came too near.

Jael looked out the window. "What's most important is, you brought Mariette. I knew you would, dear. And sooner or later I'll get to meet Kevin McKelvey, too. She's here. Meeting her young man is next." She walked over to Todd and touched his face lovingly. He caught her hand and kissed it. "You've made us a family again," Jael whispered. "Thank you. So long. So very long since we've all been together here . . ."

"Things will be okay."

Visibly, Jael brought herself forward in time. "I know. You'll make it work. You always do. He has a gift for that, Dian. Have you noticed? He and Ward, peas in a pod. It isn't that they're bullies . . . that Ward was a bully or Todd is. It's just that they persuade you, bring you around, make you see things their way. But I'm sure you know that." Jael winked lewdly at Dian, startling the younger woman. Then Dian's face lit in a grin. They reacted one woman to another, dissecting the prudish male under their microscopes.

Todd squirmed with chagrin until Jael's smile warmed him like

Caribbean sunshine. "You were always my sweet-tempered child, my little peacemaker." He blushed at the compliment, one he had heard ever since he was a kid. Jael was amused. "You are! And I'm counting on you to keep the other kids from arguing this time, too. Lord! If you hadn't . . . There were times when I came home and expected to see little corpses, Dian. But somehow Todd always broke up the fights. Pat was the oldest, but it was Todd who was my babysitter for the other two. Well, I'd better go see how one of the other kids is doing." Jael hesitated, then asked, "Do you think Mariette will mind? I don't want to intrude."

"It's hardly intruding. You live here more than she does," Todd said.

"She whines so about these suites. I can't understand what she dislikes. We just had to enlarge. The old house wasn't big enough any more. You know that, Todd." Jael nibbled on a neatly trimmed fingernail.

"I'm sure she's just blowing off steam. Ignore her. I do. She'll have to gripe a while before she admits things aren't so bad at the old place."

"Oh, how true!" Her good mood restored, Jael started toward the door.

"Are Pat and Carissa here yet?" Todd called after her.

Jael paused by the monitor array beside the door, expertly scanning the service readouts and messages. "Carissa's been here a couple of days. Patrick will fly in sometime this afternoon. He's finishing up a campaign swing through Africa, but he promised he'd be here before supper."

"Maybe we ought to drop over to Carissa's suite and say hello," Dian suggested, still using her very-correct media worker's voice.

"Oh, she's resting now so she'll be fresh for this evening." Todd was about to ask after his sister-in-law's health, but Jael rushed on, talking rapidly as she simultaneously reprogrammed some of the service monitors. "If you need anything extra, Dian, don't hesitate to call Supplies. Todd forgets about little feminine necessities, even if he is a considerate boy. We can't expect them to know everything, can we?" She winked again, then hurried out.

When she had left, Dian looked at Todd thoughtfully, waiting for him to meet her gaze. "Carissa's taking a nap? Every other time I've been in the same SE area she is, she calls you as soon as you land or pull in."

Todd clawed at his scalp, scratching a non-existent itch. "Yeah. I don't know what's going on there, either. And I'm worried. We agree she looked like hell on those recent 'casts, and come to think of it, she hasn't been showing up on any of the campaign footage recently."

"Maybe she picked up a virus."

Todd shivered. "My God! Don't say that."

Dian shrugged. "It happens, even today. Mutations are still out there looking for likely targets. Remember, I grew up with the pandemics."

"We all did. I . . . I just can't deal with them very well. Maybe I never will." He sat down on the bed, confronting the primitive fear in himself. "It's a personal hangup. I know the meds found some of the answers, thanks in part to SE Pharmaceuticals and the Antarctic Enclave experimenters. But not all the answers, and not always a cure. I guess it doesn't matter, if you're rich enough or important enough. Got a deadly virus? Put the body on ice and the tissue samples in the vault until doctors crack the case."

Dian's eyes narrowed. "That again? What is this new phobia about the Antarctic Enclave? You and Mari kept whipping each other about the place all the way down from orbit, and none too subtly. Frankly, the static's getting thick. Maybe I react because there's damned little United Ghetto States representation in that Enclave. Oh, I know a few people who are on the watchdog Human Rights Committee, sure, but . . ."

"Sorry. Forget it. It's a disagreement Mari and I are having."

"Huh!" Dian's sarcastic snort would have wilted the drapes if they had been organic fabric.

Todd didn't respond. Mariette's suspicions, and the promises she had extracted from him—they weren't going to go away. She would call in the debt, eventually. Other things wouldn't go away, either—the suite; the magnificent view; the ominous new construction, sufficient to repel an invasion; Jael's hand-patting tactics; questions about Carissa's health—and, most of all, the little case lying on the bed beside him. He was on the edge of a precipice, and very soon he would have to jump, or be pushed.

Dian tried to lighten his mood. "That was a cute little phrase:

'Mariette's young man.' Almost as cute as 'prospective member of the family.' Is she hinting we ought to take out official papers and start breeding little Foix-Saunders?"

"She certainly is. Jael's a demon for generational continuity. Old traditions. She's funny that way, considering how she kicked her family in the shins. They wouldn't have minded if she had just had an affair with Ward. But, my God, *marrying* him? Official papers and quaint old legal customs and all. If that wasn't bad enough, she deliberately had three kids. Believe me, it *isn't* because she was crazy about motherhood," Todd said with some bitterness. "We were another way of flaunting her family and spitting in their eyes, a positive embarrassment . . ."

"Hey! Don't cut her down. She's my kind." Dian added coyly, "Why do you think I transferred from university global coordination linguistics to ComLink? It *wasn't* just because I was frantic to experience sex in free fall . . ."

Todd grinned lasciviously. "But that figured in."

"Heavily!" Dian sobered. "She's family-strong, your mother. I hear it when she mouths those old-fashioned terms. Wyoma Lee was like that, too. Only her kids all died, and I was the only grandkid who didn't."

"We've been lucky," Todd said, feeling guilty again. "Jael runs scared. She watched that happening all around her. Put that together with the old-line philosophy she was raised with, and you get a woman who wants the kids to have grandkids and so on and so on. Continuity. For her, it's all tangled with Ward and how she felt about him and his being killed before all their dreams came true."

Dian locked her hands behind his neck, resting her forehead against his. "As I said, wonder woman."

"Not quite."

"Huh! See her set that servo board? Took it in at a blink. She's a top tech."

"Yeah, she helped Ward remember to eat when he was concocting his inventions, and she nursed them through patents and financial deals while he kept coming up with new ones. Saunder Enterprises is a joint effort, but she did the dirty work, then and now. Sure she's expert. She knows how to use all those crazy devices Dad kept coming up with and taught us kids how to use them, too. But she's still 'Mom'! God help us if we ever call her that, though." He had accepted Jael's dual nature all his life, yet it was refreshing to see his mother through someone else's eyes, friendly eyes. Plenty of business competitors had expressed their opinions of Jael, "that soft-voiced, throat-cutting Saunder bitch." But Dian's attitude was part heroine worship and part wariness of Jael's wealth and power and social status.

"We've got an afternoon," Todd said abruptly. "Let's forget everything for a while. Want to swim?"

Dian was agreeable. They hadn't brought swim gear, but hadn't needed to. Everything was supplied; all they had to do was take the private elevator down to the cabana. Todd carried the case along, reluctant to leave it in the room, even though he knew the staff was completely trustworthy.

The cabana, Dian commented, was fancier than all the places she had called home when she was a kid, and warmer than most of them. The little shelter was fully automated, offering remote control to deploy giant umbrellas farther down the beach, summon lifeguards, dispense cold drinks and snacks, or inflate a liquid-filled basking mattress under a tanning canopy. A high fence separated them from other cabanas and sections of the beach surrounding the house.

No one intruded. No one paged them on the com or knocked at the fence gate. Dian reveled in the luxurious isolation. Geosynch, ComLink's planetside offices, and company-supplied apartments —all came with a necessary amount of elbows-in-the-ribs contact with other people. Population growth was still matching the worldwide losses fairly well, and humanity tended to bunch up in certain convenient locations where they had to live in one another's pockets. Enough wealth, however, could still buy that precious commodity—room. Saunderhome was a mere dot among Earth's national communities. But it was special. Untouched by war or pandemics or other devastations, Saunderhome combined mankind's most up-to-date equipment with unspoiled natural beauty. Here, on this island, the frenzied pace of life in 2040 couldn't touch Todd and Dian.

They swam, splashing and frisking like kids, beach sand clinging to their wet skin. It was easy to forget there were glaciers and political upheaval and a thousand other worries. Free to do as

they wished, they became children for a while, children with adult
desires. Laughing, they sought the shade of the tanning canopy,
their bodies still glowing after the exertion of the swim. The floor
was a floating cushion, lulling the tired swimmer, or encouraging
lovemaking. They tried both, in reverse order. Teasing laughter
and sexual intensity mingled. Dian compared the sensations to
sex in null grav and declared it a tie. Todd agreed, his mouth and
hands busy.

Somewhere in the back of his mind, he thought that he had
done this before. Many times. This setting, these sensations,
though not recently. There had been days and nights of such sen-
sual pleasure. A woman he had met as a result of ComLink's
media outlets, a casual acquaintance made at a shuttle terminal or
in business dealings. When he was much younger, the woman was
likely to have been one of the staff at Saunderhome. He had always made matters plain. No strings, and the women had felt the
same way. Pat had gotten himself into some sticky messes when
the arrangement wasn't mutual. But for once, the second son had
lucked out. No strings . . .

This was different. Todd floated away in a daydream of con-
tentment, the filtered Sun gently warming his face as it sifted
through the canopy.

A persistent engine noise woke him sometime later. He listened, deciding the sound was a flier circling Saunderhome, lining
up for a landing, as he had earlier. Curiosity satisfied, Todd
closed his eyes and blanked his mind, shutting out the distant
thrumming noise, letting the mellow sensations bear him away
once more.

He was unsure how long he had been catnapping. He woke
without opening his eyes, aware of a third presence close by. No
instinctive alarms went off. Instead, he felt a comforting famili-
arity. What had waked him? A sound half heard? Perhaps it was
a scent, though he wasn't conscious of any odor which hadn't
been there when he dozed off.

His thoughts drifted. Did the species which made the alien vehicle have *Homo sapiens'* five senses? Or did they learn about the
universe in other ways? Everything now seemed to pull his mind
toward speculation about the aliens.

"Come on, kid. I know you're in there. Wake up." Sand show-

ered over Todd's bare feet in a gritty rain. Sandaled toes
scratched his legs. He jerked away and rolled over, looking up.
Pat stood arms akimbo. He wasn't alone; four bodyguards
lounged near the fence, discreetly looking elsewhere, trying to
blend in with the scenery. Pat was wearing trunks and a shirt,
unfastened, protecting his back against sunburn. Sunlight shot red
glints through his black hair. "Count on you to loll on the beach
with a beautiful woman when you should be tending chores."

"Have a heart. I'm on vacation. I'm entitled, bully boy," Todd
said. He stood up, teetering unsteadily on the liquid-filled mattress. Dian woke and propped herself on one elbow, watching
them.

Pat bowed like a courtier. "Hello, Dr. Foix. You are indeed entitled. But this lazy kid here . . ." The tone grew challenging. Pat
had shucked out of his politician's guise along with his natty
clothes.

Without warning, he launched himself, tackling Todd around
the waist. They rolled out onto the beach, making a noisy show of
pummeling each other. Todd yelped as the hot sand contacted his
naked buttocks, and he struggled to get on top of the impromptu
wrestling match.

A hard punch slammed into his midriff and another clipped his
jaw, making his vision spin. Todd quit the act, bringing up his
arms to pick off the blows, going under them and striking back.

"Hey!" he shouted, then jerked aside as Pat threw another wild
jab that slid past his ear. He countered with a fist that connected,
making Pat grunt from the force. Hastily, Todd wriggled out of
reach and jumped to his feet. The bodyguards were watching, expressionless, not about to interfere.

The sand burned his soles as he leaned forward, arms out in
defensive posture, not knowing what to expect. Pat sat on the
sand, massaging his stomach, squinting at him. "You look pretty
damned stupid, kid, standing there mother naked like that."

"What the hell is going on?" Todd demanded. Warily, he
straightened up, backing away to the shade of the canopy. He
hopped around awkwardly as he pulled on his trunks and sandals.
Pat was making no effort to move. But Todd was sure he hadn't
hurt him with those punches. They had traded plenty far worse

than that when they were both younger and less inclined to pull punches.

Dian gathered the towel around herself. She was no prude, but she wasn't yet exactly on family-circle terms with Pat and obviously was taking this situation carefully.

Pat dropped his head back, shutting his eyes and basking in the hot Sun for a long minute. Then he took a deep breath, pulled himself up, and walked toward the cabana. "Want to try it again? Best two falls out of three?"

Todd grimaced. "I just got back from three weeks in orbit. I don't feel much like playing pushover for you."

Pat spread his arms wide, his shirt snapping in the sea breeze. His expression was taunting. "Come on. I'll take it easy on you."

This time Todd gave no warning. He charged head down, carrying them both down the beach. It was almost a genuine test of strength for a bit. They wrestled half-heartedly, neither one landing any real blows. The sand was too hot for such roughhousing. By mutual consent, still grappling and straining for breath, they staggered toward the canopy and collapsed. Dian regarded them scornfully. She reminded Todd of a sleek brown cat contemplating a pair of rowdy puppies. The bodyguards merely looked bored.

Pat started laughing, holding his belly, lying full length on the mattress. Then he shook off the mood and stood up, kicking out of his sandals and peeling off his shirt. He threw several mock punches at Todd's biceps, dancing like a fighter in training. "Reef and back. I'll give you a head start, you poor weakling. Three seconds?"

"If Dian plays ref."

"For what?" Dian asked innocently. Then she called, "Go!"

Todd's sandals flew off as he ran. He hoped the med gravs would compensate for this energy expediture. It *was* much too soon after leaving orbit to be trying such nonsense.

He was counting, hearing Dian say, "Go!" once more. The sand's heat made him run at top speed. The water looked cool and inviting. He could hear Pat close behind him, panting, trying to catch up. They splashed out into the waves and dived into the deeper water.

Todd reached out in long, steady strokes. Here he had an advantage. The water buoyed him, imitating free fall. He sliced through the slow current and swam strongly for the turnpoint they had used as kids, an area of reef topped by a gnarly rock. Smoothly, Todd ducked, somersaulting, feet braced against the surface, shoving himself hard along the return track.

Plasticrete under his toes, not coral. He remembered why the artificial liner had been put there. Mari was the fastest swimmer of the three of them, and she had overdone it once. Pat had tried desperately to overtake her and had skinned himself thoroughly. Ward had dreamed up the plasticrete sponging to prevent future bloody accidents.

". . . you're mortal, you know. Just because you kids are Saunders, don't think you can't be hurt . . ."

Reaching, the water curling past his arms, body, and legs. Everything in tune. Legs scissoring, cupped hands moving the water, forcing it back. Action, reaction, the first law of getting where he wanted to in space.

I was learning the trick then. So was Mari. You're the only one who never made further use of it, Pat . . . How much you're missing, big brother! There's absolutely nothing like it on Earth.

The beach, and Dian, were ahead. The finish line. Todd touched bottom and slogged on his hands and knees, coming erect, climbing out of the water. Noisy splashing and panting at his side. Pat, trying to win. Todd's heart was thundering, but he extended his stride, overcoming the wrench of gravity and the sudden weight in his limbs. Running across the hot beach, falling into the shade, touching Dian's outstretched hand, attaining the goal. Beside him, simultaneously, Pat touched her other hand.

The two of them lay there wheezing and coughing. Dian had slipped into her suit while they had been racing. She looked down at them, still smiling scornfully. Pat finally recovered enough breath to say, "Well?"

"It was a tie."

"What?" Rebellion flared in Pat's sharp face. There were far darker shadows on his emotions than those cast by the canopy. The potential fury chained up inside him was awesome.

Todd looked over at him, glad he had won the little contest, yet knowing Pat's anger in defeat. It *was* a defeat. Pat's standards for himself were higher than anyone else could ever set for him. He had never been satisfied. No praise had ever quite fulfilled him and that demon in his being.

"Are you sure?" he asked, under control now, sounding rueful.

"I'm sure. It was a dead heat," Dian stated.

"Appropriate phrase for today." Pat shrugged as if the outcome hadn't mattered. It shouldn't have. But it did.

Todd knew acceptance wouldn't go down easy. He slapped Pat's gut playfully. "You're out of shape. Next time, you'd better not give me as big a handicap. Too much wining and dining on the political trail. Tell you what. Give us both a few days to tune up, and I'll give you a rematch. Bargain?"

Self-consciously, Pat sucked in his stomach, even though there was no visible fat there. He smiled. Not his political smile, intended to mesmerize voters. This smile was open, nothing hidden. His family grin, Todd called it. It was Pat at his best, and that was pretty damned good.

"Bargain! Next time I'll leave you out there like a beached dolphin."

"Not a chance."

They flung arms around each other's shoulders, laughing. Dian's tiny nose wrinkled with distaste. "I don't know about beached dolphins, but the two of you sure smell like beached fish."

They took the hint, wiping off the grit and sea smells with towels. Pat talked as he cleaned up. "Saw your plane at the hangar. The room monitor said you weren't in, so I figured you were probably down here. Hope you don't mind my dropping by to give you a hearty hello." Dropping by, with bodyguards in tow?

"Mind? Of course not. Though it might have been a trifle too cozy if you'd come by a half hour ago," Todd added.

Dian kicked his ankle, and he pretended agony.

Pat seemed unabashed. "Three make a very exciting party. But that never was your speed, kid. Guess I timed this right. I had to check in with 'Rissa first, anyway. Haven't seen Mari yet. Jael indicated she was kind of edgy." His face tightened again, but the cause of his anger was a long way off. "I hear you almost got it in a riot at Orleans. That's exactly the sort of irresponsible subnational leadership we need to eliminate. LeBras never *could* keep order in his district. But when it threatens our family . . ."

"That's not what's bugging Mari," Todd said.

Careful. Don't attract the sharks until you know you can fight them off.

"It's . . . it's a lot of things. Just take it slow with her, give her time to adjust. She's out of touch with the way things are planet-side. Please? You know how she is."

Pat listened intently. "I know that guy she's living with ought to belt her a good one now and then." Pat's mocking tone only partially relieved the tension caused by that suggestion. Then he brightened. "I like that big fanatic. Met him at a P.O.E. funding session a couple of years ago when he was on leave. He's a hard-headed son of a bitch, just as bad as Mari. But there's no malice in him."

"There's none in Mari, either." Pat eyed his brother, on guard, expecting a lecture. Instead Todd said, "McKelvey couldn't make it."

"Hmm. Busy being governor now, eh? Little military coup in the making up there? Well, maybe . . . hell, I don't know. The one thing I don't want to do this trip is talk politics. If I start, slug me. I sympathize with McKelvey's problems; I barely managed to get away to Saunderhome myself this week."

"Couldn't miss the anniversary . . ."

"Nope! And this year we're all together again. This is going to be the turnaround for us, kid. I just know it." Pat said, working up his enthusiasm. "We've moved apart."

"Remember, take it slow with Mari."

"I will!" Pat picked up his shirt and started toward the elevator to the house. "I'll see you kids later. Stay cool. And next time, Todd, I'll beat you!" Silently, the bodyguards followed him, shadow people.

"Do you guys do that sort of thing often?" Dian asked wryly, after he had gone.

"You mean the roughhousing? We used to—a lot. He got a lit-tle carried away there for a bit," Todd said, frowning.

"I noticed. I thought I was going to have to yell for help to pull you apart. I'm used to that sort of thing ending up with one guy at the medics', or dead."

Todd winced at the grim reference. "Just horseplay. Pat's one of those poor inhibited types. Can't shuck it off with his aides and party workers. He needs a chance to blow off some of the tension. I happened to be handy. Better me than a stranger."

Dian stopped his explanations. "Hey, it was sort of crazy to watch. Very exotic. Sibling rivalry and all. Being an only, it all seems unreal."

"You and a lot of the world. Three kids? In a time period when onlies were the rule? We took a megaton of flak about overconsuming and wasting resources and how our parents could have done something so obscene as to have three of us. I guess that made us clannish."

Dian pulled him down beside her, kissing him. "Don't apologize. I like the results." They traded volumes of understanding with their eyes. "Besides, it's good practice for me, learning to cope with your planetside exotic types—gets me in training for *real* aliens."

He silenced her with another kiss.

CHAPTER EIGHT

RITUAL

THEY remained on the beach till sundown, loath to leave the serenity it offered. The red fire spread across the sky, darkness coming with it, closing in rapidly. It took them half an hour to dispose of their soggy swimsuits and shower. By the time they had dressed, Mariette was waiting for them in the foyer outside the suite. She didn't forbear to make another crack about the mysterious case Todd was toting.

"You don't need to smuggle in a spare supply of gold, sweetie," Mari said. "You *are* at home. They're not going to make us swim back to the mainland—I don't think. We may starve waiting on the elevator, however. Where *is* that thing . . . ?"

When it arrived, they rode to Saunderhome's topmost level, an immense bubble-domed room. Hesitating on the threshold, Dian took in the oval-shaped expanse beyond the elevator doors. Then she saw Jael watching the three of them from across the room. Dian took Todd's arm firmly.

Mari led the way, descending the thickly carpeted steps to the sunken activity area. The large dining table was set for six. Saunderhome staffers stood on the sidelines near the service access, a modern electronic version of a dumbwaiter. They hadn't started relaying orders to the lower kitchens yet. Gold settings and expensive china and linens adorned the mahogany table.

"More posh," Dian whispered. Most onlookers might have taken her wide-eyed stare for admiring awe. Todd didn't.

"Put that on hold, will you?" he begged. A servant approached and offered to take the case off his hands. Hastily, Todd transferred it to a tighter grip on the other side. "Thanks, no. It's something I need for later on."

"Very well, sir . . ."

Two butlers tended bar at either end of a broad circle of chairs and couches. Roy Paige was chatting with Jael. He glanced at Todd, Dian, and Mari, then snapped his fingers to keep the servants on their toes. One asked for drink orders and hurried off to fill them. Jael was sitting in her favorite high-backed overstuffed chair. Todd had never been sure how she had managed to drag that thing with them wherever they had gone, repairing it, recovering it, always carting it on to the next in a long line of Saunder havens. It finally found a permanent home here on the island and hadn't needed reupholstering for some years now. Carissa was seated next to her in a less thronelike sofa chair. Both were intent on Pat and Mari, who met directly in front of them.

For a fraction of a second, Todd feared another war was going to break out. Pat was standing stiffly. Mari's hand was out but held in a fist, not an open-fingered greeting. They sparred silently. Then Pat's politician's mask dropped away, replaced by tenderness.

Mari responded instantly, hugging Pat. She laid her head on his shoulder and looked at Todd, her eyes moist. "You knew I couldn't resist, didn't you?" She and Pat were both laughing softly.

"You were right, Jael," Carissa said. Jael was very smug. A butler brought them a tray, and Carissa picked up a glass goblet. She turned the drink in her pale hands, sipping delicately through a straw. Her green eyes were narrowed. If she had been a cat, she would have purred.

"Sit over here with us, Dian," Jael invited, patted the chair opposite Carissa. Dian exchanged a look with Todd which told him she wasn't delighted with the arrangement. But she complied.

Pat and Mari had finally moved a little apart. Pat pulled Todd into their space, gripping his forearm. He hadn't done that in years. They locked hands, aping a fashion they had seen in a book about ancient Rome when they were kids. Pat released Todd's hand and faked a hammerlock, then let go, an arm dangling heavily over Todd's shoulder. He drew Mari into the crook of his other arm. Roy Paige began clicking off holo-mode memories of the occasion, asking them to smile for the lenses.

The mood in the room was wonderful. Todd didn't even resent being called "kid," didn't mind any of the old jokes and teasing epithets. They slipped into reminiscences about a wild party they had thrown in their teens, when they had all ended up swimming fully clothed. Mari claimed to be outraged and argued with their description of her behavior that moonlit night. Then she and Todd ganged up on Pat briefly. They switched sides again and again—none of it serious, all of it making them laugh. No prickly edges at all.

Behind them, Todd heard Jael, Dian, and Carissa talking.

". . . he looks a little sunburned, Dian . . ."

"Well, you *said* he looked pale. A little soothe-cream will cure that peeling nose. Besides, I think it's kind of cute . . ."

"It's so nice, Jael—all of us together like this. It's been simply ages, ages." Carissa. That husky, tremulous voice was unmistakable. Even when she broke into other people's conversations her voice had a whispery vocal fragrance.

In contrast, Jael's velvet, low soprano tone never lost its undernote of steely strength. From the corner of his eye, Todd saw Jael gazing at Carissa. There it was again, that peculiar possessive stare he had noticed while Pat was making the truce announcement.

"Are you sure you should be drinking that, Carissa?" the older woman asked.

"It's only milk punch."

The photo session and joyous mugging and reminiscing finally tapered off. Pat walked over to Carissa and caught her hands, lifting her effortlessly out of her chair. Her face was pink and pale like a tropical flower. Pat slipped her arm through his and started toward the dining area as Carissa said in a little-girl manner, "I *am* hungry. How did you know?"

"Know your every wish is my command, 'Rissa," Pat replied gallantly.

Roy and Todd acted as escorts for the other women. On the surface, Jael was enjoying herself, watching her successful eldest offspring leading his pretty lady to the table. But there was something else in her face. Fear. What was Jael afraid of? Todd couldn't imagine anything that had been said or done that would cause such an emotion—certainly nothing regarding Pat and Carissa. Puzzled, he let Roy Paige escort Jael to the table and led Mari and Dian himself, teasing about having two women to the other men's one apiece.

The truce continued to hold through dinner. Jael had arranged the seating so that Pat and Mari were side by side, tempting fate. But nothing bad came of it. Jael sat next to Mari, opposite Carissa. Todd and Dian were seated together at the other side of the long table. Dian whispered to Todd, wondering why Paige wasn't joining them. The black man busied himself with numerous projects and supervisory positions running Saunderhome. By his own choice, he was part of the gathering, but wouldn't spare the time to eat with them. Dian seemed somewhat mollified by the explanation. Every time Roy returned from some unexplained errand, though, she watched him curiously, apparently identifying with him to some degree.

Pat and Mari stuck to safe topics, working at it. Occasionally Jael would put in a comment. As often as not, Carissa would add a few timid words. Dian and Todd joined in when it seemed apt. As the meal wore on, Todd became conscious of a pattern, one which confused him. He hadn't noticed it until now. Had it been there all this year? Or was Mari the catalyst bringing it out? Whatever the cause, there were subtle differences in the dinner-table chitchat.

"Of course, it's not like it was when we were building Saunderhome. We couldn't run away completely from the wars and plagues. They had those in the Caribbean, too. I suppose you can never really escape your problems no matter how far you run. You'll have to deal with them eventually," Jael was saying.

Bad reminder. Todd hoped it wasn't a prelude to trouble. Things had gone so well through the krill cocktail, the soup and salad and beef entree. They ought to be wallowing in the luxuries and the good feelings. So few people could afford to eat such expensive food, and so few could brag of having an intact family circle.

Almost intact.

Mari, in Jael's view, had run away to Goddard Colony. Carissa tried to cover up the challenge, cooing over a syrup-drenched fruit dish. "These must have been picked today, they're so fresh!"

"They probably were, love," Pat agreed. To Todd's relief, his brother took up the ball and ran with it, wiping out Jael's ill-advised jab. "Picked at the peak. Mari, remember how we used to slip the lock on the garden house and sneak in and gobble all the goodies the day before the staff was supposed to harvest them?" Mariette giggled, and Pat wagged a finger at Todd. "It was your fault. You're the one who deciphered Dad's lock patent. You said it was a beep tone harmonic, or something. You little genius! Except that Dad knew damned quick it couldn't be anyone but you who did it. That pointed right back at us, and we all got grounded for a month."

"I never knew you had such a villainous childhood," Dian said, lifting one expressive eyebrow.

"Pat never lets facts get in the way of a good yarn, especially at my expense."

The servants were enjoying the evening, too, despite their duties. They didn't laugh out loud, but many were smiling, not hiding their amusement. Though some of them had been with Jael since Saunderhome was built, most were new. Todd had never comprehended why Jael wanted so many servants. They certainly weren't necessary. Ward Saunder had automated nearly everything, even the kitchens. So many warm bodies scurrying around doing menial chores had to be a status symbol, no more. And it was getting worse.

It had been bad enough. As Ward Saunder rode higher and higher, his inventions proving out with dizzying rapidity, the important people started seeking out the Saunders, at the lab in California, in Chicago, following them when they moved to the Caribbean. And the caliber of those important people kept rising. It had been years before Todd had understood what was happening. Jael had always been two women, able to wipe runny noses and discipline and read stories, yet not being there at crucial times, leaving them alone or under Ward's somewhat inadequate parental guidance. Ward meant well, but he was too easily distracted, a man thinking on a whole other plane of existence; he tended to ignore the kids, while they ran wild. When Jael was there, she cracked the whip and they behaved. She had done that and made them disappear when the politicians and businessmen arrived.

V.I.P.s came from all over the world. Many of them had looked haunted and trapped, as indeed they were, by an avalanche of events. They went away less haunted, but trapped in a different way—men who hated what they had done, but who had no choice. Jael Saunder, round-faced, soft-voiced matron, a shark feeding on bloated and floundering national leaders and their prostrate countries. How many machinations and shady deals had she pulled off in those days? Pat had started working with her when he was in his teens. He had no taste for invention but a lot of talent for Jael's brand of business. They had left lab work to Todd. And Mari had made a profession of being reckless— reckless with her life and with the family reputation.

It worked. Money and power switched hands, from world leaders' hands to Jael's small, plump ones. The graphs had shown a frightening upward line. Pat was Jael's apprentice, as Todd had been Ward's. After his father's death, he had pulled the foundations together and continued to build on Ward's work in the field he knew best, revolutionizing the world of telecommunications with his father's inventions.

Escaping, in his own way, as Mariette had.

And now Mariette had found purpose for her life. No more frivolous joy-seeking. She was as fiery and dedicated as a new mysticism convert. Her religion was Goddard Colony, and it was as if her hell-raising and sleeping around and racing at the edge of death never happened.

Boundary lines dissolved. New ones formed. Humanity reeled from blow after blow to its collective confidence. But Saunder Enterprises kept growing richer, and with riches went pomp and show. Fast fliers. Airboats. Imported foods. Rare fabrics from Goddard. A surfeit of human servants to supplement the silently efficient electronic ones.

Jackals. Todd suddenly saw them through Dian's point of view. Did she think that was what they were? It was an honest judgment, one he winced at. They had fed off the rotting carcasses in order to survive. By the time Jael was through, Saunder Enterprises was financially invulnerable, or nearly so. So what if that murderous competitiveness had left shattered fortunes and lives in its wake? She had gotten them the perks, the privileges, and the power.

It was inevitable that Pat would go into politics. Then the Saunders would have it all. In one form or another, they would have a guiding hand on Earth, in the telecom satellites, and in space, even as far out as the Moon. Only the priorities had shifted. In order to enhance Pat's power, some of Mari's would have to be jettisoned. Maybe all of it.

Todd looked at Pat, the idle conversation washing around him. For thirty-two years he had seen that face, a baby's face, a boy's face, now a man's face. He had loved the face and the person who owned it. Odd. Pat didn't look like the fictional benevolent dictator. He looked like . . . Pat. But he would *be* a dictator if he won this election. Shear the sheep and make warm coats and sell them back to the sheep. Some of the sheep, the deserving ones, might get a coat donated. But in the end, they would all be Pat's sheep.

"Well, that took care of Emory, didn't it, Mari? That whiny little kid never came west of the craters again. Saunders ruled the area. Outnumbered them." Pat laughed as he wound up the anecdote about their childhood days in Chicago. He laid his napkin by his plate and gazed around the table. "It's about time to adjourn to the theater, I believe. Mother?"

This time there was no mistake. Todd saw the dangerous flicker in Jael's eyes. Pat didn't wait for her okay. He helped 'Rissa and Mari, then walked around to Jael, taking charge.

Dowager queen. But now Pat's the king. And beginning to enjoy it. And Jael isn't enjoying taking a back seat while he runs the show.

As they moved back toward the comfortable chairs, Dian clung to Todd's arm. "It's going okay, isn't it?" she asked in a low voice.

"I guess so." Todd couldn't articulate his feelings. He was sad with a bittersweet aching, a lingering, hurtful, and slow letting go

of something he had always had. The sense of impending loss was
terrible.

The servants were gone, but Roy Paige stayed to help operate
the photonics. He took his traditional position behind Jael's chair,
his good hand poised over the projector panels. Hidden mechanisms glided the chairs about, forming a precisely measured arc.
The arching bubble dome polarized, shutting out starlight. The
room lights dimmed but left enough illumination so they could
see each other.

Anticipation gripped them. Todd leaned back, thinking that he
had helped make this anniversary ritual possible. The original
photonics were Ward's. Todd and Roy and other techs had
refined the system in the years since, updating the little show.
Ironically, because of that fine-tuning, the images would be far
more realistic than when Ward was still alive.

The acoustics were ideally balanced. There was no projector
noise. Ward Saunders appeared before them. He stood equidistant
from all the chairs. His feet rested on the carpet, not hovering un-
realistically a few centimeters above, as was the case with too
many holo-mode projections. There used to be three emulsions
and all sorts of visual restrictions created by the system's limita-
tions. Ward had identified and corrected the problems.

He was alive. There. No shimmer line. No distortion. Ward
Saunder was alive once more—as long as the projection lasted.

Ward covered his nervousness with a little stammer. He wasn't
used to serving as a model or performing, though he had the same
stunning stage presence Pat had developed into such a gold mine.
"Jael, kids . . . uh . . . a man's birthday . . . well, only comes
once a year, they say, right? I guess this is a funny way to
celebrate—showing off my new toy. But it's a pretty good way.
Thought you might find it pleasing. The old tinkerer found a
dime and made it into fifty dollars, hey, Jael?"

The speech patterns were those Ward had employed when he
was embarrassed yet inordinately pleased with himself. At work,
busy dissecting a machine or designing a diagram or sketching an
idea, he had spoken more crisply and in a heavier tone. There
had been another sort of excitement in his manner then, when he
was hunting for something. Now he had found it.

He moved toward them, turning, posing coyly, using his own

form as a demonstration of his latest achievement. He was grinning, mildly fuzzy with too much liquor—a pre-birthday binge.

Eleven years ago. It didn't seem possible. He had been dead eleven years. But the holo-mode recording held death at bay.

Ward's image made a corny bow in Jael's direction. The photonics had been captured long before this room was built. But the alignment had been carefully worked out, and the chairs were arranged to duplicate the original successful showing. As he had on that first night, Ward saluted his wife. "Jael, m'dear, you look beautiful. Ahh, don't give me that little sneer, darling. You know it's because of you, all this nonsense. Every bit of it," he said with intense sincerity. "I'd be broke, maybe dead, if you hadn't come into my life. It changed everything." He added with a ribald smirk, "Made the kids, too, huh? What would they have done without you and me?" Once more he sobered. "Thank you, my love," he said softly.

Patrick's and Mari's eyes, their black hair, their sharp features. Todd resented his genes, felt cheated, as he had so often over the years. He hadn't even received Ward's brains in compensation. No one had. Ward Saunder had been unique. He would never be duplicated, not even if cloning had been possible and they had saved some of his tissue in hopes of that miracle.

"Kids . . ." The arrangement of chairs allowed him to include Carissa and Dian in his address. But it was Pat, Mari, and Todd he seemed to look at. The effect of living eye contact was powerful, and unsettling. "I'll have to stop calling you that pretty soon. Even you, Mari. You're not my little girl any more. You're a beautiful lady, just like your mother. Beautiful and smart. Smart women run in this family." Laugh lines crinkled his merry face. "Smart men, too. You've sure got the head for business, Pat, my boy. Go to it, you and your mother. Todd, well, son, you're a top tech with a screwball way of looking at stuff, just like me. You'll have to find yourself a woman to keep you fed and dressed, just like I did, or you'll forget where you left your pants last night. Don't know about you, Mari, not yet. I'm so used to your being my baby." An apprehensive expression chased over his lean features. "You really don't have to fly and drive and speedboat faster than anyone, you know. You've got your whole life to live. Don't rush! Plenty of time. Leave the rushing around to Dad.

Reminds me, gotta make that flight to Qatar next week. Some really good stuff coming out of the Confederation Rift Labs lately . . ."

Ward shook off business speculations and concentrated on the happy occasion. But ideas always burned in that inquisitive brain. Even in his lightest moments, he never stopped wondering, speculating. "Enjoy life, kids, that's my recommendation. That's what Jael and I want most for you—for you to be happy. We wanted to bring you kids through these messes. And your mother made sure you'll never have to worry about money. My heart and my head, all in one magnificent lady." He threw Jael a hammy kiss. Then he reached out of the holo-mode frame, grabbing at something. When his hand pulled back, he held a brimming glass, lifting it high. "To us. Many, many more happy returns to us all. Is that arrogant of me, Jael? Courting the fates? You know I don't swallow that Spirit of Humanity junk. But, well, dammit, my birthday *is* my celebration for all of us. Love it! All of us here together. Let's agree. Come back home, kids, every year. You be sure they do, Jael, honey, if I get too tangled up in some wild project and forget. Every year, now," and he stamped his foot lightly upon the carpet. "Every year, we get together again right here. All of us." Again he lifted the glass. "We Saunders. Watch out, world. My kids are coming to get you, and they're damned sure coming out on top." With that, he drained the drink and hurled the glass away. Somewhere out of frame but still captured on the sound system, the sound of the crash echoed tinnily.

"Remember! Every year. Too many families splitting up these days. That won't happen here." Todd rubbed his eyes for a few seconds, his throat aching. Ward went on. "Dying, of too damned many things. They're finally getting it under control, and about time. Okay, they can call it Spirit of Humanity. Maybe that'll help some of it. But as soon as we can get that Protectors of Earth bunch to give us the land down there, we'll start on that cryogenics setup. I've got it all laid out. Remind me tomorrow, Jael, once I sober up." An eager grin split his face. He was a man in a love affair with life.

So much vitality. So much keen intelligence. Not very well organized, but incandescently brilliant. He and Jael had been a perfect team. They hadn't always been kind to each other. Sometimes the sparks flew and the team almost came to pieces. But they had been too stubborn to give up.

Jael was wiping her cheeks, sobbing softly, but she was smiling, too. Behind her, Roy Paige's head rested on the projection panels. Todd suspected the man was crying, grieving for the friend and employer who had been lost.

"Hey, Roy, let's have us another round and show 'em what we've been doing. Roy and me and Todd have cooked up another surprise for you. Sit back now . . ." Again Ward reached out of the image. A black hand extended from nowhere, handing him a fresh glass. Roy Paige, the living Roy Paige, not his disembodied holo-mode hand, slumped over the console, his shoulders heaving. He couldn't look any more. Years ago, Todd had tried to comfort the man when this happened. Now he knew nothing but time would ease the pain that would never go away completely.

Ward's image stepped aside and he gestured dramatically. A three-dimensional globe, a separate holographic image, winked into being, suspended in mid-air. It was a memory album, compiled by Ward. A rapid succession of scenes and portraits appeared. Old flat photographs and crude holographic projections made with the now-obsolete three-color emulsion process. The views showed the passing years of the Saunder family.

Ward and Jael's wedding picture. It had to be a match made in heaven. No human agent would dared have tried to bring this crazy coupling about. The financial empire's princess and the tinkerer with all those wild ideas, a man obviously doomed to penniless obscurity. Jael threw away everything for him, abandoning what had seemed, in those days, her only chance to survive. How could anyone know that her family's fortune would go under, along with so much other wealth, and that Jael would build a new one on the glittering gold of Ward Saunder's creativity?

Baby Patrick, sitting up, staring innocently at the audience—at himself more than thirty years older and sadder and wiser. Then it was Todd's turn to submit to the cute-baby-picture routine, and Mariette's. Scenes of them bare-bottomed and diaperless. Scenes of them toddling through yards or rooms of a dozen half-forgotten residences the family had occupied. The three of them playing around an old plane they'd cobbled together from junk found near the old farmhouse outside of Chicago. Todd watched them growing older, the years telescoping. Stairsteps kids. Mari had been almost as tall as Todd, for a while, during their adolescence, when she was still four years younger than he. That had driven him crazy, at the time; baby sister, as tall as he was, and nearly as tough! Todd had been scared Ward would teach her to fly before he himself had a chance at the plane's controls. That had seemed unbearably important, then. He was sure if that happened, he would die of shame, or he'd run away from home and join the Looter Troops in the newly created United Ghetto States. The images went on, speeding them through time. Todd and Mari and Pat shot up to their adult height, lost their childish bodies and faces. Todd wanted to slow down the flow. They were approaching the end too fast.

It was the present—the present of twelve years ago—and all of them were in the scene with Ward. The small holograph insert album was gone. Back to real time. They posed for a family portrait, clustering around Ward. Ward's arm, in the image, rested on Todd's shoulders. The memory was so vivid Todd felt anew that loving presence, close, touching, holding him; felt Ward's fingers squeeze his arm, and the way his father shook all over when he laughed. Ward's hand rumpling Todd's hair, a comment in his ear —and from the projection—"This damned kid's damned near as tall as I am. That's as big as you're going to get, boy. You'll bust out of your hat size if you show me up any more . . ."

It wasn't an Oedipal challenge. Glowing fatherly pride filled the words. Todd had taken that for his theme. Remember who he was, and who Ward had been. He would never be able to surpass his father, but he would try to live up to those high standards.

"Smile for the camera, Jael. Give me a kiss." The Jael in the image leaned toward him, their lips meeting. It was meant as a theatrical buss but developed into something far more loving and lingering. They turned their faces to the lenses, smiling, surrounded by their children. Happy. Perfect.

The image was gone.

Todd had studied old museum films and outdated magnetic tape systems. He had to admit a few of those quaint projections still could have an emotional impact. But when they ended, there were noises—machines clicking off, film ends flapping, or a sud-

denly blank white screen—jarring the deeply moved viewer out of
the carefully built mood. Here there was no jolt. Silently, the
image had vanished, taking with it the man they remembered with
love.

Slowly, as if the systems were aware of their grief, the lights
came up.

"If only . . ." Pat murmured after a lengthy stillness, "if only
we'd had the Antarctic facility ready, his DNA tissue samples, his
sperm . . . just six more months, that's all it would have needed."

"Ward has his legacy," Jael said. Tears dried on her cheeks.
Her eyes were very bright. "You. All of you. You're Ward
Saunder's tomorrow, the second generation. And you're going to
give us that third generation, aren't you, Carissa?"

Dian and Mariette stared at Carissa with a mixture of curiosity
and envy.

"Mother, I was supposed to tell them," Pat said irritably.

Jael flung up her hands in counterfeit apology. "Sorry! What's
the fuss? It'll be all in the family, anyway. A natural phenomenon
that's been going on a long time." She rose and walked over to
Carissa, stroking her daughter-in-law's fair hair. Todd saw that
greedy look once more. Carissa, preening quietly, didn't seem to
mind the attention.

"Congratulations," Dian said. Despite his annoyance at having
his news stolen, Pat beamed a proud acknowledgment to the
black woman.

Roy Paige had been collecting the holo-mode out of the projector. He leaned over Carissa's chair and added his congratulations
to Dian's, then said, "I'll just get this down to the safe, Jael."

"Do come back."

He shook his head. "Too tired. It . . . it always gets to me. I'll
see you tomorrow. Good night, all."

As the older man left, Todd extended his hand to Pat. "I know
how much you two have wanted this. I'm glad for you." Even as
he said that, some irrational part of him was jealous. He felt as if
they had been in a race and Pat had beaten him. "We'll have to
call you both 'Duryea Saunder,' now that you're going to be parents."

Pat and 'Rissa deserved it. Their three-year marriage had been
rocky in many ways, strained by their differing concepts of

fidelity. Somewhere along the line, Carissa had accepted the affairs, adapting to the life style with equanimity. She had wanted a baby, and so had Pat. At first there had been worries about sterility. No one was sure what all the aftereffects of the pandemics, toxins, and radiation doses would be. Carissa had been through numerous clinics. Pat had gone to some prominent medics, too. They had been pronounced sound, though doctors warned that Carissa wasn't strong and a pregnancy was bound to be difficult, even risky. Todd had thought they might have given up and was surprised to learn they hadn't and had finally been successful.

"You're going to be an uncle, kid. How about that?" Pat said.

Mariette's congratulations were less than wholehearted. "Good work. When's the baby due?"

"Late July or early August," Carissa replied, sighing happily.

Dian frowned, aware of some of the family history. "You're not going surrogate route at all, then? With your small frame, I'd think . . ."

The other woman looked apprehensively at Jael. "Oh, no. I'm going to carry it to term myself. Besides, it's too late for surrogate implantation. I don't really like that idea, anyway. It seems rather . . . unnatural."

"It's a proven technique for women who have trouble conceiving or carrying to term," Mariette began.

"Carissa won't have any trouble," Jael said firmly. "That technique's a fad, anyway. Kills more fetuses than it saves. There's absolutely no reason why Carissa won't have a full-term normal, healthy child. Lord! I went into labor at a board meeting while I was carrying you, Mariette. I barely had time to get to an infirmary. Thought I was going to drop you on the floor of the flier ambulance—like some peasant woman! I was back at the board meeting, finishing up, twenty-four hours later. There's really too much fuss made about the whole thing . . ."

"But 'Rissa isn't you, Mother," Mari objected in a heavy tone.

Pat was looking anxiously from his mother to his sister. Carissa rushed in with a cheery "Oh, I'm sure everything will be fine. Dr. Ganz says I'll have to take it easy, lots of nutri-supplements and so forth."

"Dr. Ganz is right. You'll see. A perfect baby," Jael predicted smugly. "Just as I said: Ward lives on through you children and his grandchildren . . ."

"You live through us, too," Mari put in.

Jael shifted gears, looking startled. "Well, that's true, of course. Genetically speaking, that is. You know, I never think of myself as Jael Hartman any more. I'm Jael Saunder. So it all amounts to the same thing. Ward and me, and all of you. You'll have to pick a good name, Pat, one suitable for Ward's grandchild. I have some in mind . . ."

"We'll pick one out," Pat said. Like Mariette's comments, his had a bite.

"Are you going to live here at Saunderhome after the kid's born?" Mari asked. Todd felt the trouble starting. He knew the reunion had been going too well. Carissa's long-hoped-for pregnancy would provide the excuse Mari had been itching to find.

"We haven't thought that far ahead yet. The campaign's been taking up time," Pat replied. He had been moving in subtly, edging Jael aside, taking her place nearest Carissa's chair. Carissa leaned back against his arm, basking in his protectiveness. Todd had seen the three of them in poses like this every time he had come home. Tonight he saw something new. Pat and Jael, and 'Rissa between them, and 'Rissa quietly enjoying the situation.

"Well, you have a while to make up your minds," Dian broke in, trying to lighten the mood. "You can live anywhere. And the baby can be anything he or she wants to be when he or she grows up, and can live anywhere . . ."

"Even in space." Mari wouldn't leave well enough alone. "When that baby's grown, Goddard will still be recruiting."

Worse, Pat couldn't resist the bait. "Not again! Do you have to drag that fantasy in the sky into everything? When my kid's grown up, that oversized cartwheel will just be a notation in the history tapes, and we'll be settling up the *real* concerns of mankind!"

"You narrow-minded political hack! Who the hell . . . ?"

"Drop it!" Todd thundered at them. "What's wrong with you two? We were just agreeing what a wonderful event this is going to be, how great it is that the kid won't go hungry or be cold or need to fight for a place to sleep, how proud Ward would have been to know he was going to have a grandkid—and you start clawing at each other! Back off! Both of you! Give each other a choice and a right to an opinion!"

"We'd be glad to, if the Earth First Party would leave Goddard alone."

"What are you talking about?" Pat flared. Carissa began tugging at his arm, trying to calm him down, to no avail. "If you mean that funding vote . . ."

"I mean economic strangulation and missile attacks. Over a hundred Colonists injured, fifty-eight of them dead. The last time, Todd could have been one of the casualties, too!"

A profound, shocked silence followed. Pat cleared his throat several times. Yet when he spoke, his voice broke. "Wh . . . what? What are you . . . I don't understand . . ."

"Don't you?" Mariette gazed at her older brother suspiciously. "What don't you understand? Dead? Injured? Todd almost being a casualty? A missile shadowed his ship in when he was heading for the Colony. They damned near took him out."

"Hold it!" Pat closed his eyes in pain. Carissa was huddling in her chair. Jael's mouth hung open. She seemed stunned, unable to grasp Mariette's revelations.

Dian swayed back and forth, her arms crossed under her breasts, her manner angry. "You didn't tell me it came *that* close to you," she snapped at Todd.

"I didn't want you to worry." Dian's fiery glare made Todd regret he had said anything at all. Pat was pulling himself together, looking at his brother pleadingly. With a weary sigh, Todd nodded. "It happened. I've seen the tapes, interviewed some of the victims while I was there. And I've seen the damage inflicted on the torus. Somebody took Earth First's platform, about Goddard's ability to fire down into our gravity well, seriously and hit back."

Todd half expected Mariette to go into detail, bragging about Goddard's so-far successful defense. But apparently her suspicions wouldn't let her. She didn't reveal the illegal weapons and Lunar Base fighters, said nothing about the plan to collect the missile debris in the mass driver nets and puzzle the pieces together as evidence.

"Who?" Pat asked suddenly. "You have somebody to accuse? Are you going to take it to P.O.E. court?"

"We're pretty damned certain it isn't the World Expansionists or Fairchild's party. They're Spacers," Mari replied bitterly.

"You're saying you don't *have* any proof, no names to name," Pat said, a debater making his point.

"Only killed, injured, and damaged property. Not much to you, of course. Try translating that to a direct missile hit on New Washington and see how it sits. Actually, I don't imagine our enemies really care how many of us they kill. They're more interested in crippling Goddard Power Sats. If they do that, and kill me and a lot of other people in the bargain, my share of Ward's inheritance will be wiped out, won't it? Not that it matters. Not now that the famous Patrick Saunder is assured of *his* immortality through progeny!"

"Mari . . ." She heard the warning and the pain in Pat's voice and quieted. "Whatever our philosophical differences about the Colony's worth, I've never advocated war. Never!"

"No?" Mariette wouldn't look at him. "We've heard you say, many times, that Goddard is, and I quote, 'stealing the lifeblood of Earth, draining away her irreplaceable treasures, and it must be stopped.' "

"Campaign rhetoric, for God's sake," Pat exclaimed desperately. "That's not a declaration of war. Missiles. My God!" He seemed aghast Mari could believe him capable of such an act.

"Apparently somebody didn't dismiss your speeches so lightly. They were listening very carefully and took their cues from you. So much for rhetoric. You're Earth First Party, Pat, all by yourself, the master of the 'why don't we take all those funds we're wasting in space and . . .' tactic. If you're not responsible for my people dying, who is?"

"Why . . . why hasn't any of this been released? How long . . . ?"

"A couple of months," Todd supplied. He took pity on Pat's horror and bewilderment. "They're a closed society, Pat. They clamped a total news blackout on themselves. Those who were supposed to rotate planetside postponed their yearly leaves. They choose to stay, no matter what happens. Lunar Base knows, but they agreed to hold it, even from their superiors."

"Should have seen . . . can't we see it?"

His brother was a highly intelligent man, literate, well informed about a vast number of things. But in matters of space, he had never gone past the most rudimentary knowledge. "No, Pat. You couldn't see it, even with the orbiting telescopes. There's too much distance involved. Mari's hammering it because she's mad. But she's also right. Goddard didn't tell me and didn't tell its planetside allies, either."

"We have now," Mariette announced. "We gave it to Fairchild this afternoon. Dabrowski, too."

Pat was stricken at the betrayal. "Do you know what they'll do with that information? I can hear their speeches now!"

"Is that all you can think about? Your campaign?"

Todd found himself watching Jael. Why wouldn't she say anything? She had promised they would work together to keep Pat and Mari from each other's throats. Dian wasn't a family member, and Todd didn't blame her a bit for not charging in on this. Carissa was useless when things got noisy. But Jael had knocked all their heads together often enough, physically and with words. Instead of backing him up, she was holding Carissa's hand, patting it, reassuring the expectant mother that everything was going to be all right. Possessing Carissa's attention and trust the way she intended to possess that grandchild. One more little Saunder mind and personality to mold the way she thought they ought to go. Was she thinking that the *next* time she would get everything perfect?

Todd felt as if he were looking into Jael's brain, disliking the sensation. The logic fit, though. She could step in if she wanted to. She didn't want to. Let poor Todd flounder around and play referee. Divide and conquer. It served Jael's interest, perhaps, her interest in her grandchild.

"Do you know how you look and sound?" Todd asked, ripping across the on-going harangue on either side of him. Pat and Mari stopped, staring at him. Dian nodded, ready. Modulating his tone only slightly, Todd went on. "Listen to yourselves. Look at yourselves. Yes, you, too, Mother, Carissa. How would all this infantile bickering—with Mother and Carissa playing audience—look to an impartial observer?"

There were four utterly blank expressions. Dian had picked up the case from Todd's chair. She quietly made her way to the holo-mode projector Roy Paige had left empty.

Jael was the first to find her voice. "Todd, what on Earth are you talking about?"

He couldn't repress a derisive laugh. "Earth? That's too limited. Far too limited. When I say impartial observer, that's exactly what I mean. Completely impartial. Looking at us from a distance, sizing us up. What would such an observer make of what's been going on here tonight? The almighty Saunder family, a quasi-nation, autonomous, wealthier than most existing countries on this planet, powerful . . . and we're pulling out one another's hair and backbiting like squabbling apes, or an even lower species on the evolutionary scale."

Dian was adjusting the dimensional balance and color and lining up the messenger data units. Jael glanced at the black woman, scowling, beginning to smell a rat. "I'm not sure I understand what you're driving at."

"You will, Mother. All of you will. I thought the memories of Dad would have a healing effect. But obviously that doesn't last. Maybe what Dian and I are going to show you will wake you up for now and the foreseeable future. Wake up you and the world —before it's too late."

CHAPTER NINE

REJECTED TRUTHS

"SYSTEMS green," Dian said. She leaned lightly on the holo-console, taking long, deep breaths.

Jael's expression hardened. "You seem to have forgotten where you are, Todd," she said with heavy authority. "This is a ceremonial occasion devoted to your father's memory."

"I haven't forgotten." Todd spoke gently, but he didn't retreat. "This concerns one of Dad's dreams, one that was very important to him. He was never able to pursue it to its conclusion. When he deeded ComLink to me, he gave me his dream as well. You might say it was a legacy. Does that put it into proper perspective?"

Jael groped toward her chair, sinking into it, wide-eyed and worried. She covered her mouth nervously for a moment, a rare gesture Todd remembered from his childhood. She was extremely upset when she did that. "What dream?"

"Project Search."

"That . . . that fantasy? It was never going to amount to anything, any more than the space station will." Mari rolled her eyes, seething, and Todd gestured urgently to keep her from butting in. "It was never a *new* field. Your father had lots of predecessors. All those other people who'd hoped to contact alien intelligence . . . something called Ozma, and another one was, I think, SETI. The scientists were to be commended for all that hard work—"

"And money," Todd added before Jael could.

She didn't like having her words put in his mouth. "Yes, money! A great deal of money, and for no results. I always thought it was a waste for Ward to putter around with the same idea that had been tried and found wanting. Telescopes and scanners, simply duplicating those failures . . ."

"Who were looking along the wrong frequencies." Dian didn't speak loudly, but they all heard her. "The prior searches were mostly along one or two gigahertz. And they scanned areas like M-Thirteen in Hercules. Pretty shrewd guessing, but, as it happens, wrong. We have much more sophisticated gear than they had, or than Ward Saunder had. Faster and wider scans and much sharper ears, if you care to put it that way."

Jael glared daggers at the black woman. No doubt she knew as much as Todd and Dian did about Ward's original project. But her data were old. Todd had kept things very low key when he revived the search three years ago. Jael had been undercut, shut out, and she was demonstrating it. She drew herself up. "I'm not the greedy harpy some people think I am. It wasn't the money . . ."

"Of course not," Carissa defended her.

"What's the point, Todd?" Pat asked. "I sort of remember the project. It wasn't my pet, but I did drop in on you and Dad now and then. Interesting stuff, but not very relevant to what was going on right then. The whole damned world was coming unglued—problems that make today's almost petty by comparison. Humanity needed Dad's brains working on something important, not playing around listening to star static. We needed him. We still do. Some of his inventions were the difference between life and death for millions. The viral inhibitor filter, the synthafood accelerator process, the mass driver adaptation that finally made surface transport work, the cryo medicine—all the spinoffs. Without his brainstorms, Earth would be a wasteland."

"And you think it isn't?" Mari had remained quiet as long as she could.

"No!" Pat wouldn't let her talk, overriding her with his orator's carrying voice. "Jael's right. It was a hobby Dad enjoyed, but we couldn't afford that dream, then or now."

"Are you through making speeches?" Pat blinked at Todd, who pushed on. "If you are, we can get on with it. Project Search never was frivolous. It was just a trifle ahead of time. It has finally paid off. Right now, mankind's standing at a crossroads, the most important one since we learned to talk and use tools. And we'd damned well better be equal to making the right choice about which way to go."

Whatever Pat saw in Todd's face made him change his tone. "What have you got, kid?" Mari pointed at him, but Pat took her hand, holding it fast. "Mari, hey! Whatever this is, I think maybe we ought to hear Todd out." Mari debated with herself, suspecting collusion. But she finally acquiesced somewhat grudgingly.

Todd moved around briskly, not wasting the chance. "If you would, I'd like you all to sit down again, just where you were for Ward's memorial. Mari, would you please sit next to Pat? Dian and I will be standing back here by the projector."

Grumbling and sour, Mari obeyed. At the other side of the room, Jael sat sullenly, barely tolerant of her second son's whims. Carissa reached across the space between their chairs and held Pat's hand. Todd stood between Mari and Pat, pressing their shoulders, trying to communicate his excitement with the touch. Dian cued the holo-mode systems, and the room lights dimmed once more. But she left the bubble dome exposed. Scattered starlight seemed to leap closer when the interior lights were down.

She waited. Todd prepared himself emotionally, looking up. Starlight overhead. That was fitting. "Okay, Dian, let's start. What you're going to see is a preview, a special showing just for the family. This package and some extensive corroborating material will be presented at the Global Science Council conference in a few days. I wanted you to know about it first, though, the same way Dad always showed his new inventions to us before he called in the press. This is preliminary, but it's solid. This demo works."

In the focus point facing the arc of chairs, a deep blackness formed. Opaque. Space. A blue-green-white bloated curve of Earth appeared at the lower left of the image, giving the viewers an idea of their relative position. An orbiter floated in the center of the image. Metal reflected direct solar radiation. Surfaces looked solid and edges hard and sharp. Todd was proud of the holographic quality. He had taken this one himself while closing in with his shuttle. Like many high-vacuum constructs, this satellite was a fragile-looking thing.

"This is Project Search Orbiter Four," Todd said. An insert holographic image formed on the lower right of the main projection. A monitor screen. It appeared to rest on the floor, contrasting strangely with the orbiter hanging in space. The orbiter image was revealed in harsh, unfiltered sunlight. The monitor had been photographed in an ordinary office by artificial light. Dian zoomed on the insert until nothing but the little screen showed. The readout was available at that extremely close angle.

Data jittered and froze on the screen, sketching out the orbiter's dimensions and raw specs, then hurrying on to other details. Mari forgot her anger. She perched on the edge of her chair, reading rapidly. Jael, as well as Pat, absorbed the material just as fast. Carissa could read a moderate rate feed, but this was designed for the use of techs and trained scientists—or for the wife and children of Ward Saunder.

Carissa whispered, "It's too . . ."

"Shh," Pat soothed her, concentrating on the holo-mode. "I'll spell it out later." Carissa smiled trustingly, her face and hair ghostly in the dim light.

"No immediate profit." Jael had pounced on a significant datum. She interpreted the facts as she saw them. Todd sighed. It would take her a while to absorb the rest of what he was going to tell her. Her mind was different from Ward's, but just as spectacular. Her gifts had brought the family through all the crises. She weighed value in terms of what sort of security it could buy for her family. That security had given Todd the wealth and freedom to bring Project Search out of storage. It would be hypocrisy for him to sneer at Jael's absorption with profits.

Security first. Dreams second.

Yet dreams could come true. This one had.

In the holo-mode theater, the little orbiter went through a dizzying series of changes, displaying earlier models of Search vehicles, progressing forward to its own design. The monitor distilled time and expense. Jael muttered something Todd couldn't quite hear, probably another acid comment about needless waste.

"We started with these orbiters about three years ago, but it took two tries before we got a really satisfactory model. It was bootleg research, and there was a lot of turnover and a very small working staff at any given period. Eventually we culled the staff down to a few dedicated people. About two years ago Dian hired on with ComLink, and I approached her about Project Search. She was working with the translator department, not space scans, but she was very interested. We both thought that if we actually found something, her background and training would be invaluable. We were right." Todd turned to Dian, wishing he could find a stronger compliment to thank her for her unflagging loyalty. "Beth Isaacs and Techs Anatole Duchamp and Wu Min stayed with it all the way."

Fabric rustled as his audience stirred. There was whispering. Their reactions were unformed as yet, just as the earliest data from Project Search were erratic and uncertain. The image-orbiter delivered information then, on command, sent out fresh signals, turning, hunting, fine-tuning, always seeking a target that might not exist.

The insert vied with the orbiter for attention. In the holo-mode image, a second Todd and a second Dian appeared. They were leaning over the monitor but carefully not blocking its screen, giving the camera lens a clear shot. The scenes flickered in rapid sequence, showing them and the Project Search team, poring over the readouts, discussing them, their elation growing. They reset, reprogrammed, calling for repeat scans, repeat signals, backups, and reconfirms. They tried to eliminate all element of chance. They compared their data and pictures with those from Global Astro Science's files, and from those of the orbiter telescopes and those on the Moon. They analyzed the data again and again, afraid to get their hopes up.

Jael swiveled, and Todd sensed her scrutiny in the semidarkness. "Before you ask, every bit of funding came out of my own pocket. I didn't take a thing from any of my stockholders."

The orbiter's image disappeared. A distant star field took over its part of the projection. It wasn't as realistic as the orbiter had been. The range was long and the image looked like what it was —a grainy blowup of an astronomical photograph. The monitor scene enlarged, the human figures becoming life-size, twins of the real Todd and Dian. Sound now accompanied the busy whirl of numerals and graphs on the screen in the holograph. The techs' conversations had been edited down to bare essentials, incisive comments to point up events and discoveries.

"We decided to broaden the base Ward and the earlier seekers had been using. We could, with our improvements on Ward's scan patents. The first researchers would have sold themselves for life to get such equipment."

Men and women who had donated years, searching, hoping. They were right. There *was* intelligent life beyond the Solar System. It had just needed more time for the collective human brain to produce the necessary equipment and find the exact path. Thanks to their groundwork, Todd's people had pinpointed the dream and made it real.

Dian took up the explanation. "You're now looking at a scanning sector designated nine cee jay, mid-screen, to your left. If you wish, we'll supply you with complete catalog data. We had to develop some of our own as we went along."

"What did you find?" Mari asked excitedly. "Come on! Have pity!"

The deep-space photo jumped, the image refocusing instantly. The new apparent angle was a great deal closer, zeroing in on a particular area of space. A machine-sketched bracket formed around an empty patch in the enlarged shot.

In the monitor insert, Todd and Dian cued comps and got a response. Earth's technology reached beyond Earth and lunar orbit, far beyond, spanning an empty gulf. The answer was slow. It took a while for the signal to reach its destination, be considered, and be returned. Finally, the screens put up the data. In cold, comp-abbreviated English, the letters stated: *Cnfrm. Ptrn rpt. RQ Dcrypt.* An odd series of tones and staticky bursts came from the monitor. A playback relayed from space.

"Request what?" Carissa wondered aloud. Todd was startled. She was sharper than he had realized. Obviously she could follow most comp shorthand.

"Decryption," Dian explained, "is a term borrowed from the military lexicons. Usually it refers to some general asking for a breakdown of a code. And this *is* a code, in a way. But because it's not in any human language, the comp couldn't convert it. This process is going to take considerable time to complete, but not too long, we hope."

Carissa glanced back at Dian gratefully and mouthed a thank-you. She accepted all this, unbothered by the cosmic implications.

Pat and Jael were sitting like stones, but Todd knew their minds were racing. Mari would be his ally. She was anticipating, leaning forward, eager.

Good girl. Back me up. Help me get through to them. They've got to realize that the whole history of our species will undergo a radical change.

Mari was the first to notice the pattern in the static. The monitor's electronic tone was repetitive, but so was the static, coming in seemingly random waves. Mariette, familiar with sunspot interference and other space noise, penetrated the scratchy sounds. "That's coherent."

"A . . . a message?" Jael's voice sounded very far away. "Are you saying that's an intelligent message?"

The curving half row of chairs drew Todd's eyes away from the now-familiar holo-mode re-enactment. *My mother. My brother. My sister. Carissa, and the child in her body. Saunders, all. Kevin's a Saunder, too, bound by his love for Mari. What Mari sees here, Kevin will see, and he'll understand. Dian . . . Dian already knows.*

Todd answered Jael's fearful query. "Yes, Mother, it's intelligent. It came from outside the Solar System, but we don't know exactly where from yet. We've checked, blind-tested, worked it in every human language, in clear, in code, in computerese, to every degree. We made sure. It's not natural, and it's not merely mimicking our signals. Whatever it is creates. It listens. It interprets. And it responds."

Pat was on his feet, silhouetted between the projector and the image. At Mari's yelp of protest, he moved out of the way, standing to one side. There was barely leashed terror in his hoarse voice. "Intelligent? Let me get this straight. That orbiter of yours is getting a reply? What reply? What's it saying? Where is the damned thing?"

"It's an interstellar vehicle," Mari replied scornfully. "Of course. Sit down and watch and maybe you'll learn something. You won't be able to see it, not yet. How far out is it, Todd? How many A.U.s?"

"Approximately twenty-eight, as of yesterday, and coming fairly fast. We originally estimated a year to make Earth orbit. It was making one-twentieth of one percent C, but that's gone up considerably." Mari's jaw dropped in admiration as Todd confirmed, "Faster than our best. But not light-speed, which will relieve a few physicists at the Science Council." He smiled to himself, not bothering to tell the others about the theoretical wars among the ranking minds of celestial mechanics. "We believe it's quite small, and obviously very sophisticated," he said. "We're talking a couple of months till visual contact, with the orbiting Wilson-Palo lens and the Council's big radio scanners. They haven't been looking in that region of the sky. But they will when we give them the data. It's just too damned bad the Australian scope got wrecked before the Space Neutrality Treaty went into effect. That was a beautiful eye. We certainly could—"

"A few months until you can see it and define its shape," Jael interrupted. She waved toward the monitor scene within the holo-mode. "Your data claims it's adjusting its course."

"That's right. Reacting to us."

"Maybe . . . maybe it's one of our own," Jael suggested somewhat desperately. "I remember they launched a number of deep-space craft, before I was born and when I was a child. Until funding got diverted into more useful channels."

"This thing is incoming, Mother," Todd reminded her with great patience. "The chances of its being one of ours are nil. But we held off announcing this until we could be sure. It's an alien vehicle, no question whatsoever."

His image and Dian's in the holo-mode projection resembled those of proud parents displaying a new baby. There was a bit of historical posing in their manner. They faced the cameras, aware they were going into the records along with the astonishing readouts. Feeble signals were computer enhanced and boosted. New signals were sent, new incoming data added to that building in the files. Time condensed. Confusing static became regularly spaced intervals alternated with other patterned bursts. Energy coming from Neptune's orbit began to form symbols and, possibly, letters and numerals. Dian's team responded in kind. The alien copied, questioned, returned its own queries—or at least that was what they appeared to be. It took days, sometimes, before the precious answer would come. And the most recent response was a binary readout. Not the one Project Search had sent, but the sequence intelligently re-formed and returned to

demonstrate that the machine understood what they were trying
to do.

The checks and rechecks had worn their patience thin. The tension had become nearly unbearable. Dian was tireless, and even
she grew snappy. A hundred times. A thousand. Again. No
doubt. They had it. Payoff. Project Search, out of all the scanning
efforts, had tracked down its quarry.

And now the dream had come true.

Was it going to be Pandora's box, or Prometheus' stolen gift to
mankind? There was no way to predict—whichever it was, it was
going to happen.

On the holo-mode monitor, the long-sought word appeared
after each laborious cross-check: *Cnfrmd.*

The inserts disappeared, and so did the frozen star-field photo.
Dian poised her hands over the glowing projector panels. "I can
run back anything you'd like to see again. We have a great deal
more, but it's redundant. Everything here and lots more very dry
stats. The extreme emphasis and time compression came from the
last three months, when we were positive we were onto something. The signal's been getting steadier as the vehicle corrects its
vector . . ."

"Lights!" Jael's normally soft voice was shrill with panic.

Dian obeyed. Interior illumination dimmed the stars beyond
the dome. Mari jerked around, staring at Todd. "Correcting?
How? And why?"

He thought over his reply, knowing that she, most of all, was
aware of celestial navigation's distances and problems. "We don't
know what its propulsion system is. We assume it's realigning *via*
our frequencies."

"Homing in on Earth's telecommunications, in other words,"
Mariette finished for him, nodding.

"My God." Pat breathed that prayer. "You . . . you're leading
it to us."

Dian shook her head, dismayed. Todd went on guard. "No, I'm
not. *Earth* is leading it. Hear me out, Pat. That thing's a probe. It
was coming in on Neptune's orbit when we detected it. In all likelihood, it's been programmed to prowl interstellar space, looking
for a contact just like ours. The odds are high it had already
picked up plenty before we beamed anything directly at it. Maybe

it's been talking for quite a while, saying 'hello,' trying to get an answer out of us. Only we didn't talk its language and didn't notice what it was doing—not until Project Search."

He paused, waiting to see if they would interrupt. "I can't claim I found it. I don't know if I did. Maybe Project Search is just the first Earth station that answered the com when that thing was hailing us. Now that we have responded, it's talking back. We think it can learn. We hope so. We're like two children—our species and that one out there which sent the messenger—and we speak totally different languages. We're seeing each other for the first time across a pool in a park. A very *tiny* pool, as interstellar distances go. This child, *Homo sapiens,* hasn't learned to walk or swim very well yet."

"We *can!*" Mari said fiercely. "We have the capability to go out there right now. *Have* had it for decades. If only those damned reactionary—"

"Stop it!" Todd waited for her to cool down, then resumed his explanation. "All right. Humanity hasn't been allowed to swim across the pool very far, for lack of encouragement and support. Okay, Mari? But that *other* child, the alien messenger, *can* swim. It's doing so. It's been looking for us, or something like us—intelligent life. Funny, isn't it? Both of us looking for the same thing, we from the bottom of a well, they from the top. Now it's coming over to meet us."

"You mustn't!" Jael's terror transformed her face and voice. "You mustn't talk to it any more. You mustn't let it know where we are."

Dian didn't hide her disappointment. She spoke gently. "Mrs. Saunder, we're way past that. For all we know, that probe's been coming our way for over a century, wandering at random. Maybe it picked up our first radio signals a long while ago. You must see that. We aren't doing anything to attract it. What's happened is that we picked up on it in progress. It was coming here, anyway. This way, we have time to talk to it, learn its language and teach it ours, communicate with it and find out something about its creators."

"Sending." Blood drained from Jael's round face. "It receives and sends. It thinks."

"Of course it does." Mariette didn't consult with Todd. Something in her manner alarmed him. Her excitement was fading. "And it's probably already sent word home when it first picked up an Earth transmission. I wonder where its home is?" She looked at Todd, on his wavelength once more. But the rapport was brief. She rose to her feet, began pacing back and forth. "Pick and vector and align itself, talk, interpret. Told its masters where it's going. Now it's going to have a look."

"No! No!" Jael was screaming. "Patrick! We've got to do something!"

"Try cutting off its funds in P.O.E.," Mari suggested, laughing nastily. "How does it feel to meet an entity you can't buy off or control?" Todd felt the moment slipping away from him, going off in directions *he* couldn't control.

Jael was ranting. "Our resources are stretched to the limits now . . . just recovering from the Chaos . . . can't let it . . . we have it all about to work . . ."

"Oh, shut up!" Mariette exploded. "You haven't got the slightest idea what—"

"Dammit!" Pat said suddenly. "Are *you* blind? I've got a kid brother who talks to aliens and thinks it's wonderful. Starry-eyed kid brother. That thing's a threat. You say it's faster than our fastest spaceships, intelligent, and you're going to feed it everything it needs to know about us humans."

"Everything *we* need to know may come to us in return!" Todd roared, trying to outshout him. Futile. Desperate, he kept on. "We can't run away from it. We'd better learn to deal with it. Mankind's tried that before, fearing changes and trying to stifle exploration. There was a time when we tried to halt travel by machines, vaccination against disease, anesthetics, nuclear experiments, investigation and use of recombinant DNA, seabed thermal energy drilling, building Goddard. We probably tried to stop the discoveries of fire and the wheel. But we can't! Not as long as we're human. We have to take the risks along with our curiosity!"

He hurt his throat to no purpose. Everyone was talking at once. Carissa begging them to discuss things calmly. Jael raving, supporting Pat, yet stepping on the heels of his words, turning his arguments into gibberish. Mari screaming at them both. Dian hopelessly trying, as Todd had, to spell out logic.

Unexpectedly, Mariette rounded on Todd, slapping him so

hard his head jerked from the blow. "Damn you! Oh, damn you! You knew about this when you were up at Goddard! Why didn't you tell me, tell us? You let me come down here, and all the time you knew, you . . . you bastard!"

Her hand went back again. Todd lunged, pinning her. Nose to nose with her, he used his superior strength, anticipating she would knee him, yelling into her face. "Yes, we knew! What difference does that make? What could you have done? We're in this together. *All* of us. I wanted to start straight with everyone." She hadn't lashed out yet. His face burned where she had connected. Mari didn't pull her punches. She was sniffling, angry tears gathering in her pale eyes. Todd found himself begging for comprehension in spite of his anger. *"All* of us, Mari. The whole species."

"We could have been out there already, to Mars and beyond. We *should* have been!" The tears spilled over. She twisted this way and that, trying to wrench free. Todd released her, gauging she wasn't going to strike out at him any more. "We . . . we could have met them halfway . . ."

"Met them?" Pat was a man walking in a nightmare. He grabbed Mariette and shoved her toward a chair, throwing her down into it. He stood back out of range of her fists and feet, pointing warningly, impaling her with his stare. "Meet the aliens to do what? Betray us? Ride off with them into some . . . some interstellar paradise? You'd like that, wouldn't you? You and McKelvey and all the rest of those crazy Spacers—split off and let some alien beings make us slaves, while you—"

"You stupid, contemptible paranoid." Mariette made the word sound worse than the rudest obscenity. "Invasion? Is that what you're thinking? Yes, you would. It's the *only* way you think. Everybody's out to get you, and you've got to be king and beat everybody down before you'll feel safe. Do you know what? You won't feel safe even then. You'll still be worrying that somebody's going to try to take that precious Chairmanship away from you. Well, you won't be able to beat this, and you won't be able to hide from it. You think if something doesn't suit your plans, you can lock it away or destroy it. You've got some waking up to do —a lot of it!"

"You're both paranoid!" Todd managed to yell. He was certain his throat must resemble butchered meat, but he had made them listen. "You're mad, aren't you, Mari? The alien messenger stole your piece of dessert. It's going to get here before Goddard can launch that Mars lander."

"It's Pat's fault, him and Earth First cutting off our funds—"

"Don't you start in on me again!"

Jael rushed into the next narrow opening in the verbal violence. "Pat may be right, Todd. Admit it. This alien thing probably is hostile. We've got to do something . . ."

"It's possible." Silence enveloped them. Dian eyed Todd sharply while the others gasped. "This is a first contact. We can't predict outcomes."

"You *see?*" Pat was maliciously triumphant.

Todd didn't let him go on. "It can be either friendly or hostile. My logic says any probe that sophisticated wasn't built by a species looking for new worlds to conquer. It could conquer them, anyway. It's looking for new trade outlets, maybe. Or just curious. And if it's this intelligent and powerful, we aren't going to be able to do much to resist the species that built it—*unless we can talk to their probe and find out as much as we can about its creators.*"

He was flying in circles, covering the same ground, increasingly frustrated. He had gotten too used to Dian, to his techs, to delegating explanations to his media experts. He was getting a depressing sample of what the Global Science Council presentation was going to be like, how some of the members were going to react. Was the whole damned planet becoming paranoid? Todd didn't want to claim the credit any more. Or make the presentation. Maybe he would turn the whole thing over to Dian and Beth. No, that was the coward's way out. He would have to take the good with the bad.

He hadn't reached Pat, the one person he most needed to reach. He tried once more. "Pat, they can be our friends. They can open up the whole universe to us. This is the start of a new era in human history, and you can go down in the books as the Chairman who greeted the alien messenger when it arrived."

"Can't take chances," Pat said. He glared at the holo-mode Dian was lifting out of the projector as if he wanted to grab it and smash the terrifying evidence. The fatal proof. Disaster coming.

An element beyond his control. "I . . . I have to prepare my listeners, consult the party. We have to get ready . . ."

"For what? Mass suicide?" Mari asked, shaking her head pityingly. She was pouting, a precocious child robbed of a chance to show off her special talent. Only her withering scorn for Pat was preventing another tantrum. "If they can build that, what the hell do you think you can do to get ready for them, except roll out a welcome mat? If you had any sense, you silly son of a bitch—"

"Don't talk to your brother that way!" Jael cried, advancing on Mari in maternal wrath. "I won't have it!"

Old resentment flared within Todd. *She'll defend Pat, but Mari can call me names and slap me and it's okay.*

Mariette stood her ground. "You can't order me around now, Mother, or tell me to clean up my language. I'm not a baby any more, and neither is Pat. Though he's acting like one, like a baby scared of the dark."

To Todd's amazement, Pat turned his back on both women, going to Carissa. She had been sitting very still, saying nothing much at all, not seeming afraid, even while Pat and Jael were flirting with hysteria. Carissa reached out to Pat, offering him some unseen strength he badly wanted. The scene diverted Jael's anger. She faltered, watching the pair as they shared and shut everyone else outside themselves. "I'm thinking of our baby, of all Earth's children . . ." Pat said softly.

"But not of those who choose to go into space," Mari retorted bitterly.

"If they desert us, they'll have to take the consequences."

"What consequences?" Todd asked. He was hoarse from shouting. At this rate, Dian would *have* to make the presentation to the Science Council. "You don't even know what the consequences are going to be. They may be wonderful. What's this family all about? Mother? Pat? Mari? What would Dad think of us right now? You know what he'd think. He never backed off from a new idea, no matter how risky. Never! And he wasn't ashamed to shake a rival's hand, either. We've got to try. *He* never stopped trying. He'd embrace this first contact—and you know it!"

They were a wall. Mariette, wrapping her Goddard loyalties about herself like a flag, sulking at the disappointment that the alien had put them in the shadow. Jael, empty-faced with terror, more frightened than Todd had ever seen her, unreachable in that fear. Pat, thinking hard along political lines, converting the discovery of the ages into a party campaign, organizing his paranoia into world-arousing oratory. Carissa was his comet's tail, trusting in him to figure a way out of the confusion.

"Do you know what Dad's lab motto was?" Todd rasped.

Jael was ahead of him. She recited mechanically: " 'We found a cure for cancer before we knew what was causing it.' " She wasn't there. None of this had meant anything to her at all. His childhood faith had been built on sand instead of rock, and he had never fully understood that until this moment. Ward was gone. And now Jael wasn't there for him, either. The pain sank deep, ripping out something important from his mind and heart. Incredibly, Jael sensed his loss. She begged forgiveness. "I'm sorry, Todd. It's just too much. I can't cope with this."

"Mother, there wasn't any way to break the news gradually. We weren't sure ourselves until just a few weeks ago. I've been trying to decide how to tell you. I thought the family should know first." Todd swallowed a surge of nausea. "This is . . . this is the most important thing that's ever happened. Can't you see that? It's harnessing fire. It's being Columbus and Neil Armstrong and Ward Saunder all in one."

"Maybe we can hold it back, buy some time," Pat muttered, talking to himself under the guise of discussing it privately with Carissa. She nodded, agreeing to anything he said.

"Oh, for—where have you been for the past hour?" Mari slapped her forehead in helpless disgust. "I can't believe you're Dad's son, Pat. Don't you ever think about anything but propaganda? That signal is tracking us as we orbit, all us little solar children—Earth, Moon, Goddard. There is no way you can suppress it. None. Not even if you get to be dictator of Earth and imprison or freeze every scientist who might detect that signal. Because you damned well won't suppress Goddard! We're going to be listening and talking to it on our own. Don't worry, Todd. We're not going to cross your circuits. We'll pick up on your data and follow your patterns. But we'll create our own signals." She smiled thinly at Todd. "I don't imagine Pat could suppress *you*, could he? And there are other telescopes, other listeners in orbit above us. As Todd says, not good ears, but good enough. In a few months, that signal will be bombing in, by his data. Face it, Pat! It's coming, like it or not!"

Tears flowed again, and Mari broke off her tirade. Conflicting emotions battered her. She crawled out of her chair, clinging to the back, blindly beating with her fists and repeating a litany. "Dammit, dammit, they beat us, Kevin. They beat us. Dammit, dammit, dammit . . ."

"You shouldn't have meddled, Todd," Jael said distractedly. "None of us should have. Maybe we tried to go too far. We should have quit while we were ahead."

"Mother, you can't stay ahead if you stand still. We've got to keep trying, even if the possibilities are scary." Todd laughed, and the sound was hollow in his ears.

Dian suddenly spoke up. "I remember something about your dad, Todd. I read it in an article. I think it must have been true. It sounded like something he would have said. The critics were questioning him about one of his inventions, the viral inhibitor, I believe. They claimed he was messing with nature, that maybe it wouldn't stop the plague but would wipe us all out, that he was going too fast. Ward Saunder said even the old Club of Rome used computers to plot out their doomsaying when they predicted Earth's civilization would collapse in thirty or forty years. He thought that was ironic. An old-fashioned bunch of analysts, worrying about mankind on a non-stop slide through too much growth and progress, and they used the latest technology to make their points."

"They were right in many respects," Pat said emphatically. She had touched an area he knew well. "The famines, the plagues, the wars—they came true. We're a long way from being out of that bunch of disasters even now."

"And who knows when the next one will hit?" Pat hadn't perceived that steel in Dian's personality. He pulled up short, staring at her. "You want to talk disaster, Mr. Saunder? I cut my baby teeth on it. So, will it be a disaster? You tell me. Guarantee it. Bet your life on it. I've been there, and *I'm* not going to hide and scream and say the aliens are coming to eat us. Maybe that means that knowledge is a dangerous thing. I've seen all those disasters, and I say we've got to talk to that messenger. Maybe it'll bring us a present, a solution, cures to our diseases, genuine immortality, the secrets of the universe. How do you know? You don't! Neither do we. But if you can't stop it, you'd better count on rolling with it, or finding a new friend."

Todd jumped in to help her out. "The next disaster to hit us from within could be the worst yet, Pat. We just might need the help of intelligent aliens to get us out of it. Pat?"

"I want all your data, your decryption, as soon as your people get them."

Dian dropped the holo-mode into its case. Nobody wanted to see the backup stats. They believed. That hadn't been the problem. So much for secrecy, Todd thought. They might as well have put it on ComLink. At least that would have spread the panic around generally.

"Is that an order, Pat?" Todd asked softly.

"Of course it is!" Mari pulled herself together and marched toward the elevator. "Watch out for him. He's so typical. When you turn this loose, the Earth Firsters will hit you with everything they've got, Todd."

"Mariette, where are you going?" Jael demanded, starting to follow her.

Mariette sidestepped Jael's grab at her arm. "I'm leaving. I'll rent a flier from Orleans and have it come out and pick me up if you won't let someone take me to the mainland. Then I'm grabbing the first transport heading out and up. It was a mistake to come here at all."

Jael persisted, boring in, blocking Mari's way. Surprisingly, she resorted to a caress, stroking Mariette's face. "Don't do this. You mustn't. We can work it out. We've been separated from one another for so long—that's why we quarrel."

"I don't quarrel with Todd like I do with you and Pat. He, at least, is willing to admit I might have some right on my side. But you and Pat won't let me breathe. It's got to be your way or not at all. You're stagnating, smothering yourselves on this planet, and you're trying to smother me, too." Mari giggled, and Jael's jaw dropped. "That's amazing!" Mariette exclaimed. "Do you know where I heard that? Do you remember? No, I suppose you've conveniently wiped it out of your memory. Grandfather Hartman. I was about ten, and he dropped in, unannounced. Big, noisy argument! Him saying we were living like animals in that crater and how could you turn your back on all the fine, cultural things the Hartmans had labored for, throw away their money and name and dignity—all for a crazy inventor."

Jael's face froze, the earlier tenderness gone. Merciless, Mari struck her to the bone. "I remember your slicing him up, too. I burned it in my mind, because I never wanted to forget the way you were then. 'Ward Saunder's name will eclipse everything the Hartmans ever did or ever will do,' you said with pride. 'I won't go back to that decadent stagnation. I was smothering there. Here, with Ward, I'm free.'"

Mari was eight centimeters taller than Jael, dark, thin, and long-boned, as Ward had been and as Jael was not. But they might have been identical twins confronting each other with awesome, feminine cold rage across the generations. Too different. And too much the same, because too much time had passed since Jael's rebellion against her own parents. She couldn't see the same thing happening between Mariette and herself.

Neither woman lowered her eyes, but Mari turned away. It wasn't a defeat. She continued toward the elevator, cueing the servo, hurrying inside.

Carissa tried to break the shock with trite, consoling words. No one reacted, and she gave up. At last Pat straightened up and appealed to his brother. "You must give me everything you get, Todd, please."

"This can't be political. And I'm not going to feed your campaign with data you'll twist into paranoia. Look, you'll get all you need from the public sources. Even if you dropped this holomode in the sea, there are ten others just like it. And if you destroy those, in a few weeks, a month, two, the media are going to be flooded with alien messenger speculation. Project Search has the honor of being first, but it won't be the last."

"But you have the decoders," Pat said, looking searchingly at Dian.

"That's right," she agreed. "I'm a scientist, Mr. Saunder. What I puzzle out won't be classified. But I'm not going to let it go public piecemeal. It's going to come in batches, and I don't hand it just to you or even just to Todd. It's knowledge. It belongs to the whole world, and to Goddard."

"Yes, but . . ." Pat was combing his hair with his fingers. He wasn't showing off for the cameras, for once. The gesture was completely unconscious.

Todd saved Dian further trouble. "We go to the Science Council conference directly from here. After that, the facts are available to the world. You'll have to get in line along with everybody else."

"You don't have an exclusive." Pat looked mean and dangerous. "Earth First has pull, and some military contacts. There are other decoders . . ."

"And you're the one who worries about wasting money and resources!" Todd laughed weakly. "Sure. Go ahead. Duplicate our efforts. I happen to think I've got the best team in the world. Dian and Beth and Wu Min and Anatole have been on top of this for months. If you want to make it a race, be my guest."

"You can be hurt," Pat warned. "You've got stock in SE Consolidated and SE Trans Co, not to mention all your ground-based ComLink installations."

"Are you going to shoot up my satellites and people with missiles, too?"

Pat recoiled in shock. "I didn't mean that . . ."

"Didn't you? Mari wasn't exaggerating. I was almost killed by someone who has a grudge against a Saunder-supported project—the Colony. Now you threaten Project Search—and me. Just what am I supposed to think you meant? What is Mari supposed to think?"

"It was a financial threat. I didn't say anything about missiles. I don't have any goddamned missiles!" Pat shouted.

Dian offered the holo-mode case to Todd, who said, "You're getting good at undercutting your siblings financially. But you'd better check and see if you can carry through before you threaten me. I'm diversified. A lot. I won't say you can't make a dent. But you can't cut off my lifeline like Earth First is cutting off Goddard's funds in the Protectors of Earth committees. Unlike Goddard, I won't talk secession. I'll fight you, Pat. If you want a Saunder civil war, you'll get it."

Visibly shaken, Pat backpedaled. "I'm sorry. I shouldn't have . . . don't, kid! Not us. Not you and me. We've got so much between us."

"Not as much as we used to. And what about Mari? There's

plenty of love there, too. If I didn't get through to you on anything else, Pat, hang onto this—Kevin McKelvey and that Colony
will fight if you push them too hard. And they'll fight damned
mean.

"The alien messenger is going to look at us as humans. That's
it. It's not going to distinguish between Earth First and Goddard
or cities or seabed installations or primitive farms. We're all the
same species, and we ought to act like it. You keep up your present course, and there may not be any Saunder name for that
baby to inherit. We just may kill ourselves off before the messenger ever gets close enough to shake our hand or deliver a warning
to us, if it turns out to be hostile. Think about that. Think *hard*."

He and Dian started for the elevator. Jael stopped them. She
waited. Obediently, hurting inside, Todd gave her a good-night
kiss. He peered into those eyes which were so like his own. What
he saw was discouraging. "I wanted this to be happy news,
Mother. It would have made Dad happy, you know."

Reluctantly, Jael nodded. "Yes, it would have. You're very
much like him. It's just that . . . that the rest of us don't have
your courage." Todd didn't trust himself to speak. Jael whispered,
"Mari . . . where did I . . . why did it go wrong? Please . . ."

"I'll talk to her, or try to," Todd promised. The weariness returned to him full force, a burden he didn't think he could take.
He kept promising. He couldn't turn her down. Todd attempted a
smile, but couldn't manage it. "We Spacers are supposed to speak
the same language . . ."

"The language of the alien messenger," Pat said. His voice was
ice. He was staring at the now-empty holo-mode projector, thinking. The wrong thoughts. There would be no soothing, persuasive
speeches from Pat Saunder, no famous voice to guide humanity
toward the coming event, to help it accept the alien contact. The
future seethed with panic and fear—all the wrong things.

It seemed like ten kilometers to the elevator and hours before
the doors opened. The holo-mode case weighted Todd's hand and
arm. The wonderful discovery. Mankind's future. The news—*we
are not alone.*

Neither was he, but it felt that way. Dian offered the solace of
her presence, comforting for the beloved people he was losing. He
barely sensed her hand on his arm or heard the elevator doors

172 Juanita Coulson

slide shut. It seemed an appropriate ending to a disastrous evening when the cage began to sink back toward the private suites two levels below. They weren't going all the way down, but they had taken one hell of an emotional knockdown.

"It'll work," Dian said gently. "You'll see."

"It's got to. For all of us."

CHAPTER TEN

☆☆☆☆☆☆☆☆☆

THE ENEMY AMONG US

THIS press conference disguised as a "science meeting" had been a mistake. Todd wondered if his original announcement hadn't been a mistake, too. He couldn't hide the discovery, but perhaps he should have found an alternate method of breaking Project Search's news to the world. Handing out the data at the year-end Global Science Council conference meant he personally had to take the credit or the blame. And there had been plenty of both in the hectic ten days following that brief moment of glory.

The scientific community had, for the most part, accepted the data. Dian and Beth and the others had been very thorough, the evidence solid. Only a few diehards withheld final judgment until they could confirm the discoveries with their own observations. Todd didn't resent those honest skeptics. After all, doubts and double-checking were what science was all about. The real danger came from another small group within the Council. They believed, but unfortunately they interpreted the data just as Pat and Jael had: alien invasion! There weren't many of them, but some had impressive professional credentials. They had provided the Earth First Party with potent ammunition when they gibbered that the incoming vehicle was certainly the forerunner of a deadly attack from beyond the Solar System. Pat grabbed that weapon and took off on a new stage of his campaign at once. His speeches *sounded* like sweet reason: "We must remain calm. We must

prepare ourselves to deal with this unknown menace from afar."
But the reaction had translated into global panic and, coinci-
dentally, an explosive growth in Earth First's voting rolls.

Dr. Albrecht, head of the Council, and other scientists had
rebutted Pat's speeches as best they could, but too few listened to
them. As the unrest and paranoia mounted day by day, Albrecht
had pleaded with Todd to help them. Todd had pointed out that
he wasn't in Pat's league as an orator. No one was. And if the
world's most respected scientists hadn't been able to get a fair
hearing while the populace was in its present mood, the only
thing likely to change that was time and the alien messenger's ac-
tual arrival near Earth. Yet Albrecht had persisted, kept wheedling, reminding Todd it was his responsibility as the sponsor of
Project Search. Wearily, knowing in advance his efforts would be
futile, Todd had acquiesced.

Futile indeed! A waste of time. Todd gazed out over the mea-
ger audience gathered in the Council's New Washington meeting
hall. Frank Chabot and one of Todd's top media teams manned
the front row, giving the event full coverage. They weren't at all
crowded. Worldwide TeleCom and Riccardi's Incorporated Network had sent mere second- and third-string apprentices, token
representatives. ComLink's rivals were strangling this press conference before it could reach the air. Not that they needed to. Todd
and the savants sharing the dais with him couldn't compete with
Pat's speechmaking. Protectors of Earth was holding an emergency session at the same time as the conference, with Pat as their
star attraction.

The rest of the attendees consisted of a few archivists and
specialty reporters working for research organizations and a scattering of professional curiosity-seekers who had passed inspection
at the door. Screening out undesirables had proved necessary.
Early the previous week, during another public meeting, the
Council had learned that the hard way, when hecklers broke up
the conference by screaming that the scientists were traitors,
selling Earth out to the alien monsters. Dr. Albrecht had been
forced to call for troops to restore order.

There were troops protecting them now, ready to quash any
disturbance before it could get out of hand this time. Soldiers
lined the back wall of the room and tried to blend in with the

decor. Troops . . . and an officer. An important one. A general?
This gathering hardly seemed worth sending a brass hat to super-
vise. Todd peered curiously at the man, searching his memory,
sure he had seen the officer somewhere else. P.O.E. insignia. The
relays clicked in his mind. Ames. Of course. General Ames had
been on the platform with Pat and the other dignitaries when the
Trans-Pacific truce had been announced. Ames's presence there
was understandable. But what was he doing *here?* Unwillingly,
Todd recalled Pat's words: "Earth First has pull, and some military contacts."

"You can be hurt."

Was Ames part of Earth First's network? Todd hesitated to call
it a conspiracy, but that term was creeping into his thoughts more
and more often nowadays. The near-riots at the science press
conferences, the insanity spreading across the globe every time
Pat ranted about aliens . . . and was Ames here to command yet
another thrust at Project Search? Surely the project's enemies
would be more subtle, more devious. Still, the idea made Todd
uneasy. He hastily glanced away from Ames, lest the general become suspicious.

Dr. Bjornberg leaned toward Todd. "Where are all the rest of
the reporters and observers who should be here?" he whispered
angrily. "You are the communications person, Mr. Saunder. Can
you not command . . ."

"I can and I have, as much as possible." Todd gestured to his
media staff. "It seems Protectors of Earth is a bigger draw."

Another scientist growled, "Chairman Li Chu *deliberately*
scheduled this so-called emergency session to conflict with our
meeting!"

"Naturally." Todd was mildly surprised that *they* were surprised. By now the rival media personnel were packing their gear,
looking bored, sneering as the attempt to put down paranoia had
come to an end. Chabot kept working, riding his boss's hobby
horse faithfully, seeking out individual interviews with the best-
known people on the science panel. But how much of the worldwide audience out there was watching any of this? Todd knew the
figures must be pitiful. They hadn't convinced anyone who wasn't
already on their side. Up the coast, in P.O.E.'s HQ in New York-
Philly, Pat would be amassing staggering audience totals, millions

upon millions of people hypnotized and taking in his every word —believing, their terror feeding itself as a result. And the golden voice would lead them on, telling them to trust Patrick Saunder to save them from the invaders. Vote Earth First Party!

"Just outrageous," Dr. Albrecht was complaining. Todd nodded absently, watching a black face at the rear of the room. General Ames watched back, his expression unreadable. Finally he turned and left. As he did, Todd found he had been holding his breath and let it out. Albrecht was still ranting. ". . . pearls before swine. They're incapable of understanding what we're trying to tell them."

"Possibly," Todd conceded. He was in no mood for arguing with those allegedly on his side as well as coping with Pat's intransigent opposition. With a shrug, he signaled Chabot to give up a bad job. Gratefully, the last techs made their way out. As the other doors opened and closed, an ominous roar of hundreds of people burst through. Fairchild and some of the public had showed up at earlier Science Council meetings, to cheer on the decryption progress and show support. Nobody except reporters showed up this time. CNAU Civil Order Enforcement had advised against it.

Todd wriggled into his coat, collecting his holo-mode materials, stepping down off the platform. Uniformed enforcement officers waited by the V.I.P. doors, hands on their side arms. Paramilitary escort. They insisted that he needed it now, while the public temper was running so high.

Bjornberg and Albrecht and several of the more stubborn Council members followed Todd out along the balcony. Unbreakable plexi protected them and the enforcement escort from a hail of brickbats and junk thrown by the crowd gathered on the plaza. It was the incident at Orleans Port again. But these weren't starving rioters. They were howling and throwing things at the enemy—Todd and the scientists, the people who had brought the bad news and dared try to claim the alien should be welcomed, not fought against. The plexi wall shuddered under the onslaught, but held. Todd noted enforcement sharpshooters perched in catwalks near the ceiling. So far, they weren't shooting. Chairman Li Chu's Spirit of Humanity edict held a lot of power in New Washington. Enforcement had strict orders—no return fire unless someone injured the parties they were guarding.

Would that help? A sacrifice? Someone they could kill?

Just as well I don't have a martyr complex, because I'm not remotely convinced my death would satisfy them at all. I doubt it would even slow down Pat's campaign much.

The scientists were yammering at him, pleading, insisting, as they had ever since the presentation. They believed, and they wanted to take over. No violence, but in a subtle way, theirs was also an attack.

"Foolish to keep a separate facility, Mr. Saunder . . ."

". . . your father would have . . ."

Ward. Strictly speaking, Ward Saunder hadn't been a scientist. But his contributions to scientific progress had been undeniable. The Council hadn't been able to ignore the iconoclastic tinkerer, and they had extended the membership to his son, an honor Todd had been proud to take, despite the elitist factions and stodgy element of the group. Since the presentation, he had learned that these influential, brilliant men didn't understand him and his motives any better than they had understood Ward and his.

"I know what my father would have done, Dr. Bjornberg—exactly what I'm doing." Todd walked along briskly, forcing them to pant to keep up their wheedlings.

"Should consolidate the decryption attempts . . ."

"Combine your facilities with ours in Lausanne . . ."

They came to the end of the balcony walkway. Enforcement troops checked the door before opening it and letting the Council members through. Another ugly blast of sound hit Todd as he exited onto the roofed trav-park area. The mob was kept at bay by a close-meshed repeller fence. But there was no plexi, and the voices battered him.

"Spacer bastards! Traitors! Going to sell us to the aliens!"

"They want to make slaves of us!"

"Gonna tell the monsters all about us!"

Pat's speeches, reduced to ravening paranoia. Todd paused and looked dispassionately at the contorted faces and waving arms. Dian had predicted this. He had known himself, in that part of his mind which hadn't wanted to acknowledge this facet of humanity as well as the dreamers and idealists. They were part of *Homo sapiens,* too, and they were scared.

"Gentlemen and ladies, we've had all this out before," Todd told the cluster of scientists. "I've made my decisions. You'll get everything my team finds. We're forgoing the usual publication lapse period, simply to accommodate the need to know. But Project Search retains autonomy. No, that's it. No more." Enforcement held the heavy doors of a military transport vehicle open for him, waiting. Todd stopped on the step to tell the Council leader, "And, Dr. Albrecht, if you try to stage a media reassurance session like this again, I can promise you that Chairman Li Chu and my brother will cut the ground out from under us—again. Really, I've gone along as far as I can. But please leave future media judgments to me. I can propagandize a lot more effectively, I'm sure."

He climbed inside, letting the enforcement troops shut out further arguments. A box on wheels and treads. Locked away. Protective custody, so that Todd Saunder could travel five blocks from the Science Council to his office HQ in New Washington. He knew there were other heavily armed transports surrounding them as they rolled the short distance, girding one passenger in a bristling array of weapons.

The area was, normally, a quiet one. It had escaped the Chaos burnings. The streets and buildings were old, original structures or restored with a view to turn-of-the-century styles. Angry mobs simply didn't intrude here. Not until Todd Saunder and Project Search had electrified the world and some of the mobs had tracked down the address of the project. Air travel, so far, was safe. The mobs were too poor to do anything but roam the streets. Enforcement kept them off Todd's property, off everyone's property. Yet they continued to prowl and shout curses, blaming the messenger for the message. Other astronomical outlets were detecting the signals now, other scientific teams working on the decoding. It didn't matter. Todd was a Saunder. The name came with a built-in memory jogger, thanks to Pat's global exposure and fame. Todd Saunder was the target of their hate, and likely to remain so.

"Sorry about this," Todd murmured, jouncing on the hard seat.

"That's all right, sir. We're paid to preserve the peace." The brown face was an expressionless mask, as Dian's could be when she didn't want anyone to know what she was thinking or feeling. All the officers riding in the transport had the same sort of faces. Nothing readable. No fear. No anger. No recrimination. No approval.

Police had changed drastically in the last few decades. After the old monetary system collapsed and comp account economics went into high gear, the nature of crime altered. Law enforcement changed with it. An ident was needed for goods and services, and stealing an ident was useless unless you stole the card holder's handprints. There were supposed to be ways to get around that problem, but they weren't available to ordinary thieves. Then the famines and plagues started, and unemployment rose to fifty percent or higher. Things really got rough. Civil insurrections followed. Police became paramilitary. They wore full weapons and armor and carried chest pack cameras to record their activities and those of anyone they detained, restrained, or were forced to kill. The instant cams had eliminated a lot of legal red tape. Of course, the United Theocracies and other ardent Spirit of Humanity supporters with Protectors of Earth had fought enforcement procedure through all Earth's courts. To a standoff. Enforcement watched its step, but it didn't hesitate to put down a genuine life threat.

The human dichotomy of the decade—life is precious, and life is cheap. Attitudes existing side by side. No wonder humanity was confused and looked to someone like Pat to give it some logical rules to follow!

"That bunch looked pretty nasty," Todd said, knowing the officers weren't prone to chitchat; but he was restless, cooped up, unable to see where they were going.

"We'll handle them, sir. They got out of hand a bit last night, a kilometer west of here. The Third Millennium Movement held a rally at the park, and some anti-Spacers attacked them."

"Killed thirty people," a woman officer chimed in. "Had to shoot a few."

That statement was positively garrulous for these stony-faced enforcers. Todd glanced from one to the other, trying to detect some emotion. Pride in containing the riot? Bloodthirsty satisfaction at killing some of the mob? Disgust that it was all caused by a civilian delivering news about a space machine no one could even see yet?

Nothing, just as before. Whether they were keeping crowds back while the exterminator corps went in to wipe out a few million rats in city areas or shooting rioters who got out of hand, these troops were trained to reveal nothing to the outsider. They reminded Todd of the bodyguards Jael and Pat were hiring now —cold, frightening, ruthlessly professional. And he wasn't sure they were answerable to him, even if his taxes were helping to pay their salaries.

"We ought to put in some controlled-violence arenas, like the Hispanics did," one man said. "Let the bastards kill each other." Personal opinion!

It was the only one Todd was to hear. The transport grumbled to a stop. Doors thumped open. Guards with shotguns, automatic weapons, and bulletproof shields led him out of the rolling box and across the pavement to ComLink's door. Other CNAU troops were patrolling the normally quiet business street. There were more guards posted outside his offices. No mobs here, yet, and the enforcement troops intended to keep things that way, obviously.

The ranking officer saluted Todd as they reached the door. "Sir, if I might suggest? You're a flier? Better use air transport, you and all your important people, next time. You and your corporation are sort of an attractive target right now, if you take my meaning."

"I do. I'm not used to a bodyguard," Todd said shortly.

"That might not be a bad idea, either, sir." The officer wheeled and started shouting orders to his personnel. "Tighten up there! Get that transport down to the intersection! We're going to keep things settled!"

Inside the offices, ComLink and sanity still existed. Todd's elderly security guard, all they had ever needed until now, scowled at the enforcement troops, then smiled warmly at Todd. Mikhail Feodor, Elaine Putnam, and a dozen other top ComLink executives crowded around Todd, all talking at once. They had seen the Science Council debacle, sympathized, cursed the cretins who wouldn't listen. And they had a pile of decisions for him to make in a hurry. They were good, as Dian had often noted, teasing Todd, saying he was lazy and delegated authority strictly for that

reason. Yet they hadn't brought trivia. Riccardi and his other
rivals needed countering, and only Todd Saunder could give the
word. He flipped through the readouts while Mikhail and the rest
looked on.

"This one, and boost the Pacific link. No, don't increase the
rate on these entertainment leasers. We need their good will.
Elaine, if you can give the science outlets any more push, do it.
Color it good. That's where we need the entertainment types.
Hire." She grinned at the tactic, and Todd grinned back. "Okay,
we're setting the telecom business back fifty or sixty years, back
to when 'network' meant an entertainment source. But, dammit,
we can't afford to coast on just supplying services and news.
What good is owning the company if I can't make it a mouthpiece
for my hobby?"

That brought a round of approving laughter. Most of them
hadn't hired on with plans of working to reach an alien intelligence. But now that the boss had pulled it off, company loyalty
turned in his favor. He had paid well and been lavish with the
perks, when deserved. Pride went with the job, pride in being able
to read and write and think in an era when the bulk of humanity
reacted too often out of emotion.

"You're stretching it pretty thin, boss," Putnam warned him.
"That's why I wanted to boost the rate on the dramas and com-
edy leasers."

"Sell a few more voter-response outlets to my brother. Pat's got
the money, and he always needs the votes," Todd suggested
sourly. It was a joke that stung. A few of his people grimaced. "I
know you can do it. What have I got you for, if not to let me
loaf?"

The impromptu conference broke up, his supervisors and execs
drifting away to their own upper-story offices, leaving Todd with
Iris Halevy and her staff of front-door screen experts, as Iris
termed it. They handled the calls, the off-the-street traffic, as
efficiently as ComLink's upper echelons tracked the heavy stuff.

Todd eyed the metal shutters Enforcement had insisted he put
over the front windows, ruining the view for Iris. Bodyguards!
Then he looked at the scene on the big wall display beyond Reception. Miguel Falco, ComLink's crack media interviewer, had
cornered Pat just as the Protectors of Earth assembly session ad-

journed for lunch. The boss's brother was big news, even if the boss and his brother were temporarily on the outs these days.

". . . quite a bit of panic around the world. Would you care to comment, Mr. Saunder?"

"Earth First's position is on public record, Miguel. I've said again and again that people should remain calm."

"Yes, but people have reacted strongly to your speeches, sir. You don't feel your oratory has agitated some . . ."

The handsome face stiffened in indignation. "Certainly not! Anyone who says I'm whipping the public into a frenzy had better come up with some pretty solid proof, Miguel. I have *never* advocated civil disorder. We've got to be well organized and work together to combat this alien invasion."

"You *do* think it's going to be an invasion, then? You haven't changed your mind on that?" Falco made sure his techs caught him in the lenses along with Pat. The interviewer was a ham, but fortunately one without any political ambitions, or he wouldn't have been worth keeping on ComLink's payroll.

"No question whatsoever. Until we know otherwise, we must assume the alien is hostile. Why else would it be coming here, if not to scout for an invasion?" Todd gritted his teeth, forcing himself to listen despite his frustrated anger. What angered him the most was that Pat could make statements like that and the people bought it, just as they bought tainted peace treaties and all the other political fast deals Pat palmed off on them. He spoke, and they signed up.

"Your brother's Project Search scientific group is the one that discovered this alien vehicle. He says we can't know if the alien's hostile, that it's probably friendly and can offer us all sorts of help for Earth's problems . . ."

Pat's bodyguards moved in close, ready, if necessary, to get the pest off their employer's back. Pat forestalled them. "Yes, Todd's little group *did* spot the signals first. You must understand, Miguel, that my brother's a bit of an ivory-tower type. He means well, but he's far too trusting. He even believes we should keep handing over funds to Goddard Colony, while people here on Earth are starving. We just can't afford to waste our resources, especially now, when we need all our strength to combat that alien." A benign, patronizing smile lightened Pat's face as he gazed into the ComLink's cameras. It was his salesman's smile, the one that clinched the deals and piled up the votes. "I don't blame my brother. He thinks he's doing the right thing. And we must remember, because he detected the alien machine so soon, now we have a better chance of defending ourselves . . ."

Todd didn't want to hear any more. Pat could make black seem like white and vice versa, and millions would swallow the guff. He went across the reception area to the front building section he had converted for Project Search's use.

He stood inside the door, surveying, his mood easing. His baby. He was cooperating with the Global Science Council closely now, of course, feeding them the data as soon as Project Search confirmed. And he had had to resist a lot of very tempting offers of help—too much help, much of it actually disguised efforts to get on his bandwagon. But Search was still his and his alone—with a little help from a very bright woman named Foix and some loyal, hard-working ComLink top techs and translators.

Dian noticed him and waved. She didn't come over to greet him. She was busy doing some language cross-checks with Beth Isaacs. Todd didn't feel neglected, well aware he was an interloper here. He was a capable translator and top tech, but not up to the team's abilities. It was enough they acknowledged his leadership and let him look over their shoulders.

The staff had grown quite a bit in the last two weeks. The old-timers needed help, had needed it for weeks, though they had been reluctant to open up the ranks. They had developed a Goddard Colony closed-circuit possessiveness about Project Search and disliked sharing. But the furor resulting from the presentation to the Council drew eager would-be recruits by the hundreds. Anticipating that, Todd and Dian had their pre-selected possibilities already spotted, so when the people applied to them, the clearance checks had already been run. They had started right in. There were over thirty ComLink translator techs and interpretive specialists involved now, splitting the work into round-the-clock eight-hour shifts, leaving Todd in their wake.

He found an empty terminal and cued up the available data, knowing his action wouldn't interrupt anything currently in progress. Translation was discouragingly slow. He had anticipated it would be, but that didn't soften his impatience. Todd cushioned his chin on the heel of his hand, gazing at the moving letters. Two weeks' intense effort, high gear, new staff to assist. And so far Project Search had broken down a grand total of three symbols, and *those* weren't yet guarantee-confirmed. Dian kept telling Todd what he already knew—that until certain vital keys were translated, they weren't going to pick up much beyond the messenger's ident signals, its rearrangement of their words, its pattern for "repeat," and another for "ready to run."

The signals continued to adapt and adjust to Earth's signals. They had fed it some very intricate sequences, and it had handled all of them. Todd's estimates of the intelligence of the machine—and the species which made it—kept escalating. So did his hope.

They *couldn't* be hostile!

Yet did he really have anything but faith to assure that? He didn't know. No one did. Yet.

But the point had been made—better the possible devil we know than not knowing at all. The trouble was, thanks to Pat's rabble-rousing, that too few humans felt that way. The day of judgment was approaching, and they seemed determined to make Earth into a living hell even before it arrived.

Todd was getting a mild headache, staring at the screen. He rested his eyes a moment, putting the monitor on hold, looking around the room. Heads bent over other monitors. People reading old language books. *That* was a strange sight! Young techs reading paper books. But nobody illiterate in print media could be recruited for Project Search. There was simply too much invaluable information stored in places the worldwide telecom ed systems didn't touch. Thanks to Todd's Science Council connections, Search had been able to raid university and institutional back files and musty libraries everywhere. He had achieved a malicious triumph when Pat's military connections discovered to their consternation that their frenzy to update and computerize everything worked against them in this translation job. Todd suspected Pat's staff had hired its own bunch of translators and that they were trying to twist what little data was available to back up Pat's paranoia theme. They had issued two releases, and the media science commentators had managed to reduce them both to jokes, explaining the silliness of Pat's scientists even to the layman.

But the paranoia continued. Most of the public didn't really care what the alien messenger was saying. The mere fact that it was there was the trigger. Fear happened without the higher brain areas ever becoming involved.

I'm not sure you'll want to deal with a species as emotional and fear-oriented as we are, alien people. I hope you're tolerant. We'll grow up. Eventually. I hope.

The last two weeks had gone from nervous to tense. How long would it take for things to settle? *Would* they settle?

He cued the monitor again. The screen split. Nine miniature frames showed him the progress, distilled into basics. Updates on the orbiter's input and outgo. They were getting some relays from the lunar backside telescopes and transmitters, too. Todd hadn't expected that much cooperation from Lunar Base Copernicus, not after Mariette's performance. Goddard was still maintaining virtual com silence, and the military was making noises about relieving the entire command of the Lunar Base. In theory, that meant Kevin would be posted back planetside, too. Todd wasn't going to hold his breath waiting for that to happen, though.

They had some now-recognizable key phrases. Correction, *probable* phrases. Dian insisted on qualifiers until she could hold a language in her hand and read it in three dimensions.

1. Hello. I am Alien Messenger.
2. Please repeat your last message.
3. Do you copy?

And there were pictures. Nothing like a holo-mode or even a distinct two-dimensional image. But there were visuals, hampered by the enormous gulf between the two stations, yet coherent. One of them, when Todd had displayed it for the Science Council, had caused pandemonium and fierce debate. One faction insisted it was an alien interpretation of a plaque Earth had sent into space decades earlier, and that therefore the alien had encountered the plaque, learned from it, and was returning Earth's message as a form of greeting. A large faction disagreed violently. To them the images represented the alien species itself, and in *that* form it was indeed a greeting.

Todd had liked the first interpretation, but he wasn't sure he believed it. Things would be so much simpler if the alien *could*

speak a human language, had learned one years before it had
contacted Project Search. But Todd wasn't convinced. The concept made him shiver.

If it had happened that way, the aliens were so far ahead of
them in knowing about *Homo sapiens* that Project Search could
never catch up.

And if the *second* interpretation were correct . . .

The image, static broken, filtered through twenty-eight A.U.s of
space, seemed to depict two bipedal figures. Humanoid. If it was
what it appeared to be, the image was showing them the rough
outlines of its makers.

The figure image hadn't come through the orbiter's scanners
until the day after Todd and Dian left Saunderhome. Beth Isaacs
had greeted them at the door of the Science Council conference
with the news, relayed to her fellow techs stationed at the conference. They had all been very excited and had debated on the spot
whether to include the new data, knowing in advance they
wouldn't be able to keep it back. It was the most startling thing
yet found.

What would Pat and Jael have done at the birthday memorial if
I'd shown them that? Maybe it's just as well they had time to ad-
just to the shock before that got sprung on them, too. Humanoid?
Definitely smarter than we are, to have built that vehicle. And
who's teaching whom the other language?

Project Search was turning out to be a rather humbling experience.

Beth Isaacs' training with the dolphin-human teams of Sea-
Search Rescue was serving them well. Five of the new recruits
came from the same background. They had all had practice talking to an alien species, though that intelligent beast was a native
of Earth. Beth had observed with a smile that it was just a slightly
bigger step to communicating with an intelligent alien from somewhere else.

Todd could see her working over a monitor, her dark, short
curls and sharp profile eerily lit by the screen's glow. Other
Search workers leaned over her shoulder. One was scribbling on
some paper, not wanting to leave the readout in order to record
what he was thinking on another monitor. They could read, write,

and translate. The cream of humanity's ability to reason, and they worked for Todd Saunder.

Dian finished what she had been doing and left her station, coming over to sit beside Todd. "Read any good monitors lately?" she inquired with a smile.

"Everything you and the team put into them. I feel like sitting in front of the screen day and night so I won't miss a single exciting development."

"You'll get a sore ass and tired eyes, doing that."

"Should I set up shorter team hours?" Todd asked, concerned.

Dian shook her head. "No, we're just as eager as you are. It's fatiguing, but we all hate to see our duty rotations end. Just when we think we might have something, another team takes over. But it's a friendly rivalry. We're afraid it'll be the other one to break the key instead of us." She paused and stared at him, and a tingle of anticipation worked along Todd's gut. He felt what she was going to say before she spoke. "Like now."

He held his breath a moment, wanting to savor the news. "Close?"

"Very, very close. Things starting to fit. Still a hell of a lot we have to put together, even with the comps doing the work. But it's there, Todd. I can damned near taste it. A week, maybe. I may be wrong, but I don't think I am. Beth doesn't think so, either. We're practically there. It'll be baby talk, pidgin English—but it'll be genuine communication."

"And we can touch them, prove they're friendly, end this damned paranoia and talk of invasion," Todd said almost prayerfully.

She looked at him anxiously, reaching a deeper part of the emotions. "Was it worth it? What's happening between you and your family . . . ?"

"It was worth it," Todd replied without hesitation.

"Are you sure?" She was as adept at breaking down his code as she was at deciphering the alien messenger's signals.

"Not entirely. It hurts. But we can't go back. I knew that from the start."

"Are you getting enough sleep?" Dian asked abruptly.

"With you spending most of your time here and knocked out

completely when you're not on duty station? Of course I am," Todd said, giving a lewd smirk; Dian rolled her eyes.

"Todd . . ." He heard the change in her tone and eyed her intently. "I think maybe we should hire some extra security."

He turned her statement over in his mind, feeling cold. "Why?"

"We're starting to get some threats, calls from the outside. Someone apparently tapped into our circuits to the Science Council reference files. I don't care if they listen in when we call to get some obscure datum, but the tap lets them call *us* . . . and they have."

Todd knew such problems had existed in the Twentieth Century, before feedback com private lines were instituted and anonymous calls eliminated. "I'll tell CNAU Enforcement . . ."

"Won't do any good. They're using some kind of scrambler lock."

Todd was shaken. "Military? Spies? Spying on Project Search? That's crazy! We're handing data out to the media as fast as we get it!"

"I don't think that's what they're after. They're not trying to steal the data. They want us to shut down. The last call came to Beth. The guy told her she'd better get out of the project while she was still alive. Huh! That one rattled us pretty badly."

"When did this happen?"

"That one? About an hour ago, while you were at the meeting. That's why I didn't call you to tell you about it. The earlier calls were just annoying. This one sounded mean," Dian explained.

Todd stood up, his anger building. "I'll get some military specialist techs on the case right away, maybe borrow some from Mari's sources. Dammit, this is a private corporation. Scrambler locks! What right have they got to spy on us? Nobody's going to tap into my lines anonymously. I'll take it to the top in P.O.E. if I have to." He added with some chagrin, "This is galling— ComLink, circuit-tapped. But I'll take care of it. Rely on it."

Dian stood up, too, reaching on tiptoe to kiss him. "I always do."

Todd gave her a confident smile and left her to her work. But once outside Project Search, a wave of doubt rose. Muscle. More muscle, and heavy tech counterdeterrents. Damn. He had to get his people some protection, yet he hated the idea of still more armed guards and outsiders poking around his property. Clutter, getting in the way of his people. Jael and Pat traveled everywhere with squads of sharpshooters, muscle, and rough-tactics specialists. Did that mean the entire family would have to?

He gazed around the reception area. Iris, busy filtering calls and answering dumb queries, she and her staff efficiently fielding the more obvious nuisance communications for ComLink's New Washington HQ. If someone was threatening the people in Project Search, adjacent to this reception area, were Iris and the others safe? Troops, outside. But what if the voice behind the calls had an unknown force to override those troops? Inside the building, there was only old Charlie, who had never had to do more than oust an obstreperous salesman. The new shutters and the enforcement police ought to handle trouble, but . . .

He would have to hire a security adviser, he supposed. More ident checks. Heavier com locks. Insulting Todd's people. Maybe if he removed Project Search from the line of fire . . . but the data feeds were here. And *would* that eliminate the problem? Remove them to where? The new recruits weren't space-oriented. And no planetside location would be any safer than this one, probably less so. As far as that went, space side wasn't safe, either, not after what had happened at Goddard.

"Mr. Saunder?" Todd came up out of his bleak speculations, glancing toward Iris. She indicated her desk monitor. "Call for you, but they say it's personal, want you to take it in your private office."

Todd sighed and walked over to her desk. On the big display screen behind her, a paid-for political speech by Pat was droning away. More paranoia. More anti-Spacer propaganda. Things like that tempted Todd. He could pull the plug. Pat would have hard going without ComLink's outlets. Riccardi's Incorporated Network and Nakamura's Worldwide TeleCom facilities weren't nearly as good, and they would cost Pat ten times what he was paying into Todd's accounts. If the rest of the family wanted to play rough, he could, too. How would big brother talk to the world without SE ComLink's translator-splitter and all those lovely global systems?

He knew what that would bring. Suits and countersuits within the family structure, tearing them apart even more. The gaps were getting pretty large, anyway. Maybe there wasn't much more to lose.

"Did you get a name?"

Iris bit her lip. "They used your private line number, boss."

Then it had to be Pat or Jael, or maybe Carissa. Todd wouldn't allow himself to hope it might be Mariette. "Okay. Hold any other incoming. You can transfer and say I'll be there in a minute."

Deep in thought, he took the elevator, moving almost by reflex. He realized he had been immobilized inside the cage at the fourth level for at least a minute with the door open, the elevator waiting patiently for him to get off at his destination. Todd roused himself and stepped off, walking into his office.

"Okay, Iris," he said, then waited. The screen flipped, green dead space. The lower light indicator showed him Iris was off the line and had safety-locked the incoming call, so the circuit was clear. Where was the important other end of the communication?

Maybe it *was* Carissa. She was going to have to stay in New York-Philly quite a long while, maybe until she gave birth. Pat had taken her to an obstetrical specialist after Ward's anniversary memorial, and the doctor's orders had confined 'Rissa to the family residence there. Complete bed rest. She had com and monitor contact with her family and friends and the outside world, of course. Yet it was bound to be a situation to try the spirit. Everyone felt sorry for her. Todd tried to rein in his impatience, reminding himself of 'Rissa's problems.

Seven, maybe six months to go and she would be free again. And if all went well, at its present rate of acceleration, the alien messenger might be approaching Jupiter's orbit by then, or perhaps be even farther along on its course toward Earth. Two new arrivals—the little third-generation Saunder and the alien messenger.

"Carissa . . . hey? Are you there?" Todd said, punching the override to assure the connection was responding at the other end. Maybe 'Rissa was handling two calls simultaneously and hadn't noticed he was ready.

'Rissa's baby. And Jael acting possessive of it. How would she have felt if it had been Mariette who was pregnant, or Dian?

Those babies would be out of Jael's chance of controlling—Spacer-oriented parents and children . . .

The screen went blank momentarily.

Then the room shook all around Todd. Adrenaline raced along his veins before his mind could focus on what was happening. He gripped the edges of the console as the temblor faded.

Earthquake? In New Washington? There had been a few quakes in this region over the centuries, and some bad ones in the Carolinas, but . . .

The room shook again. The screen jittered, came on, and Iris Halevy's frightened face peered out at him. "Rioters! Mr. Saunder, we . . ."

She was falling away from him, screaming, bodies shoving between her and the screen. Todd heard other people screaming, glass breaking, and loud, crackling noises.

Shadows and light, flickering across the confusion—fire! Right below him! On the first floor of ComLink.

Todd bolted out, skidded to a stop in front of the closed elevator doors, remembering. The circuits wouldn't let him, and he shouldn't go that way, anyway. Not in a fire!

Stairs!

He wheeled and ran to the end of the corridor. The automatic opener didn't function, but the fire regulations, reinforced throughout CNAU after six thousand or more people had died in a United Theocracies prayer meeting, demanded that the door operate manually. It did, though Todd had to throw his entire weight against it to force the heavy door open.

He ran down the plasticrete-lined stairs, ricocheting off the walls and using the rail to keep himself from falling headlong. Todd winged breathless gratitude to the Spirit of Humanity that he hadn't been in space for several weeks. He was fully readapted to Earth gravity. Panting, his heart thundering from the adrenaline jolt, he was still able to move, and move fast. The strength was there, now when he needed it.

Todd exploded through the main-level rear stairwell door, loping down the hall. He could see the flames licking through the front window-wall—or the space where the window-wall had been. The whole front of the first-floor opening to the street looked smashed, a cavernous door torn through the structure, the protective steel shutters blown apart. Gunfire sounded from the street.

As he tried to stop his rush, the old security guard met him at the reception gate. The man was bleeding profusely from a head cut. Iris was supporting him. She, too, was bleeding, her clothes torn, hair falling in her face.

"Too many of 'em, boss . . . tried to . . ." The elderly guard groaned and slumped against a wall as Todd and Iris eased him down to the floor.

Todd looked around in rage, wanting something to hit, someone to pay back. "Where are they?"

"In Search!" Iris wailed, pointing.

As she did, the door of the translation rooms burst outward. Noise pounded Todd's eardrums. Dust and fire billowed through the new-made doorway. The screams were starting again, louder, from inside the room.

"Dian . . ."

Todd paused only to tell Iris to call for more police, then ran for Project Search, leaping over monitor consoles and the wreckage of Iris's reception desk. His staffers were lying everywhere, some dazed and hurt, others simply cowering in shock. He didn't see anyone who didn't belong there, but there were people outside, standing beyond the broken window and throwing things through the fire burning the frame, fighting enforcement officers.

A man crashed into him at the doorway. Todd staggered, giving as good as he got, and threw the intruder off balance. No one he knew, and the man had a club. Todd wrenched it away and raised it, and the stranger bolted for the outer office.

Clutching the weapon, Todd spun around, roaring into a melee. "Dian? Dian! Where are you?"

"Here . . . !"

Project Search was in shambles, fires blazing in a dozen points around the large room. Other men were toppling files, kicking in monitor screens, hitting Todd's people.

He charged them, heedless of the odds, unthinking. "Hey! Get out! Let's go . . . !"

They ran over him, not even stopping to hit him. Feet brushed his head and body, and someone kicked his legs and belly in passing. Not deliberately. He was merely an obstacle to their escape.

Todd rolled over, coughing in the rapidly accumulating smoke. He couldn't get his breath for a moment, his brain refusing to operate properly. "Di . . . ?"

"Help!"

The systems went into gear again, shakily, but functioning. He half crawled between the wreckage, coughing harder. A blast furnace heat poured over him from the main storage banks of the translator files.

Todd pulled himself upright, using an overturned console as a support. Dian was flailing at something up ahead, the fire a deadly, wavering bright curtain at her back. People were clawing their way past Todd, some of them helping others.

"Get out!" he ordered unnecessarily. "Get everybody out! Stay away from the front windows!"

He moved to Dian, one arm up, frying, the heat making him look out through squinted eyes. His hair felt as if it were singeing off his scalp, his flesh blistering, searing, sucking him dry. He heard Dian's voice.

"Beth! Beth's . . . oh, God! Help me, Todd!"

Dian had stripped off her own tunic and thrown the garment over Beth to put out flames. Todd forced himself to lower his arm, then took off his shirt, wrapped it around Dian, and shoved her toward the door.

"I won't leave her . . . her and Anatole . . . he's . . ."

Todd could bear the briefest glance deeper into the room, where Dian was pointing. A body lay there, the head thrown back grotesquely, the mouth opened, the clothes blackened and bonded to the crisped dark skin. He gagged, desperately fighting to keep from vomiting, as he picked up Beth.

The woman arched in agony, moaning. "Don't, don't, please . . ."

Dian was cradling Beth's head, hurrying alongside Todd as they both stumbled away from the worst of the fire. Todd felt pieces of skin coming off on his hands where he touched Beth. Helpless, hating to hurt her, he let Dian guide him, struggling to reach fresh air.

Smoke was a boiling, angry sea, closing in on them, fingers of

flame reaching out through the clouds toward them. Todd had no
sense of time, parts of his brain going numb.

Have to get out. That way. Dian. Right here beside me.

"Hang on, Beth . . ."

"Over here," Dian urged in a raspy voice. "There's a clear
path! Beth?"

The body in Todd's arms continued to jerk and writhe, making
his task nearly impossible. Beth was tall, and her long legs and
arms made a good purchase difficult.

*I'm hurting her. Her burned skin's coming off every place I
touch her. But I've got to . . .*

Water! Or liquid of some kind! He didn't care what it was. It
was wet and cold, drenching him, Beth, and Dian, beating back
the smoke and the fire. The stream wasn't so powerful he couldn't
move, though. Gulping and spluttering, he waded through the
spray.

Air—cold and smokeless—hit them next. Men in heavy insu-
suits were circling them, trying to hurry them along. Firemen.

"Get that big stuff in here! We got a bad one!" one of the
firemen yelled over his shoulder. He leaned close to Todd,
bellowing in his ear. "Anyone else in there?"

"Ana . . . Anatole . . . dead. He's dead."

"Okay! We'll get the body."

Todd and Dian were out in the middle of the wrecked reception area by now, helping hands guiding them. "Medics! Beth
needs a medic," Dian was crying. "For God's sake, someone help
her!"

Iris and some other staffers and a couple of the firemen cleared
a space on the floor. One of the firemen had emergency-aid
equipment, was throwing some kind of gel sheet over the dirty
floor, then reaching out to help Todd.

Beth wasn't twisting about so badly now. Todd didn't know if
that was good or bad. He hoped it meant she wasn't in as much
pain. He knelt as carefully as he could, lowering her onto the gel
sheet. The fireman moved in quickly, examining, soothing, wrapping Beth in the sheet.

Not fast enough. Through smoke-abused eyes, Todd had already seen too much. Beth's long legs were seared red, some
places blackening, blood seeping out. Her arms didn't look too

bad, but her chest and left side were hideous, her hair was half gone, and one side of her face was badly blistered.

"Anatole," Beth whimpered. "He . . ."

Dian bent over her, trying not to get in the fireman-medic's way, afraid to touch the other woman but speaking gently to her. "We'll get him, Beth. Just rest. Gonna be okay . . . okay . . ."

She was shaking with suppressed hysteria. "Are you hurt?" Todd asked. He wasn't sure it was safe to touch her. He had caused Beth so much pain, out of necessity, and he didn't want to hurt Dian, too.

"She can't hear you right now, miss," the fireman told Dian.

Dian sank against Todd, the pent-in tears welling up. She bawled helplessly while he held her, no longer worrying whether he might touch a burned area. She needed the holding more than his excessive caution.

Wu Min and several of the new techs were sitting on nearby pieces of wreckage, most burned or bleeding. Some looked as if the attackers had hit them with clubs. Sirens and loud feet and clattering equipment assaulted their senses. There were more medics coming in now, taking over the extra patients from the fireman who was treating Beth. One of the techs refused an injection, insisting too loudly that he was a member of the New Genetic Coalition. No foreign substance would enter his body. It was a genuine religious conviction, and the man probably spoke in sincerity. Yet, considering his condition, it seemed like lunacy to object to a pain killer when his arms were oozing pools of skinless tissue.

Todd knelt in the middle of the holocaust, embracing Dian, wanting to hit someone, wanting to cry. He couldn't. No target. And his eyes felt burned dry.

"Mr. Saunder?" Someone was draping a cool, wet garment around his shoulders and bare back. Todd peered up, blinking. A dark face. A helmet. Enforcement. One of the officers who had escorted him from the Science Council meeting, a thousand years ago.

"My people . . . help my people . . ."

Iris was fussing over the elderly security guard, a fireman-medic alongside her. That poor guard! He never had a chance. And the enforcement troops posted outside?

Todd heard sporadic gunfire, not as much as before. There were shouts and incoherent curses from the streets, troops angry that the quarry was getting away. Wind gusted through the broken window-wall and ruined shutters. A few flakes of snow were settling over the wrecked furniture.

"We will, sir," the guard promised. The mask-face gave way for a split second. "We'll get them. Those sons of bitches killed five of my people. Full-scale attack. Wasn't rioters. Organized . . ."

Another officer, one wearing an investigator's ident, leaned over Todd. "Take it easy, Mr. Saunder. We'll get them," he repeated. "I understand you got some of your employees out of that fire. Nice going."

Todd didn't feel like accepting a hero's compliments. The reminder of Beth had made Dian stiffen and beat her fists helplessly on his chest and cry still louder. Todd cradled her head on his shoulder, gently stroking her smoke-saturated hair.

"Who did this?" he asked between coughs. "I want you to find out who did this!"

The investigator was talking softly into a porta minicom, apparently conferring with some distant superior. For all Todd knew, the man was calling an arson squad.

Arson? Civil insurrection? The officer's bitter remark rang in Todd's mind—*organized*. The same anonymous threatener who had warned Beth she would be killed if she didn't leave Project Search?

The CNAU Enforcement people wouldn't find them. Organized. Hiding behind military scrambler locks. A lot bigger than the criminals and rioters the troops were equipped to handle. Anything this well planned wouldn't leave handy tracks and handprints pointing to the perpetrators.

Wouldn't leave a brand name on a missile heading for Goddard Colony . . .

Enforcement troops were trying to make order out of the mess, helping the firemen-medics lift people onto stretchers, holding curiosity-seekers outside the windows. "No-good bastards," one of the officers snarled. "Ought to take 'em all out and shoot 'em . . ."

How often had that been said? During the past decade? The past century? Centuries before then?

"I . . . I got a good look at one of them," Todd said, then had to pause and cough.

"That's great!" the investigator exclaimed. "We'll want you to check our files, sir, when you're okayed by the medics. We'll take you and the lady to Emergency Facility."

"Not necessary." More coughing, seeming to pull Todd's lungs inside out.

"Better do it, sir. You take care. We'll catch these bastards."

Todd peered toward the doors of Project Search. No doors. Nothing within the big room now. The firemen apparently had knocked down the conflagration before it could spread to the other floors. At least that meant no one else would be hurt.

Project Search. The consoles, the tapes, the data banks, all their carefully amassed material—gone. Some might be salvaged. But most of it was ruined by fire or water or chemicals. There were duplicates elsewhere. They could rebuild. But the focus, the excited, concentrated, dedicated effort, all those wonderful minds and the talent, working together on the messages that would change the future—broken, burned, some of them dead, most of them hurt.

Two men climbed through the debris, carrying a stretcher. They had thrown a cover over the body. It didn't help. That was ComLink Master Tech Anatole Duchamp.

"Find them! I want them to pay," Todd said in anguish, making his tortured throat and lungs obey.

"We will, Mr. Saunder. We will."

A vain promise. They would probably try—unless spies within Enforcement's own ranks had tipped off the anonymous enemies, helped them break through Enforcement's blockade.

Medics were tenderly lifting Beth Isaacs, sliding an invalid carrier under her. Todd desperately wanted to help but knew he would just be in the way. Somewhere behind him, investigators were whispering, comparing notes, their words knives entering Todd's blistered back and dazed brain.

"See this? Custom. Fire burst. Military. Lab?"

"We can try." Todd could envision the man shrugging, accepting the futility of the effort in advance, but agreeing to go by the book.

"No handprints. We aren't going to nail those goons who did it or whoever hired them. This was pro. Lots of money . . ."

"Yeah. Somebody wanted these people very, very dead."

CHAPTER ELEVEN

COMPUTERS CAN'T LIE:
PROGRAMMERS CAN

DR. ALBRECHT was a nice guy, but he wouldn't take no for an answer, no matter how many times Todd repeated it. Short of being rude, Todd decided the only way to evict the man was to escort him to the door personally and see him on his way—hoping he wouldn't turn around and come back to take up where he had stopped.

Todd cued the elevator, willing it to hurry.

"This terrible, willful destruction of your project—barbarism. That's what it is, my boy."

"I agree."

"Have the police no idea who could have perpetrated this villainy?" Albrecht wondered. He tended to talk like that. Too many lectures in front of the university's vid cameras, probably.

"No. They're working on it." The doors opened, and Todd resisted the urge to shove Albrecht inside. He waved the man ahead and stepped in beside him. "Apparently the incendiary was a military device, very sophisticated. The thugs could have put it in a pocket and brought it in. Armed forces all around the globe use the same thing. It'll be very tough for the police to trace."

Albrecht made sympathetic noises. "Then your enemies—the enemies of science and Project Search—are indeed formidable.

You *must* see the wisdom of the Science Council's invitation. If your Dr. Foix and the other personnel wish memberships and privileges, I'm sure the Council would be amenable . . ."

Todd didn't bristle at the bribe offer. Albrecht meant well. He just didn't operate on the same frequency as Todd and his people.

"Doctor, I appreciate the offer. But it's really too early to make any plans. My people are still in the hospital."

Except for Anatole. His genetic inheritance is on file in SE Antarctic Enclave. But Anatole himself, the good, decent, intelligent person he was, is dead.

"Terrible," Albrecht opined again. "They're coming along all right, I trust?"

Todd winced at the reminder. "We don't know yet, for a couple of people. They're at the Texas Burn Facility, undergoing treatment. Dr. Foix flew down to spend some time with them yesterday and see how they're getting along. They couldn't have any visitors at first. At least now Dian can go in and see Beth and Anaya briefly."

Mentioning Beth inevitably brought visions of her lying on the gel sheet, of the emergency-room attendant carefully washing bits of Beth's skin off Todd's blistered hands. One week wasn't long enough to lose or even soften a memory like that. It still made him queasy.

Reaching the ground floor didn't shut Albrecht off. He kept on with his pitch as he and Todd strolled down the corridor toward the front door. The smoke smell still permeated the walls and door frames and floor. The debris had been picked up. New supplies replaced the wrecked furniture. Iris was back at her desk again, though looking very pale, glistening burn bandages on her hands and one cheek.

"I . . . wish you would seriously think it over."

"I will, Doctor. As I said, it's just too early."

"All the training, not to mention your files. You did say you have duplicates of all the material? Good! Good! Good scientific precaution. Of course, one never expects such a terrible thing as *this* to happen to the main file in a research project, still . . ."

A new security guard was tending the door. He wasn't alone. There were six other people, subtle, jacketed, looking as if they were trying to blend in with the rest of Todd's staff. They couldn't. They might as well have worn signs advertising them as security personnel.

Project Search was closed. The arson inspector's seal was still on the makeshift barricade that had been put up to replace the shattered doors. A stink of fried metal, plastic, stagnant water, and something sickeningly sweet managed to get past the barricade, reaching Todd's nose, reminding him.

The front window-wall was gone, too. New steel completely boxed them in.

Albrecht was gazing around, clucking. "Such destruction. Terrible!"

"It is that. And expensive, too," Todd said acidly. He winged a cue at the new door guard. The man reached for the monitor trigger but didn't press it, waiting. If he opened the door too soon and they couldn't get Albrecht to take the hint, it was going to get very cold inside the reception area. New Washington was back to its normal January temperatures—normal, that is, since the glacial outbreak had lowered northern hemispheric temperatures around the world.

"Oh? I hadn't thought about . . ."

Todd smiled bitterly. "My mother tells me that before the Death Years businessmen could collect insurance on such damages. That must have been nice. Now we just have to save back enough funds to take care of ourselves, or gamble that nothing further will happen to us."

Albrecht grabbed Todd's hand, pressing it, playing fond uncle. "We want you, my boy. The Science Council stands ready to support you and fund you. You really can name your own ticket, as they say." He chuckled fatuously.

Put Project Search under their banner. That's the price of their generosity. They'll pay. They'll probably be willing to pick up the tab for the medical bills for my people, too. Everything transferred and to go on just as it was before the unknown enemy broke in and firebombed us.

Only Project Search wouldn't continue as before. It was an independent operation. The Science Council was a confederation. Todd could predict the outcome if he accepted Albrecht's generous offer. Every linguist and self-proclaimed expert on the alien messenger and its creator species would want to get into the act.

Advice, bad, good, indifferent, and mostly emphatic. And he would be in their hire and would have to listen to it all, just as he was enduring Albrecht's babbling now. A bit of courtesy to a fellow Science Council member was quite another matter from having to follow the dictates of three thousand plus voting members of that body. They would take control if that happened, and Project Search wouldn't belong to Todd Saunder any more.

Jael would somehow find a way to get the funds Albrecht was dangling *and* keep Saunder autonomy. Todd didn't know how she had accomplished that in many of the deals she had pulled off, but he freely admitted she was a genius at it. He was momentarily tempted to contact her and ask her to wheel and deal on *his* behalf, this time.

He never had, though, and it was too late to start. She had provided the financial security that enabled him and Ward to put ComLink together. But she hadn't needed to deal for them. The deals had already been made, before Todd was old enough to need them. He had stepped into Ward's shoes and been on his own ever since.

"I'll think about it, Dr. Albrecht. You'll have to give me some time, though. I need to talk it over with my colleagues." Iris was raising an eyebrow at him. She winced and touched her face, regretting the silent facial sarcasm.

Albrecht pumped Todd's hand, taking the equivocal answer as probable assent. "Good! Good! I'm sure they'll agree it's the best thing to do." As Iris was fetching the man's outerwear, Todd gave the door guard a sign. For a moment, they shivered in the sleet blowing in while Albrecht dawdled over his farewells. Finally, he left, and Todd signaled the guard to close the door quickly.

Todd pinched the bridge of his nose. Fairchild was making a speech on the big main display screen. Pro-Spacer. That was a refreshing change. She was pro-alien messenger, too, as one would expect from the Third Millennium Movement's spokeswoman.

Todd turned back toward the elevator. "Iris, I've got some work to do. Hold any calls until I tell you otherwise."

"Yes, sir."

He stopped and looked at her kindly. "You all right?"

She tilted her chin up bravely, ignoring the burn bandages. "I'm fine, boss. You and Dr. Foix just take care of Beth and Anaya and the others who were hurt."

"We will. Dian said she'd give Beth your love."

The medics might help his people, but what was going to help Project Search get back on its feet? He hadn't yet really studied the financial aspects. At first he had been too preoccupied with the murderous attack and getting Beth and Anaya to the medical facility that might save their lives. For four days, they hadn't known if Beth even had a chance. The doctors in Texas said her lungs were burned. Not until two days ago did Todd feel he could head back to New Washington with a clear conscience. He had left Dian with Beth and Anaya, and she had called this morning to say Beth was out of danger and she would be taking an afternoon flight back.

The good news was welcome. But it also meant he now had to come up for air and look at the rest of what had happened. He had been doing that in the back of his mind all week. He didn't like what he saw in his mind's eye—red splashed across Com-Link's Project Search accounts.

But the funds would come from somewhere. He had some stock he could let go. A few more global rental circuits hadn't been tapped. And if his salesmen got busy, they could steal some more accounts away from his competitors.

What had Pat said? *You can be hurt.* Financially, and otherwise. That was a disturbing thought, one Todd hadn't yet faced squarely. And he hadn't yet figured out who had placed that mysterious call on a top private line, calling him away from Project Search when the attack had come. A ruse to protect him? Why? He thrust the speculations away as he would a terrible nightmare.

Money. He needed it. Poetic justice? Was he now paying for the funds he had quietly borrowed from his own corporation to finance Project Search? It wasn't illegal. As he had bragged to Jael, not one stockholder had lost. Todd Saunder had footed the entire bill. Sometimes it was money. And sometimes it was the use of time and other people's equipment that you had to justify to yourself.

Bootleg research. His time and money, other people's property, or time, or data, in some cases. The term covered a lot of territory. Ward Saunder had tried to spell it out for his son a long time ago.

Chicago. The crater towns, springing up like mushrooms west of the war-racked city on the lake. Ward, hired away from a lab in California, now working for another firm at the edge of the Midwestern United Ghetto States. It was after closing hours at the plant. Everyone else had gone home. Jael had taken Pat and Mari to a clinic to have their eyes checked and had dumped Todd on her husband, glad to get rid of at least one cranky kid for a while.

Todd, sitting on a lab table, his stubby child's legs dangling while he watched wide-eyed as his father ran through an experiment. "There! Did you see that? That's called replication, Todd. Haddad's got something with that formula, because I can produce the same results right here, every time." Ward hesitated, frowning. "It'd be better if I could have my own lab to do it in, though. Someday I will. Your mother guarantees it, and she always keeps her word, eh?"

His father's long-fingered, acid-scarred hand rumpled Todd's hair lovingly. "I pay for these materials, Todd." He spelled out the rules. "You always play fair by your employer if possible. Fair pay for fair equipment. Well, mostly adequate equipment, in this case. But the space to work in—that's priceless. They don't realize it, up in the front office. They waste their time and their engineers and inventors every day. I told them what I was doing. They just don't think it's important. But it is. You keep your eyes on the gauge. I'll run it again . . . see? Right down to a point five. Almost inertialess. And if we incorporate that with Haddad's experiment, we can turn the continental rapid-transit system upside down and make the damned thing finally work! Just wait till I tell your mother about *this . . . !*"

I told them what I was doing . . .

So did I, Dad, but not until the results of the experiment were in my hands. Did I cheat, by your standards? No, I robbed myself for the time and the personnel and the equipment. I'm the only one who got hurt—me and the people who've been so loyal to me . . .

He left the elevator and went inside his office, tiredly cueing the door shut. The room was semi-dark. A glow from ComLink's commercial net filled the wall of monitor screens to his left. Surface media and satellite link, following him everywhere, even into the sanctuary of his office. Todd started toward the desk.

He wasn't alone.

Very slowly, he turned, peering into the shadows opposite the monitors. "Who?"

A figure was faintly limned in one corner, caught in the constantly shifting light from the screens. The figure didn't respond to Todd's query. Todd backed away, groping, hitting the master override on his desk and flooding the room with bright overhead illumination.

He stared at the man in the corner. No weapon, at least none visible. The stranger was nondescript, a Scandinavian, it appeared. Blue eyes and cornsilk-white hair, a lot of fuzzy blond beard. As Todd continued to look at the silent form in the corner, it hit him. Wrong. The package wasn't quite coordinated. The features didn't suit the Scandinavian genetic type, and the skin color didn't match the hair color as it should have. Todd puzzled over this, mental relays tripping. "Gib?"

The shuttle pilot's familiar choppy laughter tore away the remainder of the disguise. "How did you spot me?" Gib Owens asked. Without waiting for an invitation, he sat down.

Todd hulked over the pilot. "What does that have to do with this masquerade?" he demanded.

Amusement slid off Owens's bearded face. "My survival, that's what it has to do with. Mine and Goddard's. Come on, Mr. Saunder, how did you identify me?"

Todd frowned and shook his head distractedly. Then he said simply, "I know you. And . . . the coloring is off. The hair looks too freshly bleached. And the beard's what—a good fake? Your genes aren't Scandian," Todd finished.

"Then I guess I'll have to try something else the next time. This was a quick job. We figured it would get me through without being detected. Worked, too. Came in on one of your Pacific shuttles on the Indus run. Took the surface systems to New Washington. They checked through my papers all along the way. But they might be a little sharper when I head back." The young pilot appeared to be planning some alternate disguises.

Delayed shock caught up with Todd. He slumped into his desk chair. "You slipped planetside aboard one of *my* shuttles?" Gib's expression was bland. He wouldn't explain how he had accomplished that, what ComLink employee he had changed places with, where the obviously forged papers must have come from. "Are you going to tell me what this is all about? Why this espionage routine?"

"Necessary, sir."

Todd glowered at him. The disguise seemed juvenile, but Owens was in earnest. So were the people he worked for. "I don't like people hiding in my offices, Gib."

"Sorry," the pilot said. "Right now, I'm a sub on your regular custodial staff. Got the regs to prove it, too." Owens sobered, then went on. "You really should tighten up your security here, sir. It's too easy to break through. I mean, I was sent planetside because I'm a late file at the Colony and my chances are better; the enemy is less likely to have a package and be able to spot me than it would some of the more experienced men. Not that I'm not experienced," he added proudly.

"I know the security's lax, but it's better than it was."

"We heard about Beth Isaacs and the others, Mr. Saunder." Owens was coldly angry, sharing Todd's feelings. "The police catch anyone?"

"Not yet."

Mariette had predicted that Todd's Project Search announcement would lead to retaliation, people trying to strike at him, at his project. They couldn't stop the *real* messenger, so they had tried to stop Todd Saunder. Todd hadn't fully appreciated the danger he was in. He hadn't believed Mariette, thought she must be exaggerating. Even after he had seen the destruction at Goddard, he had clung to that naive hope.

"It wasn't the first time. The first few days Project Search was operating downstairs, saboteurs tried to tap into our global lines. ComLink was disseminating the data so no one would be ignorant. We had enough alternate channels to go around them, but that tipped me off—or should have." Todd thought of the missile shadowing him and Gib Owens in orbit. The last time he had seen the pilot was when he stopped by the Colony Sickbay, just before he and Mari left for Saunderhome. "How's your head?" he inquired.

"Oh, just fine." Owens was embarrassed. He touched his scalp lightly. There was no apparent scar. Makeup? Or superb medical care? Gib smiled in gratitude for the question. "Are we masked in here, sir?" he asked tonelessly.

Todd had to translate from Goddard slang. "We can be."

"Would you cut in a circuit?"

Exasperation mingled with curiosity. Todd cued the desk panel, activating his privacy circuits. The sound on the wall screens garbled and dampened to white noise. Nothing but incoherent murmuring would be apparent from outside the cubicle. The effect would completely cover their voices and jam any attempt at electronic eavesdropping. Originally, Todd had installed the device to prevent snooping by his business competitors. ComLink security had beefed up the output early this week, after the attack on Project Search. Todd looked at the glowing panels under his hands. Security. Had they done enough? Were he and Gib *really* safe from detection?

Owens had a doubt on the same score. "That'll probably take care of it," he said unhappily. The pilot reached into his tunic and fumbled with some sort of fastener, then withdrew a mini-tape and handed it to Todd. "The governor and your sister send their loving regards, Mr. Saunder."

"Gib, I'm having an awful lot of trouble swallowing all this cloak-and-dagger gibberish." Owens was maddeningly uninformative. Waiting. Todd tossed the mini-tape in his palm, then dropped it in the "read" slot. An image snapped up on his desk monitor. Visual garbage.

Owens smiled tolerantly, then offered Todd a thin strip of intricately formed alloy metal. It appeared to be some exotic combination of materials somehow combined with layers of silica. "Try that in your translator-splitter circuit, sir, if you would."

Todd recognized the form of the tiny key Owens had given him. More military borrowing. They had adapted Ward Saunder's translator patents and extrapolated them into cryption-decryption devices. The key Todd held was the only thing that would unlock the meaningless smear on the screen.

"It's not for replay," Gib warned. "One run-through." Goddard had also borrowed the mini-tape self-destruct option. Todd would have to get this message right the first time or forget it.

Owens's young face, behind the beard and the makeup, was hard, older than his years. Their harrowing ride in the shuttle must have been just part of his recent experience. Had he been on Goddard when the earlier missiles had hit? Sharp, combat-ready, willing to die, if necessary, so that Goddard would live.

Owens stood up, headed for the door. Todd stared at him. "Where are you going?"

"The tape will give you everything you need, sir. I haven't been briefed on its contents. It's safer that way." The look he gave Todd was rather cheerfully fatalistic. "If I don't know, I can't tell anyone we don't want to find out about it, now can I?"

Once, Todd had thought corny lines like that only occurred on vid dramas, part of a theatrical game. But this wasn't a game. The young pilot meant every word and knew the risks he was taking. He nodded, then was gone.

Todd looked down at the decoder strip Owens had left, turning it over several times. After a long moment, he inserted the key in the translator circuitry and waited for the screen to clear.

Kevin McKelvey's image gazed out at him. Mari was leaning familiarly on the back of Kevin's chair. "Hello," Kevin said. The mini-tape was very crisp. Todd doubted the new worry lines in that rugged face were caused by imperfect resolution in the recording. The strain of leading Goddard Colony and fighting off unknown enemies was showing. "Mari's filled me in on what happened at Saunderhome, of course. I assume you heard Fairchild's subsequent speech at Protectors of Earth assembly, revealing the missile attacks."

There was a pause while Kevin considered how best to express himself. Mari rubbed his head, whispering too softly for Todd to hear. McKelvey's broad shoulders straightened. "Pat has gotten word to us *via* Fairchild, promising that his committees will investigate the missile attacks. So far, we've seen no movement down there. We're trying to give him the benefit of the doubt, as you requested. Meanwhile, we're watching him make political capital out of your material about the alien messenger vehicle. His mobs are attacking our people planetside, just as the missiles struck at us up here." He didn't keep the bitterness out of his tone, but his resentment wasn't aimed at Todd.

Mariette cut in, her voice a bit startling after Kevin's deep rumble. "Pat's stalling, Todd. We know he is. He's refusing to deal with our planetside intermediaries and agents. And it's *not* just because he's busy pulling strings and lining up votes. I'll bet he's not talking to *you,* either . . ."

Reflexively, Todd opened his mouth. Then he felt sheepish. He hadn't done that for years, not since he was a child. It was foolish to argue with a recorded image. His reactions had reached something deeper in him than his lifelong experience with vid media. He listened morosely while his sister and Kevin went on talking.

"We're going to give you an update on what we've collected with the mass driver net," Kevin said. The screen separated into two sections, one showing the data readout. "Electronics are Asian, probably Nippon Associated or a good copy. That doesn't mean they made them, of course. These pieces of reassembled guidance fins are CNAU-manufactured. The part of a triggering device seems to be Maui-Andean in make. Nothing direct, naturally. But these are all staunch Earth First nations—or their leaders are. And they've been involved in some of Earth First's shady deals in Protectors of Earth, and against our supporters." Kevin's huge hands clenched into fists, drawing Todd's eyes momentarily. The barely contained fury didn't come through in his voice, which was remarkably calm. Nevertheless, in his own way, Kevin was as much a political orator as Pat was. Kevin's captive and willing audience was Goddard Colony, and he didn't have to fake their sentiments at any point in order to convince them he would be their best choice for a leader.

"There have been two more attempted attacks, Todd," Mari broke in. "Our units stopped them in lower orbit. No damage. But they certainly aren't giving up or going underground, whoever they are. In fact, they're stepping up the rate."

"They're stepping up the firepower, too," Kevin said grimly. "From now on, we're using the toughest equipment Lunar Base Copernicus can spare." He answered Todd's question, anticipating it. "The Moon's regularly scheduled supply ship is two weeks overdue. No adequate explanations, according to the base commander. And his previous supply was partially contaminated. They detected it in time to prevent an outbreak of neo-anthrax."

Todd's jaw dropped. The viral mutation warfare system was Earth's worst nightmare, after what it had lived through in the Death Years. The latest pandemic of neo-anthrax had been brought under control in 2030, but everyone suspected the strain still existed in secret labs, somewhere. If Kevin was telling the truth, that suspicion was based in fact, and someone was trying to use the deadly material to wipe out the Moon base. "The short-

ages put them on critical mode. We helped them out, or they
would have been forced to lift ship and abandon. We're not over-
supplied right now, either. But we'll make it. So will they."

Worse and worse. Lunar Base Copernicus and Goddard were
separate legal entities. They had cooperated in the past, but obviously the loan of classified military equipment constituted a
breach of orders on the lunar commandant's part. By all implications, the pair of them were one step away from joining forces totally in defiance of all legal connections with Earth. Didn't anyone at Protectors of Earth realize what was happening up there?
Or did they know and not care?

Let the erring sisters go . . .

They couldn't *afford* to let the space colonies go, and whoever
was putting missiles up in killer orbit and sending neo-anthrax to
the Moon knew it. The Spacers had a terrible advantage if they
chose to fight back—Earth's gravity well. Push far enough, and
there would be a war in space, with firepower raining back on
Earth to repay the death and destruction dealt to the Colony and
her allies on the Moon. Innocent bystanders, perhaps billions of
them, would die, on Earth and in orbit.

From the little screen, Mari was now addressing him. "Todd,
we had to confide in you. We depend on you, trust you. We hope
you'll keep your promises, even if Pat won't keep his."

A picture, a taped image. They weren't speaking to him
directly. Yet elapsed time and distance didn't matter. Mariette
and Kevin were there in the room with him, and they were calling
in their debts.

A live-action scene began on the second half of the screen. The
picture was quite crude. Todd narrowed his eyes, studying it
clinically. Poor transmission? No, he saw the problem. The
recording had been made under difficult, hurried conditions,
probably with woefully inadequate equipment. A hidden lens?
The man's name escaped him temporarily, but Todd was familiar
with the visage, and not in a pleasant context. Part of the North
Asia groups. Not a petty dictator. The head of secret police in his
national area. He was an enforcer who kept his name and picture
out of the media. How had Mari and Kevin obtained this recording of him?

Then Todd concentrated on the man's words. Instatranslation

converted the language smoothly, though the lips weren't in synch. Ward Saunder's inventions served the audience, again. The instatranslator must be operating with a scrambler, too. That enforcer wouldn't have let them get away with taping him if his security people had detected them. Considering what Goddard's agents were up against, the poor picture quality was forgivable.

". . . do not pressure the Human Rights Committee again or you will regret it most deeply. If you do, your leader will cease to exist. We will make sure that, despite the sanctions, any further effort to communicate with Antarctica will result in your beloved Kuwai's immediate termination . . ."

The screen tore up briefly as the hidden lens fought to maintain its focus. When the picture steadied once more, the little man's eyes were awful. He relished the prospect of killing his victims. Expertly, he touched the unseen audience's very soul. "You do not fear for yourself or your brave allies. This I understand. You will die, and your preserved seed in the tissue banks in Antarctica will die. I promise you this. You and your inheritance will be gone—*forever!* And your beloved leader? He, too, will die. He will never awake from his frozen cell.

"You will cease all your rebellious meetings and publications at once! Any further opposition, and I will carry out my promise without delay! Break off all relations with these Spacer people or pay the price. You will receive no further warning!"

The insert image winked out. Mari and Kevin glanced at each other, gauging what effect the scene might have on Todd. They seemed to be wondering if he would think it was a fake.

Todd wished he *could* dismiss it as a fake. But it rang all too true. The tone, the references, everything pointed to that nasty little faction of Earth First, to its most ruthless and fanatically planet-oriented faction. Such an ugly threat suited their style.

But did they have the ability to carry through on that threat?

How much had the anonymous agent dared in smuggling that recording to Goddard? SE Antarctic Enclave. Incorruptible. Watchdogged. Reachable *via* remote-relay vid view of any of the confinees. It *had* to be off-limits to any political conflict.

"That son of a bitch means it," Kevin said. Mari was nodding, her pale eyes reaching across space and time to Todd. That was

the way Pat had looked at him when he first began to comprehend the implications of the alien messenger.

Mari was shaking with anger. "That's not the only thing threatening our agents. That's one of the few we were able to catch on
a recording, though. We can't betray that agent. His life is at
stake. His life, and that of his leader. There are thousands who
may be in jeopardy."

They showed him a quick series of other recordings, obviously
made at several different places. Someone making a pleading inquiry about a relative, a dissident who happened to be a supporter of Goddard. The response:

"No, we have no record of your uncle. No, no conviction notice. We really don't know where he is. Sorry."

Someone else trying to find out why credit deposits supposedly
registered to a Spacer political group had mysteriously vanished.
Legal runaround, the more frustrating because the people behind
the readout wouldn't come forward and tell the lies to the
bankrupted inquirer's face:

"No record. I have no record of that account. Please check
your number again and be sure you have cued the monitor cor-
rectly . . ."

And another attempt, in another language:

"We are not permitted to give you that data, madam. I am
sorry, madam." Off screen, an enraged, impotent woman yelling
that the data demanded was that regarding her own son. Imper-
turbable, the readout continued. "That data is classified, madam.
If you wish to register a complaint, please go to the Department
of Civil Information and request Form 8568-T. Thank you . . ."

T? T for Terminated?

The screen coalesced into one image—Kevin's and Mari's.
"That's only a sampling," Kevin said. "Such things are happening
constantly to our supporters. Maybe to other people, too, the
third parties that also oppose Earth First. I don't hear anything
about Earth First supporters running into those situations. I
doubt you do either, Todd. But Third Millennium, the Expansionists, the Serene Future people over in Asia, the Energy Now
Party, the Socialist Communalities, even United Theocracies for
Peace—they are being wrapped up in threats and red tape and

dumped, more and more frequently. If the enemy can't beat us fairly, they're going to erase all the rest of us, it looks like.

"We'll give you a key list. Each of these particular people has been specifically threatened, through his relatives, political followers, or some other person who cares about his survival. Each of them is a confinee to SE Antarctic Enclave, or has dropped out of sight. You can't keep the list," Kevin said as an afterthought.

Todd blinked as eighteen names flashed on the screen. Time pressure was heavy. He worked to memorize the data, the faces, the idents. He hadn't known some of these people were even up for trial! Other names he recognized from ComLink's news reporters—people their countrymen considered troublemakers. *Some* of their countrymen. Three of the potential political problems had avoided that designation by volunteering to go to the cryogenic preservement facility during the earliest years of the polar Enclave. They had done so to spare their followers war and death, thinking that by removing themselves from the scene, those they loved would be safe. Others had been sent there after trumped-up trials. Some came from nations which themselves had ceased to exist when they had been gulped up by larger national entities.

The data stayed on the screen while Kevin's voice-over explained, "The confinees can be seen, in theory, via holo-mode linkups with the global telecom network—yours. You have a monopoly, Todd. It's a minor department of ComLink. Maybe you aren't aware that certain requests to see relatives' or dissidents' holo-images never reach the processing system. They're being thwarted in their own countries. They're not allowed even to ask. Neither is anyone else. They get put on hold or told there's a technical problem. If you complain to P.O.E.'s Human Rights Committee, you get the same shuffle around and go nowhere. If that isn't a conspiracy, we don't know what it is. We can't get past the red-tape barricade. We've tried. We can't even clear some of the financial nonsense out. It's 'classified,' even stuff we have a right to see. Maybe you can get around it."

Kevin split the screen again, so that Todd could see him and Mari and the eighteen names, reduced, simultaneously.

"Two of the people who've smuggled data to us have disappeared within the last month. Mari made some discreet checks on them when she was planetside. Nothing. Maybe they've been shipped to the Enclave, or dropped into the Pacific. We don't know and can't find out. They join a growing list, one five years old in some cases, as long as Goddard's been in existence and factions on Earth have been fighting our *right* to that existence," Kevin said grimly. "We're sure these eighteen have vanished, for all purposes, off the face of the Earth. And the Human Rights Committee won't let us into Antarctica or into their sealed records to check on them . . ."

"They can't, under law," Todd reminded him, to no avail.

Kevin shrugged, as if he had heard Todd's comment. "Who gets it next? Who vanishes next? Whose credit disappears next? Yours? You can be damned certain it won't be Pat's, or any other faithful Earth Firster's, such as Galbraith's or Riccardi's or his satellite network's. *There's* a pair we're keeping our eyes on! Them and Weng and Ybarra and some others. They all have too many good reasons for wanting Goddard out of their economic and political hair. You say we're paranoid and have to maintain our lifeline to Earth. Well, someone's chopping that lifeline in two, killing our people, engulfing our financing. We're asking you to help, as a trusted ally."

Mari leaned forward, peering directly into the lens. "We *do* need you. And you need us, Todd, whether you realize it yet or not. Use our agents, our allies. Trust Fairchild. She can put you in touch with some sane people in high places who might not come out openly for us, but would do it for you. A general or a second-in-command politico. We don't think they're *all* against us down there! Fairchild will help us, to the limits and beyond. Todd, please?"

The images vanished. The eighteen names remained for a full minute. Then the tape ended. No playback. If he didn't know them now, it was too late.

He sat and thought for a long time, the white-noise garble from the wall screens humming. None of these claims was proved. He had only Mari's and Kevin's word for the accusations. And, in counterargument, he had Pat's adamant insistence of fair dealing and his own knowledge of SE Antarctic Enclave's operations. Todd admitted to himself that it had been a while since he had checked up on the Enclave; it wasn't his concern. Besides, the place was under P.O.E. franchise, off-limits except to authorized personnel.

He had seen a sign with those words at Goddard. Secrets. In Goddard's case, most likely secret defense systems and weapons. Was there something going on in the Antarctic that was illegal, too?

When he had left the Enclave after helping set up the sophisticated com and electronics network there, Todd decided he had been there enough to last him the rest of his life. He wouldn't return while he could still function, though of course if he fell terminally ill or had an accident . . .

As Ward Saunder had.

I have to know, Dad. It's a problem, a riddle, and I have to know. It's like breaking the alien messenger's language. Finding out the facts, even if they're terrifying. Knowledge is better than ignorance.

"Intercom, connect me with Iris Halevy on level one, main desk." The screen cleared, and Iris's face appeared. "Iris, would you . . ."

She wasn't hearing him. Iris grimaced and punched at her monitor's manual keys, muttering, "What's the matter with this thing? All I'm getting is garbage."

Todd realized what was wrong. He removed the translator strip from the slot and slipped it in his pocket. Immediately, Iris's expression became sunny. "Oh, yes, boss?"

"I'm going to be on my ultra-private com circuits for a while. Would you relay any vital calls to George or Elaine? They can handle everything I would."

"Will. Oh, boss, you're supposed to pick up Dr. Foix at three."

"Oh, God, yes! Thank you for reminding me. Would you please call Arrivals and leave a message in case I'm delayed a bit?"

When Iris had cleared the line, Todd activated his full privacy com circuit and contacted Protectors of Earth Archives. The Brasilia installation was obligated by international law to maintain complete available records on every citizen, living or dead, who had been alive during the past thirty years. In theory, anyone could talk to the computer. In practice, doing so wasn't that easy. The system was set up to discourage casual inquiries and needless comp traffic. But it was supposed to cooperate with a reasonable customer. Yet it didn't. From the beginning, Todd detected resistance in the system. His suspicions increased.

He didn't go straight down the list of eighteen. That would be too obvious. Goddard's agents would have probed regarding these same people. He skipped about randomly, calling for data on innocuous people, investors he knew personally, people he had met socially who might well become SE ComLink shareholders. In all ways, he attempted to make this look like a legitimate business data search. In nearly every instance, the names he called for were solid citizens. Here and there, at widely separated points in the inquiry, Todd inserted a few of the eighteen names.

The records on people he knew were handed over without a quibble. Potential Saunder Enterprises investors didn't exactly roam the streets in rags. He had expected the comp's cooperation there. On the selection from the eighteen, the response was cold and reproving: CONFINED TO SE ANTARCTIC ENCLAVE.

Todd let six responses like that go by without challenge. At the seventh he let the comp sit there, holding the telltale readout a minute. "Need further data," he finally said. "Check to see if property confiscated." A safe and logical request if he was running a financial search.

DATA IS CLASSIFIED.

The suspicions stirred around in Todd's belly like a pitcher full of ice. "Recheck data. Confinee records are not closed. Property confiscations under term of conviction in subject's Maui-Andean nation must be entered in public record. Answer."

This time the comp made *him* wait while it thought over the specific demands and rules. Todd wasn't surprised by the response when it came.

DATA IS CLASSIFIED. IF YOU WISH TO INQUIRE FURTHER, PLEASE FILE REQUEST FOR UNSEALING OF CLASSIFIED DOCUMENTS AT THE DEPARTMENT OF . . .

Todd tuned it out. He made a few more phony requests, considering whether to try again. Once more might be safe. He got the same results. Classified. Unavailable. He changed the tactic slightly and said the confinee had an outstanding debt owed Todd Saunder and restitution could be claimed from the confinee's relatives or estate. The comp wouldn't budge. He was talking its language, but it refused to open up.

He cleared and established another secured line to SE Central Financial in New York-Philly and started talking to a different computer. Here he had what he hoped would prove an extra advantage.

"Todd Saunder, clearance classification Priority A-One. Lock this on full confidential, my readout only. Do not record dupe of inquiry or data requested."

"Yes, Todd Saunder. How may I help you?"

Todd crossed his fingers. He hadn't done that since he was a kid. He desperately wanted Mari to be wrong. Let the damned computer spit back everything he asked for, no quibbling, everything neatly printed in green and white, all the people and their property exactly where they should be.

It didn't. Several times he interrupted the data request to remind the computer whom it was dealing with. He made it search its programming to confirm his clearance rating. The Saunders were equal. They had A-Ones, and no one else in the firm—or anywhere else in the world—did, not with *this* computer.

Nonetheless, the damned machine was holding back on him. He hounded the comp about one of Goddard's supporters who hadn't been convicted, according to the records, but who suddenly had disappeared. "Look, I know Kirpalani isn't at that address. And what do you mean, no funds registered? He's got two hundred prime shares of ComLink stock." In his agitation, he slipped out of comp phase and had to pull himself together and phrase the questions properly, not that it did any good.

He turned to another attack angle. "Van Eyck's confined? Confirm." The computer went through its little ritual. Todd didn't let it off the hook. "Clear Human Rights Committee, Protectors of Earth, available-access view circuits. View of Van Eyck."

Todd demanded to see the frozen body which lay 16,000 kilometers away.

"Time requested, Todd Saunder. Relay connect necessary."

"Go through SE Central Expedite, Emergency Relay," Todd ordered it.

Computers had been a subsidiary industry of ComLink from SE's beginnings. It wasn't Todd's preferred field, but he hadn't forgotten the way these particular systems were set up. Not many

SE employees still working with the company knew about that
Expedite command. It was strictly for use by a Saunder, and the
computer would undoubtedly read back through its little memories to be certain it was okay to let him through.

"Executing, Todd Saunder . . ."

That was one form of reply. Yet for some reason the dispas-
sionate machine-voice's words sent a chill down Todd's spine. He
shivered and added a stern qualifier. "I wish the view held until I
release."

No acknowledgment. He started to repeat the order when the
screen shimmered and he was seeing Van Eyck. The man seemed
to float in his cryogenic cubicle. The color wasn't normal, of
course. It wouldn't be. Preservement monitor readouts skimmed
across the bottom of the screen, establishing that Van Eyck's
body was being held properly in suspended life, ready to be revived when time and the political or medical situation would
make that possible.

The image vanished. Todd jumped and leaned forward,
addressing the SE Central Comp angrily. "Regain image. I wish
the view held until I release."

There was a very long wait. The image did not return. At last
the comp voice said tonelessly, "Maximum allowable viewing
under Human Rights Committee regulations is one minute. Time
must not be exceeded. View of image will not be restored."

"Break connection," Todd ordered curtly, not even allowing
the machine the usual ritual of signing off politely.

The computer had lied to him. Why? The maximum allowable
viewing time under the original Human Rights Committee regulations was *not* one minute. It was open-ended. If the privilege was
abused by a confinee's relatives and friends or by the merely curious, the limitation factor clamped on and one minute was it.
Todd couldn't imagine hordes of interested people demanding to
see Van Eyck. It was possible the Goddard agents had abused the
privilege and triggered the limit. But the *Expedite* should have
overridden that.

Just what hadn't the system wanted him to see?

Todd did some more mental replaying, since the computer had
denied him its services. He formed Van Eyck's body in his mind's
eye, studying it, reading the monitor figures. In order, seemingly.

Shouldn't he have been able to see other cubicles beyond Van Eyck's? According to the confinee numbers, Van Eyck's body was preserved in the middle of a fully occupied section of SE Antarctic Enclave. At the angle the camera had been using, Todd should have seen at least a suggestion of the other cubicles in the line.

Frost on the scanner? Not possible, not the way those scanners were built for Antarctic usage. Unless the techs were letting efficiency slide. That didn't seem likely, not with P.O.E. franchising the Enclave and with Human Rights Committee tours checking up on the techs twice a year and reporting back to the P.O.E. assembly. And the Committee said everything was as it should be.

Was it? He didn't know! He had asked the questions, and he still didn't know. At least when he was trying to communicate with the alien, there was ample reason for the problem. This one didn't satisfy. He couldn't be sure. Maybe there were security checks going on. Political machinations. He kept out of politics, didn't like it. Now he was running up against walls he might have been able to breach if he had known a bit more about how these other comp systems were now programmed.

But if that *wasn't* the reason . . .

Asking the questions hadn't produced any real answer. It had just given him more questions. This was something he would have to dig at, and dig hard. He had bragged, not realizing how deeply the data was buried—or hidden. Now it was more than pride driving him. The possibility that Mari's accusations might be valid wasn't going to go away until he broke down those barriers and found out what lay behind them.

A light was flashing at the lower left-hand corner of the screen. Todd unlocked the privacy circuits. "Yes, Iris?"

"It's getting pretty late if you're going to the terminal."

"Thank you. Tell Bob and the crew I'll be up to the hangars in a minute or two, please."

Todd removed the white-noise override from the wall monitor screens. In place of the masking murmur, a babble of conflicting voices and music rose, each individual screen vying for attention. Documentaries. News. Dramas. Comedies. Religion. Politics.

Which was which? There were times when he couldn't separate it all any more, couldn't tell truth from illusion. Todd dimmed the lights and left, heading for ComLink offices' roof.

CHAPTER TWELVE

DEADLY GAMES

NORMALLY, the hangars and company piers were available to all his executives and top techs. But on the advice of his new security chief, guards had been posted and access carefully restricted. The precaution seemed sensible, after what had happened to Project Search. Todd passed through the ident and regs checks just like the rest of his staff. The security guard smiled tolerantly at him and waved him through the electro-protected gate onto the roof flier strip. The guard's stance wasn't quite military, but uncomfortably close to that.

The mechanics held the door open for Todd. They had already made sure he had a spare coat stashed in the luggage holder, too. He thanked them with a thumbs-up and sealed himself into the two-seater, running through the takeoff checks. Everything green. He was piped through to CNAU Flight Control. His ident let the distant traffic regulator note his takeoff point, vector, and destination.

"Recorded. Cleared for the New Washington regional guidance systems, Todd Saunder. ETA commercial domestic terminal at 1500 P.M., Atlantic Time."

Todd checked his watch and frowned. He would have to boost it to get there before Dian's flight arrived. He triggered navs and power; the flier lifted and sidled off the edge of the building.

Once cleared, he pulled up to his assigned altitude, circling to get onto his proper vector. As he swung southwest above the fifty-story buildings being erected under CNAU's urban revitalization program, Todd could see crowds thronging the streets far below. Whose office or residence or commercial outlet was getting smashed and burned now? Whose people were they hurting or killing?

He engaged primary drive and headed toward the terminal. Much of his route went through the oldest surviving sections of New Washington and its southwestern suburb cities. Empty sky-scrapers and burned-out husks of businesses and apartments lined the flight path. Broken eyes of windows peered at Todd. Limbs of metal frameworks were rusting away in the elements. Stone had crumbled and fallen hundreds of stories to the streets. Plasticene facing had scorched and melted into meters-long icicles, dripping down the buildings. Far off to his left lay the waters of Atlantic Inlet. The day was clear but cold, visibility excellent up here.

There were other aircraft in the lanes. Todd kept watch on his monitors, but Traffic Control was maintaining distances okay. He spotted some Enforcement Patrol fliers, a number of commercial craft, and a few private-ownership fliers such as his own. Some-times he kept track of idents, just for curiosity's sake. Today he didn't bother putting them up on his screens.

He kept mulling over the conversation with the Protectors of Earth and Saunder Enterprises computers. It didn't make sense. He would have to talk the situation over with Dian. She could help him get his thoughts in order . . .

Traffic. Someone behind him and above, and dangerously close. For a fraction of a second, Todd assumed it was an en-forcement officer, close-checking his idents, on the alert because of all the rioting. But the expected enforcement hail didn't come.

"Ident approaching aircraft," Todd demanded of his monitors.

The flier leaped off the screen at him. No enlargement. True viewpoint. The mysterious craft was no more than fifty meters to the rear and closing fast. Very sleek flier, military design, one-way view canopy to hide the person at the controls.

It bore no identification whatsoever.

Unmarked vehicles—of any kind—were illegal. What was this cretin doing? He was begging for Enforcement to ground him for life. And the sooner the better! It would make the skies safer for everyone.

"Do you read, vehicle on Delaware Ten Zero vector? You are intruding."

They were flying at high speed through an area thick with teetery old buildings. He had to get hold of that pilot! This was not merely reckless, it was suicidal.

No reply. The pilot refused to acknowledge. Enraged, Todd called a general distress, summoned Enforcement and CNAU Flight Control's observers to pick up on this lawbreaker.

Com circuitry roared in a burst of static. Todd tripped the relays and sent the transmission again. Nothing. Backups green. Scrambler override!

The unidentified pilot was knocking Todd's distress call right out of the sky! He wouldn't let him call for help! And he was using illicit military equipment to stop Todd.

None of this could be happening! A missile couldn't have tracked his shuttle up toward Goddard. But *that* had happened!

A red bolt slashed by under Todd's left wing. The flier rocked in the shock wave. Todd fell over in a steep dive, power on full. The streets, a hundred stories below, swept toward him for a horrible instant before he righted the craft on the other wing and began to climb.

His heart was trying to slam its way out through his breastbone when another bolt came at him from a different angle. Missed him by meters, and not very many! Nav monitors screamed warnings, pinpointing a second intruding aircraft.

Another unidentified! Right and high above him.

Once again Todd put the flier over in a dangerous dive and rolled sharply. But all too quickly, the pilots overcame his tactic, working him between them, each trying to force him into the other's sights.

Todd banked again, steering frantically. He triggered the automatic mayday. That probably couldn't penetrate the scrambler override, either, but he had to try.

The third bolt almost hit his canopy. Red shock patterns danced in Todd's eyes. When they cleared, he was heading straight for a row of old dwellings towers and had to elude at dangerous speed.

They weren't going to let him get away. They meant to kill him. The attacker ahead of him now was racing to a turnpoint. There it would come for him head on, and the pair would pin him in a cross fire.

Time froze. He and Pat and Mari, riding mini-flitters, skimming the waves and buzzing Saunderhome. Too young to realize they were mortal, they had re-enacted sky battles out of ancient vid dramas. Mock warfare. Jael took away their flying privileges for weeks every time she caught them. But it hadn't cured them of the reckless game.

Now that form of flying came back to Todd. It had brought him punishment when he was a kid. Right now it could prove his salvation. He was part of the beautiful machine, wheeling, dipping, cutting under his attackers as he doubled back on his own vector. He had eluded Pat and Mari that way more than once! But this was no game. Death waited three hundred meters below —if he weren't disintegrated in mid-air first!

The tactic worked for a moment, giving him precious seconds. No way out. Not the way he had been going. And their override made chances of outside help nil. He couldn't count on an Enforcement Patrol happening on this melee. He would have to get himself out, if he could.

His initial surge of fear was gone. Very steady, he boosted the little flier to maximum before they spotted what he was doing. Atlantic Inlet was too far. So was the terminal. And CNAU Enforcement HQ might as well have been on the Moon.

The attackers had been driving him away from inhabited streets, deeper and deeper into the Chaos-riddled sections. How old were those pilots behind him? Old enough to remember when this area was populated? The transcontinental missile strikes and burnouts hadn't destroyed all the lofty structures. But many of those that were left were studded with hot places and cordoned-off hectares of land and buildings. No section for a sane flier to enter.

No options. Todd thought of the city he had known in his youth. The ship's programs couldn't help. They hadn't been set up for these maps. Recall and instinct would have to do the job.

A blackened series of towers flashed by on his right. Memories clicked. A collection of dishes and antennae had once blossomed on those roofs, part of Ward's original ComLink Corporation. The landmark gave Todd confidence. He hardly reacted when another energy bolt lanced by. Its strength was attenuated, proof he was putting considerable distance between himself and his pursuers.

Braced for the upcoming turn, he leaned into the bank, nearly rolling the flier. The little aircraft peeled hard. Todd forced himself to keep off the retros as a skyscraper kissed paint from the flier's undercarriage.

He gave it a count of three, then leveled. Then he dived.

The abandoned street was narrow, deeply shadowed, and thick with fog which rose from the ruins below. Todd stood on the foot brace, resisting the gees. That wasn't Caribbean surf down there, but rubble and an unforgiving pavement. He searched through the darkness, his nav guides probing the greenish glow of their readouts lighting the cockpit eerily. Todd cut his running idents to try to hide himself.

They were tracking him, of course. Anybody with a military override scrambler system would certainly have full tracking scan ability. They would home in on Todd's own circuitry output.

That meant he needed a mask. Where? The streets helped. They were crooked and pinched with dozens of right angles and erratic intersections suitable for putting buildings between him and a clear signal contact. Each dart into a bolt-hole, though, was a replay of that harrowing swerve which had led him into this abandoned section of the southern city. Todd balanced the craft expertly, appreciating anew the flier's superb handling. He abused its structural integrity again and again.

The flier's warning systems chattered, picking out radiation spots. His ship didn't like those. Neither would the attackers'. Standard shielding could serve all three of them only for a short period. But compared with a direct weapon hit, old, weakened radiation was a small worry.

Todd flew still lower. Rubble rose in stories-high heaps. Broken windows glared at him. Jagged ruins of penthouses loomed above. He was so far down in the bowels of the empty city that a fine, dirty mist filled the air everywhere. It bred in the accumulated garbage at street level.

Vision was severely limited, but he didn't dare rely too much on his instruments. Todd swiped irritably at the condensation forming on his windows. Then he spotted another cramped intersection amid the gloom and hurtled into it.

He almost couldn't complete the maneuver.

Smoke-scarred brick and the gaping teeth of shattered window-walls rose out of the fog like nightmares. Collision point, dead ahead!

Somehow, he kept himself calm. Todd tapped the retros delicately, avoiding a fatal yaw. The brief burst of braking fire spilled over the dirty bricks and through the broken windows. The flier skidded wildly, scraping something hard and unyielding.

Only a moment . . . and then he was free, moving clear, still banked over on his side, whistling down a snaky alleyway. Todd exulted, too in love with flying to be afraid.

Amazing himself, he righted the flier, slumping heavily against his safety webbing. He switched to manual on the com. He couldn't break past their override, but maybe they would start talking to each other at a range close enough for him to hear them.

If he could find the alien messenger's signal in the infinite reaches of space, he ought to be able to locate those bastards following him. They probably had a multisystem, Todd speculated, remembering the military specs he had read to update his knowledge after the shuttle ride to Goddard. Okay, that meant they would be using an unusual frequency for their two-way com between each other, to coordinate their attack. He rejected the normal frequencies, hunting, hoping they were too busy hunting *him* to notice that he was eavesdropping once he *did* find the frequency.

They weren't very imaginative. Far end of the band. Static clearing, words coming through. Todd pounced on the setting. He had them!

". . . no more full fire. Risky . . ."

Were they afraid a lot of firepower might be detected on CNAU Enforcement's scanners, or what?

"Over. He's in here someplace. Where's he going . . . ?"

Todd grinned cockily for the first time since the hair-raising encounter had begun. He blocked the output feed so they couldn't hear him and muttered nastily, "Where you're not going to find me, you son of a bitch."

The sooty mist opened a trifle. The alleyway was ending. Not good. Ahead lay a wide street. That would cancel out the maneuvering advantage of his small flier and let them get a straight shot.

Then Todd's attention was caught by black maws high along the sides of the skyscrapers lining the avenue. Missing windows had left entire floors of the old structures open to the elements. Hundreds of them, like lofty steel and glass caves, beckoned the fugitive. Nav scans told Todd that the craft were coming after him low. He cut everything but motive power, and the screens went dark. He was blind, and so were his attackers if they tried to track him.

He climbed, navigating eyeball mode, lifting above the alley buildings before he merged with the avenue. The flier spanned the wreck-littered four lanes and kept climbing. Wiping more condensation off the windows, Todd burst free above the mist.

There! That one! He couldn't say what made him select that particular ruin. Intuition? He swung over hard, not cutting speed. He didn't dare lose it now, or he would be splattered all over the side of the building. He flew through the center of an immense, broken window-wall and simultaneously hit retros full.

The interior wall rushed toward him. Retro fire billowed along his glide path like a blue-white carpet. The little flier slued and began to roll, the left wing tip aimed at the floor. He was split-seconds away from an out-of-control cartwheel.

The awful moment lasted forever. Todd leaned back and right, hard. Then the skids came down, scraping, braking . . .

Forward motion ceased.

The flier was at rest, upright, and intact, turned on its axis to parallel the interior wall and the window. Todd hastily completed the crippling of his ship, cutting all power.

He sat very still. His breathing sounded unnaturally loud. He could hear blood rushing through his temples and ears, too. Only now was he aware of these physical sensations, his body protesting what he had put it through. Todd felt sick and hoped he wasn't going to throw up. After a few seconds, the nausea settled to a bearable level and he peered out at his surroundings.

The burned-out floor he had picked as a haven was cavernous, low-ceilinged, and dark. The only light came through the broken window-wall. Todd cracked the canopy slightly and listened. There were dripping noises, possibly from broken conduits and condensation falling from the ceiling. Then he heard the distinctive high-pitched whine of flier thrusters.

How many? One, or two? He tried to gauge speed and distance from the sounds. Without his accustomed electronic tools, he was thrown back into the more primitive era of hunter-and-quarry flying.

The whining dopplered. Immediately afterward, another power system's sound rose in pitch, then dropped abruptly as a second craft flew past the skyscraper. They weren't flying at his story level, Todd guessed. Lower, but not by too many stories.

In a few minutes, they came back. Search pattern. That wasn't very encouraging. How long were they going to hunt him? And how thoroughly?

Todd flexed his shoulders and twisted his stiffening neck. It would be nice if Dian were here to soothe away the tenseness. With a rueful smile, Todd realized he was going to be a lot later picking her up at the shuttle terminal than he had anticipated.

His hand was resting on his thigh. Suddenly, Todd became conscious that he was touching the decoder strip Gib Owens had given him. He sat up very straight, blinking, and took the key out of his pocket. He stared at the darkened com panel.

Scrambler lock. They didn't expect him to have one. They hadn't bothered to use one themselves. Either they hadn't cared if he overheard them, or they assumed he would be too stupid to eavesdrop successfully.

Todd cursed himself for not having remembered the key earlier. Fumbling in the semi-darkness, he fed the decoder into the com's translator slot. The thing would work as well here—in reverse!—as it had in his office. Gingerly, he cued the com. The faint green glow seemed like a cheery electronic campfire, holding back the jungle.

He had contact. And the com's readout reassured Todd he was safely hidden behind a masking wall of static.

". . . couldn't have made it over to the Inlet."

"How did he get away? That bastard sure can fly . . ."

"We gotta report . . ."

Report? To whom? Todd's growing curiosity was chasing his
shivers and nausea into oblivion. He studied the hateful voices.
Neutral inflection, like ComLink's media 'casters and enter-
tainers. You had to train to achieve that sort of voice. The pilots
could be from anywhere. They were talking in English, but there
was no ethnic or regional tone at all in their words.

". . . must have cut his systems. There's nothing registering,"
one of those flat voices complained.

Todd smiled. Damned right he had cut his systems, except for
the scramble-locked com! And he didn't intend to fire up again
until those predators were out of his range.

"Look, we *have* to find him, at least confirm he didn't ident
us . . ."

"He didn't. Hell, we did the job . . ."

Todd strained to hear. The whining of their engines was gone.
They must be prowling other streets now, still hunting. If only
they would let something slip! A name. A takeoff point. Anything!

"Gave him a scare . . ."

"That's all we were supposed to do. They said spook him, scare
him off . . ."

They? Who were *they?* A fake! A phony attack! They had
never meant to kill him at all, just scare him off. Off from *what?*

Todd hated his immobility, wanting to strike back and shake
the answers out of them. Who the hell wanted him scared badly
enough to stage that risky aerial chase? He *could* have been
killed, despite the intentions of the pilots!

". . . prefer a clean job, like that Spacer pilot. That's one of
them we won't have to worry about any more . . ."

What? Whom were they talking about now?

". . . go home. Saunder'll report this to Enforcement. They'll
hunt around and file it and forget it . . ."

The signals moved rapidly. Todd boosted gain, wanting to cap-
ture every scrap of information he could. He switched on navs,
knowing now that they weren't going to track him back *via* his
circuitry and kill him, as he had believed they would. He swore at
his having been duped. They were drifting off the navs. Could he
fire up and hope to catch them? Todd checked the readout, knowing there was no chance.

The voices were fading, other signals cutting in as static.

". . . lose bet . . . other team bragging . . . got Owens on that African transp . . ."

Icy shock dashed away Todd's anger. Gib Owens? Dead?

The signal was almost gone. He boosted gain to maximum, hanging on as long as he could.

". . . fucking Colonists. Won't . . . no slipping that one past us again . . ."

". . . too bad about the civilians . . . Spacer's fault . . . sent him . . . should have known we'd . . ."

There was nothing there but static. They had the range to cross the continent in those ships. They had left to report their successful "scare mission" to an unspecified "they." Todd switched to a commercial frequency. A newscast was in progress. Absently, he removed the scrambler lock and replaced it in his pocket.

". . . no survivors. The Nairobi shuttle, with three-hundred-twenty passengers and crew, went down without contacting Global Flight Control. Sea-Search Rescue Director Capra speculated that equipment failure may have been the probable cause of the crash. A more complete analysis is expected when Protectors of Earth's seabed salvage teams recover the wreckage from the ocean south of the Cape Verde Islands. All indications are that no lifesaving gear deployed. Director Capra says that in a Mach Five system failure, the physical properties of air and water produce such resistance that . . ."

The weight of Todd's hand fell on the manual cutoff and the voice stopped. Fresh nausea rose in his throat. He understood the implications of systems failures at Mach 5 far better than the announcer did. She was merely reading copy, speaking dispassionately so the ComLink translator-splitter could send the news out in every human language. In plain English, there was no hope. They would probably never even find much wreckage. It had become part of the Gambia Abyssal Plain on the ocean floor.

Gib Owens, cocky, young, an expert pilot, a combat-ready Goddard Colonist, a trusted courier, a nice kid. Dead. And hundreds of others had died with him.

"Too bad about the civilians."

The mysterious "they" who had sent the pilots had sent another team, probably saboteurs. "They" had killed 320 people in order to take out Gib Owens.

Gib, asking Todd how he had seen through his disguise, saying a flaw might cost him his life. The forged papers hadn't worked. Someone else had also seen through his disguise. Or someone had betrayed him.

Three hundred and twenty people. Pawns in a cold war between Earth and its first space colony.

In the new mysticism, which the majority of Earth's population claimed to accept, life was infinitely precious. They followed that belief more in theory than in practice, but it had changed the penal laws, altered the attitudes of even those participating in war. Life must be preserved, or at least saved for the human gene pool. Killing was a savage thing out of Earth's past, something man must somehow put behind him, led by the Spirit of Humanity. But now and then you have to make a few sacrifices in order to get the damn Spacers . . .

Todd sat very still, not seeing the flickering com screen continuing the now-silenced broadcast, not seeing the burned and blackened walls around him. He was seeing names and idents that weren't quite right, and a picture remote-relayed from Antarctica, which a computer had cut off much too soon. He was getting advice from an enforcement officer telling him to take the air route henceforth and avoid trouble. Friendly counsel, honestly intended? Or had it been a method of steering Todd into the path of two assassins? Mari, on the tape, begging Todd to consult Fairchild, to get in touch with Goddard's secret allies—"people in high places . . . a general . . ." Like General Ames, P.O.E. Enforcement's second in command? Was he one of the anonymous friends of the Spacers? Or was Ames yet another factor in an enemy conspiracy? In his mind's eye Todd saw Ames staring hard at Pat while he made a truce announcement, and Ames lurking in the back of the hall when the Science Council tried to quiet the public's fears about the alien messenger. Coincidence? That Ames showed up where he did and when he did? That people were saying and doing things which later seemed to tie in with deadly events? Was Todd letting his suspicions run wild? Or did he have good reason to be on guard?

Whom could he trust? Whom could he depend on?

Games. He and Mari and Pat flying mock combats through the palms girdling Saunderhome. But *this* game was different, and very deadly.

Gib Owens, delivering the tape with those eighteen names. Todd had tried to check them out, unsuccessfully. And a short while later, he was forced to fly for his life. Another coincidence? A straight dive into the Atlantic at Mach 5 might look like a co-incidence, an accidental systems failure, too. But Todd knew it wasn't.

What about a frozen prison under the Antarctic glacier? Were systems failures going on there as well?

"Was all this really worth Gib's life, and the other lives, Mari?" Todd's voice broke. No! The question was unfair to Mari. He was asking the wrong person. He flinched away from the alternative, the accusations forming in his mind.

Who wanted Gib Owens and the knowledge he might have shared out of the way? Who wanted any inquiries aimed at certain confinees in SE Antarctic Enclave dropped?

Two puzzles, maybe interrelated in ways Todd didn't yet understand. But the pieces surrounding them were making frightening sense. When someone had firebombed Project Search, a mysterious call had taken Todd out of target range—a call on a circuit available only to top-level Saunder Enterprises personnel. And when Todd had made his probes of P.O.E. Archives and SE's computer system, he had done so with his own top-privacy circuit. Had the same unknown enemy tapped in and found out what he was doing and decided to discourage him from trying that again?

Possibly. In fact, it was the most logical explanation. And it broke every law and required access to systems supposedly locked against everyone but the Saunders.

Protecting him from the firebombing, instructing the assassin pilots to scare him, but not kill him. Someone in power within the conspiracy had taken great pains to keep Todd Saunder alive. But it was okay to kill Anatole and Gib Owens and 320 people on the Nairobi transport. What was special about Todd Saunder? Why was he exempt?

He was exempt because he *was* a Saunder.

And the chief of assassins might have to answer to someone very close to the family. Perhaps someone who *was* family.

Todd's mind and emotions shrank, icy cold. He withdrew into a personal eye of the hurricane deep within his being.

His next move was going to take careful planning. It could be —*would* be—tricky and very dangerous. He couldn't afford to make mistakes. It only took one, for Ward Saunder or for his too-curious second son. Todd mulled the risks as grief and rage strengthened his determination. First he would have to call CNAU Enforcement and report this incident, as "they" anticipated he would. Follow their schedule, for now. Don't arouse their suspicions. Not yet.

But before this thing was through, "they" were in for some surprises. Big ones. He was going to find the answers. He owed it to Gib and the other victims. And he owed it to himself, and to the species the alien messenger had crossed light-years to meet.

CHAPTER THIRTEEN

☆☆☆☆☆☆☆☆☆

WARNINGS

Todd had begun to shiver and sneeze from the damp of this place. He was still mildly queasy, but he cued the systems and checked the outside. He knew they weren't waiting for him, weren't trying to kill him—unless by accident—yet he almost wished he could fly out and meet them and give *them* a bit of a scare for a change.

Getting out of the building wasn't as tricky as getting into it, but still, doing so took some careful maneuvering. Once he was out in the open air, he followed the four-lane avenue, heading back to the heart of New Washington and CNAU Civil Order Enforcement. Follow the regs. He contacted CNAU Flight Control and apprised them of his radically changed flight plan, and that he was on his way to report a whopper of a complaint against two other fliers, not that it would do any good. Then he called Iris.

He talked over and around her surprised questions, wondering if the experience was showing in his face that much. "Tell Dian . . . please. I'm due there right now, and I can't make it until later."

"Boss . . ."

Impatiently, Todd went on. "And have Bob send over a mechanic team to CNAU Enforcement. I put this poor beast through hell and need it checked to be sure it's okay. Also, reserve a cou-

ple of seats on tomorrow's orbital flight out of Orleans. I'll be
spacing, and Dian will probably be going with me—"

"Boss!" Iris finally broke through, sounding harried. "Your
mother's holding on another line. She wants to know where you
are. I think she just got back from a campaign trip with your
brother. What shall I tell her?"

Todd sighed. "You might as well tell her I'll be at CNAU Enforcement. Otherwise she'll ride everybody ragged. Where's
Falco?" A quick check informed him the crack ComLink interviewer was in the city, finishing up an assignment. "Get him and a
tech team over to Enforcement HQ, too, as soon as they can
make it. I've got a news release to get out under an interview
cover. I want it to go global, so tell them to bring full translator
gear. Got all of that?"

Iris nodded. "It'll be there, boss."

With genuine affection, Todd smiled at her. "You're a gem.
How about a raise? Starts yesterday. I'll put it through before I
lift off tomorrow." She was grinning widely when he broke the
connection.

Todd landed in CNAU Enforcement's V.I.P. strip. Rank had
its privileges, and Saunder Enterprises fed plenty into the public
coffers of Central North American Union. The session with the
police went about as he had expected. He had to edit his complaint. Some things he didn't want to reveal—the illegal translator
strip, for one. Yet he could, with convincing anger, put on a
terrific performance as an outraged citizen who had been attacked
and nearly killed. There were questions and more questions, and
recorded forms for him to affirm with his handprint. There was a
space for signatures, though a lot of complainants had to sign via
a comp printout. Todd impressed the higher brass and working
investigators by using a pen as if he did it all the time.

He wondered if Falco had arrived yet. They would probably
keep the reporter and the techs outside until the questioning was
over. Jael would also be showing up soon, if she ran true to her
habits.

The chief investigator was making noises as if the formalities
were over. Todd was about to excuse himself and leave the rest of
the digging to Enforcement when a com call interrupted them.
There had been a slip-up in communications. Todd realized as he

listened that he wasn't supposed to hear the incoming report. Confidential police business. He couldn't hide his shock.

". . . matches the descriptions you just put out on the Saunder attack incident ninety minutes ago. Both pilots are dead."

It didn't make sense. The wrecked planes and the pilots had been found less than thirty blocks from where Todd had hidden in the ruined building. He had watched his attackers leave the area. They had been much farther away from him than that when their com signals faded. It was very unlikely they had doubled back, or they would have spotted him when he finally emerged from his hiding place.

". . . idents on bodies confirm probable Serene Future connections. One of their splinter groups, Chief . . ."

The ranking officer was looking unhappily at Todd. He didn't want to be obvious and shut up the reporting officer, not when Todd Saunder was president of the world's most powerful telecom network. There were laws about the suppression of information that should be available to the public. "Uh . . . thanks, Williams. Full investigative teams will be there in ten minutes. Seal off the evidence." The chief nervously turned to Todd. "We don't know anything for sure yet. It'll have to go through the labs. I'd appreciate it if you'd be discreet about this, Mr. Saunder. Wouldn't do to go blabbing it until we have some proof. Could be a frame-up."

Todd was positive that it was indeed a frame-up. The Serene Future political party was part of the Spacer coalition, fighting for Goddard's rights in Protectors of Earth's assembly. True, Serene Future had reacted very badly to the news about the alien messenger. It was as panicky and paranoid in that regard as the most rabid Earth Firsters, though for different philosophical reasons. But Serene Future was a mystical movement. Its members had been known to commit suicide in protest of the death penalty, one of the most extremist and eccentric actions yet produced by the Spirit of Humanity religion.

The dead men couldn't have been those who attacked him. Dupes. More pawns and sacrifices. The logic was obvious. And Todd wasn't so sure the blurted com call from the officer in the field was an accident, either. Maybe he had been *meant* to hear

and believe so that his suspicions would focus on Serene Future
—and not on the real culprits.

*I'm becoming as paranoid as Mari. But, like her, it isn't para-
noia when they really are trying to get you . . .*

"No, I won't broadcast it, Chief. You have my word on that.
But I want to be kept updated on what you find out," Todd stated
sternly.

"You sure will, sir. Soon as we know anything definite."

The suspicion had been planted. The lid clamped on. Todd
would play the enemy's game, for now.

Miguel Falco's ComLink team and Jael, accompanied by a
horde of muscular bodyguards, arrived at CNAU Enforcement
HQ simultaneously. When Todd came out of the building, they
were engaged in a hot argument, as hot as Falco dared. One of
Jael's bodyguards had fetched Todd's coat out of the flier. He
shrugged into it as the ComLink interviewer closed in on him.

Jael advanced on him, too.

"In a minute, Mother."

"I've got my trains waiting. Your mechanics are taking that
plane of yours apart. Iris said you have to pick up Dian. That
poor girl has been cooling her heels for—"

"In a minute!" Todd said loudly. He didn't have Pat's wonderful, carrying voice, but he had recovered his volume, after the
hoarseness caused by the Search fire. Jael reeled back, stunned,
looking up at her son as if she didn't recognize him. "Dian's going
to wait. She knows me. I sent her a message. Right now there's
something I've got to do. It won't take long, but I'm going to do
it, Mother. Do you understand?"

A slow, deep flush spread up from her fleshy chin to her forehead, the reddening skin standing out in contrast to the white er-
mine fur fringing her coat hood. Her velvety tone was gone. "I
understand," she said harshly. "We're going to talk about this
later, Todd."

"No doubt. Miguel . . ." He briefed his media star quickly,
priming Falco on which questions to ask and how to stage the
brief interview. Jael's bodyguards began fanning out to form a
fence around them, keeping curious CNAU troopers away. Beyond them, out on the V.I.P. airstrip, Todd noticed some of
ComLink's mechanics busy dismantling parts of the swift little

flier. Troopers watched them, some fingering the scrape marks on the flier's belly and speculating on what the craft had been through.

Falco's techs framed him and Todd and signaled go. "Listeners of Earth," Falco began, shamelessly borrowing from his boss's brother, "we're here with a late-breaking bulletin. Todd Saunder, president of SE ComLink, has just been attacked by two unidentified hostile pilots and was nearly killed. Police are investigating right now. It looks like an assassination attempt, isn't that so, Mr. Saunder?"

Todd hadn't been in front of a lens for a few years, but he hadn't forgotten the techniques. He pulled old talents out of storage, letting some of his leftover fear show. Pat termed that the Everyman Syndrome—show the audience you're human and that you can be scared, too. Pat needn't be the only actor in the family.

"Yes, that's right, Miguel. It was very close. I'm a pretty good flier myself, but those guys meant business. For a little while there I thought I was done for. Finally managed to shake them . . ."

Jael butted in, breaking her own rules about staying in the shadows. "This is simply terrible, Miguel . . ." Hastily, *sotto voce,* Falco introduced her to the audience while Jael went on. "The police must solve this thing quickly and bring those men to justice. No one is safe these days! It's exactly what my son Patrick has been saying—that we have to bring some order to Earth before we slip back into the Chaos. They've even made attempts on Patrick's life, you know, during those tours in South America and Europe . . ."

"Do you think this latest attack is really aimed at your older son, then?"

Todd hadn't interrupted, but Jael was aware of his burning stare. "Well, I wouldn't say that. They're trying to hurt *all* my family, and I think they must be caught and punished to the fullest extent of the law. I don't want to make any insinuations, but it could be some of Patrick's enemies, striking at him by attacking Todd . . ."

"We see you brought some bodyguards with you, Mrs. Saunder. Is that going to be common practice from now on?"

"I fear so, at least until the campaign is over. There's too much at stake . . ."

"Especially with a new little Saunder in the making, too, right, Mrs. Saunder?" Falco obviously thought it wouldn't harm his standing with the family corporation if he alluded to the expectant parents' happy announcement to the media a couple of weeks earlier. Then he swung back to the man paying his salary. "Todd, any speculations why they might be after you specifically?"

Todd timed the pauses as best he could, copying Pat's skillful delivery. "This attack might have been aimed at the family, and at Pat's campaign. But I believe it has something to do with Project Search, because I'm sponsoring the contact attempt with the alien vehicle."

Jael's motherly facade was crumbling, and the lens techs tactfully trimmed focus away from her, concentrating on Falco and Todd.

"They burned out Project Search's New Washington headquarters last week, and now this attack on me. Just put two and two together," Todd said coldly.

"It's obvious you and your brother differ in your attitudes about this alien messenger, Todd. He says it's a scout for an invasion from space. You don't think so?"

They had covered this territory before, many times, since the Science Council presentation and the worldwide release of the news. Usually Todd had let more media-comfortable spokesmen talk for him. Now he took the initiative. "No, I don't. I think it's the greatest opportunity ever offered to mankind. Our future for centuries to come will be different—and better," Todd said emphatically. He couldn't express his own uncertainties. Not here. This was the time to do his own propaganda spreading. "But there are people who hide their heads, who aren't willing to reach out for the wonderful opportunity that's coming. These misguided, frightened people are the ones who scare me. I sincerely believe they're the ones who sent fliers to attack me and firebombed Project Search and killed a man and hurt eight innocent people." Jael had turned her back on him, refusing to look at or hear him. Todd breathed deeply, hoping to convince the viewers he was taking a reluctant but absolutely necessary step. "I can't

allow any more of my people to be hurt, and I'm not going to
play target myself. So I'm transferring Project Search to space."

Jael reacted, whirling around, her mouth open in disbelief as
Miguel Falco picked up his cue. "When is this going to happen,
Todd?"

"Immediately. Some of my people are still in the hospital, of
course. But all the equipment and translation linkages will be
moved to space. When my staff has recovered, they'll join us in
orbit." Falco moved in close to him for a two-shot, contributing
his presence to the concluding statements, grabbing a little ego-
flattering broadcast space for himself in the bargain. "Project
Search will go on. These people who are trying to stop me have
failed. When the alien messenger reaches Earth orbit, about a
year from now, my people are going to be the ones to go out and
meet it—as friends, not as frightened, cowardly enemies who
would burn or shoot innocent people. Rely on it."

Falco wrapped up. Todd waited to see what Jael would do. She
didn't speak. After a long moment of glaring daggers at him, she
marched out across the airstrip toward the SE Trans Co spur.
Todd and her bodyguards followed. There were three cars, two
security brackets and one for the illustrious passengers. Todd
wasn't overly fond of modern rail travel, but he climbed in the
private car and sat with Jael. The propulsion systems took them
up to speed very rapidly, and they connected with the direct line
to the terminal.

Silence was a black cloud enveloping them. They hurtled
through the tunnels at top speed, magnetic resistance nil. Jael's
car was the best money could buy, custom-manufactured by the
same people who catered to kings and dictators. She could live in
this car, if she chose, and live far better than most of the world's
population was living right now.

"Mother," Todd said softly.

"You talk too much."

Well, that was something. At least she wasn't shutting him outside with her silence any more.

"I inherited that from Dad. He always said what he thought,
and not always at the best possible times for other people," Todd
reminded her.

She still refused to look at him. "Ward didn't propagandize."

"He did when he believed in a cause. So do his children. Pat hasn't got a patent on using my network to broadcast his message of hate—"

"Stop it!"

"That's what it is, Mother—hate. Hate for the aliens he doesn't even know, won't make any real effort to understand, through their communications. The only reason he wants my decryption data as it comes in is so he can build it into still *more* hate propaganda and whip the whole damned world into a paranoiac frenzy. Get them so scared they'll vote straight Earth First Party. Isn't that the strategy, Mother? He manipulates. He always has, and you let him. You egg him on, don't you? Nothing's too good for Pat . . ."

"Stop it!" Jael was on the verge of tears, angry tears. But there was something else in her face. "You don't understand—*won't*. People are *scared*. They'd be scared whether or not Pat made speeches. You did this to them, Todd. Acknowledge it! You and that damned alien thing. You had to find it, didn't you?"

He tried to break in, to explain again that his detection of the vehicle was academic. Discovered or not, it was already altering vector before he had made any moves to communicate with it.

Jael wouldn't listen. "Your . . . that thing is bringing all our worst nightmares to life!"

"Not *my* nightmares. And not Dad's. He had confidence in the future, in his ability to meet it and cope with it. What's happened, Mother? You used to feel that way, too. I've seen you digest his patents, learn to operate devices half the world's techs couldn't begin to comprehend. You're not some dithery, uneducated, stupid nonentity. You're Jael Saunder," Todd said with fierce familial pride. "You showed us kids how to be tough, taught us that knowledge was the key. 'Outsmart them all, and live.' Do it now. Outsmart the idiots who can't see anything but a menace in contact with another intelligent species. Dammit, we're *Saunders!* You told us we're the cream. It ought to be we, the intelligent ones, who talk to that alien and give it its first impressions of what humanity is like. Do you want it to see some slavering United Theocracies crazy, ranting about how cosmic rays are destroying his liver and his precious soul? Or should it be a bunch of goons smashing windows and clubbing people and setting off firebombs to destroy what they can't understand? Mother? I want you to be proud of this, of what I've done."

Jael shook her head, the white streak in her hair gleaming in the car's interior lights. There was defeat in her manner, a deep, pained anguish. "I . . . I can't. I used to, but I can't. Not any more. It's too much, Todd. Too fast. I could absorb it when I was younger. But now . . . just . . just give me time, time to get things in order. Pat's . . ."

"Don't bring Pat into this," Todd pleaded. "I realize you're involved in his career, but what about *my* career, and Mari's? Yes, Mari has a career now, too. You may not like her taste in housing, but she's got purpose to her life now, a damned important purpose, for her and Goddard and the future of Earth."

"And Mars? I know what they're doing, those fools. We can't afford it! We've got to pull together and get Pat elected to the Chairmanship first. You're going to wreck it for him—you and Mariette and all this damned space travel!"

Jael and Pat had resisted, violently, when Todd had broken the news about the alien messenger. He had assumed they would see the inevitable in time. Pat had the ability and the intelligence. But his motives were skewed. So were Jael's. She wanted the alien messenger to disappear. It was complicating Pat's straightforward rise to political power. And right now, she wanted Todd and Mari to disappear, too. Either that, or to come home to Mama and confess their sins and admit they had been doing wrong and misbehaving. Come home and be her little loving, obedient babies again. But they had never been all that obedient, even as children. Jael was still trying to make that ideal fantasy—the perfect marriage despite all opposition, three perfect children despite the criticism she had taken for opting to *have* three children during famines and disasters—be true. She was attempting to rewrite history, working with her children's lives.

Todd noted her unshed tears and the age lines Mari had mentioned. Time. Too many years of making history happen, fighting and clawing and building an empire for her children's sake. Jael wanted money and power. For herself, yes. But even more for her children. Nothing would defeat them. She had accumulated enough wealth and clout to make her family invulnerable—invulnerable to everything but the passing of the years.

If Mari had gone into the entertainment media, Jael would have accepted that. She would have made Mariette Saunder the reigning, dazzling queen of Earth's dreams. Pat was running the political show, king of *his* arena. The "good" child, the peacemaker, the second son, got to play behind the scenes and rule Earth's all-essential telecommunications, making Jael's dynasty and her global control of rulers and their populations possible.

Instead, the children were taking unexpected turns in the road, wresting control away from Jael, going in directions she didn't want them to. Mari first, now Todd.

And if Pat rebels?

Todd had never known a Jael Hartman Saunder who wasn't a fierce, ruthless fighter, a magnificent little bird of prey defending her brood. And he had never known her to reject new ideas. Those had been Ward's life, and she had made them hers.

"Mother, why is it always Pat who gets the breaks from you? Why don't you tell him to ease off on Mari and me? I've been settling their squabbles and taking second place to Pat all my life. Okay. He's the star. I don't want to be a media event. But I'm damned sick and tired of being taken for granted—the 'good son' who never gives any trouble and always caves in on his own wants to help you boost Pat, sometimes at his expense."

Jael caught Todd's hand and held it tightly. "I love you, Todd. I don't take you for granted. It may seem that I do, but I don't. And I love Mari. Believe that. I don't always approve of what she's doing with her life, but I love her. I love you all. We're family. There will always be a Saunder family . . ."

"Will there? Not at the rate we're going, Mother. I almost pity that baby Carissa's carrying. If this is a sample of family solidarity, we're going to end up scattered and forever estranged—if goons set off by Pat's speeches don't kill me and Mari before that happens."

She looked at him, her gaze piercing. Love. And a terrible, dark warning that had no name. "If you hurt Pat's chances, or that baby's . . . don't do it, Todd. I'm going to keep this family going. No matter what my failings. No matter how old I'm getting."

Ward Saunder hadn't possessed Pat's strange, compelling stare. He had had the unusually pale eyes, but not the power that came from within. That was Jael's. She still had it.

"We're here," Jael said suddenly in a non sequitur, letting go of his hand. "Do you want me to come into the terminal with you?"

Todd started. He hadn't realized they were slowing down, gliding to a stop. "No, no, that's okay. I'll go find Dian and be right back."

"We're going to the complex in New York-Philly." Jael's tone didn't allow an argument. Todd paused at the car door, looking at his mother. She softened the order slightly with an explanation. "I want you to talk to Pat. And he wants to see you. He was upset about this attack. So was Carissa. It'd help her if she could see you weren't hurt. Please, Todd?"

He nodded curtly and stepped out, hurrying toward the Arrivals lounge. Three of Jael's bodyguards followed Todd, over his protests. Todd shrugged and let it go. Dian had been sitting patiently, apparently reading an old book, eliciting curious stares from the other passengers in the immense lounge. She looked up before Todd called to her, smiled, stowed her book in her hand luggage, and hurried toward him.

The guards busied themselves looking elsewhere, granting them a moment of privacy on the busy concourse. Todd didn't want to let go, but they had to breathe. Dian finally leaned back and peered up at him. "Okay?"

"I'm fully functional. Bad case of leftover mad, but that's burning off. Now I just feel lucky."

"Lucky? Quick. Outdodger from what Falco said in his follow-up." It was plain she had seen his impromptu interview outside CNAU Enforcement. "Iris said you were okay, and you looked good. But I believe in an eyeball check . . ."

"Not here in public," Todd teased. Dian wouldn't release him. He had never seen her so concerned, not even when they had been in the fire at Project Search. "Beth and the others?"

"Pretty good, considering. Beth's asking when she can get back to decryption." Dian's smile was shaky. "I told her we were ready when she was. She'll like what you said, if they let her watch the broadcast. Some of the others will have to get used to spacing . . ."

"Yeah, well, we can work out the details of the transfer later. Iris tell you about lifting ship?" Dian felt the hidden meaning under that, even though Todd had said nothing to anyone about his real plans. Her expression wasn't quite her United Ghetto States mask, but close. She was open to him, but not to the body-guards or any other onlookers. She would go along, possibly tell him he had been crazy not to try something to fight back earlier.

"I'm go, now that Beth's out of danger."

Dian's arm slid around his waist. Side by side, they walked out-side to the waiting cars. Along the way, Dian eyed the body-guards. "I should have been with you," she said softly. "You shouldn't have had to take it alone."

"No. Beth needed you. She hasn't got any family. Besides, I had enough to scare me shitless without worrying about protect-ing you, too."

"Huh!" Dian said mischievously. "Scared? You scared for me, lover? Careful! That's practically a commitment, as your mama would say."

"Tell her about it. She's in the car," Todd countered, enjoying Dian's abrupt shift to consternation. She wasn't sure whether or not he was teasing her, until she actually saw Jael. "Don't go full decibels on me, now. I never could stand decibels and brains both in the same woman."

The door had snapped open as he spoke. Todd had meant for Jael to hear. He seated himself beside Dian, opposite his mother. Jael took the bait. "He's a liar. It runs in the family, Dian. His fa-ther could make you believe the Sun rises in the west. Never pay any attention to those big mouths." She leaned forward, pressing Dian's hand, sharing a revelation. "The trick is to watch the wheels going around in their manly little heads. Gives them away every time."

"Oh, I will!" Emboldened, Dian added, "Have to watch his hands, too. Those speak for themselves."

"Indeed!" Jael laughed heartily, a frank, earthy laugh Todd had always loved to hear. "That *also* runs in the family. It's the first thing I noticed about his father, the lewd rascal! Carissa's been known to say the same thing you did. These Saunder boys are chips off the old block in every regard. I'm glad you're onto his tricks. That saves me giving you an awful lot of motherly advice. Forewarned is forearmed . . ."

Todd was grateful to see her in a cheerier mood. He played butt of the joke, pretending offense. And he carefully stayed away from any comment on Pat's notorious womanizing. This wasn't the time or place to bring it up, now that things were settling down once more.

Jael remained in good temper. She even asked solicitously after Beth and the others who had been injured in the firebombing. Dian relayed thanks for the flood of gifts and get-well messages Jael had sent to Project Search victims, saying the patients had been very touched by her concern. So had the doctors, Todd learned. Jael had hired world-renowned burn specialists and flown them to the Texas facility at her own expense so that they could consult with the staff doctors on the very best treatment for Beth and the rest.

They rode on through falling darkness. It wasn't much past five, but evening came soon in January in this latitude. They used the well-maintained special rapid-transit tracks skirting Atlantic Inlet. In kilometers, this was the long way around New Washington from the southern terminal to New York-Philly. But in safety factor, at the speeds they were running, it was the best option.

Todd let Dian carry most of the conversation for him. The two women got along very well. There was none of that patronizing air Jael adopted when she was talking to Carissa, and none of the animosity that always seemed to rise to the surface when she met Mariette. Dian wisely stayed away from discussing the alien messenger or her translation work regarding it. They talked about past history, Jael bringing up her admiration for Dian's grandmother. Wyoma Lee Foix was worth quite a few minutes of mutual agreement and anecdotes Dian could share from her childhood in the Chaos days in the United Ghetto States.

Todd didn't mind being excess conversational baggage, relieved of the necessity to think of safe topics. He didn't want to remember that moment of terrible warning when he had seen deep into Jael's soul.

Shore lights and the tracks winked and shimmered in the reflections from the great Inlet. Todd looked out into the twinkling darkness. Atlantic Inlet—one more leftover from the wars. How many wars, over how many millennia? How long had man been fighting man? Were they ever going to stop? Some people believed such conflict was inevitable, citing the mythology of brother warring against brother in the beginning of creation. That was an idea Todd didn't want to accept, both for intellectual reasons and for personal ones. There had to be a maturity coming to them.

We've been very resilient, fortunately. We've had to be, since we're our own worst enemy and a very formidable one. How resilient are we now? I hope we can come out of this current fratricidal madness and survive.

The ride was incredibly smooth. He hadn't taken a trip with Jael in her favorite transportation for quite a while. He had forgotten how seductive the very faint sway of the car could be, the strange, noiseless movement as they raced northward at nearly air-transport speed. Acceleration had been imperceptible, but they had built up enough velocity to reduce the waters of the Inlet and the lights on the other side of the car to smeary ribbons of light and dark. They left Atlantic Inlet, and now the megalopolis was around them on every side. Todd had confidence in Jael's engineer. She hired none but the best. Yet when he rode in a vehicle he wasn't handling personally, there was always an uneasiness in his mind. If anything went wrong, they would be dead, fused into a telescoped lump of humanity and metal in a matter of seconds. It wouldn't really make any difference, in that event, if Todd were operating the cars or an experienced engineer were—and chances were far better that nothing *would* go wrong with an expert in the lead car.

Bodyguards in that car, too, and bodyguards in the car behind them. The way Jael Saunder traveled these days. So did Pat. ComLink footage on the campaign showed more and more armed muscle surrounding the candidate and his mother. Carissa hadn't been on screen these past several weeks, not after the doctor had made plain what the risks were. Idly, Todd wondered if Jael's train was also equipped with the high-powered weaponry those bodyguards were trained to use. He wouldn't have been surprised. Very little was surprising to him any more. The train probably had a military scrambler system, too. Pat had bragged, not idly, that he had military connections, some very impressive ones. They were buttering up the future Chairman of Protectors of Earth, no doubt thinking ahead to their next world peacekeeping forces' budgetary session.

The courtesy monitor had announced their ETA the moment they had left the terminal and offered a silent, running commentary on traffic conditions and minor news bulletins no one had cared to read. Now, as they began to decelerate very gradually, the ETA figures rippled and changed, adding at first seconds, then minutes.

Jael noticed, letting the conversation lapse. She spoke to the com, demanding an explanation from the driver. He was profusely apologetic, repeating several times that SE Trans Co guidance had to bump their ETA because of a higher-priority traffic jam at their destination. The engineer wasn't pretending his earnest apologies. Jael Hartman Saunder wasn't used to waiting. She demanded to know *what* higher priority could bump her out of line and make her tap her toes, wasting valuable time.

"Mr. Patrick Saunder put through the order, Mrs. Saunder," the engineer replied tonelessly. "Something about a Supreme Council of P.O.E. meeting they're having at the complex . . ."

"Patrick didn't tell me about that," Jael said, stricken and angry.

"Maybe it came up suddenly, one of those spur-of-the-moment things," Dian suggested, trying to calm the older woman. Todd shook his head, warning her not to interfere.

"Are they leaving?"

"Yes, ma'am. We should be in the train park in three minutes."

The deceleration, as smooth as the climb up to speed, continued to step them down. The endless city and suburb lights coalesced out of the smears top speed had caused. At a crawling pace, the three-car mass driver adaptation cut in normal propulsion, edging toward the waiting entry at the end of the street. The area around SE New York-Philly Complex was parklike and beautiful, especially at night, with light reflecting off little ponds and shadowy groups of trees bordering the buildings and plaza. Above the massive horizontal dark slit that was the door to the train and vehicular park area, Saunder Enterprises Mainland HQ towered. Office lights were still on in many of the levels. SE busi-

ness activities never ceased. However, the train passengers
weren't going up to the offices, but down into the buried sanctuary, the private residence six stories below street level.

Apparently it *was* a business session for Pat, even within his
subterranean apartments. As Jael's three-car train slowed to a
crawl, Todd saw, along the curve of the tracks ahead, other
V.I.P. trains and vehicles leaving the parking area. One train
passing them on an adjacent track bore a Presidential seal.
Galbraith. He must have traveled up from New Washington to
confer with the next Chairman of P.O.E. Todd speculated this
had probably been a political plotting session, then. Galbraith's
Social Traditionalists forming a coalition with Earth First and
World Advancement parties, carving up the world. Galbraith had
hoped to run for the Chairmanship himself, until incumbent Li
Chu acknowledged Pat as her political heir. At one time, decades
ago, when part of the Central North American Union had been
the United States of America, President Galbraith most likely
would have been the favorite in the election. Now, Galbraith's
office was a joke, a puppet administration operated by Protectors
of Earth. Galbraith was old, a never-powerful leader who was virtually politically impotent, trying to ride Pat's coattails and thus
hang onto what clout he had. For Todd, the man had proved his
weakness by his actions these past few weeks. Galbraith had first
said nothing at all about the electrifying news Todd Saunder
brought the world. When he *had* to respond, he echoed Pat, down
to the last frightened demand that CNAU mobilize and "prepare."

There were other trains, carrying generals, potentates and
financial moguls, plus vehicles belonging to delegated managers
of Pat's various Saunder Enterprises corporations and numerous
other bigwigs. The trains and cars must have clogged the parking
area and taxed Trans Co's guidance system. Now they had all
cleared out, and Jael's train was given permission to proceed.

Jael was fuming, not hiding a bit of it. Todd didn't say anything out loud. But he thought that his mother had better get used
to waiting in line. She had been a dowager queen of a global empire for so long, she assumed that was the way it would always
be. But when Pat received the Chairmanship, he would be too big
to have Jael tagging around at his elbow everywhere while he

conducted Earth's business—and too necessary to cater to her and her taste for luxury and preferment while men and women of genuine political power cooled their heels. From now on, it would be Jael Saunder who would cool her heels. Perhaps that was a result of Pat's rise to power that she hadn't foreseen when she had first set out to buy him the Chairmanship.

They glided into the now-empty parking area, a huge tunnel with access for trains and vehicles and supply equipment at both ends of the building. Forty stories of offices, SE Mainland HQ's heart, soared above them. The elevators to the private residences were on their left. Bodyguards handed Jael and Dian out of the car, escorted the three of them to the cages. More new military-type equipment flanked the cages, scanning the elevators to be sure nobody was trying to sabotage anything. Another price of political popularity? Todd wondered.

They rode six stories down, entering a bombproof hole in the ground. There were still more guards in the foyer outside the bottom level, and an assortment of men and women in mufti, including the bosomy blonde Todd had first seen a few weeks ago when Pat had made the Trans-Pacific truce announcement. She was posing as an "aide" now, as were all the others in civilian clothes. Some actually *were* aides. Most of them were flunkies, though, or thinly disguised undercover bodyguards who wouldn't be suspected as such because they didn't look the part.

Jael led the way back toward the private apartments. Servants appeared out of nowhere, offering to take the coats they had been carrying since they left the train. Dian glanced up at the security cameras in every corner, then looked at Todd. He nodded, very sour. Watching them. Always. As if they were in danger even among their own army of private bodyguards.

The door of the recreation lounge opened, and Roy Paige came out. He brightened when he saw Todd and Dian. Jael was busy telling one of the wardrobe servants something. Seeing that, Roy edged close to Todd. "I'm glad you're here. Maybe you can do something." Todd frowned in confusion as the black man explained. "He's been drinking. A lot. I never saw him drink so much. He can hold plenty, I know; so do you. I think it's all this political stuff. They're closing in on him already, and he hasn't even got the election sewed up. Making plans about what they're gonna do—what they expect *him* to do—once it's in the bag . . ."

"Well, it's what Pat said he wanted," Todd said uncertainly.

Roy looked as if he might cry. "He didn't show it while they were here. Now it's all coming out. He's hurtin', Todd. Poor kid." Pat *was* a kid to this man who had loved and worked alongside Ward Saunder. Roy took Todd's arm with his remaining real hand, squeezing it hard. "He needs you. He needs *somebody*. I don't know what's happening here." Jael was sending the servant on her way, turning around, noticing Roy. Hurriedly, speaking in a teary whisper, Roy Paige finished, "He's never gonna live to get as old as his father, the way he's going. He's gonna break."

CHAPTER FOURTEEN

A DYNASTY DIVIDED

MORE aides and guards stood about inside the recreation lounge. They were clustered near the main door when Todd, Dian, and Jael entered. The aides immediately began fawning on Jael, ushering her and Dian toward an island of comfortable chairs nearby, offering to fetch them drinks from the bar in that area.

At the far end of the long room, Pat stood at another, larger bar, all alone. Had he sent his aides into exile, or had they fled from his temper? He was pouring himself a drink. Even from fifteen meters away, Todd could see his brother's hands shake.

Todd left the women in the flunkies' care and walked toward Pat, who was making a media production out of selecting chunks of ice from the antique bar refrigerator, dropping the pieces into his glass, splashing liquor on the marble counter top. Suddenly, he looked up at Todd. Wary, Todd stopped and waited three meters away from his brother.

He saw what Roy Paige was worried about. Pat and Mari both had a tremendous capacity for alcohol, but they built up to an explosion point eventually, and then all hell broke loose. Pat was very near that stage now. He abandoned his meticulously built drink and eased his way around the bar. As Pat came close, Todd smelled his breath, heavy with rare pre-Chaos whiskey. Nothing but the best.

"Damn you, you little bastard," Pat said without rancor. His voice was slurred, the wonderful eyes not quite focused. He grinned and hugged Todd clumsily, shaking him. "Damn you for scaring me like that! You okay, kid? No singed places?" Half sincere, half clown-act, Pat examined Todd, patting his pockets, grabbing his chin, forcing him to turn his face first this way, then that. Todd bore the manhandling stolidly, considering it a small price to pay to keep Pat under control. "You must have come through pretty clean. You *look* clean. Huh? Doesn't he look clean, Mother?" Pat didn't wait for Jael's answer from the far side of the room. He kept on rambling. "Real clean, clean enough to make me sound like a prize jackass in that cute li'l global cast you made with Miguel . . ."

For an instant, Todd squirmed inwardly. Then he was annoyed with himself. He was reacting like a naughty kid caught joyriding in his brother's car. "Well, any excuse to spread the good word. Hell, you do that, right?" Todd said with mock joviality, encouraging Pat to relax and laugh with him. "Besides, I had to blow off a little steam. Got pretty wild up there. Once I cooled down, I figured it was a good chance to plug my hobby. Why the glare? Hell, it's the same thing I said a week ago when they interviewed me after that firebombing at Project Search."

This time the tactic didn't work. Pat wouldn't laugh along with him. "Nobody listened to you talking—then." Then Pat softened the sharp words. "I'm sorry about your people, the man who got killed . . . God, I'm sorry!"

"Jael told me you're paying for their treatment. You didn't have to do that."

"I want to!" Pat declared earnestly. "We're Saunders. We stick together. No one hurts us or our people. We knew what kind of expense that med treatment would mean . . . had to, kid." Todd thought of the dead and injured Goddard Colonists and considered asking Pat if his generosity extended to them, too, but he held his tongue. Pat returned to the first subject. "You're right, though. Grab the publicity while it's hot. I'd have done the same thing. Smooth move, your calling Falco like that. Push the pet theory, huh? Isn't that what Dad used to do? But shit, kid, don't get yourself killed doing it. You know, I think it's all because of this decoding stuff of yours."

He hung his head, breathing hard. The liquor was affecting him heavily. So were the pressures of the campaign. Bodyguards. Constant security. People checking his elevators and trains and fliers to make sure no hidden bombs or assassins were aboard. They probably went through Pat's closets searching for insidious poison hidden in his clothes, too. V.I.P.s leaning on him and wheedling. Axes to grind. And always more speeches to make. Look handsome for the people. Tell them what they want to believe. Make them love you, follow you, vote for you.

Todd had often been jealous of Pat's physical beauty, his tremendous stage presence, the women who flocked around him. After so many years, and seeing the price Pat was paying, that jealousy was almost gone. Fame was picking Pat Saunder to bits. Each greedy admirer left less of the man for Pat Saunder himself.

"Can't you put it on hold, kid, this decoding stuff?" Pat said. "Huh? Just let me get this damn election over with and I'll channel funds all over the place to your de . . . decryption. Promise!"

Todd couldn't resist the impulse. "Are you going to send funds to Goddard, too?" he asked.

Pat winced, his handsome face taut with pain. "I can't! Can't! It's campaign strategy . . ."

"Come on, Pat. Is it? Are things really that simple? Do you think you can turn off all the anti-Spacer hatred after the campaign's over? As for Project Search, I meant what I've said all along. If my people don't decode the message, other scientists will, and they just might bungle the job. I want the job done right, and my people are the best." He knew he was piling too much on Pat, more than his brother could comprehend in his present condition. Piling things on him, the same way the V.I.P.s and the adoring public were.

"Yeah, yeah." Pat waved a hand as if to shoo away insects. Then he brightened and changed subjects again, suddenly cheerful. "Two of 'em? Were they crack fliers? Damn! That must have been exciting, huh? Shit! I wish I'd been there. Bet you peeled 'em off, just like we used to scrape bugs off the palms at Saunderhome." He was vicariously enjoying Todd's close call. They were adolescents again, reminiscing about buzzing the island, affectionate conspirators.

"A little bit scarier than those dumb stunts," Todd said. "They zigzagged me all over the old capital. I almost decorated a building a few times. I started thinking maybe it was a good thing my sperm's on file at the South Pole." Despite the momentarily happy mood, he found himself watching Pat narrowly, looking for a re- action. Pat's inhibitions were down. Would he reveal something, act as if he knew something secret about SE Antarctic Enclave or a computer that wouldn't obey its programming? There was no flicker of guilt. Todd felt immense relief at that.

Pat slapped Todd's shoulder exuberantly. "Hey, right! We're on storage down there, safe and sound against the slings and arrows and all that stuff. Tucked away for posterity, our li'l sperm and eggs. Good old Enclave! Dad had a terrific idea there. That's the kind of altruism I like. Pays off. And we can brag that it's all for the good of humanity, right?" Across the room, his aides and guards eyed him worriedly. No one gave them any orders, how- ever, so they stayed where they were while the candidate sneered at his own campaign philosophy. "We ought to drink to altruism, kid."

He spun around, gesturing, nearly pulling Todd off balance. "And look at the perks! Look at this beautiful bombproof cave. Ippolito built this place on blood. That's funny, isn't it? The big- gest arms dealer in modern history. Old bastard made *billions!* He couldn't count all his money and properties." Giggling, Pat grabbed Todd around the neck in a loose bearhug and whispered loudly, "Remember how Ippolito panicked and came running to us? Deadly disease, the doctors told him. And he begged us to put him on ice till they found a cure. Name our price—*any* price, he said." Pat straightened and peered owlishly at Jael. "Oh, you got him good, Mother."

He lurched to the bar. Todd followed him, trying to get the glass away, muttering that he wanted a drink himself and would build Pat a fresh one. He didn't have a chance to pull the switch and make a watered drink for his brother. Those pale eyes were focused and glittering, and an anger line appeared between Pat's black eyebrows. He had reached another stage of drunkenness, one beyond slurriness and good-natured floundering. He closed a strong hand over Todd's and forcibly took the glass back. "I want to drink a toast to our illustrious mother, the woman who made all these wonderful altruistic benefits possible." Then he drained the glass.

Jael was finally moving, Dian following her warily. The guards
and aides hung back, trailing Jael, but not very eagerly. Pat
watched his mother approach. "We stripped poor old Ippolito absolutely naked. He wanted immortality on ice, and we gave it to
him—at a whopping price. Cleaned him out. Mother showed the
bastard no mercy. If he's not a Saunder, he's shit. Right,
Mother?"

Todd glanced at Dian. He hoped his expression was as unreadable as hers. He was embarrassed, and he hurt for Pat's sake. He
wanted to cut through his brother's self-loathing, but Pat had the
power on full.

"And we're his beneficiaries. We're going to inherit the whole
damned planet—you, me, and Mari. No, I forgot. Mari doesn't
want any part of our old planet, does she? Just you and me, then,
kid. And me making speeches about the wasteful consumption of
Earth's priceless resources. Look at this place! The old boy built
it so no missile could touch it. Spent half his fortune to be safe,
buried here, surrounded by obscene luxury. Now he's in a frozen
box, and all this is ours. Talk about wasteful consumption!"

Pat was talking faster and faster, as if wanting to spit it all out
before Jael could stop him. "They force it on me, Todd. 'Take
everything, but let me live into the future, even if you have to
freeze me to do it.' 'Vote for my bill; don't ask why my people
are starving.' 'Look the other way while I enslave half my population; I'll pay you for your silence.' And I take it, Todd. They
offer it to me, and, God help me, I take it. It's a damnable habit
now. They keep telling me there's always more where that came
from. And there is! I'm addicted! I'm living like a goddamned
emperor, and I haven't even won the election yet. They already
own me, those—those leeches!"

He gripped Todd by the shoulders, pleading. His eyes were
haunted. "I'm a hypocrite, kid. But I've got to pay it all back.
Somehow. It won't be free. They give it to me, but it's got strings.
Oh, God! How am I going to keep all these promises I'm making?
I've got to. I will! You believe me, don't you, kid?"

"Sure, sure, Pat. You always keep your word," Todd soothed.

Pat shook him hard, agitated. "Right! Right! I knew I could
count on you to see what I'm talking about. I'm going to make it.
I am!"

"Pour some wine, Patrick," Jael cut in. She was at Todd's elbow, speaking in her threatening, tightly controlled voice. "Not all of us care to drink rye."

"Just Dad and me and Todd, huh? Like father, like sons." Pat's manner turned testy. He made the words a challenge.

"Ward never drank like a fish and then babbled . . ."

"No? Didn't he? I seem to recall a few evenings in our happy home when he let you know what he thought of all your wheeling and dealing and the way we were growing up. *In vino veritas,* and all that. Maybe Dad didn't have as much truth locked up in his soul as I do. He couldn't! *He* wasn't a hypocrite. Hell, who cares if I babble? No one here but us Saunders and wallpaper people." He grinned and wriggled his fingers contemptuously at the cluster of guards and aides. Then he leered at Dian. "You're almost a Saunder, aren't you, sweetheart?"

Dian placated him with an assenting nod. Jael was about to continue scolding Pat when he went to rummage in the wine racks behind the bar. With a frown, Jael watched him wipe the old bottle and begin extracting the cork. His hands were remarkably steady now, Todd noticed. He hoped Pat had burned off the worst of what was bothering him.

Not all of it. He was still an explosion looking for a place to happen. "Say, kid, 'Rissa wants to see you. She heard the news and got worried. Wants to press the flesh and make sure you're okay, you know. Go on. Give her a kiss and make a pass at her and cheer her up . . ."

Jael glanced warningly at the ubiquitous security monitor cameras in the corners. "That's not wise at the moment, Patrick. She's probably been watching this little performance of yours, on her closed-circuit screens. She'll be upset. Let me calm her down before—"

"You stay away from her," Pat said curtly.

"Patrick, be reasonable. She's pregnant."

"No!" Pat's sarcasm would have melted the marble bar top. "Now how did *that* happen? Suppose it was something I did? Butt out, Mother. You play doting grandmother when I say so. Otherwise, go tend to your power brokering. You had your chance to be a frail, pregnant female."

Jael wouldn't let it go, even though Todd signaled her frantically to change the subject. He sensed Pat's rising anger as Jael pushed on. "I was much stronger when I was carrying you and the others. Carissa needs help. I have plenty of experience . . ."

"Don't you just! Iron woman! Drop the kids on the carpet while you're at a board meeting, slicing a competitor into bite-sized pieces. I've heard it all, Mother, too many times. Carissa's having this baby, not you. She'll do a damned sight better job raising the kid, too, than you did with us, for my money. *Lots* of my money!"

"If you'd just calm down and be civil . . . I told you I'd take care of it," Jael persisted, her tone dangerously patronizing. "You have your hands full with the campaign. I can take charge of this little feminine matter and see that the very best—"

Pat grabbed the half-empty whiskey bottle and raised it over his head. The bodyguards took a few steps forward, then stopped. Decisions were impossible. Whom did they protect? The shining political star, or the woman who had hired them?

"That's no good, Pat," Todd warned tensely. "Put it down, please."

A series of emotions warred over Pat's sharp face. "Right again, kid. It's not the time. Not yet!" Then, quite deliberately, he smashed the bottle to pieces on the counter top.

Reflexively, Todd wheeled, shielding Dian. Splintered glass flew. The bodyguards and aides finally had to act. They moved in on Jael, Pat, Todd, and Dian.

"Are you hurt, sir? Dr. Foix? Did you get cut?"

"Mrs. Saunder? Please, let me get a cloth . . ." A woman aide mopped daintily at a splash of whiskey soiling Jael's expensive clothes.

"Mrs. Saunder? Sir?" Pat was a smiling statue, refusing to reply, enduring their ministrations. They pried the remains of the bottle's neck out of his fingers and examined him for cuts or blood. People swarmed around the bar and picked up shards of glass, blotting at stains, fussing. "Maybe we'd better call the medics," one suggested.

"That won't be necessary," Jael said. "It seems no one is injured." She was trembling with rage, yet not letting it erupt into tears or yelling. "Patrick, how could you?" she asked in a soft voice. "That was outrageous. A childish tantrum."

"But fun! Damn, that felt good!"

"You can't expect to behave like that after you're elected," Jael replied icily. "You'll have the dignity of your office to—"

"Wait! Just wait!" That dangerous glitter returned to Pat's eyes. He seemed cold sober now. "Get this junk out of here," he ordered his aides, indicating the broken glass. Then he turned to Jael. "Maybe it was a tantrum, Mother. But it's something that's been coming a long time. If you're too blind to see it, I'll spell it out for you. No, don't put on that little tolerant sneer of yours. I'm not your baby boy any more. I'm thirty-five years old, and that's *my* wife, and *my* baby. Not yours! Got that? Keep your damned hands off. Quit trying to live my life—*and* Todd's, *and* Mari's! God! That's probably why we're losing Mari. You couldn't let her be, could you? Got to run everything. Saunder Enterprises and all us little Saunders. Toe the line. Salute sharply there! And most of all, mind Mama. *Not any more!*"

The bodyguards and aides began to leave, toting piles of broken glass and sopping bar towels. They looked back over their shoulders, and Todd read their mixed motives. They didn't want to get dragged into this. But they hated to miss the juiciest part of the fight. The famous Saunder clan, screaming and slashing at one another. Todd assumed Jael had signed them on to a strict protection-of-privacy contract, or this fracas would be all over the rival media in the morning. Pat's political opponents would love to get their hands on it.

"Don't you turn away from me, Mother! I've got one hell of a lot more to say! We're going to settle this!" Pat didn't stop glaring at Jael as he addressed his brother. "You don't have to put up with this, kid. Go on, Todd. You and Dian see 'Rissa . . ."

Todd felt like a rat leaving a sinking ship. Dian wouldn't let him hesitate. He knew she was right. A bodyguard shut the door on the yelling. A wall monitor screen showed Pat going at it again. Then the screen went blank. Jael or Pat had pulled the plug. The watchers weren't going to be allowed to witness this event, under the guise of protecting them from harm. No eavesdroppers invited.

Dian took two steps to every one of his until Todd realized he was practically running back to the private bedroom suites. He slowed down and allowed Dian to catch her breath. "Pat's held too much in, ever since he was a kid. It explodes now and then. But never this bad. He used to be able to work things off roughhousing with me, or racing boats or fliers with Mari. Maybe he ought to hire a sparring partner, one of those bodyguards. But when would he have time for exercise now? He's on stage all the time. And all those responsibilities. Roy Paige was right; they're killing him. And Pat hates to lie. Political fast talk to please the crowds, sure. But not all those promises he knows he can't deliver."

"You think he's lying?"

That was a knife, the blade ice-cold, thrust in Todd's gut. "I don't know. At least I hope I don't." Dian looked up at him, puzzling out the words. They didn't say any more, conscious of the watchdog wall monitors. But she nodded. They would discuss it later, where there wouldn't be anyone else to hear. Todd returned to the painful family argument. "I've seen him and Mother butt heads plenty of times. This one's different. For one thing, this time he's going to win."

"Cutting the apron strings, now that he's going to be a papa," Dian said soberly. "Painful but necessary. It has to happen. Older generation. Younger generation. That baby's the next generation. It'll have to cut loose from Papa and Mama someday, too." Dian pointed to the door to her right. "I'll stop and chat with the doctor. You go on and see Carissa."

Saunder money had converted one of Ippolito's room-sized wardrobe storage areas into a small obstetrical facility. Day and night, trained med staff remote-monitored Carissa and the fetus. Todd checked to see if it was all right for him to go on into the bedroom suite. They cautioned him not to tire the expectant mother and granted permission.

Carissa was propped on mountains of pillows, as was her wont. Todd had spoken to her on the com several times the past week, and he had always seen her in pretty much the same situation—a small, pale face and figure in a huge bed, surrounded by frilly cushions and coverlets, monitor terminals and prescribed medicines cluttering the side tables and the shelf above the bed. The only thing that had changed from the last time he had spoken to her on the com was that this time she was wearing chic blue bedclothes, not green ones.

As he pulled up a chair, Carissa stretched her hands to him. "How are you?" he asked. "You look beautiful, as always." Ritual compliment, expected.

Carissa drew him forward, kissing him on the mouth. It was more than a sisterly peck. He had been through this routine before, and resisted it as he had before, acutely uncomfortable. Nothing ever came out in the open, but it had been there since Pat met Carissa three years earlier. Todd had never voiced his feelings, preferring to bury them, not wanting to create trouble. He had thought the pregnancy would eliminate that subtle seductiveness in Carissa's nature. Obviously it hadn't. When he didn't respond, she sighed and sank back on the pillows. "Oh, I'm fine. Tonics and vitamins and viral shield medications, the works."

"You have to follow orders. That's a very important little fella you're growing there," Todd said encouragingly. She was studying his face, looking worried. "I'm okay, too. Not a scratch. Honest. They dented my flier a bit, but not me."

"I'm so glad. The reports sounded awful." She was silent a moment. She *was* beautiful, more beautiful than Todd had ever seen her. Dian had referred to something called the glow of pregnancy. That must be the explanation. Carissa's pale fragility was now enhanced by a special form of new beauty. Despite all the concern for her, she didn't seem particularly sick or weak. She looked pampered and was enjoying it. But her endearing little smile was gone. "Todd, couldn't you stop them?"

The monitors at her bedside. Jael was right. Carissa had seen Pat and Jael going at it. "They won't hurt each other. It's just a lot of noise. I've been through it before."

Carissa wasn't convinced. "They cut off the signal. Pat doesn't want me to see them, to be with them . . ." Her lower lip protruded in that silly little-girl pout that was so cute. The doctors were making her a prisoner for the next six months. She had been promised a window on the world so she wouldn't miss anything. Pat had taken away her toy, not letting her participate—even if it was an ugly family fight she was missing right now.

"He just doesn't want to upset you, 'Rissa. You know you have to take things easy. They're . . ."

"Arguing over me," she finished for him. She had put her finger on the situation astutely, but her green eyes were innocently wide.

The effect was disconcerting. "Maybe I should be flattered, but I'm not. Pat's not even whoring around as much as he used to. Oh, don't look so shocked, Todd. I'm not *that* naive. But he's squabbling with Jael so much, with *everybody*. It scares me." She let go of one of Todd's hands and absently stroked her abdomen As yet, there was no visible sign of her pregnancy.

We can't see the incoming alien vehicle, either, but it's there. And this baby's going to grow up in a future that's forever changed, because of that other, as-yet-unseen newcomer.

"'Rissa, it's just that they're both under so much strain right now. They worry about you and the baby and about that campaign. Things will smooth out eventually, I'm sure of it." Todd was lying. He wasn't sure of anything any more. He had a momentary urge to ask Carissa about the Antarctic Enclave, but that was ludicrous. Aware of Pat's affairs or not, sharper than she looked or not, she wouldn't know anything about the reprogrammed computer or the missing people on Mari's list. He realized, with an inner start of surprise, that he had missed the chance to ask Jael if *she* knew anything about it. Pat was too drunk now, and he hadn't shown any guilty reaction to Todd's remark. But Todd had ridden to the terminal with Jael. He could have asked then. He hadn't. Todd examined his reasons, frightened: *Don't ask. If she refuses to answer, she reveals something by it—covering up for Pat, perhaps. Better to assume she'd react as Pat had, blankly, knowing nothing.*

Why can I seek knowledge, accepting the risks, when it comes to the alien messenger, but not when it comes to my own family?

Carissa was talking, not expecting him to answer. "I can't campaign with him until the baby's born. I hope that won't hurt his chances with the voters." She plucked at the antique, silken coverlets. "He worries so much. About that alien machine of yours . . ."

"It's not my machine, 'Rissa. I found it, that's all, like someone spotting a comet through a backyard telescope. An amateur, stumbling onto something big. But now that I *have* found it, I want to talk to it, communicate with it. That's terribly important, 'Rissa, for you and your baby, for all the other babies about to be born now and in the future. It's tomorrow."

"I . . . I'm trying to understand that. So is Pat. He really is."

Todd longed to use her as another means of communication, one that could reach Pat where he had failed. Pillow talk? He had denigrated Carissa's talent for that. But she was pregnant, and Pat obviously was very proud and possessive. There was a chance that would change things, change them around the way Todd prayed they would go. If they could just repair the breaks in the connection . . .

"Don't be angry with him, Todd," Carissa said sadly. "Jael's mad at him so much these days. And he's so afraid everyone will judge him without hearing his side of the story. Afraid they'll jump to conclusions."

"That's my situation regarding the alien messenger," Todd said, seizing on the analogy. "We shouldn't jump to conclusions about the aliens who built it. We can't even talk to that little machine yet, not really. I want to hear its makers' side of the story—just as I'd want to hear Pat's."

She stared at him a while, then said, "I'm scared." Todd started to reassure her, thinking she referred to the supposed menace of the alien vehicle. "All these bodyguards and weapons," she went on, "we've never had so many before. Jael and Pat say they want to make sure no fanatic or enemy breaks through and hurts us . . . hurts the baby." Again she stroked her abdomen, looking at nothing, plainly worrying about the dangers of being an attractive target.

Todd heard someone come in, glanced over his shoulder, and saw Dian. She smiled and greeted Carissa, standing on the other side of the big bed. Carissa nodded and continued as if there had been no interruption. "Pat said something about 'full strike and counterstrike ability.' Missiles and all that. He said I'd be safe anywhere in the Saunder empire. Isn't that a funny way of thinking of it? Empire!" She saw their shock and went on ingenuously. "Oh, yes! At Saunderhome and the Swiss estates and Manila— everywhere. Pat said it was all taken care of and I shouldn't worry about him or Jael when they're away from me on the campaign. They'll have bodyguards and armed vehicles . . ."

"Are they really in that much danger?" Todd asked weakly, exchanging a worried look with Dian. "Why do they need so *much* firepower? The Trans-Pacific war's over now. These riots aren't that much of a threat to *him*. Pat's the world's most popular politician," he finished with some bitterness.

Carissa snuggled into the pillows, smiling like a cat. "Yes, I know. He's going to win. All the predictors say so. Wouldn't it be nice if we could all be together again at Saunderhome this summer, after the baby's born? We could watch the election returns from there."

A lovely wish. Impossible. Not in that space of time. Goddard's enemies weren't going to go away. Neither was the alien messenger. All the paranoia Pat's warning speeches were causing now would still be there, probably intensified, in August and September.

" 'Rissa, would you do something for me?" Todd said suddenly. She was lightly raking her nails across his palm, but he managed to extricate his hand without being obvious. "Would you try to make Pat see that the alien messenger needn't be an enemy we have to fight? Make him understand that—"

"It's for you and your baby, Carissa," Dian chimed in. "You don't want that baby to be involved in an interstellar war, do you?"

Three years ago, Todd would have thought that argument futile, used on Carissa. He hadn't seen beyond the little-girl manners and the sweet, husky voice. Now he knew Carissa was thinking it over, comprehending more than she seemed to.

"No, of course not. No one wants that." She didn't reach for Todd's hand again, but she held him, sensing the two of them were looking for an excuse to leave. They didn't want to tire her, yet she clung to their presence. Carissa's head turned, her blond hair swirling about her shoulders. She looked at one and then the other. "You have to promise *me* something."

"If we can," Dian said, taking the words away from Todd lest he be tempted to agree to too much without knowing what the commitment involved.

"Don't judge Patrick, not without a trial. He's afraid that's what you'll do." Carissa giggled childishly. "I'll be your spy, try to make him understand about the messenger." The silliness evaporated. She was deadly serious. "And you, if I need you, you've got to help. I don't know how much longer I can keep them from . . ."

"Carissa," Todd explained carefully, "Dian and I will be in space. It's not safe for Project Search down here, and I can handle ComLink from orbit just as well as from Earth." Dian eyed him sharply, again reading things underneath the words.

The woman in the bed shrugged off his excuse. "You'll come. I know you will. You'll have to, Todd." There was a hint of desperation in her voice. Todd didn't know her nearly as well as he knew Pat, but, as he sometimes was in talking to Pat, he became convinced Carissa was sincere about this. No act. No little-girl melodramatics, "Don't judge him until you talk to him. Help me. Help me to help them."

Reluctantly, unsure if the bargain was an honest one, or if he had even a small portion of the reasons behind it, Todd took her hand once more. "I promise." Dian sucked in her breath, disapproving. "I'll come. I'll help." Todd forced a very shaky smile. "After all, as Mother always told us, we Saunders have got to stick together."

CHAPTER FIFTEEN

MASQUERADE

When they left the underground apartments, Todd turned down the guards' offer to bring him whatever vehicle he wanted as a stand-in for his damaged aircraft. Wary of any train or car that might be bugged, Todd shook his head and led Dian out of the immense structure. The guards stared after them, bewildered, unable to believe a Saunder would go out into the city on foot, without an escort.

The broad avenue north of the SE Complex was brightly lit and patrolled by CNAU Enforcement. Crowds were smaller there, now that it was past midnight. Still, the bustle of people and traffic provided a kind of haven, anonymity amid the night life. The sounds were white noise, covering conversation, letting two people talk about dangerous secrets.

Dian had been remarkably patient. Grateful for that trust, Todd let the accumulated rage and frustration boil out. Dian listened, appalled. As he detailed the suspicions and the terrible proofs, she shook with empathic anger and fought back tears. "Damn them!" she exclaimed in a whisper. "I just felt it, ever since they destroyed Project Search . . ."

"Just the offices. The project's going on," Todd insisted, his arm about her.

Dian leaned against him, still shaking. "Everything fits. I just knew it. Anatole and Gib and what they did to Beth, and now you . . ."

"No. Killing me would have been breaking their orders." Todd added grimly, "But the next time they might not be so fussy. I'm not going to give them a sitting target any more. From now on, I'm taking the initiative."

"We are," Dian corrected him. Her tone left no room for discussion. She sniffled and wiped her eyes, and asked with blunt simplicity, "How do we beat them?"

"First, I'm going to Antarctica." Street noises surged around them as Dian sucked in her breath and held it for a long moment. "They have two targets," Todd continued, "and I'm connected with both of them. They want Project Search shut up. They can't control it and it threatens Earth First's campaign. But now I've started to poke into something else—the anti-Spacer conspiracy. Somehow the SE Antarctic Enclave is critical to them. And I intend to find out what's so damned dangerous to them that they're killing people for it. The computers are rigged. They can be bypassed, but only an eyeball check is going to tell the real story. I helped Dad build that installation. I know what makes it tick. And I'm the one they made mad. I'm going."

Dian cocked her head, peering up at him. Shambling drunks and night workers hurried by them; late partygoers moved in and out of the all-night stores lining the street. Yet they were alone on an island of shared knowledge. "I guess . . . I can't talk you out of it," she said. "You're too damned stubborn."

"You ought to recognize stubborn from personal experience," Todd teased.

They strolled along side by side. Todd could almost imagine the wheels turning within Dian's quick mind. "You have a plan?" she asked. "Or are you just going to walk right into that top-security polar Enclave?"

"No. I'll have to swap idents with someone who has a clearance. And I better do it soon. The semi-annual Human Rights inspection tour takes off in less than two weeks." Todd frowned. "I thought maybe one of the maintenance staffers, coming in to relieve someone else at the station . . ."

"Uh-uh," Dian said firmly. "No good. You think anybody could slip a ringer in on ComLink and not be noticed?"

Todd thought about Gib Owens masquerading in just that way. "Probably not," he conceded unhappily. "Suggestions? You've been up to something. I hear it in the sly way you asked that."

"Yeah. Might be a way I can get you in, as a member of the tour."

Todd stopped walking, taking her by the shoulders and staring at her intently. "Who do I pay? Genuine idents? My God. That'd be worth . . . but Mari's people must have tried that."

Dian was contemptuous. "Didn't work. I checked. The Committee members are thoroughly screened." She took pity on his confusion. "Remember I said I knew people on that Committee? Well, after you and Mari kicked each other on that ride down from Geosynch last month—nagging back and forth about the Enclave—I decided to do some checking myself. Old times. Curiosity. This person I'm thinking of owes me, wants to pay. And he's the type who can't be bought. Not for money. But I think he will do it, for loyalty and for what you're digging at—and he's on the team that's heading south in February."

Todd kissed her, oblivious to their surroundings. "You're marvelous. That's the most important part of getting in there . . ."

"You can't go looking like you," Dian told him, smiling.

Todd envisioned Gib Owens's unsuccessful disguise. But Dian wasn't referring to a Scandinavian type. Her source would be a United Ghetto States citizen. "Well, rumor has it Ward's grandmother came from a good family that could trace its line back to slave days," Todd said, returning her smile. "A bit of hair dye and some darkening of the eyes . . . the genes are right."

"You're gonna get that tan you've needed, finally." She linked her arm through his and they started walking again, quickly now, almost in lock step. Dian leaned against Todd's shoulder, chuckling. "You'll look terrific."

"Fairchild. I'll contact her. I *need* contacts, and Mari said we can trust her. If we go roundabout, through some of my lesser-known subsidiaries, I think we can get the message to her without tipping our plans. And the accounts the computer wouldn't give me—got to dig those loose, somehow."

Dian jerked her chin down emphatically. "That's my field, breaking codes. I've got contacts, too. We'll take them from all sides, like they've been hitting us."

Todd flung up his arm, hailing a commercial transport approaching the corner station nearby. He hurried Dian forward as the driver opened the doors for them. "Right now, we get to one of ComLink's airparks and pick up a flier. I made a big public announcement this afternoon. Tomorrow we're going to be on that shuttle, heading for orbit. And we've got an awful lot to do before that ship lifts."

Dian dropped back into the seat, catching her breath as Todd relayed their destination to the driver. They felt the acceleration when the transport hummed up to full speed. The driver was pushing it, noting Todd's ident and thinking that pleasing a Saunder with his service would be good for a nice bonus. Dian indicated the chronometer on the control panel. "Today. We've already started on a new twenty-four-hours."

Todd set his jaw, his mind racing, plotting an incredibly busy—and dangerous—schedule. "Today. And we've already used up an hour of it."

The remaining hours before liftoff were nerve-racking. Before they were through, he and Dian were both running on adrenaline. If they had been able to make direct contact to call in the debts and obligations they needed, things would have been easy. But they couldn't collect those debts openly. They had to resort to dodges, intermediaries, innocent-sounding inquiries, running, burning the com circuits raw, both of them aware of a deadline in the very real sense of the term.

Neither one got any sleep until they lifted ship that evening. It was a positive relief to be cut off from a telecom or—for a while—any need to watch one's words and veil one's meaning in codes. Todd closed his eyes, almost relishing the dynamic pressures of lower launch stages, and free fall sent him off into much-needed dreaming.

It didn't last. An attendant woke him barely two hours into the flight. Message. Dian roused, peered across from the couch next to Todd's, apprehension visible in her face, Warily, Todd cued the individual monitor in front of his flight couch. Printout. No voice. That was unusual. The message was even more unusual. Put to anyone save himself and Dian, it would have seemed quite ordinary:

URGENT. TODD SAUNDER. ANOMALY REGISTERING AT COM-
LINK TRANSLATOR SAT FOURTEEN. NEED IMMEDIATE EX-
ECUTIVE JUDGMENT WHETHER SCRAP OR RESTORE. WILL
AWAIT YOUR ORDERS. SIGNED: COMLINK MELBOURNE.

Melbourne ComLink division was a sales and entertainment
office. It wouldn't send a message regarding a glitch in one of
Todd's remote satellites.

But Fairchild's secret network *had* received a message and sent
him an answer:

YES. GO ABOUT YOUR BUSINESS, PER OUR INSTRUCTIONS. WE
WILL CONTACT YOU.

Dian's eyes glowed with relief. Todd faked a yawn, canceling
the printout. The attendant glanced at him, and Todd shrugged.
"Not really important. Some techs get excited easily." The man
smiled sympathetically. Todd let himself float once more, daring
to build his courage. He and Dian had sent out the bills—and the
payments were already starting to come in!

They couldn't head directly for the isolated satellite. There
were things that had to be done at Geosynch, and loyal staffers
Todd had to take into his confidence. He and Dian agreed on
which people were solid. No arguments. There weren't many of
them, but they were absolutely essential. The world had to be
convinced that Todd Saunder and Dian Foix were in orbit, busy
reconstructing the shattered pieces of Project Search, preparing to
renew contact with the alien messenger.

That *was* going on. So were certain secret hologrammatic
recording sessions and coded exchanges with certain people
planetside and at other orbiting locations.

Then, all too soon, with too little rest to sustain them, Todd
and Dian boarded one of ComLink's tiny maintenance shuttles
and went off on an "inspection" orbit, checking various translator-splitter sections of the network. They reached Relay Fourteen
six hours later.

For a while, they thought the wires had been crossed, that they
had come to a rendezvous with no one to meet them. And for
several bad minutes Todd feared that they had been tricked, that

maybe the enemy had penetrated the codes and the message hadn't been from Fairchild's people after all.

Then the little station's short-range com came alive abruptly. "Permission to come aboard, Mr. Saunder?"

No preliminaries at all. Startled, Todd checked the nav screens. They said there was nothing outside for thousands of kilometers in all directions. The voice signal, though, was on docking vector, closing very fast.

"Military," Todd declared, putting the obvious together. Dian looked wary. "They're masked against detection," he said. "We can't see them. Wouldn't hear them unless they opened their scramblers. At this range, nobody else will pick up that signal, either. That's impressive hardware. Must be brass, to have that on his ship. Mari *said* some of Goddard's potential allies held very important positions on Earth." He leaned toward the com. "Come aboard."

Final approach, docking—all very smooth, and accomplished with an invisible ship. Not until the air lock cycled and a man stepped through the port did the person behind the mysterious voice become real.

"I—I know you," Dian blurted as the black man removed his helmet.

"So do I," Todd said. He laughed sheepishly. "General Ames. I thought you were on the other side. When I saw you at the science press conference, I figured you were spying on me, maybe had even ordered up the firebombing and those pilots later on."

Ames seemed bemused. "That's good. Keep thinking like that, for public consumption. Supports my image as a hard liner." He anchored himself amid some empty webbing, as at home in space as he was giving orders at Protectors of Earth Enforcement HQ. This man *was* big brass, commanding thousands of troops.

"And you're not a hard liner?" Dian asked suspiciously.

"No. If I were," Ames said without resentment, "I would have blown you out of space, knowing what I do about your adventure with a scrambler lock and your overhearing those assassins. And the fact that you've gotten hold of one Ed Lutz planetside, who happens to be a member of the P.O.E. Human Rights Committee assigned to inspect SE Antarctic Enclave. You need a doctor with the ability to alter ident handprints, hair texture, skin coloring, and eyes. You need top-secret, non-detectable transport back to Earth in order to link up with Lutz and switch places with him before the inspection tour. Have I got it correct?"

Todd sagged in his webbing despite the lack of gravity. "You didn't get all of that from . . ."

"Fairchild? Not entirely. I have my sources. And incidentally, I made sure the 'other side,' as you put it, *didn't* get those sources." Ames had honed all of his original accent out of his voice. Like the assassins, he spoke telecomese, uninflected English. But there was something in the way he had said that last that chilled Todd.

"I . . . I don't want anyone else to die," Todd said weakly.

"Who said anyone died?" Todd couldn't read that black face and was afraid to press Ames on the matter. The man's tone didn't change, but there was even more steel under the words. "You'd better trust me, Mr. Saunder. I'd say time was of the essence in this case. You want the doctor? You want the transport Earthside when he's done his job? Yes or no?"

"I didn't expect . . ."

For the first time, Ames smiled. It was a charming smile, if you didn't look at his eyes. "Didn't expect such fast service? Fairchild's agents have their own timetable, and it's crowding me. I can't spend much time up here, either. I've got places planetside I have to be seen. Frankly, Mr. Saunder, I don't approve of this whole thing. It's not a civilian's line of expertise. If it weren't for Fairchild's asking me . . . I don't know why the hell you're doing this yourself instead of letting one of your subordinates try the infiltration."

Todd met the dark gaze levelly. "Why are *you* here, General? You say it's risky for you to be away from Earth right now. Why didn't *you* delegate this mission? If you want a job done right . . . and besides, I've got the motivation, more than any of my subordinates will ever have."

For a tense moment, the men stared at each other. Finally Ames nodded. "Okay. Let's move. Give me your specs, and I'll have what you need. There's a doctor who can do what you want, as long as he gets a sanctuary in space until this current mess settles down. Agreed? We'll work out something for Dr. Foix's friend Lutz, too, if necessary. We don't always succeed, but we *try* to take care of our people." He paused and shot a warning glance at Dian. "But once he leaves for Antarctica, he's on his own."

Dian sought to hide her fear. "She knows that," Todd said with some heat. "I won't have it any other way. I may not be as much of an amateur as you think I am, General. Or maybe I am, if I'm trusting you."

Ames sighed and gave up. There would be no more warnings. "Okay, Mr. Saunder. As of now, we're in business together—trying to save what's left of that planet before it disintegrates."

The next six days were even more hectic than the preceding ones. Ames came through, the doctor he delivered to orbit protested that surgery in free fall had *not* been part of his training. But after the initial protest, he went ahead brilliantly, so brilliantly Todd wondered where an honest physician would learn such a trade. The mela-tabs that darkened Todd's reshaped face and altered handprints as well as the rest of his skin were a wealthy-class fad to produce quick-tanning and pseudo-Negroid coloration. They were also supposedly employed by criminals and espionage agents who could afford the expensive treatments. Handprint alteration, of course, was illegal in every nation on Earth. The ident system would be useless if the technique became generally available. Dr. Tedesco also had the medications and equipment to kink and dye Todd's hair, as well as to change the color of his irises to a Negroid brown. When the doctor was finished, the face looking back at Todd from the mirror was virtually unrecognizable. The shock was bearable when he reminded himself that the changes were temporary. Besides, it was all in a very good cause. A life-and-death cause. Life and death for Earth and *Homo sapiens* . . . and for Todd Saunder.

He owed a lot of people before the six days were done. Ames, Fairchild, and many more whose names he wouldn't be told, not if they all wanted to survive. But if what he was going to attempt pulled Earth out of its current nightmare, that ought to even the ledgers. Then . . . it was time to go. Time to pay the bills.

He and Dian went planetside on board a fully masked and scrambler-concealed military vessel, landed at a secret port in the Mediterranean, hopping westward by a complex pre-planned route toward the Central North American Union. Had Gib Owens followed this same course, thinking it would hide him?

Todd thrust his qualms aside. The decision had been made. Time to carry it out. They entered Dian's old territory. She became Todd's guide, leading him through the maze of a mid-continent boom town to a ramshackle train station. They mingled with the crowds and headed north toward the United Ghetto States. The train was a filthy and smelly disaster, the tracks dangerous. The company that owned the line was corrupt. That was one more item on a long list of projects Pat had promised to do something about, once he got the Chairmanship.

Todd stared out at dismal scenery as the train crossed the Illinois plains. The landscape would have been depressing even had it not been winter. The outlands of much of the continent were factory farms or owned by the Old Earth religious factions, and in this season all the area was frozen and barren. No one got off at any of the little way stations en route, and the engineer put on reckless speed to avoid being stopped. A year ago, in a notorious incident, a unit of the Old Earth evangelical army had commandeered a train at one of these villages and executed the passengers and crew as "demons who put a curse on our land." The only safe way to get through this region without taking to the air was to move as fast as possible and stop for nothing.

Most of the passengers were heading north for the mid-winter holiday break. They were construction techs or service workers catering to that industry. A lot of rebuilding was underway along the northeastern shores of Lake New Madrid. Civilization encroaching again, now that the earthquake's map making was finished. The fact that so many people had sought work at such a distance from their United Ghetto States didn't say much for the economic picture in those enclaves. But the economic picture wasn't exactly rosy in the Central North American Union, come to that; it was just a little better than in the U.G.S.

Todd was thoroughly inside his disguise, looking like any other nondescript black man riding the train. Dian's prettiness was hidden by a straggly wig and makeup. Nobody paid them any attention. At journey's end, they piled out of the train, moving with the throng, just two more work-weary people coming home. The roof of the big antique train depot had been blown away in the Chaos wars. As a result, the concourse was dotted with little drifts of snow that fell from the cracked ceiling. Todd kicked through a pile of the stuff, thinking that snow must mean the climate was shifting once more. Enough winter precipitation could nourish the spring crops. Maybe U.G.S. and CNAU would have enough food for everyone, for a change, this year.

The old depot was well east of the crater towns where Todd had grown up. Dian showed him the way through Chicago's confusing streets. Some sections were nothing but rubble left over from the Chaos. Others bloomed with new construction, rivaling any of the showcase areas in the East and along the Gulf Coast. In general, though, employment was far below P.O.E.'s global target of fifty percent, and the condition of the city and its people was evidence of slow growth and poverty. They boarded a motorized skid carrier and rode in the open, enduring wind and pellet snow, until they reached Lutz's section of town. After leaving the municipal transport, it was a five-block walk. Todd wasn't sure his feet were still attached to his legs by the time they reached the security fence of Lutz's apartment building.

This would be the first real test of Dr. Tedesco's talents. Todd pulled off his glove and pressed his right hand against the ident plate. The whorls and indentations on the skin were no longer his, if the surgery proved out. The system was programmed to recognize only legitimate building occupants. It read the print as Ed Lutz's, lit up promptly, and opened the gate. Letting out his breath, Todd escorted Dian inside.

They climbed the stairs to the third story and used the key Lutz had smuggled to Dian by a very roundabout courier route. They tried to look as if they belonged in this place as they hurried on in. The moment they did, Ed Lutz closed and locked the door behind them.

Todd looked at the man curiously. He couldn't say he was exactly seeing himself. He hadn't been born with brown skin, kinky reddish black hair, or brown eyes. Yet the features were remarkably similar, just as Dian had said they would be. The holo-mode the doctor had worked from hadn't quite shown the man himself. Now Todd could make real-life comparisons. In many ways, the resemblances were superficial. Yet it was a very good match. Ed Lutz didn't have any strong facial characteristics. Like Todd Saunder, he was the type other people tended to take for granted, visually.

"Man, you *do* look like me," Ed Lutz marveled. His accent wasn't too heavy. That was another bonus. Todd had ingested hyperendors to enhance his memory, and he had been copying Lutz's voice patterns off a tape Dian had acquired. It was a relief that he needn't worry about duplicating a thick United Ghetto States inflection. "Dian claimed we could be related," Lutz said, "but I thought you'd look more like your brother."

"I should be so fortunate," Todd replied with a chuckle. "If I did, maybe this job would be simpler."

Lutz shook his head. "Uh-uh! Can't get in without idents. And your brother, rich as he is, can't buy 'em."

"But we can be given them, for old times' sake, huh?" Dian peeled off her ugly wig. "How are you, Ed?"

"I'm here. And I wouldn't be, if it wasn't for your grandma."

Guilt was eating at Dian, guilt that she was involving an old friend in such danger. "Ed, you know you don't have to do this. You can still back out even now. They've already killed people."

"Yeah, so you told me." Lutz was angry. "Firebombs. Crashing planes. Mean stuff. That's why I *want* to help. I never came out much, politics style. But that's damn wrong. Made up my mind for me." He moved to a dispenser and drew them three cups of caffa liquid. Todd sipped greedily at the hot stimulant.

"You'll lose your Human Rights Committee credentials for helping us. And whoever's trying to wreck Project Search and Goddard Colony will want to hurt you, too, Ed," Dian warned.

Across the room, on a muted vid monitor, Fairchild was making a speech. Not her usual campaign speech. She had all but withdrawn from the race and was throwing the full force of her Third Millennium Movement into an effort to counteract the anti-Spacer and anti-alien propaganda. Todd hoped someone besides Ed Lutz was listening to her.

Things were getting worse around the world, and the descent into insanity seemed to be increasing exponentially. ComLink had been lucky. No further incidents since the firebombing and the attempted assassination. No need. Todd had supposedly removed himself from Earth, run away. One enemy they had sent crawling. Now they were going after others—and they were beginning to confuse friend and foe. The fanatics were, in effect, attacking each other, like a family tearing itself apart. While Todd and

Dian were dropping down from space, getting back in this arena
called a planet, somebody had blown up one of Nakamura's subsidiaries, a key power station in the Asian energy network.
Nakamura was Todd's competitor, an anti-Spacer. But they had
attacked him, anyway. Thousands of people had frozen to death
in the North Sino regions and Japan when Nakamura's station
went. Normal logic wouldn't work against people who could do
things like that.

Dian and Ed began reminiscing about the bad old days. "I
been tryin' to repay you for years," he said. "Told you last summer, huh? Sent you that note. Didn't really expect to have anything you could use, though. You want to get to the Enclave, you
will. Hadn't been for Wyoma Lee, I'd have died from that bullet
wound. She sure saved my life, and a hell of a lot of others. Besides, it's time for me to move on, I think. I kinda like that offer
of yours, Mr. Saunder. 'Bout a job and a place to hide out until
all this gets straightened out."

"Guaranteed," Todd assured him. "The pro-Spacers promise
they'll do their damnedest to protect you. Arrange a new identity
for a while. ComLink's a big enough outfit for you to get lost in.
Besides, I can always use a top computer tech. You might have to
spend some time in a backwater office or an oceanic rectenna station, temporarily . . ."

Lutz laughed. "Won't bother me. I travel light. Might even get
me a trip into space, huh? Never been there, but I'd like to go."
He was a few years older than Todd, a man Earth-bound by economics and circumstances, yet not afraid of the world beyond the
sky as so many planetsiders were.

"Free fall's tricky," Dian warned him, smiling.

"I got a strong stomach. Hey! You sure are beginnin' to look
like Wyoma Lee, know that? Sound like her, too. You were just a
dirty-faced kid last time I saw you. Wyoma was about to send
you off to school, get you smart and out of this mess. Did, too,
from what I see on the vid. *Doctor* Foix! Wyoma would be proud
as hell. Doin' you and your man this turn is payin' Wyoma back,
just a little. Debt I've had on my mind a long time. May she rest
easy."

He spoke out of grim times. Todd's own memories of the
Chicago crater towns and the brushfire wars of the Teens had left

nightmares which still haunted him. The three of them had made it out of that environment, by different methods. Now terrible events were bringing them together again in the same area.

The black man drained his cup. "Somethin's not right, down in that Enclave. Truth is, Mr. Saunder, me and a lot of other people who go on the tour been wondering 'bout things. But we're just li'l-bitty fish. We know the rules: Keep your mouth shut and sign here. I went on the first tour and a coupla others, these past five years." He offered Dian and Todd refills on their caffa, then looked intently at Todd. "You're a big fish, Mr. Saunder. A mighty big fish. You sure you want to do somethin' like this?" General Ames's pointed question, more politely phrased.

Todd felt Dian's scrutiny and replied with a nervous laugh. "There have been times, this past week, when I've asked myself that. I *have* to, Ed."

Lutz nodded. "Yeah. I guess I do, too. You know, Wyoma Lee ain't in the Enclave. Maybe that's why *I* have to, Mr. Saunder. There's other things movin' me this way, but that's an important one. I got my idents ready for you. And I checked to be sure—nobody's going on this tour who knows me. But I got to tell you, you won't see nothin', just monitors showin' the frozen people. The Committee big shots ask a bunch of stupid questions, same stupid questions every tour, far's I can figure out, and the top techs grin and answer them . . . same stupid answers every time, too . . . and then we catch the next flight north outa that oversized snowdrift. Can't see that we're doin' any good."

"Didn't they take you down onto the preservement floor at all?" Todd asked.

"Nah. They say we'll melt the bodies if we do that."

Todd smiled. "You won't. The setup's too well built to be bothered by the small amount of body heat a tour group emits, even if you weren't wearing insu-suits." Ed Lutz looked utterly blank. "The self-contained insu-suit," Todd explained, "is what you wear to go into the preservement area so you won't get cold or leak any body heat and strain the cooling mechanisms. They don't use those on the tours?" Lutz slowly shook his head. Obviously he had never seen or worn the equipment. Todd weighed that fact. "Interesting. I wonder why. Something else to investigate. Sounds like the Committee hasn't got the faintest idea how

my father's cryogenics systems operate. They *should*. The big
shots are supposed to be instructed in—"

An unpleasant thought struck Todd forcibly. Collusion?
Payoffs? How high did this conspiracy run? The black man's
speculations seemed to be going in the same direction. "Maybe
they've got all the same tricky ins and outs the Spacers have,
huh? These people been carrying messages back and forth these
past few days, settin' up this deal between us, Mr. Saunder.
They're efficient. Scary the way they can do things and show up
when you least expect 'em." He read the apprehension in Dian's
expression. "They already tried to shoot you down once, Mr.
Saunder. How you know they won't catch you this time and stuff
you in one of those boxes and freeze you?"

Todd wouldn't let Dian voice her second to that worry. He
forced a grin and replied with more confidence than he felt. "Because as far as they're concerned, I'm not going to be in Antarctica. Todd Saunder is in space, at Geosynch orbit. So's Dian. I'm
cruising around, minding my corporation's business, out of everyone's hair. The last place they'll look for me is on the tour of the
Enclave."

Bewildered, Lutz asked, "And what are you goin' to do when
you get there?"

"See what changes they've made, if any. They've made some,
or you'd know about insu-suits, just for starters."

"Todd helped build the Enclave, Ed," Dian told him. "He
knows more about the equipment and the way it functions than
the Committee does, maybe even more than the Enclave techs do.
He even knows how to get around the security systems."

"If they didn't alter those to serve some nefarious purpose,"
Todd added sourly.

Lutz sighed. "I hope you find whatever it is—and stop all this
meanness. It's just gettin' damned bad. Better stop it." He tried to
put a bright face on the situation. "Way these Spacers been doin'
things, getting this all ready for you, it ought to work. You're me
now." Again he stared admiringly at Todd's disguised face, then
looked at his own hand and at the clever bioelectrical-embedded
prosthetic handprints Todd now wore.

"He'll do," Dian said. Like Todd, she was trying to project
more assurance than she felt. "I noticed the resemblance between

the two of you when I first met Todd. But it never seemed important. Until this stuff about the Enclave came up. Then I remembered your note, and seeing your name on the Human Rights list."

"*My* name," Todd reminded her with a sly grin. "*Ed Lutz*." He examined his palms, hoping. The tissue implant, like his artificially darkened skin and irises, should last at least a week—long enough, if all went well. "The blood type's a good match, fortunately. But if they start taking DNA samples, I'm in trouble. Dian and I worked out a scheme to get around that, too. It isn't just the espionage experts who've contacted you who've been busy, Ed. I've made my own plans. Don't worry. If the disguise doesn't work, Dr. Tedesco promised he'd refund my money."

The joke fell flat. Ed didn't get it, and Dian didn't think it was funny, not considering the risk involved. Todd hurried on to business. "How long before you're due at the Committee rendezvous in Buenos Aires?"

Lutz glanced at a chronometer. His notification printout from P.O.E. was propped alongside the timepiece as a reminder. "About thirty-six hours."

"And your job leave is cleared?"

"Yeah. Boss likes the funds P.O.E. grants him for letting me take the tour. Civic contribution, you know? I don't get paid enough, anyway, and then he gets the bonus because I'm volunteering to freeze my balls off. I'll be glad to be shut of him and the job. I been a model citizen, playin' the big shots' game too many years. And if you'll take me on without references . . ."

"Dian's your reference," Todd said earnestly. "I'd never argue with *that*. Now we'd better get started. I want to fine-polish your speech and body movement patterns until I can pass for you."

Dian and Ed Lutz laughed. Todd was mystified until Dian explained. "That's a very old term, historical. Wyoma Lee said *her* mother remembered some black people trying to pass for white. They felt they had to do that to get away from prejudice and have a chance at the so-called good life." She and Lutz looked at each other and laughed louder.

"And you're doin' the passin', this time, so you can freeze your balls off instead of me!" Lutz exclaimed, doubling over and slapping his thighs in merriment.

Unoffended, Todd grinned. "Oh, I don't intend to freeze. Just find out if some other people really *are* frozen." He didn't elaborate further. He got busy with his final homework. Dian had briefed him as well as she could, and he had used Lutz's holographic image as a model. This was his last chance to perfect his role before he had to play it in front of a potentially hostile audience. Dian acted as judge, or as director, of the rehearsal. Todd aped Lutz's mannerisms until fatigue forced him to nap. Then he woke and went at it again.

After one last run-through, Dian declared Todd ready. "I'd better be." Todd adopted his version of Lutz's voice and accent. From the other man's startled expression, he knew the imitation was a good one. "Good's I'm goin' to get."

"Oh, I wouldn't say that, lover," Dian returned slyly. "I've got lots more to teach you. But not here. You just be sure you're on that plane when it comes back north."

Todd was wearing some of Lutz's clothes, carrying others in the case he would take with him. He couldn't give himself away by even the slightest slip, such as a garment that might belong to Todd Saunder, but never to a comp tech from the United Ghetto States. Todd waited patiently while Dian reassembled her own disguise, converting herself into Ed Lutz's new sexual interest. Lutz put on his own coat. They would leave the apartment, by a different exit, at the same time Todd headed for the shuttleport to start his trip.

"*Sure* they won't miss you and come huntin'?" Lutz asked again, more concerned for his surrogate's safety than for his own.

"Sure. For the next week, if anyone calls me in orbit, they'll get a very messy holo-mode image of me saying I can't hear them, can't clear up the transmission, and maybe we'd better make connections later. That happens often enough on other telecom systems. And some of my satellites *are* past due for maintenance checks," Todd said, winking at Dian. Then he pointed at Lutz and returned the man's concern. "When I leave here, you disappear. Dian will show you how and where."

Dian made a face at him. "You take care of you. I'll take care of Ed and me." Then, as Todd turned toward the door, she came close, speaking intimately. "You *do* take care. Hey, and you stay away from those sperm and tissue banks down there. I don't intend to have your precious assets wasted away on anyone but me," she finished, attempting to lighten the mood.

"I'm already on file in the Enclave," Todd told her with amusement. "So are you. Our immortality is secure." His grin slid off, doubts resurfacing. "I think. At least that's what I'm going to find out."

Lutz eyed them with mixed fondness and curiosity. But he didn't ask questions. Dian had promised that was one of Lutz's admirable points. Yet Todd felt he could read the black man's thoughts. He must be wondering about a lot of things. The news about the unsuccessful attack on Todd's flier had been snapped up by Saunder Enterprises' competitors with more than a little malicious glee. One of the arrogant Saunder clan, nearly brought to grief. Speculations had buzzed. Nobody but Todd and Dian—and Ames—knew about the exchange he had overheard between the two pilots. As far as CNAU Enforcement was concerned, the pilots were dead. Todd realized that concealing the overheard conversation would hamper any investigation Enforcement could make, but he wasn't willing to trust them—to trust *anyone* very much now.

Seabed rescue units had abandoned their efforts to recover wreckage or parts of bodies from the African plane crash. They would never find anything there, any more than Enforcement's investigators would make anything out of those phony, sacrificed dead "pilots" and the phony planes. Gib Owens's memorial would have to depend on what Todd Saunder discovered in Antarctica—and what he did with the information he happened to find.

Intercontinental connections went just as smoothly as Todd had hoped. He pretended to doze during the flights from Chicago to Orleans Terminal and through the long Sur Atlantique flight. When he arrived in Buenos Aires, the rendezvous time was still more than twelve hours away, per the Human Rights Committee's plan. It recommended the tour members use pre-departure time to sleep and adjust to time-zone changes. Todd did just that, blending in with the local scenery and continuing to rerun his memories of SE Antarctic Enclave, boning up as thoroughly as he could. He had picked his own brains and every available file since he had left SE Mainland HQ in New York-Philly a week ago. He

and Dian had staged a convincing departure for Geosynch HQ
and made plans. It had been an exceedingly busy eight days.
They had barely had time to contact Ed Lutz and learn if he
would agree to the wild scheme, and to find the doctor to convert
Todd into the man he would stand in for. He didn't dare sleep or
relax too much. He had planned as carefully as possible, but the
chance of a glitch was appallingly high.

A familiarization meeting in P.O.E. Assembly Hall at the terminal was scheduled just before departure. Again Todd had surprisingly little difficulty losing himself in the crowd. "Ed Lutz"
was one of forty citizens, computer-selected to be honest and un-
biased, a sampling of observers from around the world. Tour
guides passed out mini translator-splitters to those who didn't
speak English or Argentine Spanish. Holo-mode presentations,
very simplified ones, told the tour members what they would be
seeing once they arrived at the Enclave. The ten big shots, as Ed
Lutz had tipped Todd, were the only semi-permanent members of
the Committee. They held the indoctrinators' fawning attention,
and they did nearly all the talking and questioning for the entire
group, suppressing any attempts by the "little fish" to assert themselves. The Committee pecking order was being firmly established
before anyone got any pushy ideas.

At the boarding gates, Todd went through the ident check—
palm and finger prints, full comp scan. The Enclave personnel assigned to screen the fifty Committee members waved him past
without a second glance. Todd held his breath as he walked
through the tunnel, half expecting to be called back. Nobody
stopped him. They had triplechecked the idents' authenticity, but
had taken *him* for granted.

He was relieved, and surprised, hardly daring to believe the
masquerade would work that well. Dissidents' and criminals' relatives had tried to bribe Committee members and Enclave personnel in the past, wanting to smuggle themselves south to see their
imprisoned loved ones. None had succeeded. According to the
records, Enclave security was reputedly the best in the world.
Mari and Kevin said their agents hadn't been able to get through.
Yet they hadn't spotted a bogus Ed Lutz. Had none of the other
attempts involved this form of disguise?

Maybe. And maybe he was reaping benefits from a lifelong sit-

uation. Pat had adopted one of Ward's epithets and flung it at his
bodyguards—"wallpaper people." Ward had told them that
phrase when they were kids, then had to explain what "wallpaper" was, and why some people were fated to forever melt into
the stuff: ordinary, physically unremarkable, unmemorable people.

Like Ed Lutz. Or like Todd Saunder. Never in his life had
Todd been so grateful to be a "wallpaper" person. He had
gambled on the fact of his paternal grandmother's having come
out of the Chicago ghettos during the last century, thinking that
would give him a genetic advantage in impersonating Ed Lutz.
But now it appeared it was important to have an undistinguished,
common-man look.

Whatever it took, to get the job done and to survive.

The takeoff was routine. Everyone tried to relax for the first leg
of the trip, the jump to Marambio in Antarctica. Two of Todd's
seat neighbors were Committee members from the Maui-Andean
Democracies and Nippon-Malaysia. The hard-won truce held, but
the two former enemies were stiff with each other, making group
socializing difficult. Todd hoped their hostility would keep the
rest of the passengers nearby preoccupied and further dampen
any curiosity about "Ed Lutz."

A badly garbled announcement came over the com, and smeary
lettering formed on the view screen at the front of the cabin.
Todd scowled at the poor workmanship. Around him, other techs
echoed his sentiments. "They should endeavor to put their equipment in proper order," a Sino Committeeman said in carefully
correct English.

A European chuckled. "We'd do it for them if they'd pay
us . . ."

"I hope they provide warm meals this time. Soon enough to be
cold." The speaker looked like a Polynesian, and Todd smiled at
him sympathetically. He himself wasn't looking forward to the
climate, summer at the pole or not.

Some people cracked jokes, trying to ease the mood of a serious mission. The Committee members wouldn't be here if they
hadn't volunteered out of civic pride for the honor tendered them,
as Ed Lutz had. But their attitude toward Antarctica and SE
Enclave was mired in apprehension and distaste. The world now

accepted the need for the Enclave, to preserve life and to relieve the collapsing capital punishment system. Still, members tried to laugh away the plane ride and the knowledge about where they were going.

In retrospect, SE Antarctic Enclave was a radical concept. It had looked, for years, as if Ward Saunder would never win permission to carry it through. Even after the successful cryo revival of a volunteer, even with the critical loss of lives during the Death Years and the Chaos, mankind had balked. Ironically, it hadn't been the threat of more human deaths which had swung the vote in Protectors of Earth's Supreme Council. It had been the extinction of the wild elephants. Science confirmed, in late 2028, that there were no more wild elephants anywhere on Earth. Nor were there any rhinos, big cats, or giraffes. The whales, the Global Science Council decided, had come through centuries of slaughter and toxic pollutants and probably would make it, just barely. But the other exotic wild creatures which had colored man's wonder and imagination for hundreds of generations were forever gone. The elephant, especially, had provided a rallying symbol for the Cryo Preservement Movement supporting Ward Saunder's plan to build the Enclave. The powerful beast, the epitome of strength—and man had managed to wipe it out in its natural form. That had happened to thousands of species on Earth, to millions, but never with the impact of the elephant's extinction. Somehow, that had triggered the change. Votes fell on Cryo Preservement's side. Antarctic land was donated. Treaty arrangements were made. The Human Rights Committee's watchdog system was established. The vanished elephant had made it possible to preserve the seeds of *Homo sapiens* and some of the species' bodies, hedging against the future. Man had realized, nearly too late, that he, too, could disappear and leave little trace that he had ever been on Earth.

What the alien messenger "movement" needs is a poignant symbol, something to reach the heart of mankind and convert its opinion . . .

Todd alternately checked the view out the window and on the cabin's courtesy vid screens. They soared south over Mar del Plata and the island dots that used to be the Falklands, now called Southern Pacific Neutality Point Five. Within the plane, the ambient temperature was a comfortable twenty-five. The ocean was still fluid below them. But on the distant horizon, a white continental mass was already visible. The sight chilled the otherwise cheerful group.

"Getting cold," someone complained. That wasn't true, but the comment brought general agreement. The effect was psychological, and it seemed to grow chillier, the farther south they went.

"I wish I'd been tapped for the October tour," another passenger grumbled. "It wouldn't have been so cold, then, when I got home. They say it's summer here now."

Skeptical laughter rang out. Again the complainer had been correct. But people huddled in their seats and put on their coats, fighting off an iciness that wasn't there. With morbid interest, they watched the changing scene outside. The courtesy screens gave them the pilots' view, a more complete look than peering out the window afforded. Monitor arrows showed a landmark to the west.

The readout, in several languages, told the shivering Committee members that they were passing the Strait of Magellan and Cape Horn. There was little to see in that direction, even in computer-enhanced form. The gloomy Strait soon fell behind, and other views showed them the glaciated continent with its outlying archipelago.

They took the sixtieth parallel in, the route Saunder Enterprises' supply shuttles used to fly when Ward was building the Enclave. That meant the pilots would have to adjust their course east soon, if they intended to make landfall at Marambio for transfer to the Enclave shuttle. Even as he thought that, Todd felt a subtle seat-of-the-pants alteration in their movement.

The courtesy screens showed intermittent clouds and sea-level storms. There was one clear patch, where they could see tabular iceberg tows going along the Drake Passage. Daredevil rigger ships herded floating freshwater storehouses. The Indus and Sahel contracts paid well, well enough to tempt men to risk their lives towing the bergs to warmer regions. Horrendous winds rushed the coast and beyond, seeming to engulf the ships and icebergs. The plane flew on and the clouds closed over the scene below, leaving the fate of the riggers in mystery. The passengers could only hope that they all rode out the sudden storm in safety.

Plane travel in Antarctica could be dangerous, too, as Todd well knew. This was a time when ignorance would have been bliss. There were far too many accounts—and he had read most of them!—of whiteouts and katabatic winds which bred impassable blizzards, confusing and blinding pilots. Planes had crashed on Antarctica's lonely peaks and volcanoes, in areas so remote the bodies had never been recovered. They had become part of the continent, locked in the ice, but, unlike the occupants of the Enclave, past all hope of revival.

Saunder Enterprises Antarctic Enclave was located in the heart of the vast, unforgiving land, very near a place once named the "Pole of Inaccessibility." If they went down there, anywhere but right on top of the base, it would be the same for them as it had been for the earlier airborne travelers lost in the South Pole's merciless reaches.

And the same as it had been for Gib Owens, hitting the ocean at Mach 5.

CHAPTER SIXTEEN

☆☆☆☆☆☆☆☆☆

FROZEN SANCTUARY

TODD tensed as the pilot completed the vector change and pushed them over in his descent. There was nothing at all to see outside now. Sweeping snow and clouds obliterated the polar landscape. He wished the pilots would throw up their readings on the screen, even if he was meters away from the controls. But he couldn't express that wish, not out loud. Ed Lutz was a comp tech, not an accomplished amateur pilot. In theory, the readings wouldn't mean a thing to the man Todd Saunder was pretending to be.

Despite his habitual worry during a landing, there were no problems at all. He had endured worse touchdowns under far better weather conditions.

There was a delay. For several long, upsetting minutes, they sat, uninformed and building grim fantasies in their minds. Todd had been through that, too, and always resented it. After, in his estimation, far too long a wait, an attendant emerged from his cubicle, told them to deplane, and ushered them to a lounge. Station personnel said the outlook was good. The freak storm was blowing itself out quickly. Passengers stood around, staring at the station view screens, watching gravity-driven winds sucking polar air and snow off the glacier and seaward. Sastrugi, rock-hard sculptured waves of ice-snow, formed a white ocean around the station. Some blizzards could bottle up a station for days or weeks. Todd hoped this wasn't one of them. No one wanted to talk

much, and no one wanted to go outside and take a look at the
"real" Antarctica. Some people were grumpy, not yet adjusted to
the time changes. Nearly all of them were showing some stress
after an hour's flying in bad weather.

But barely two hours later, they were told to board the Enclave
shuttle. It was a smaller ship than the wheeled aircraft that had
carried them from South America, but far more modern and better equipped. This shuttle was designed to take a lot of polar
weather and could land on the glacier itself. Todd felt a lot more
confident riding this bird. But he feigned uneasiness like the rest
of the lower echelons, fussing with his safety belt and so on, listening closely to the attendants' instructions on crash procedures.
He knew there had never been a crash on the Enclave run. But
precautions were heeded far more closely now than earlier, simply because of the daunting terrain.

They were airborne again. No viewplate this time.

They ascended steadily. Antarctica was a high continent, the
highest on Earth, thanks to thousands of meters of ice. And SE
Antarctic Enclave was carved into the loftiest plateau of this frozen land.

Finally, descending, at a very gradual rate. Todd squirmed with
impatience. More tests coming up, of his disguise and of his
suspicions.

They bumped along on the skis with minimal discomfort and
came to a full stop. They waited. Then, very slowly, they moved
forward. Todd heard a faint squeaking across the snow, extremely
cold and packed snow, and air temperatures to match.

Some blasé passengers had dozed during the flight. Others had
read their instructional packages again. Todd hadn't felt the need,
not of such basic material as that; the hyperendor medication had
put his mental faculties and memories into high gear, long enough
to last out this venture. Enclave attendants moved among the passengers, helping those who had translators to adjust them for op-
timum effect. The ranking attendant addressed the Committee via
her jewel pendant throat mike, another one of ComLink's handy
devices, and another of Ward Saunder's patent spinoffs.

"Ladies and gentlemen of the Committee, we have arrived at
Saunder Enterprises Antarctic Enclave. Please remain seated until
we descend to docking level . . ."

On cue, the ship started to drop, very slowly. They had been sitting on a parking platform and now were being lowered into the glacier. Todd had been through this procedure numerous times before, when he was helping his father at the facility. But he still didn't like the sensations.

"Per schedule, we will tour the preservement chambers first. Tours of the tissue banks, the cloning experiments, and the cryogenic pharmaceutical laboratories will be available later to those who are interested. If you have any questions at any point, please ask one of our Enclave personnel. We are ready to help you, and one of us will be near you at all times."

Todd hoped that wasn't strictly true. He needed to be alone, at least for a while, if he was to carry out what he planned. He studied the woman greeting them. She was older than he would have expected. When the Enclave was being built, the volunteers staffing it had been young and idealistic, for the most part. The Antarctic wasn't always kind to those who weren't in their prime. This lecturer, though, appeared older than Pat, maybe nearing her forties. She obviously wasn't part of a youthful, high-turnover staff roster. She spoke, and the other attendants acted, with a faintly smug air of superiority. Todd recognized the pattern. Isolation syndrome. He had seen it show up on occasion with his Geosynch techs, although term service there was generally much shorter than it would be at the Enclave. And he had seen such smug pride at Goddard, and watched it turning into secessionist drives. In theory, these Enclave staffers were the employees of the Human Rights Committee and of Protectors of Earth, despite the Saunder Enterprises badges they wore. The Enclave was chartered, and heavily funded, through P.O.E. Yet the staffers behaved as if the distinguished visitors were silly, uninformed tourists, and patronized them.

Dedicated, elitist—like Goddardites, and even like Project Search teams. Such people developed a fierce loyalty to their own causes. And they could be damned good at keeping secrets, as Todd had reason to know.

Where better to hide secrets than in frozen storage at the bottom of the world?

Motion ceased. Todd detected faint noises up front. The pilots, buckling down monitors and logs and readying the craft for the maintenance crews. Doors sucked open at either side of the passenger compartment. V.I.P. Committee members were already on their feet, familiar with the routine, trooping out. The lesser members, like "Ed Lutz," followed, moving uncertainly, gawking as they exited the shuttle.

The area immediately around the docking platform was sheathed in metal and plasticene. It could have been any docking platform on Earth; the arrival and departure bays in every terminal were much the same. But overhead, the resemblance ended. A massive elevator shaft of ice rose hundreds of meters toward the glacier's surface. The shuttle had been lowered so gently it hadn't seemed they could have been descending so deep. Maintenance lights were strung down the length of the vertical tunnel, showing the gleaming, icy walls. At the top of the shaft, there was blackness, a heavy weather door blocking any trace of sunlight penetrating the translucent upper layers of ice.

The Committee, surrounded by uniformed Enclave staffers, was now standing at the bottom of a very deep hole. And the door to the surface was locked. Images of intolerable temperatures and surface winds were racing through other minds besides his own, Todd knew. He had been through this before. In effect, they were all at the mercy of their guides and environmental life-support, just as if they had been transported instantly to orbit. This was different from space living. Gravity pulled at Todd, and the atmosphere lacked that recycled quality he associated with Geosynch HQ. He was on Earth, yet imprisoned and isolated, along with the other Committee members, shut off from the rest of humanity.

The guides started to lead them out of docking. When some of the newer members objected to being rushed, the Enclave staff patiently explained that Maintenance needed to get the temperature down to run certain checks. "We are always conscious of the effects of body heat here," the chief guide explained with a sweet, scornful little smile. They kept the Committee moving. The V.I.P. members cooperated, scowling at any of the lower echelons who held up the line or tried to ask questions. Very quickly, the tour was steered through a heat lock into the Core, the central section of the Enclave. With monitor screens supplying multi-views, the guides gave them a rapid look at the facility. The personnel lived

in the Core, kept their records here, managed the holo-mode
relay system to show the world, if necessary, live—or suspended
animation—views of any of the "confinees." In dizzying sequence, the members were shown the sperm, ova, and DNA storage areas, the P.O.E.-sanctioned human cloning experimental
labs, the pharmaceutical sections, and other scientific and commercial divisions.

The lesser members could ask questions about these areas and
even get a few straight answers. But the V.I.P.s, again, quashed
them, eager to get on with the business of the tour.

The staffers led them out from the Core. The Enclave was built
in a series of concentric circles. The inner one, not quite a kilometer in diameter, contained the Core and the adjacent labs and
production areas. Outside that, reaching more than a kilometer
from the Core's rim, the preservement chambers began. Before
they could go there, they had to be dressed for it. The staffers
took them to Suitup and handed out bulky, heavily insulated gear.

No insu-suits. None in sight.

Along with the others, Todd accepted the coat liner and parka,
the padded cap, overlarge mittens, and thick-soled boots. The
implications of the cold-weather gear chastened many of the tour's
rookies. They were grateful for the staffers' help, needing extra
hands to fasten all the togs and seal strips and zippers. The
staffers solicitously made sure those who required translators had
them. Everyone was cautioned to use breath masks over mouths
and noses to prevent frostbite. The tour members waddled obediently after the similarly garbed staffers.

Why? Where *were* the insu-suits? The obvious answer struck
Todd. Insu-suits weren't for curious tourists—not if the Enclave
had something to conceal. It was too easy to see out of a properly
sealed insu-suit, too easy to stay warm and not worry about heat
leakage damaging the cryogenic facility. Plus, this bulky gear
hobbled the Committee, severely limiting their ability to snoop or
wander into any place the staffers didn't want them to go.

There must be insu-suits hidden somewhere, for use after the
Committee left. He would have to locate one, once the staffers
were looking the other way.

"Your luggage will be placed in the guest quarters. After we
complete the preservement tour, we will return to the Core for re-

freshments. If anyone wants to take the subsidiary tours then, we'll arrange them." Most of the group, those whose faces weren't completely swathed in scarves and hoods, looked bored by the offer. Todd kept his manner neutral. He knew about the labs, had set up their monitoring and com systems, in fact. But a mini-tour just might suit his purposes. He would keep the option in mind for later.

The guides divided them into five groups, three staffers to a group. Then they were led to a row of trav-carts in the corridor outside Suitup. Todd got in a cart with a Rift Country delegate, a Frenchman, and a woman from the Greater Mediterranean Confederation. The guide driver took off quickly. Each group of ten Committee members had its own route. As they followed the beltway girdling the Core, one by one the little triads of trav-carts dropped away, taking separate radiating corridors heading out toward the preservement area. Todd's group took the corridor along the East Forty Degree Longitude line. The others must be equidistant from his tour, he knew from the pre-tour indoctrination materials.

Divide and conquer. Each group was taking a different spoke of a large wheel. It reminded Todd of Goddard Colony, though this time there was no shift in gravity and his position was horizontal to Earth's surface, not related to the axis of a torus. The aspects were reversed, too. The Goddard torus was teeming with life. The outer concentric circles of SE Antarctic Enclave were frozen sanctuaries holding thousands of bodies neither alive nor dead.

There was no way these five small groups could survey those thousands. By separating them, the staffers further insured they had no chance of coordinating their tour. In intent, the system allowed the Committee to make random and impartial studies throughout the preservement chambers. In actuality, it gave them a hit-or-miss, superficial run-through, proving absolutely nothing.

Ed Lutz had been scornful of the tour's effectiveness, and so was Todd, now that he saw how it was being conducted. They were seeing just what the techs wanted them to see, and nothing beyond that. The Committee would report back to P.O.E. and quiet down, once more, any rumors of foul play.

Only the rumors were getting louder, and some people didn't believe the Committee's reports any more. With good reason!

The corridor was a long, descending ramp. Scanners set in the walls at regular intervals peered at them from behind insulated screens. ComLink's techs had installed those. Todd watched for any alterations as he rode past. No new interlinks. Same narrow field. Safety scanners, installed mostly so that an injured staffer could call for help from such a station. But they weren't well designed for security searches. The Enclave assumed climate and location provided their security. Nobody got in here who wasn't granted entree.

Todd's fellow trav-cart passengers peered around uneasily. He hoped none of them was claustrophobic. Ice millers and sophisticated glacier drillers had cut the corridors right through the continental ice sheath. Intellectually, Todd knew the engineering specs, knew the ceiling and walls weren't going to close in and seal them in the glacier, crushing them with trillions of kilotons of ice. Emotionally, though, he wasn't sure.

They were approaching a baffle wall and a heat lock. The last of the lab and storage sections. Beyond that wall lay the preservement chambers. The trav-carts swung in neat U-turns and parked, ready for a hasty getaway once the obligatory tour was over. Whisk the shivering snoopers off scene before they could ask for anything not suitable for their eyes . . .

"Mechanized equipment is not permitted past this point," their lead guide explained. Another lie. Todd was breathing hard from the effort of climbing out of the cart wearing so many clothes. Committee members used to warm climates were beating their arms about themselves and stamping their feet. Condensed breath and frost generated by their bodies hung in a cloud around them. Their footfalls, despite being muffled by the boots, echoed. Todd's eyelashes grew sticky, riming with the chilly fallout. Humidity crystallized and fell or hung suspended in frigid air. Some Committee members were growing white coatings on their eyebrows or on bits of hair peeping out of their caps. No one asked what the temperature was. No one really wanted to know.

When he had been working here, they had kept it minus eighty and lower, Todd remembered. With insu-suits, minus one hundred was nothing. In this old-fashioned gear, a ten-degree drop felt like fifty.

He watched closely as the guide opened the heat lock. Had the staffers made any modifications? No. Still a simple tog trigger. Secondary insul wall operated by sensor plate. No print lock.

They went through one at a time. Occasionally the heat sensor tripped, and the guides made the next in line wait until the systems compensated for the additional load on their circuits. Eventually, all ten Committee members and the three guides were on the far side. A faint throbbing sound underfoot suggested buried machinery, hectares of it. Indeed, there *was* that much machinery maintaining the cryogenic chambers.

They were in a refrigerated room lined with monitor screens. "We are in monitor room twelve A," the lead guide announced. The screens blinked and showed them what lay past the outer wall. Row upon row of cryogenic cubicles reached seemingly to infinity. The immensity of the preservement facility was difficult to grasp. The glacier had been scooped out for a kilometer or more, all around the Core. It formed a deep, vast natural storehouse. Pillars of ice, reinforced by plastimetal tempered against the extreme cold, had been left to buttress the ceiling and distribute the incredible weight above. The screens' views showed catwalks extending from the balcony beyond the monitor room and running out over the sunken main floor. "This way, please. We have auxiliary monitor screens placed for your convenience along the maintenance bridges . . ."

The outer heat lock opened. The rapidly condensing body heat from the group billowed out and up toward the shimmering roof. "We have very efficient temp and humidity control, especially in here," the guide told them. "We have to, for the protection of our confinees. I must caution you—do not attempt to go down to the main floor! Your body heat could kill the confinees."

"They say we'll melt the bodies if we do that . . ."

Todd squirmed, wanting to challenge the lie. This group *might* strain the cryogenics systems if it descended to the main floor *en masse*. But even in this ridiculous gear, they could go down in groups of two or three without harming the preserved people in any way. With insu-suits, they could stay down there for hours, comfortably, and not raise the temperature one degree. He gritted his teeth on his anger, trudging with the others out onto the catwalk.

As they progressed along the narrow bridge, the awesome proportions of Saunder Enterprises Antarctic Enclave silenced all complaints about the cold. Even Todd was stunned. The facility had been much smaller the last time he had seen it. As the bodies continued to arrive, the glacier millers had reamed out more and more space, reaching deep into the ice. Todd squinted, trying to decide if the feeling of distance was an illusion. It could be created by holo-mode. He couldn't be sure. The preservement area *appeared* to extend indefinitely, though that couldn't be true. The floor below was filled with preservement cubicles, surrounding the Core, going out beyond the limits of his vision. Neat rows of meter-wide cubicles, each three meters from the next one in line. The cubicles perched on thick stems—umbilicals feeding from the ice-encased cryo systems underneath, going up into the sealed boxes on the frames above.

The guides halted at an auxiliary monitor screen. Numb, gulping frosty air, the Committee members huddled around them. The guides showed little effect from the cold. The lead guide's voice was steady, not shaken by chattering teeth. "One of our first admissions to the Enclave, ladies and gentlemen: Dr. Jacob Elias, cubicle one zero jay ee." The monitor zoomed on extreme close-up of one of the myriad boxes below. Smoothly, the guide explained. "We are equipped to accept confinees even during the Antarctic winter, if the shuttle ships can deliver them to us. We are here to serve Earth and its future generations. Dr. Jacob Elias was admitted July 12, 2030."

Dr. Elias's torso was discreetly masked to honor his privacy, but his face was in plain view. The kindly countenance was unquestionably that on modern history tapes. The face was real. Even via a holo-mode monitor screen, the man was alive, waiting in frozen sleep.

"Dr. Elias is dying of type B neo-anthrax mutation, as you know. His people wanted to save his artistry and his beloved person for their children and their grandchildren's time. When he slipped into coma, he was delivered to the Enclave. We have preserved him with all care, until the day when medicine can cure him . . ." The hope was that future doctors, yet unborn, could save that incredible mind and those gifted, musical fingers, putting his ravaged body back in working order.

They had been able to preserve Elias. July 2030. Just months too late for Ward Saunder, even if they had been able to recover his body from the ocean. The sperm and ova and DNA banks went operational in March 2030. By July, the preservement chambers were in business, too. They could take this gentle man whose music had brought solace to a stricken world and spoken across language and culture, across battle lines. When he fell ill, while only in his fifties, the imminent loss had been unbearable. The world clamored, demanding something be done to save him. And Saunder Enterprises Antarctic Enclave was ready. Dr. Elias had been one of its prime claims to altruism ever since.

The guides handed out ultra-scan binocs to those on the tour and pointed out the cubicle. Todd peered down at the floor. He couldn't see much more than he could on the auxiliary monitor. It wasn't good enough. It wasn't eyeball. He *had* to get a close look at some of those cubicles, and at the circuitry supporting them. There were ways to bypass the relay monitors and security systems, if one knew how.

A few sections away from Elias lay Natalya Petrovna, the conscience of Asia, the rescuer of thousands of suffering children, during the last years of the Chaos. She hadn't succumbed to the plague or fallen in war. Age had crept upon her. She had gone to the Enclave willingly, speaking prayers to the Spirit of Humanity and believing wholeheartedly in the hope of life the polar installation offered. Her example had encouraged many others to take the same course. It had even comforted condemned criminals and political dissidents sentenced to the Enclave against their will.

There were other famous, much-loved names in this section below the catwalk. !Kanagai. Gupta. Solana. Loos. Huang. Hirota. Zelinski. Su'biyya. Spirit of Humanity embraced them all, whether Muslim, Buddhist, Christian, Havurah Judaic, pagan—whatever religion or thought of the future they might have possessed. This icy fortress was now their mausoleum, and their hope of resurrection.

The guides showed them a number of confinees, then led them

farther along the catwalk. They stopped at another monitor station twenty-five meters away. This time the displays on the screen weren't so heroic. Here were some dissidents, artistic rebels, political malcontents. Almost none of these had volunteered for this living death. But the monitors showed them waiting just as peacefully and safely as Dr. Elias and Natalya and the rest of mankind's revered elite. Todd wondered where they kept their crop of billionaires, such as Ippolito. Probably safe in the honored sections. But presumably the Human Rights Committee wasn't interested in them. The rich customers could pay for their own upkeep and watchdogging. They weren't sponsored by Protectors of Earth. Technically, the Committee shouldn't have been overly concerned about heroes like Elias, either. Again, there was plenty of funding from such people's own governments, and they would come here willingly. It was the true confinee who should be the object of the inspection. Yet only now that they had come this far into the preservement area had they begun to reach some of those people—and the genuine criminals, the capital punishment confinees, lay still farther out.

By now, some Committee members were shivering so badly they could barely see the monitor screens. Chattering teeth sounded through the mufflers and breath masks. Todd estimated they had come much less than a quarter of a kilometer. But already, the agonized tour members must be thinking that inevitably they would have to walk *back* that far to the monitor chamber and then take a further cold ride until they reached the warmth of the Core.

Cold, terrible, overwhelming cold seeped into Todd's marrow. Racked by shivers, he stared along the catwalk. Did he imagine he saw the icy ceiling curving gently, forming an arc? The perspective gave the impression of the Earth's shape, a shape he shouldn't be able to see from this vantage. The preservement area seemed endless, horizonless.

No! It *did* have a horizon, and an end. Vast as this place was, it was finite. He *knew* that. But he could no longer think clearly, too seized by the cold.

Todd was hypnotized by the beauty of the ice, by the symmetry of the countless rows of cryogenic cubicles. Awkwardly, his movements hampered by the heavy clothing, he looked right and left. Somewhere port and starboard around the huge circle, there were other catwalks, other tour groups, other shivering Committee members, other smirking Enclave staffers.

"W-we'd better . . . better go b-back," the ranking Committee member of their group said. "We've s-seen enough."

"Spirit of Humanity, oh, yes!" someone else whimpered.

The guides were sadists. They stopped, but they didn't immediately begin retracing their steps. "If you're sure, sir. We will be happy to give you a complete inspection swing. Our facilities are totally available to your Committee. We wish you to be satisfied . . ."

"Sat . . . satisfied," the man chattered. He was quaking under his mound of furs. "Au . . . author . . . authorization . . ."

"Hurry," a colleague pleaded.

"Right here, sir." The guide held an authorization-form plate out for the senior Committee member. "You needn't remove your glove. In fact, we advise against it. The sensor will pick up your handprint through the fabric, sir." The guide had to steady the man's quivering hand until the record was made. "That'll do fine. We can complete the data when we get back to the Core. This way, please, ladies and gentlemen."

He didn't have to invite them more than once. They wanted to run, but they couldn't. They shambled along, the guides aiding them. A couple of people nearly fell. The guides supported them as they all lurched for the comfort of the monitor chamber. It seemed a very long way off. Todd wasn't ashamed of his shuddering, as grateful as the others when they slipped into the anteroom and then through the second heat lock. Still needing help, they crawled into the trav-carts, huddling there.

"Have you home in a jiffy," the guide driver cheerily assured them. If Todd had had the strength, he would have knocked the man out of the cart and pounded his head on the icy floor. Instead, he crouched in the seat, wishing the condensing moisture would form a bubble around him and keep out the cold.

CHAPTER SEVENTEEN

ILLUSIONS, AND BETRAYALS

TODD was no good for anything for more than an hour after they reached the Core. With those from the other returned tour groups, they sat in the lounge sipping hot krill soup and caffa. Gradually, it occurred to him that some of the newer Committee V.I.P.s were trying to live up to their oaths. They had retreated to the Core with everyone else, and they were just as cold. But when they recovered a bit, they started demanding further surveys of the confinees, insisting on seeing numerous political dissidents and criminals.

The Enclave staffers, as usual, were scornfully cooperative, though they hid their contempt very well. "Certainly. This first view, madam, is from preservement circle fourteen, file twelve." The guides cued a you-are-here map on the monitor screen insert to pinpoint the location. Half a kilometer out into the glacier beyond the preservement heat lock, farther than any of the Committee had been able to go. Remembering the cold, many of those watching shivered violently and gulped their hot liquids. "Subject two on the list you presented, madam—the rebel Chandrur, circle fifteen, file eight." The holo-mode showed the criminals and dissidents, one by one, just as it had showed the heroes. But here they could watch in considerably more comfort. "Former Presidente Ramirez, circle thirteen, file two. Opposition Coordinator Takao, in circle fourteen, file . . ."

Around the Enclave map, scattered selections, all of them far beyond the catwalk positions where the Committee had stopped. Guides ticked off the requests methodically. One of the members broke in, saying, "It'd take *hours* to see them all." Some of the die-hard idealists who were taking the job seriously groaned as they realized the truth of that. "But—but we have a duty to Earth, to the people . . ."

"We can extend the length of your tour, of course," the chief guide suggested, "so that you may perform your checks from here or on site. A week?" She was warmly courteous. But Todd didn't miss the malicious glitter in her eyes. She was enjoying the idealists' shock.

"A—a week? Isn't there some quicker way?"

"I'm afraid not, sir. A week is hardly adequate, actually. If you will consult your orientation materials, you will see that we have over one hundred thousand available cubicles and more being set up every day by our staff. If you will give us your lists, we'd better get started. If you wish, we can suit up again and return to the preservement chambers for eyeball inspection as soon as you're ready."

There was a lengthy pause. Todd could feel the mental wheels spinning, the ideals shattering. Hearing the stats, making resolutions to see each and every confinee on the Committee's current inspection list, was one thing. Trying to carry out those resolutions while coping with death by freezing was quite another.

"You see the impossibility of your demands, Tovar?" the V.I.P. Committee leader said with annoyance. His young colleague grimaced, but he knew he was defeated. His support was gone. More tolerantly, his ranking superior told him, "Don't feel bad. We run into this on every tour. You couldn't be expected to realize the immensity of the task. It's all right. We've worked out a method to fulfill the Committee's obligations without killing ourselves in the process."

"Full rapid scan, sir?" the chief guide asked. "As usual?"

"Yes, yes, get on with it, please. You have the lists . . ."

Todd sat back, sipping soup, saying nothing. Collusion? That, or a Committee member who liked his comforts and took the easy way out. Some of the younger members had brought up the matter of insu-suits. They had been sloughed off with pat explanations of insufficient equipment and late tests that questioned the integrity of the suits' heat retention. Doubtful, overruled by their seniors, the youngsters had quit fighting, especially after being stunned senseless by the cold. They were dedicated, but they had learned to live with the global political system—good, cooperative, peaceable citizens, or they wouldn't have been selected for the Committee in the first place. Todd wondered if their consciences bothered them, or if they would end up being paid off in perks and favors if they continued to raise a fuss.

Or were there nastier methods of removing them as a problem?

The guide raced through the lists of dissidents and criminals the Committee had been assigned to investigate. The holo-modes provided good imagery. The staff hadn't let the systems slip since ComLink's techs had installed them ten years ago. No, eleven, Todd corrected himself. This was February 2041. The last gasp of summer for the South Pole.

Below the lifelike images, readouts checked the states of preservation on the confinees. Everything in order. The dissidents and criminals didn't die in prison, before firing squads, by electrocution, or in a noose. They weren't dead here, either, according to the data. Until political affairs settled or time found a cure for criminal insanity, they would remain here.

One holo-mode winked out, and another replaced it. Locators marked the widely scattered cubicles around the outer circle of the Enclave. The onlookers were starting to thaw, resigned to accepting this easier method of inspection. They commented on how serene some notorious warlords looked, or how ready to wake up and speak once more various fallen rulers now seemed. The list was a sampling from all P.O.E.'s member nations and quasi-nations—murderers, political mavericks, defeated generals, rebel writers and artists—the scum of humanity and the politically unpopular and the just plain unlucky.

"How many more, sir?" the chief guide asked. "This *is* a bit of a strain on the equipment."

As the Committee leader sped up the requests, Todd eyed the woman guide sharply. She didn't seem aware of his scrutiny. A strain on the equipment? Gobbledygook! Ward's patented cryo modification holo-system could handle a thousand times this load. It was so efficient, maintenance was virtually nil. And it was energy-thrifty. No heat problems at all, if it was properly installed —and this equipment was. Yet no one reacted to her statement. The data wasn't in the familiarization material, and even a tech would have to dig a bit to locate it. Weren't there any techs on the Committee with that sort of training or knowledge of where to look? Todd surreptitiously studied the faces around him. They accepted her statement. They honestly didn't know. Who had set up the Committee to eliminate such expertise? More collusion?

Ed Lutz wasn't supposed to be an expert in these systems, either. That meant that Todd would have to pass himself off as very lucky and bumblingly stupid, a fortunate hit on the right combination—if he got caught.

The requests finished after more than an hour. The systems were still working without visible problems, as Todd had known they would be. There was an audible sigh of relief when the Committee leader finally called a halt. Energies were running down. Most members just wanted to sit around the lounge and continue to recuperate. When a guide offered an inspection tour of the labs, there were fewer takers than anticipated. Enough, though, that Todd saw his chance to lose himself in a crowd. He went along while others returned to their sleeping quarters or chatted with Enclave staffers, fascinated by the life style in this miniature nation at the bottom of the world. Fourteen Committee members, Todd with them, followed a lab supervisor in a leisurely stroll through the tissue-storage file rooms.

This part of the Enclave had been a natural outcome of the Death Years, the Chaos, and the plagues. Gene pools dwindled or died out completely in many areas of Earth. Family lines which had existed for generations ended. Some previously established tissue banks had been destroyed in the wars or contaminated, the genetic materials lost. When Ward Saunder first proposed the Enclave, it had seemed the ideal solution: neutral territory, honored by every combatant, a land where even valuable minerals were too costly to extract. There was nothing the Antarctic had that the warlords wanted. But science, and Earth's heritage for tomorrow, *did* want it, and the Saunders had made it available for their use.

The collection process was by no means complete; would never, in theory, *be* complete. But so far more than a billion samples had been gathered and stored here. More and more nations were taking advantage of the proffered service every year. Todd's own tissue samples were on store here.

". . . a form of insurance, a guarantee against future disaster," the supervisor was saying.

"If that terrible alien invasion kills most of us, we'll still be able to reproduce and fight back."

Pat's propaganda, following him even here. The original intent of the Enclave's tissue banks was being lost in the new wave of anti-alien paranoia.

"If necessary, perhaps we will perfect cloning and produce perfect warriors to fight the aliens in space." The Committee member didn't use his translator, but his strong Rift Country accent still identified his origins. The comment brought protests from a United Theocracies country member. "Cloning is against nature. It must not be done."

The lab techs hastened to explain that human cloning was decades in the future. The Enclave had only recently received P.O.E. permission to begin the simplest experimentation that might, eventually, lead to genuine human cloning many years ahead. The near-fanatic United Theocracies adherent didn't believe them. He kept questioning, trying to catch the techs in a lie.

"Cloning feeds my people," an Indian representative said. "The earlier cloning of plants and fish and fowl . . ."

"We are not talking of plants and fish and fowl," the religious hothead retorted. "We are here to guarantee the sanctity of human life!"

The techs tried to calm him. "What this gentleman says is true. Cloning *has* fed millions, and clothed them as well. The technique produces quick-maturity fowl and fish and a variety of grains, edible crops, and fibers, as listed in your briefing tapes. Nowhere here will you find human embryos *in vitro,* as your propagandists claim . . ."

A few others, like Todd, were staying out of the argument, moving up and down the aisles, peering curiously at the labels and readouts on the storage chambers. It wasn't that cold in the labs, so the impulse to stick together for warmth was gone. None of the guides was paying close attention to them. Instead, they were preoccupied with the noisy United Theocracies Committee member.

Todd glanced around warily. No Enclave personnel or other members were in sight, and he was near an auxiliary door to the maintenance corridors. The hyperendors he had consumed put his memory at top power. A map of the Enclave shaped in his mind. That way, and then to the right, and down a narrow passageway. Maintenance Suitup. There ought to be some insu-suits *there!*

It was almost too easy. Gib Owens and the Goddard allies who had "disappeared" might have thought their jobs were equally easy. Reminded of that, Todd kept his guard up as he made the run down the empty corridors. Finding the suits was no problem. The adaptafabric outfits weren't name-tagged, and there were plenty of them. That lessened the chances that someone would take a spot inventory and notice one was missing. Once he was suited up, his face was partially hidden. That, too, would be a help. Even so, he waited until a duty watch of lab techs went by the outer door before he slipped out into the hall.

The big question—had there been some secret updating in security? That was a gamble, had been from the beginning, one he had to take. No scans. None in sight. No ident print locks, either. Those hadn't been developed when the Enclave was constructed. None had been installed since. Theft and break-in weren't high-priority problems here. There was little need to demand print identification from the regular Enclave staffers, most of whom lived here for six months or more on a duty tour.

Todd avoided the trav-carts. Those *were* likely to be inventoried and tied in to the main computer logs. He had neither the time nor the patience to tinker with one's guts and block out the tracking system. Clad in an insu-suit, he would be warm enough, especially while exercising. He had made good time getting around the Enclave years ago. He still could, if he had to, and he did.

He ducked under the monitor screens lining the corridors, running in a crouch until he could straighten and lope along. So much to do! So damned little time! When he reached the heat lock, he was breathing hard. Warmed and filtered air sucked into the helmet, whistling in his nostrils. He rushed past the monitor screens and past the second heat lock, out into the preservement chambers.

Slowing, Todd moved onto the balcony near the catwalk, gazing out over hundreds of hectares of gleaming coffins for the living. The eerie sensations of a couple of hours earlier returned, intensified. Then, he had been with other persons. Alone, the immensity of the Enclave struck him even more powerfully and roused atavistic fear.

He had been very much alone before, in a spacesuit, hanging outside a shuttle in orbit, the only living being within thousands of kilometers. This emotion was stronger. No high vacuum, though minus eighty degrees centigrade was sufficient to kill him fairly quickly. Gravity, and plenty of air for the insu-suit to warm and filter through to him. He was alone, and yet he was not. He was the only breathing, mobile human being here, surrounded by thousands of helpless, frozen men and women. He was alive, and they were utterly at his mercy. Sophisticated equipment linked them with revival and a future existence. But Todd Saunder—and many other people at the Enclave—had the technical knowledge to disconnect those links and destroy these sleeping prisoners.

I could kill them. All of them, or some of them. At my whim.

The sense of omnipotence shook Todd as few concepts had save the discovery of the alien messenger. To his horror, he knew a momentary thrill, an almost perverse, gloating feeling of power he hadn't realized was in his nature. Aghast, he slammed a lid on that monster in his being and hurried to the edge of the catwalk and the maintenance ladders leading to the lower floor.

The instant of temptation and ugly self-knowledge was gone. Todd was back in business, scrambling down the ladder. He hesitated, searching his memory and looking around. Then he climbed over the low reminder shock barrier, set to keep maintenance crews from accidentally carrying certain equipment out into the cubicle aisles. He started running down those aisles, scanning the section monitor readouts, hunting for particular, pre-chosen chambers.

Sounds were mildly distorted by the insu-suit. The steady hum of the buried cryo machinery was like a million heartbeats throbbing in unison. Now and then, far away, there were cracking noises, shiftings in the ages-old ice man had invaded. Nothing to cause alarm, the engineers had promised. But those natural complaints from the glacier would stay with the Enclave. If humanity wanted to use the Antarctic, that was part of the worrisome price.

Individual shock barriers surrounded each cubicle. Todd ran carefully down the middle of the aisles and cross-aisles, not ready to cross those invisible fences yet. The secondary barriers were the last reminders Maintenance would get, and they were guaranteed to prevent accidents. They could bite, and hard.

From the corners of his eyes, he saw the frozen faces as he ran. Men and women, dark and fair, red and yellow and black and brown, every nationality and genetic strain and ethnic type. Monitors tabbed their names and conditions. Row upon row of living ghosts—waiting, waiting . . .

Limbo. The opponents of Ward's Enclave concept had flung rougher expressions than that at the Saunder quasi-nation when Protectors of Earth was considering franchising the facility. Ward had turned the rebuttals over to Jael, and she had done a thorough job of crushing the opposition, as usual. Not limbo but hope, she had said—and was not hope preferable to certain death?

Not everyone could afford the privilege. Not everyone was fortunate enough to have a sentence commuted to open-ended imprisonment in the Enclave. Executions still happened, in some countries. But far fewer now than then, thanks to the Enclave and to the militant Spirit of Humanity religious movement.

Yet death was not vanquished. Ward Saunder had never said it would be. He offered a scientific tool to hold it at bay, no more.

An item from a historical tape flashed in Todd's thoughts. Alfred Nobel. Another genius inventor. He, too, thought his invention would free mankind from its own violent nature.

Todd's steps slowed. He was beyond the privileged sections, into the far vaster ones holding unwilling confinees. The first cubicle to his right contained a woman. She was young, not pretty, African. Strong features, rigid with defiance. Elizabeth Gola, author of the Right of Independency Manifesto. She wasn't one of the eighteen on Goddard's list. But her face and form attracted Todd. He had to look up at the cubicle. The body was suspended a few centimeters above his head, resting on the life-giving support stem channeling down to the cryo machines and temp regulators.

Her defiant face intrigued him, won his sympathy. Without intending to, Todd reached out, then caught himself before he touched the shock barrier. "Sorry," he said, feeling foolish for talking to someone who couldn't hear. "I don't have the time. I'm not far enough. Need another eight frames . . ."

He covered the distance at a jog. The exertion of touring earlier, without an insu-suit, was costing him. No problems with chill factor, but gravity bothered him. Todd smiled ruefully. Age and acclimation taking over. He was becoming too fond of spacing. Each time he went planetside it took longer to readjust. This time he had rushed it. Long enough, though, to pull this off.

He stared up at the cubicles on either side of the aisle. Beyond, the containers reached to the sub-surface glacial horizon. He had a better viewpoint than he had had on the catwalk, and he had come deeper into the preservement chambers than he had up there when he tried to assess distance vision. Not real. Some of it was, but not all of it. The area wasn't as immense as it had seemed. Part of that awesome distance range was holo-mode, damned good, too.

Would the V.I.P.s on the Committee believe him if Ed Lutz said the endless horizon of cryo cubicles was exaggerated? Probably not. Even if he told them as Todd Saunder, there would be doubts.

I'm not exactly Earth's most popular person right now, thanks to the last wonderful news I brought them . . .

He checked the section screens for confinees' names. Prandathra, Swenson, and DeWitt. Bustamonte, Van Eyck . . . Djailolo. He had been one of the losers in the recently ended Trans-Pacific war. Todd recalled the Malaysian Lunar Base pilot, one of Gib's friends, yelling in grief-stricken outrage when he had read Djailolo's name on the confinee list during Pat's speech. Djailolo had not only made the mistake of opposing the winning rulers on his side, he had also been a booster of Goddard Colony and the Spacers, and he *was* on the list of eighteen names.

"You've paid for supporting Mari and Kevin, didn't you?"

Todd sadly asked the man in the box. He stepped closer to the cubicle, studying it. Intuitive alarms went off. Something wasn't right. Todd knelt, squirming under the shock barrier and the transparent coffin, examining the maintenance stem. The tiny readout monitors looked okay. Everything appeared fine. He had expected that. But his jangling, inner alarm didn't shut off. It was tightening into a painful tension.

He crawled back out into the aisle, then stood, staring up and down the files. Possible? All too possible. But where did it originate? In the maintenance stems feeding from the cryo machines? Or from the Core? If it was the latter, he would never get past the systems.

Practicalities convinced him. Core mode would have taken a massive amount of special programming. Too hard to cover up the input from Saunder Enterprises' supply sources. Much easier to tinker on site. Out here, past the shock barriers, working with the original system, selective removals and replacements would work best, and most efficiently and convincingly.

Selective. The word sent a wave of revulsion through Todd's viscera. He swallowed hard and forced himself to move along the rows of confinees' coffins. They had thrown all the unfortunates together at random. A political gadfly who had never harmed anyone was placed beside a depraved mass murderer, a man too deranged to help with medico-psycho techniques, and too deadly to try to lock away from society and take the risk that he might escape.

Who had made the selections? Who had put them together like this?

Todd located three more of the names on the Goddard list and checked each maintenance stem for anomalies. He didn't touch anything at first, until he had eyeballed thoroughly. Then he went to work. Disable was simple, if you knew what to look for, and he did. Ed Lutz might be capable of this, too, if he had been instructed. That could be an alibi, if needed. Again and again Todd glanced over his shoulder, peering out from under the coffin where he was working, hoping his insu-suit audio would pick up any warning sound.

The half-buried circuitry yielded to his skilled probe. Same old casing. Same old guts. Eleven years old and still working superbly. Except for one small detail. Output for the obligatory holo-mode relay system—that eye of the world, demanded in P.O.E.'s Enclave charter. As Todd himself had tested, this relay was supposed to provide, instantly, a confirming three-dimensional view of any confinee—hero or dissident or criminal.

Todd examined the program set, growing more contemptuous and angry by the second. No precautions taken at all. No feedback. No trigger mechanism to register at the Core. Why bother? Ward Saunder had designed the system so well, so intricately, one tiny adjustment would be undetectable.

Unless you were Ward Saunder's son and had watched him build the original device.

Satisfied that he wouldn't call down hordes of Enclave personnel on himself if he went further, Todd removed the small circuit trigger and cradled it in his gloved palm. He scooted back and stood up, facing Van Eyck's cubicle.

The computer would give him only a minute's worth of looking. Now he could look as long as he wished, or until he was caught. But *what* was he looking at? Van Eyck, another Goddard supporter, accused—falsely, by Mari's claim—of murder, convicted, and confined. He slept in icy suspension. Cryo support kept his body and brain safe for the future.

Todd didn't want to find out. He glanced down at his hand, at the circuitry base, his thumb moving, pressing the crucial set. Resisting what he knew he would see, he looked up once more at the cubicle.

Van Eyck was gone.

He had probably been gone for months, ever since he had been "confined." He had been replaced by a holo-mode image. In that future he and his supporters hoped to see Van Eyck would have no part. Time was on the Enclave's side, and on the side of Van Eyck's enemies. The term of his sentence was indefinite, and, like most of those confined to the Enclave, his confinement could be pushed forward again and again to suit the politics of those who had sentenced him.

Todd released the set trigger. Van Eyck was visible once more, secure and frozen.

Todd replaced the circuit. Then he went up the aisles, quickly repeating the test. At first he checked the other names on the list,

those people Mari was worried about, the names Gib Owens had
given his life to deliver. He found more like Van Eyck. Too many
more. He couldn't cover them all. But of the six within this section, five were gone. People presumed safe and preserved in the
Enclave, some for three or more years—gone. Gone while Goddard was being completed. Gone while the Trans-Pacific war
went on, while the alien messenger was coming to greet a supposedly intelligent species.

On impulse, Todd ran to an area that seemed restricted entirely
to criminals. No political dissidents. No possibly moralistic motives for wanting these people out of the way in order to save a
country, a people from war or political disaster. If not for the
Spirit of Humanity movement and Saunder Enterprises' altruism,
none of these criminals would have survived to reach the Enclave.

They hadn't survived *after* they had reached the Enclave, Todd
discovered. None of them. The rate in these cubicles was one
hundred percent. In these outer sections, the ones no Committee
members ever reached, even via the catwalk, there were only
rows of holo-mode images. The cryo machinery throbbed, sus-
taining nothing.

The rows reached into the distance. Somewhere, another holo-
mode form took over, projecting an illusion of endless distances.
There was no reason why all the cubicle space *couldn't* be used,
and with minimal expense. But it wasn't. Someone—for whatever
reasons—had decided to turn off thousands of people. Wipe them
out. Yet continued the sham, the lie to the world, that these thousands were humanely preserved, living into Earth's future.

His boots scuffing on the frosty floor, Todd walked back into
the political sections, where there were fewer criminals and more
innocent confinees. Djailolo was dead. Van Eyck was dead. Bustamonte was dead. Ngoro Kwami, Theda Ryan, Yuri Mikhaila-
vitch, Toshiro, Pandrachagishipim . . .

He had no heart to make a list. Enclave Core probably had
one, locked and security-sealed. And somebody, somebody in authority, probably had one—the higher-up who had laughed at the
Enclave's charter and ordered these mass executions.

They *were* executions. Maybe the world wouldn't care over-
much about the dead criminals. Humanity was as much at war

with itself over capital punishment as it had ever been, this past century or so. The Enclave cubicles given over to the murderers and saboteurs and terrorists were a compromise, a concession to shut up the tenderhearted. But the political losers, the artists who adopted causes their governments opposed—they, too, were dead. Honest and worthy people, some submitting bravely to their sentences, exhorting their followers not to rebel in their names and risk death. Time, they had said, would prove them right and their causes just. No blood must be spilled! Condemnation to the Enclave was not, after all, death. With pride, they had accepted confinement, a badge of membership and their heritage for the future. Someday, when Earth was free, they would awake and return to lead their happy people.

Someone had canceled that plan—and the people who believed in it.

Gone. No one left to revive.

New horror struck Todd. What about the tissue, storage labs? If the unknown perpetrator had killed the people, would the hidden assassin hesitate to remove all other traces of those persons' existence?

The body, the tissue samples . . . the future. Wiped out. Tomorrow was never going to come.

It was as if Ward Saunder had never lived, never dreamed of building a refuge of the Death Years and the Chaos. The refuge was no refuge now. It was a grave. Worse! Those who might have mourned over buried loved ones didn't even know their relatives and admired leaders were dead. The scientific advances, the successful revival of the cryogenics volunteers—wasted!

Why?

Mari's accusations, proved. Yes! But much more. Other trade-offs and bargains made. Goddard wasn't the only threat to some tyrants and financial barons. How convenient to find a way to make absolutely sure an enemy would never come back to haunt one! In public, for the world, one boasted of altruism and magnanimity, of death sentences commuted to Enclave confinement, of a business rival "unfortunately" caught in a frame-up and sentenced to that frozen prison. In private, worry ceased. The threat would be erased, if the price were right. How high a price

for secrecy and the ability to play the generous victor yet murder
one's foes, too?

Who?

That question was far worse than the why of it.

Saunder Enterprises. The Saunders. The Enclave was theirs,
entrusted to them by the power brokers and the powerless alike.
Todd tried to erect mental walls to fight off the logic. He couldn't.
Unwillingly, his mind replayed Pat's dedication speech, on the anniversary of Ward's death after the Enclave had been established
and placed under the charter of Protectors of Earth.

". . . a sanctuary, a haven, a refuge from mankind's madness.
Never again, my Listeners, will we let them die! Saunder Enterprises gives this Enclave to the world—to protect us from the
criminal and the criminal from himself, to save us from prejudice
and political shortsightedness, to wait out the uncertainties of disease and war and economic chaos. There they will rest undis-
turbed and safe, they who would otherwise die. They will wait,
tomorrow's heritage for Earth, to waken to a bright and wonderful future . . ."

Did Pat know? Was he responsible for this hideous travesty?

Chinks appeared in that mental wall. Doubts battered against
it.

Not Pat! Todd refused to accept the despicable idea. And
yet . . .

*It's ours. And the Enclave is under Pat's division of Saunder
Enterprises. He has to take the responsibility.*

*So do I. Ward let me play second in command while he was
building the Enclave. I should have guessed, then, what the temptations would be. The watchdogs don't know what to look for, or
are easily bought off. I know what to look for, and I didn't. And
now it's too late, for thousands of these victims.*

"They're cutting our throats, Todd. Some supporters are bailing
out, and some are simply disappearing. No wonder those who are
left are too scared or weak to resist! Whoever's doing it wants to
break Goddard. And they want to destroy everything on Earth
that Dad stood for. Earth First! Earth First Party has to rule it
all! And if they can't rule us, they'll try to wipe us out of existence!"

His feet had brought him back to the cubicle holding the African woman. Elizabeth Gola. Dissident. He came out of past nightmares to waking agony. The woman in the box could be Dian. There was no real physical resemblance, but there were similarities, all the same—the stubborn set of the full mouth, the tense skin around the eyes promising trouble for whoever opposed this woman. If she woke, she would once more bestride her continent, rousing the poor and the landless, creating trouble for the petty dictators and moguls.

If she woke . . .

She was no criminal. Nor was she one of the wealthy who had bought life-graves in the Enclave. Gola had no claim to artistic genius. She was merely an intelligent and idealistic reformer—a problem. Those who had sentenced her proclaimed that in the Enclave she would not be a martyr but would probably outlive those doing the sentencing. Did she have a husband, a lover who hoped to live that long and meet her again? Children? Certainly she had followers, who depended on the watchdog Committee to assure that Elizabeth Gola and all her fellow prisoners were safe.

Todd especially didn't want to know, this time. But he was compelled to find out. Gola's humanity appealed to him, and she was helpless to speak for herself. Reluctantly, he slid under the cubicle, removed the crucial base, returned to the aisle, looking up. For a long minute, he stared at the woman, not moving. Then he pushed the set to *Off*.

Elizabeth Gola did not exist.

CHAPTER EIGHTEEN

☆☆☆☆☆☆☆☆☆

COUNTERATTACK

HE went further, taking a risk. Todd disconnected the cubicle shock barrier. Then he returned the holo-mode set to its place. Elizabeth Gola once more appeared within the box. But now there was nothing at all between him and her.

Nothing at all. Not even the cubicle itself!

He put out his hand tentatively, and thrust through the shimmering cryo box. His fingers touched Elizabeth Gola's frozen face, went into it, beyond it.

The sensation was gruesome, awful.

Todd took a step forward. He now stood in the space where the cubicle wall should be. The machinery underfoot was a sham, too! It might feed power to *some* cubicles, those heroes and billionaires. But not here. And the outer rings were ravaged and empty.

He drew back, shaking his arm violently as if to shed the presence of the non-existent woman. The reaction was intensely emotional, one he hadn't experienced since he was a boy and Ward had first shown him the effectiveness of a good holo-mode projection.

Not just the victims! The whole damned installation! Fake!

Somebody paid. And somebody was saving one hell of a lot of funds by this little "economy"!

Todd turned away, nausea roiling in his gut. He stumbled

blindly under the cubicle's image, groping for the maintenance stem, restoring the circuitry to its original place. Holo-mode and shock barrier were solidly implanted once more.

A light was flashing on the section monitor to his right. Security alert. He must have it triggered it when he removed the barrier. Guards would be coming here very soon.

He sought to control himself, putting his intellect back in charge. Pat had taught himself to act, to move and convince an audience. Now it was time to find out if that talent ran in the family.

Along with a talent for killing . . .

No! He couldn't allow that thought to surface. Not yet!

Footsteps were echoing in the immense glacial caverns. He would be able to hear the guards while they were still some distance away. If they were running to intercept him, they wouldn't be paying too much attention to the scanners. That gave Todd a chance for one more clinching detail for his act.

Deliberately, he approached the restored shock barrier. Even being braced for it didn't help when the current lanced his left thigh. Todd gasped and fell back, dropping to his right knee. He knelt until the pain diminished to a bearable level. Then, carefully, he got to his feet. The insu-suit fabric was seared open where he had contacted the barrier. Cold was starting to penetrate its inner layers. He hoped the guards weren't going to enter into a long, on-the-spot interrogation.

Of course, they could make a very *short* session of it if they shot him on sight!

He positioned himself just outside the shock barrier and looked up at Elizabeth Gola's false image. To create the emotions he needed, Todd thought of Dian and imagined her trapped in that cubicle, forever locked away from him.

There were four guards. He saw them coming from his right, their shapes distorted by the curved edges of his insu-suit faceplate. They were wearing side arms. Todd resisted an impulse to dive for cover. He couldn't give them any reason to shoot.

They surrounded him, blocking all chance of escape.

"Sir?" the guard leader's filtered voice said. "This is a restricted area. What are you doing here, sir?"

The man was coldly polite, like all Enclave personnel seemed to be. But Todd heard the threat, the steel under the courteous inquiry. Steel? Or was it ice?

Todd continued to stare at Gola. He felt the guards growing uneasiness. The challenge was shifting. Another polite voice repeated, "Sir, what are you doing here? You were told this was a restricted area. Body heat on the main preservement floor endangers the chamber occupants . . ."

Only a scant few of them, compared with how many are supposed to be here!

Todd yearned to throw the lie in their faces. Instead, he gulped and encouraged the lump in his throat until he could say with appropriate hoarseness, "I . . . I had to see her . . . see her *real*. Not on those . . . those screens. She was so brave. The Right of Independency Manifesto . . ."

The guards stirred, looking at one another. Todd behaved as if he were barely aware of their presence. Their expressions became pitying, so much so that Todd had to work to keep his fists unclenched. The bastards had the cruelty to pity a naive outsider who believed their lies. They had caught the poor fool where he shouldn't be and assumed—as Todd hoped they would—that Ed Lutz was mooning over one of his ideological heroines. Misguided, but not particularly dangerous.

"She *is* brave, sir," the guard leader corrected Todd. "She's not dead."

Hypocrites! Euphemisms, hateful, worse than the truth, rose out of the past. One of Jael's sanctimonious rich relatives, intoning at Ward's memorial service. "He's not dead, my child. He's merely sleeping." But *this* usage was the most hypocritical of all! These guards knew the truth. They had to. Yet they mouthed the same words, and without the excuse of piety.

Another guard took up the lie. "Eventually, the Affiliation of the Rift Countries and the other African nations will resolve all their differences, sir. Then people like Elizabeth Gola will return to their homelands and lead their countries to a better world."

More platitudes. More promises that could never be kept, for Gola and the thousands of others.

"I had to see her," Todd repeated, making his voice shake. He didn't have to feign his sorrow, or his trembling. His leg was starting to hurt a lot. With calculation, like a man entranced, he reached out toward Gola's non-existent cubicle once more.

The guards pinned him and dragged him to safety in the center of the aisle just before he touched the shock barrier again. Inwardly, Todd was grateful to be rescued from that second heroic performance. He wasn't sure he could endure another shock without yielding to an undignified yelp, one that wouldn't suit Ed Lutz's adoring, hypnotized stance at all. He struggled with the guards just long enough to seem believable, then sagged. They supported him, suddenly very solicitous.

"You're hurt, sir. We'd better get you back to the medics."

"Had to see her . . ." Todd said faintly, giving the performance of his life. *For* his life.

"But you *have* seen her, sir. And you wouldn't want to risk her chances of revival, would you?" Todd blinked at the man, pretending to consider his logic. The hard voice was soothing. "You've seen Elizabeth, and now we have to take you to the Core, sir. Temperature problems here can be extreme. Please, sir. This way."

Todd slumped, allowing himself to be half carried, half-dragged. The guards weren't rough with him, but they didn't dawdle. As they passed the section monitor screens for Gola's block of cubicles, the guard leader stopped to run a security check. Todd held his breath as the others hustled him onward. How thorough and expert would the man be? And how persuasive had Todd's act been? In a few moments, he heard the guard leader's footsteps overtaking them, and then the man was out in front, leading the way once more.

His act had worked! The guard hadn't stayed at the monitor long enough for any sort of replay. And each additional hour of readouts would bury any tiny evidence of tampering in a blizzard of new data. Todd didn't need an indefinite cover-up, anyway— one just long enough to permit him to get away. Once the news broke, it wouldn't matter. They could falsify data, but they couldn't bring the dead back to life . . .

I'm making a habit of breaking shocking news to the world, of late. For all the panic the alien messenger news caused, though, I'm still proud of that. I always will be. But this . . . I'm not

*proud of what's been done at Saunder Enterprises Enclave. I'm
sick and ashamed—and mad!*

His escort heaved Todd over the outer maintenance shock barrier and pulled him up the ladder to the catwalk. He no longer
had to fake unsteadiness at all. Shock was setting in, physical
pain underlined by emotional stress. Unabashedly leaning on the
guards, he staggered with them through the heat lock. Trav-carts
were parked just beyond the doors, and he fell into one of the
seats with a groan.

The guards didn't talk to him during the ride back to the Core.
They kept up a busy chatter on the com, however, reporting to
their Enclave superiors. Todd tried to brace himself for the next
tests—medics and questions. It was going to be hard to concen-
trate, even with the hyperendors' help. Burning cold spread
across his leg, a growing distraction that was swamping his
thoughts.

Where were they? At the outer perimeters of the Core. The
trav-carts veered sharply, taking an auxiliary corridor toward
Medical. Todd was thrown against the cart's side rail and cried
out involuntarily. The guards muttered something that might have
been an apology and pulled him back upright again.

Enclave medics, Todd found to his relief, weren't too interested
in why he had gotten burned, only in how to treat the injury. He
wrapped himself in Ed Lutz's United Ghetto States accent and
mannerisms, shrugging off their attempts to administer narc-
synths or other sedatives. He needed his mind as clear as possible.

"This is going to be unpleasant, Mr. Lutz," the physician
warned in an understatement. "Electro-stimulus will be rough in
these dosages. We can give you some—"

"I c'n carry it. 'M all right! No drugs or blood! 'M New Genetic Coalition!" Todd put all the fervor he could into that boast.
It was something that wouldn't be on Lutz's idents, but also
something they would be inclined to accept, if his act continued
to convince.

A few Committee members peeked in the emergency-room
door. Some were whispering with the Enclave guards who had
brought Todd here, obviously being briefed on Ed Lutz's peculiar
behavior and rule-breaking.

Todd almost forgot to perform when the medics began shearing the insu-suit away from his wound. As Lutz, an alleged New Genetic Coalition adherent, he had bragged he could stand this without an injected or inhaled pain killer. As Todd Saunder, he wasn't so sure.

He had bumped a barrier that wasn't at full-shock capacity when Ward was building the Enclave. This injury was worse. He could only compare the pain to the time he had had a brush with a ray, fifteen years ago, in the waters off Saunderhome. Pat had pulled him out of the water, or he would have drowned, doubled over with pain and stunned almost unconscious. The accident had bought him a flight to Gulf Central Medical Facility, one of the best-defended and safest areas still around during the Chaos. It had also drawn the family together anew, in a time of heavy stress for Jael and Ward's marriage. They had all stuck close by Todd, while he was out of his head with fever and then recovering.

Pat, saving my life then, and now I'm going to . . .

Todd braced himself as the medic trainees debrided the insu-suit fabric out of the wound and removed dead skin. The chief physician talked while he worked, damnably cheerful. "Don't see too many of these. Our staffers learned, the hard way, to stay off those shock barriers. Hmm. Doesn't look like we'll have any necrosis or permanent scarring here. You're pretty lucky it didn't bite you harder . . ."

It would have if I hadn't been set for it and had floundered around and hit it several times in reaction.

"Had t' see her," Todd said through clenched teeth. "Up close."

"Well, you certainly did that. I hope you're satisfied. Painful price to pay for satisfying your curiosity, I must say." As Todd continued to mumble, the doctor patronized him, as the guards had. "Yes, of course, I understand. Gola's a wonderful woman. A true heroine. Now just lie back, please."

It occurred to Todd that the medics probably had a lot more experience working with comatose and sedated incoming confinees than they did treating alert and resistant patients. There were undoubtedly occasional injuries among the Enclave staffers, but, as the doctor had said, most of them had learned to avoid the sort of wound Todd had suffered. The medics were alternately rough and then gentle and apologetic when their procedures brought agony.

"Stimulus current is working nicely. There'll be some swelling. You'd better see your own medic when you get home . . ."

Todd climbed out of a haze of pain, realizing the ordeal was nearly over. *Part* of the ordeal. The medics had disconnected the equipment. A glistening protecta-cover was over his wound. No one had noticed anything unusual about his skin color or hair texture. No one had tried to take a DNA or blood sample for close analysis. His religious protests had held.

The next step in the ordeal followed immediately. The Committee V.I.P.s and top Enclave staffers closed in on him as soon as the medics were done. The one concession they allowed was a glide chair. They steered him to the Core supervisor's office for an impromptu trial.

Someone had fetched Ed Lutz's idents from Todd's assigned sleeping quarters. Todd assumed that meant they had gone through the rest of his gear as well. From the looks on their faces, they were disgusted and disappointed, plainly having found nothing suspicious. They had spotted the New Genetic Coalition propaganda Todd had packed with exactly this sort of excuse-making in mind. A guard tossed some of the lurid printouts on the Enclave supervisor's desk. She looked at the material and grimaced derisively.

"Very, *very* ill-advised, Lutz," the senior Committeeman lectured Todd.

The supervisor consulted with her guards. "Lutz has been on three previous tours of the Enclave, according to his idents. He's never attempted anything like this before. Why this time?"

The Committeeman waved at the propaganda on her desk and took the need to reply away from Todd. "There's your answer, madam. These new cults. Appalling! They go over full power. Waste of good training. They simply lose all common sense, become obsessed with this 'natural existence' fad and all manner of hero worship . . ."

There was general, condescending agreement to that. Todd roused himself and pretended to argue, protesting that he was no fanatic. He remained in Lutz's persona, slurring his words, both imitating Lutz's accent and reacting to the pain. It was the right tack to take. The condescension grew. Several of the guards had already dismissed him as harmless and compared his stunt with previous uproars at the Enclave. "The Committeeman's got it. Remember that Serene Future crazy last October? That cretin almost smashed through the heat lock with a trav-cart. Kept babbling that it was 'ungodly' to lock up people away from the Sun." The other guards chuckled and nodded.

Then someone wondered, "How did he know where to get an insu-suit?"

Dangerous question—one that had to be fielded exactly right. The supervisor pursed her lips, watching Todd intently. "Lutz? Can you hear me, Lutz? How did you know where to get that suit?"

There was no one in the room except Enclave guards, the supervisor, and three high-ranking Committee members. The question didn't surprise any of them. It hadn't surprised the medics that Todd, a non-Enclave person, was wearing a suit, but inquiries weren't their job. Collusion again?

"Lutz?" the supervisor demanded, speaking sharply.

Todd jerked in the glide chair and moaned, not looking at her directly. He mumbled, "Read . . . read old tape 'bout . . . 'bout buildin' the Enclave. Said . . . said there was special suits . . ." He lapsed into more moaning to gather his thoughts. "Didn' do nothin' wrong. Gotta right. Had to see her. On the Committee . . ."

"Not any more," the senior Committeeman said angrily. "You have forfeited your position, the honor given to you, and all future rights to serve on Protectors of Earth's esteemed branches."

"Read about it, eh?" the supervisor repeated thoughtfully. "We'll have to plug that hole. We can't have such things lying around available in the antique tapes. Might give others ideas like this one. Shouldn't be taught to read, most of them. Just complicates matters. Make a note, Vaca. We need a thorough library scouring to tidy up . . ."

"Yes, ma'am."

Todd squinted at them, feigning bewilderment. "Had to see 'er . . ."

The Committeeman shook a finger at him. "You deserve a public rebuke. At the very least, we will make sure your employers know you have lost your accreditation. You don't understand even yet, do you, you fool! Your reckless fanaticism could have endangered the future revival of the very woman you're so concerned about!"

"I . . . I saw her! Gola," Todd said dazedly. He stared at a point ten centimeters above the Committeeman's head and let a dreamy expression come over his darkened face. "I saw her. Elizabeth Gola. I c'n tell 'em I did . . ."

"Who?"

The supervisor sneered. "His fellow fanatics, of course. You're wasting your time, sir. Indeed, he *doesn't* understand."

"Should . . . should we let him talk?"

New alarms shot adrenaline through Todd's veins. The pain in his leg flared until the supervisor replied with a shrug, "Why not? He's at liberty to do so, under P.O.E. law. We'll make no attempt to stop him from relating what he saw in the preservement chambers. I *do* trust the Committee will make plain how he took chances with Gola's life, and with thousands of other lives."

"Of course!"

No, they wouldn't try to stop "Ed Lutz." In fact, they might even subtly encourage such publicity. They didn't want tour members going where they weren't watched. But on the other hand, "Ed Lutz" seemed sure he had seen the real Elizabeth Gola, safe and sound in her cubicle. What better unsolicited testimonial to quiet the persistent rumors around the world and in orbit and prove that all was well with the confinees?

"Saw her," Todd mumbled.

They weren't even paying attention to him any more. They talked around him as if he were a piece of furniture. "At least this one didn't do any real damage, not like that crazy two years ago who tried to smash the labs to destroy the 'human clones.'" The guards snickered openly, and the supervisor didn't stop them. "They *do* fall into these strange delusions. I must insist Lutz be kept under guard for the remainder of the Committee's stay at the Enclave."

The rest was remarkably easy. They scolded him. Told him again he was going to lose his Committee credentials. Todd had foreseen that, and Lutz said he no longer cared, if it helped find the truth. That it had. The business of the insu-suits remained thorny. The supervisor toyed with the thought of wiping Todd's mind with hypno drugs, but the unrepentant "fanatic" raised such a howl about the prospect they decided it wasn't worth the bother. He realized, from their attitude, they had already mapped their strategy for dealing with Ed Lutz's revelations. When he left the Enclave, he could expect to be watched. How long, he didn't know. They would let him ramble about seeing Elizabeth Gola close up. But they would make sure he was made to look like an idiot if he elaborated on *how* he had achieved that. No problem. It would be easy. A nobody from the United Ghetto States, a naive new mysticism convert . . . Todd knew, all too well, the power of manipulative media methods and undercut propaganda. By the time the Enclave agents in CNAU and the Committee members who were cooperating with them got through, Ed Lutz would be a forgotten person. The only thing anyone would remember about his revelations would be that he had seen the African heroine, safe, frozen, ready for the future. Very neat.

Ed Lutz was a pariah. They took him back to the infirmary and posted guards at the door, barring contact with other Committee members. Obviously, they didn't want him contaminating the innocent, not until they had gotten their counter propaganda tightly organized.

Todd dozed but didn't allow himself to sleep deeply. It seemed like a long time until the tour windup. They had set aside a barless prison for him on the shuttle flight back to Marambio—a separate seat, close to the V.I.P. section and well away from the other lower-echelon members. An Enclave attendant sat beside him throughout the flight, making sure he didn't mingle or talk to anyone. At Marambio, they kept him aboard the shuttle until everyone else was on the commercial plane for the flight to Buenos Aires. Then they escorted him to another set-apart seat. There were no restraints, no obvious signs that he was under arrest. But it was very close to that. Other members watched him with wide eyes and whispered behind their hands about the rebel. The flight north to Argentina seemed to take days, not an hour and a half.

No one detained him at the Committee's Arrivals lounge. But by now the rest of the Committee had gotten the message, even if they hadn't been told exactly what it was "Ed Lutz" had done to incur the V.I.P.s' wrath. No one spoke to him. People who had been sociable to Todd on the flight down avoided him, sunshine allies, treating him as if he had the plague.

He had to wait while everyone else completed a series of forms and vid recordings, attesting they had completed the tour and were satisfied with what they had seen. No one asked Ed Lutz to make such a recording. The P.O.E. staffers kept him in the lounge until everyone else had departed. Then they let him go.

Todd wasn't alone. He spotted the men following him immediately. Enclave agents? Protectors of Earth? The smothered fury he had been nursing ever since he had discovered the truth at the pole sank, cold fear rushing in over it. They were tracking him still. He couldn't let go of the act, not for a while. "Ed Lutz" trudged to the international terminal gate and boarded his shuttle for Orleans. So did the strangers who had followed him from the Human Rights Committee lounge. Nicely arranged. Tickets in hand well in advance. They had known his itinerary and were going to stay right with him all the way.

Curiously, their dogging him like this was a relief. Todd hadn't been sure how far the conspiracy extended, or to what lengths it might go to crush leaks. On the long flight back from Antarctica, he had thought, far too often, about Gib Owens and the passengers on the Nairobi shuttle. Ostracism had been a picayune nuisance, in comparison with that.

But they *hadn't* sabotaged the Enclave shuttle. And now, with these trackers accompanying him on the flight to Orleans, it looked very much as if the passengers around Todd—innocent people—were safe, too. It meant they had bought his story—the Enclave supervisor and the guards and the V.I.P. Committee seniors. Bought "Ed Lutz" and his mooning attempt to see Elizabeth Gola, just as the voters bought whatever Pat Saunder offered for sale with his voice and pale eyes and handsome presence.

But even if these clumsy watchers meant no harm—just wanted to monitor "Ed Lutz" and possibly keep him under control if he started spouting to the media—they were going to be a hell of a problem. How could he shake them? Ed Lutz had to vanish, because Todd Saunder had to reappear. Todd Saunder had important things to do, and he couldn't do them while towing this embarrassing comet's tail of snoops.

Nominal landing at Orleans. Still no sabotage. Todd wasn't

breathing normally yet, but he was almost amused to note the
men trying to be unobtrusive as they continued to trail him
through the vast terminal. Just one domestic flight to make, and
the trek to Lutz's apartment, and maybe along the way he would
find a method of ditching them . . .

Todd rounded a corner and three burly men closed in on him,
hemming him in toward a wall. "Ed Lutz? Protectors of Earth
Enforcement," the biggest one said, flashing an ident. Mask-faces
again, as hard or harder than those of the Enclave guards.

"What do you . . . what is this?"

Over one of the brawny shoulders crowding him, Todd saw his
other unasked-for problems come to a halt. The men who had
tracked him from Buenos Aires drifted toward one another and
conferred in hurried whispers, confused, staring at the sudden
group of muscle surrounding their quarry.

Todd tried to twist aside, looking frantically for a way out of
the wall. A heavy hand clutched his arm, pushing him hard.
"Hey! What the hell . . . !" They were shoving him, a door
banging open on a dark passageway. Some kind of terminal access, for employees only. Todd struggled violently, punching and
kneeing.

He was fighting robots. They dragged him abruptly sideways,
through yet another door. Where the hell were they taking him?
And why? He was beyond fear, going cold with stunned surprise.
It wasn't supposed to happen like this. He had made all the plans,
how to get out of the Enclave, what to do if he uncovered what
he suspected he would . . . the plane hidden on the roof near
Lutz's apartment . . .

These human elephants weren't any part of the plan.

"Damn you! Let me—"

A solid arm clamped across his throat, cutting off his air and
the words. Other hands pinned his, and someone snarled. "Shut
up! We'll explain later." The third man was leaning against the
closed door, ear to the plasticene as he listened for sounds from
the other side.

Red and black lights danced behind Todd's vision, a roaring in
his head. The steely arm was mashing his carotid, sending him
down into unconsciousness. Fear . . . anger . . . all of it fading,

being engulfed in sorrow. He had failed, never had a chance to talk to Pat. And Dian, he would never . . .

"Let go of him, stupid. You're strangling him." Dizzy, blood suddenly rushing up his arteries and into his brain, Todd became aware he was free. The arms that had been pinning him, choking him, were now propping him up. Lights still danced at the edge of his vision, but he was able to see. He blinked at the three men. The biggest one was holding up a hand, cautioning Todd to be quiet. He said softly, "Sorry. We had to get you away from them in a hurry, before they could close in."

Todd leaned against a pile of storage bins, gingerly shaking his head to steady out the ringing in his ears. The man posted by the door was still listening, but his attitude was more relaxed than before. Apparently whoever he was guarding against—the trackers who had followed Todd from the Southern Hemisphere?—had gone away. Todd was reminded of himself, hiding in the burned-out building in New Washington, listening to the assassin pilots searching the airspace outside his metal and glass cave.

He almost smiled. The effort hurt, activating abused skin and muscles all the way down to his collarbone. *"Are* you P.O.E. Enforcement?"

The biggest man smiled back at him. "Yes. A particular faction. Not all Protectors of Earth swallows Earth First's party line. We're Spacers, like Mrs. Fairchild. General Ames has kept in touch with some of your people . . . a Mikhail Feodor, a Putnam . . . and with some Goddard agents. We got here to back you up as soon as we could."

Todd's own words echoed in his mind! *"It pays off to delegate authority, if you pick the right people."* Mikhail, Elaine, and a lot of *very* loyal people, people who cared about the future.

"You might say, Mr. Saunder, that we're McKelvey's ground troops. We know what's been happening up there, what certain elements on Earth are trying to do to our base on the Moon. It's criminal, and we've tolerated it long enough. We don't live on the Moon or in a habitat, but we believe in what you and Mrs. Fairchild are saying," the trio's leader explained earnestly. "I apologize for the rough stuff. Speed was essential. We couldn't let them catch you, or let you get any further as Ed Lutz. They located the plane you had hidden for your getaway. It's been booby-trapped."

Todd sucked in his breath. It hurt to do that, too. He glared at the muscular type who had headlocked him. The elephant had the grace to look sorry.

"Dr. Foix's waiting for you, she and some of the others. We'll take you there. Big things are starting to happen, sir. We've got to stop it." The spokesman hesitated, then said bluntly, "A war. The cretins are pushing it, and it's about to blow up in all our faces, worse than the Death Years, worse than the Chaos."

Todd dared to let go of part of his held-in emotions for the first time in hours. Maybe the species *was* worth saving, if there were still people like these, like Fairchild and his ComLinkers, willing to risk service oaths, political careers, and their lives for humanity.

"We'd better go, sir . . ."

Todd massaged his neck, walking along with them through a maze of passageways. The men knew Orleans Terminal far better than he did, which was humbling. "That was a good stunt, if a trifle rough," he said by way of forgiving them. "It ought to keep those Enclave types busy for a while, wondering where Ed Lutz disappeared to and who he's talking to about what he saw at the pole. By the way, do you know who booby-trapped my flier?"

"Not precisely, but it was somebody working for Saunder Enterprises . . ."

He was sorry he had asked, but not surprised. Saddened, though. The surprise was in a shadowy alley a half-kilometer from the terminal. The men were using an old methanol-powered, internal-combustion-engined vehicle. Todd hadn't seen one of those for twenty years. The antique blended in well with the construction slums lining the rubble-strewn highways leading east. Todd peered out the grimy window as they rode along, seeing the shacks, the burned-out warehouses. He thought of the synthafood riots which had almost killed him and stopped Project Search before it was announced to the world. Those riots started here, in these miserable hovels. If they had stopped him, that would have changed a great many things that had happened in the weeks since. For better, or for worse? No turning back, then or now.

They followed bumpy, twisting roads into the city. The land north of Orleans had changed drastically after the New Madrid quake had sucked up so much of the river.

But the Gulf shore still got enough rain to keep vegetation jungle-wild. Tropical flora threatened to take over parts of the centuries-old buildings and parks. Again Todd felt like laughing. These three burly Third Millennium Spacers, and *he* was president of ComLink, head of the project which had spotted the incoming alien, hands across the light-years. And the Enclave, dream of the future, an awakening from cryogenic sleep. Transglobal and orbital flight, at speeds impossible forty years ago. And they were riding in a car left from the previous century, scraping along at forty kilometers per hour on quaint, air-inflated wheels!

They left the crooked thoroughfare and weaved down a dirt path toward some trees. Not until they were within ten meters of the trees did Todd realize the things weren't there. Holo-mode, a good one. The driver behaved as if they were real, carefully detouring around the trees, then steering inside a cavernous structure. An abandoned food storehouse. Todd hoped all the rats had been exterminated before these Fairchild supporters moved in. The place was now a command post and a hangar. Military-equipped fighter and shuttle craft crowded the area. Com monitors were everywhere. The structure bustled with hundreds of people intent on very serious business—the business of saving *Homo sapiens* from itself.

Dian met Todd with a tight embrace as he emerged from the old car. For several minutes, he couldn't speak, didn't want to, relishing being alive and close to Dian once more. Finally, she pulled back. "I'm going to convert. I've been praying to Beth's Spirit of Humanity, and you're here, and okay! Oh, God! I've been so scared!"

Some of ComLink's other key personnel were in the hangar, too. Their relief at Todd's return from limbo was heartwarming. Mikhail Feodor, his broad Slavic face split in a grin, pumped Todd's hand while others swarmed around them yelling greetings. These were the ones in on the secret, who had risked their lives to pull off Todd's crazy invasion of the Enclave. Touched by their welcome, Todd mock-scolded them. "What are you doing here? You're supposed to be up at Geosynch or keeping your heads

down in the planetside offices." Then he looked tenderly at
Dian. "How's Beth? And the others?"

"They're doing fine. Ed said he'd hide out in space, just to see
what it was like, since he had to hide, anyways. So it was arranged." Dian gestured toward a lean, uniformed black man edging through the circle surrounding Todd. Ames. The second in
command who had never grabbed publicity, except to pose as a
hard liner. Another man, like Todd and Ed Lutz, who specialized
in blending in with his background, increasing his value when he
decided to commit treason and help Pat Saunder's political rival
and the Earth First's candidate's own brother. His face had lost
some of that inscrutable mask, though not all of it.

"General," Todd said, nodding. "Thanks. You made it possible, right down to rescuing me out from under those goons at the
terminal."

"I still wish you hadn't done it, Mr. Saunder." Ames gave a
pained sigh. "But it's done." He paused, his eyes narrowing. "I
gather it paid off."

"Yes, it did. And *I* wish it hadn't—"

Ames didn't let him go on. "That happens. The thing is, to use
what we find to stop something worse from happening. Like now.
I know McKelvey. I served with him some years ago. But he
won't trust me now, or any other Earth-based officer. I can't say I
blame him. It means I'm going to have to ask a civilian to do
something he shouldn't meddle with—again. And this time it *is*
me doing the asking, not you. You're our connection to Goddard,
Mr. Saunder. I just hope to hell you can keep them from coun-
terattacking. You've got to."

Startled, Todd gawked at him, and Dian broke in. "It just
started, Todd. Goddard's gone on war status. They were hit with
a new wave of missiles while you were en route from the pole.
And this time they struck back." Her dark eyes filled with tears.
"They were ready. They disarmed one of the incoming birds and
got a tight ident. They found out who . . ."

Ames finished for her, his manner dripping contempt. "Riccardi. Not only has he been providing guidance with his com sats,
but Goddard's agents tapped into his line—an unscrambled line
—when he was making plans with President Galbraith."

The revelations stunned Todd—Goddard's proof against its en-

emies, while he had been in Antarctica gathering a different sort
of proof.

"Riccardi's apparently been using his satellite network to handle
the missile launches," Ames explained. "He helped the anti-
Spacers mask orbital build-points with holo-modes. In retaliation,
Goddard hit him hard with *their* missiles, and they've got some
heavy stuff, thanks to the Lunar Base. They've had the capability
for some time. We knew it, and we've been hoping to God
nobody would push them into using it."

Mikhail Feodor broke in, his voice shaking. "They hit Riccardi's northwest Geosynch, boss. Killed everybody on station."

Riccardi. Todd's business rival, one who had often played very
rough. Had he united with Goddard's enemies because he hated
Todd and anything Todd was supporting, like the Colony? Or
had there been more to his murderous opposition?

"He . . . Riccardi was on his inspection rotation this week,
wasn't he?" Todd asked, knowing the answer, remembering his
rival's schedules very well. "He was on that Geosynch with his
staffers. Dead." The faces around him registered horror. Enemy
or not, Riccardi depended, as they did, on the orbiting HQs.
They, too, had been riders in such satellite villages and knew the
terrible vulnerability of those structures. They envisoned themselves trapped in Riccardi's situation, sudden death ripping open
the hulls and pouring them and their air out into high vacuum.
Todd shook his head in bewilderment that Riccardi had invited
that retaliation from Goddard. Had blatantly asked for it. And
had let his enemy find out about it when he was stupid enough to
use an open circuit to talk to his conspirator. No wonder Ames
was so contemptuous of the dead anti-Spacer. "What about
Galbraith?" Todd inquired.

Ames made a rude noise. "The CNAU President's in over his
ears. So's Ybarra. And Monte. And Weng."

Weng. Boss of that vicious little secret police chief on Mari's
tape. The pieces all falling into place. The hyperendors weren't
wearing off; Todd's thinking was sharper than it had ever been.
The petty tyrants, and factions within their countries, turning
more and more to Goddard's cheaper power. It wasn't only anti-
alien paranoia. It was economics. And the greed, the brutal tyr-
anny, were far more dangerous than Earth's fear of the unknown.

The fear was random. The greed moved with calculation. Kill Goddard. Kill its enemies in the Enclave.

And kill Todd Saunder, who might find out the truth.

Todd took a deep breath and held it. Ames and the others were watching him. "Pat can stop Galbraith, probably pull the strings to stop the others, too. I'm sure there are some you haven't named, General. If you can give me the data, I'll pile it on my brother and make him listen—even if I have to put a gun to his head."

"That's already there, Mr. Saunder. Goddard's gun. Her missiles. I'm expecting their declaration of war any hour now. Killing Riccardi wasn't the end of it. His heirs are frantic for revenge, and the other conspirators are cornered. They fight and win, or lose everything."

"But we're the ones who really lose," Todd said with cold anger. He glanced at Dian. There was something in her eyes, something deep and terrible. "I found it," he said simply. "Exactly what I didn't want to find."

She was nodding. "So did we. The buried accounts. The erased idents. The other end of the conspiracy. And something else." The eyes were brightening with a light that illuminated the immense hangar. Todd's pulse quickened in response as Dian spoke. "The key. The critical piece. The alien's still meeting us more than halfway. And I feel sure that means it sprang from a civilization not too impossibly different from our own. It all broke, just as Beth and I felt it would. That's why they firebombed us, Todd. They listened in, knew how close we were. Now *real* communication begins. We were this close when they . . ." She held her thumb and forefinger a centimeter apart. Then she frowned. "You were limping when you got out of the car."

"Staged the burn, the plan we discussed. Necessary. It's not important."

"Are you all right now?"

"No. But it has nothing to do with my leg." Todd's anger was returning, redoubled. "General Ames, where's my brother right now?"

Ames indicated a nearby monitor. Spy monitor. Even Patrick Saunder wasn't immune. Protectors of Earth guarded him, guarded their star member and probable future Chairman. But

P.O.E. watched him, too. "Scheduled to arrive at SE Mainland HQ in about an hour. Chairman Li Chu is calling an emergency session of Protectors of Earth for this evening. Your brother undoubtedly intends to make a speech . . ."

A speech arousing Earth, whipping her billions into more xenophobic frenzy as a result of Goddard's strike against Riccardi's satellites.

"He'll make the speech," Todd promised. "But not the one he expects to. I'm going to replace his speech writers. If I have to, I'll override him with ComLink's translator-splitters around the world, and Pat knows I can. I've never done that, but I will—edit his words, use his voice to say what I want to say, to reach the world." Mikhail and the rest of Todd's people were shocked at the threat, but nodded, ready to go against all their ethics if they had to.

"You'll have help," the military man said tersely. Todd tried to read his face. He couldn't. Ghetto face. McKelvey's face when McKelvey refused to let down the walls. Coup d'état in the making? Galbraith about to lose his Presidency in an overthrow? And Weng and his secret police, about to disappear as they had made so many others disappear? Todd was afraid to ask for details.

"Hold off, General. Let me try it my way first. Can you get me to my brother? Is Earth on war status, too?"

"We'll get you there, Mr. Saunder. But first, let's swap data. Cover all the possibilities. Then, if . . ."

If I'm killed, the facts I learned in the Enclave won't be buried with me. And if I can get through to Pat, I'll need what the general and all the agents and Spacers and the rest of this hidden network have uncovered, to clinch the arguments.

"Todd," Dian said shakily, "sabotaging your plane, someone from Saunder Enterprises . . ."

He held her very close, taking and giving comfort. "I know. It's a risk. But I have to try. For all of us. And you'll have to back me up, with ComLink. You and Mikhail . . . everyone." His people were agreeing, very sober and determined. "General, can you protect my people?"

"We'll certainly try, Mr. Saunder. And your satellites. We need those." Ames and his fellow military conspirators were caught in a difficult situation. "We're sympathetic to Goddard, want to stop the madness. But we'll have to commandeer your equipment to fight a possible counterstrike from Goddard. The one on Riccardi came too fast. The next ones . . ."

"There won't be a next one," Todd returned flatly. "Dian, if I don't—" She tried to stop him. He went on, drowning her out. "If I don't make it, finish Project Search. Meet the aliens for me, if any of us are still here."

"We'll meet them together," Dian said, her chin going up.

Todd fed his data to the staffers in the hangar. Computers relayed to other computers, a global and orbiting network. Goddard wouldn't open the circuits. Todd was dismayed. Ames shrugged, not surprised. The state of things. Worsening steadily. Ames *was* surprised and appalled by the extent of murders in the Enclave. And Todd absorbed as much as he could of the corroborating data. Family matters. Family disgrace. Saunder Enterprises. He was cutting his heart open, spilling his heart's blood. But these people had a right to know.

ComLink, Fairchild's Third Millennium Movement, the civilian and military underground that General Ames represented—working together to stop an impact with disaster.

Dr. Tedesco had sent counter remedies, via Dian. Todd took the first dosage in the treatment that would return him to being Todd Saunder physically. It should be having a noticeable effect by the time he reached Pat, enough so he would be recognized. There was a flier waiting, and a bit of an argument when Todd insisted he was going to fly her. The co-pilot's motives and his chase pilot's were strong. But not as strong as his. He intended to outfly them all.

Time was telescoping. The future, terrible or wonderful, thundering toward them. By the time he was geared for flight, his irises were already faded to blue, his skin lightening, some of the kink relaxing from his now-undyed hair. Todd moved by reflex, boarding the flier, familiarizing himself with the systems. Outside, on the hangar floor, Dian was watching, waving, seeing him off. A million years ago—Dian, waving, seeing him off for Goddard, Gib Owens riding co-pilot at his side.

The flier lifted, sidling, almost but not quite out of control. The big man who had led the rescue team at the terminal was his co-pilot. The trooper inhaled sharply, clutching the safety bar, and

Todd grinned, getting even for the rough treatment earlier. "Hang on," he warned. A lot of ship was under his hands and voice. Enough, he hoped, to get him to New York-Philly in time to prevent a species' extinction.

He pushed propulsion, zooming through the opening hangar door, barely clearing obstructions. People dived out of his way. Todd flew straight into the holo-mode of the trees. "Good imagery," he complimented the Protectors of Earth enforcement officer. "But not as good as my father's inventions are capable of. I saw just what they can do, when their use is perverted, in Antarctica." Wide-eyed, the other man braced himself. Behind them, the screens showed Todd's chase escort, scrambling to catch up with him, flying out of the hangar in his wake.

Invisible fury exploded rearward in a full-power launch. Todd's flier leaped into the sky, gees slamming him and the P.O.E. trooper back in their seats. Data tore across the screens faster than most human eyes could take it. Todd noted what he needed, flying on instinct, mock-attacking Saunderhome once more. The other man was priming the military gear, on the com with the chase fliers trailing them. They were scrambler-masked from CNAU Flight Control—which might still be loyal to Galbraith and the anti-Spacer conspirators. The screens read heavy weaponry on board Todd's ship and the others. They would fight their way through to Pat, if they had to.

Todd reached for sub-orbital altitude, high above the slow-moving civilian traffic. Earth lay far below, her ugliness and old scars lost from this height. Earth. Humanity's birthplace. Earth, at the bottom of a gravity well. And Goddard, priming a counterlaunch. The Earth First Party had clamored for a war, in its own way, and was likely to get it. Species' suicide was a voice command away.

He pushed his flier to Mach 3, aiming eastward, still accelerating, flying over old battlefields. History. Man's conflict with himself. Brother against brother . . . and against sister. The ship became a two-passenger defensive missile, its target an underground castle, and a man with a golden voice.

CHAPTER NINETEEN

THE DEBTS COME DUE

HE walked into the V.I.P. train-and-car parking area. The storm troopers protecting Saunder Enterprises Mainland HQ weren't expecting that. Nobody arrived here on foot. The guards specialized in screening vehicles and their occupants. Todd almost made it to the elevator bank before they noticed him and swung around, training their weapons on him.

Todd raised his hands and walked on toward them slowly, his voice cold and firm. "I'm Todd Saunder, in case you don't recognize me. Patrick Saunder's brother. If you shoot me, you're going to have one hell of a mess to explain to the family." The guns and electrostingers wavered as he kept coming at them. "I'm going down to the apartments to see my brother. I know he's here, so don't give me any nonsense about his being on a campaign tour. Are you going to get out of my way, or do I let ComLink go live to the world with my execution?" Carefully, not wanting to move their nervous trigger fingers, Todd pulled aside his flight coat and let them see the chest relay miniaturized lens he wore. Nuñez, Falco, Chabot, and the other media hotshots had taught Earth how much could be captured and sent out to the world via such a tiny device. One of Ward Saunder's spinoffs. One of hundreds. The guards edged back, reluctantly. One of them whispered into a security monitor.

"Tip him off. That's okay. A lot of surprises come with my package. You can't ruin them by warning him I'm on the way."

But if the surprise never got there?

Riding down in the elevator, Todd didn't dare breathe. Guards, checking these elevators for bombs and booby traps, ostensibly to protect their employer. If they knew how to spot one, chances were they also knew how to plant such a device—and remove an unwanted intruder.

But nothing happened.

The aides and inner-fortress bodyguards didn't try to stop Todd when he stepped out into the subterranean foyer. They watched him with animosity and muttered among themselves, earning his sneer. He went on into the apartments and used the complex's own spy monitor systems to narrow his search. Pat and Carissa were in their bedroom suite.

Carissa might be a problem. What Todd had to say could cause severe shock, possibly bring on a miscarriage. Despite what was at stake, he didn't want that. There had been too many deaths already.

And this death would be that of a little Saunder.

They looked up as he walked in. They had been told about his approach. Carissa was tremulous and puzzled, smiling uneasily. Pat was hard-faced, ready to strike. But he was confused, too, reacting out of that emotion and what his guards had told him about Todd's words and actions.

"Kid! What the hell . . . ?"

"Todd! Where on Earth have you been? I've been calling your space station for a week!" Jael, on the com at Carissa's bedside. Todd glanced at the screen. Jael was sitting in her office at Saunderhome, palm trees visible out the window panel beyond her head. The dowager queen in her castle, as Pat was in his.

"Hello, Carissa," Todd said gently, ignoring the screen and Pat. He kissed his sister-in-law's cheek, squeezed her hands. Then he straightened and looked at Pat and at Jael's image. "Can we adjourn? Elsewhere. I don't care where in this cave. But we'd better be private and masked—fair warning. You're going to answer some questions, and you may not want the whole world to hear us when you do. Not yet."

"Todd, how *dare* you burst in on our conversation like this!"

Pat had gazed steadily at Todd ever since he had come into the room. Unlike the last time they had seen each other, Pat was now cold sober and very much in possession of his faculties. And of his intuition. "We'll do as he says, Mother."

"Pat, don't leave me!" Carissa wailed, clutching Pat's arm. He kissed her and summoned the doctor and nurses, leaving her in the women's care. "Pat! Pat! Please don't cut me out like this . . ." The medics were giving Carissa something to calm her down when Pat led Todd out of the room.

Todd followed him through the labyrinthine apartments. He didn't recognize most of these rooms any more. Pat and Jael had changed everything radically. They had changed themselves, too, perhaps. Too much. Pat stopped at what was obviously his staff's security command center. Five mufti-clad "aides" gaped as Pat pointed at the door. "Get out. And if I find any of you sons of bitches have tapped into my private lines *again,* you'll end up stationed at a Saunder Enterprises seal farm in northern Greenland. Out!"

They went, fearing him and hating him, not hiding their reactions. A massive series of doors closed, sealing the brothers in. Their sole contacts with the outside world were the shimmering monitor screens. Pat spoke to the systems. "All right. Transfer Jael Saunder's call to this station. Terminal one. Full scrambler lock on the connection. I don't want anyone else with us. Emphatic. Execute."

Jael appeared on screen one. She was seething, predictably, furious with both her sons. "I hope you have a good reason to—"

"How about murder?" Todd asked, wasting no valuable time.

"What?" Pat blinked and shook his head, then flared at him. "What murder? Goddard again? You blaming me for that? And what's all this talk about my guards shooting you?"

"Goddard. Yes. You are to blame." Todd hesitated, regarding Pat intently. "You don't know? You honestly don't know?" He wanted to believe that, more than anything in his life. "I *did* expect a challenge, or to be shot on sight. The plane I was going to take here was booby-trapped, by Saunder Enterprises techs, Pat. It would have blown me out of the sky. The only reason I'm here is because some Spacer supporters spotted the attempt on my life and provided alternate transport, military style, with weapons and

masking scramblers. Just like your private ships carry. You and
Mother are getting pretty damned good at assassination preven-
tion measures. Does it go both ways? Prevent it? Or cause it? Is
that what we've come to, Pat? Murder? My murder? Three hundred and twenty innocent people on the Nairobi shuttle? People
Galbraith's trying to kill with anti-Spacer missiles? Or thousands
of people in SE Antarctic Enclave, people supposedly saved for
the future? But they've been eliminated, down to the very
cubicles they should be resting in. I suppose it doesn't matter,
really. I mean, what's the difference if it's one or a few thousand?
It's all a body count, right?"

Pat forced a derisive laugh. "You're mad. That's the only explanation possible." Fighting. Still fighting it. Pat Saunder wasn't
a quitter, and he wouldn't give up easily, not with his honor and
his future at stake.

"Second system," Todd commanded the adjacent screen. "Put
me through to ComLink Central. And don't stall me. I know
they're ready. Connect." He looked at Pat and at Jael's image.
"You want this scrambled, too? I'll give you time to get your
alibis together. The only fair thing to do, for the family." No
reply. Todd shrugged and added on a scrambler lock. The systems refused it. They would respond only to Pat or to one of his
clearance-rated "aides." His face an impending hurricane, Pat
gave the order.

Dian appeared on the second screen. Like Jael's, her image
wavered slightly under the influence of the masking circuitry.
"Got it, Todd," she said. She split the screen. A staticky,
machine-created set of shapes and figures formed in the lower
frame. A voice, high-pitched yet growling. Imitating its master's.

"Earth . . . Earth . . . Vahnaj . . . Vahnaj . . . Earth . . .
Vahnaj . . ."

A name! Todd grinned, delighting in the present Dian had
given him amid so much grief A name for the alien. Its world's
name? And what they called themselves, most likely, as the intelligent species which had originated on Earth were the Earthmen.

Todd couldn't hold back the tears. He wiped his face with the
backs of his hands, not ashamed of his joy. But this wasn't the
time. He hadn't wanted this to happen here, under these condi-

tions. Dian had no choice, he knew. Yet the wonderful discovery was tainted, thanks to what his family had done.

Pictures. Machine-made, a little jerky because of the communications difficulties and the astronomical distances involved. A human figure! Spelled out in a rapid-fire series of static blips, compressed, rippling dots and open spaces. No, *two* human figures! Male and female. Copied from the Voyager plaque, as some idealistic Science Council members wanted to believe? Todd doubted it. Dian and Project Search had sent a similar mode weeks ago. That was probably the image the Vahnaj messenger had picked up and copied. Replaying humanity to itself, but with more clarity than any of the previous signals. Now Todd understood Dian's excitement. Words, a name, figures . . .

Another picture. Two more figures. Male and female. Not human. Humanoid. Distinct and subtle difference in the images, reproduced side by side. Human and Vahnaj. The average height, calculated against the spectrum wavelength Dian had supplied originally, was a bit taller than that for *Homo sapiens*. The head was broader, flatter on top, perched upon a very long neck and steeply sloping shoulders. A long torso, abnormally so by human standards. Slender appendages. Three fingers and an opposing thumb, shown in quick extreme close-ups formed of the on-and-off static. The images shifted, ultra-sophisticated, close-ups and side-by-side comparisons of the two species, the machine supplying the contact point for *Homo sapiens* and Vahnaj to view each other for the first time.

Todd wondered if the messenger had sent the images back home. They wouldn't have reached there yet. Might not for years. The *real* Vahnaj. Not their images. Again he wanted to weep at the awesome concept.

The four figures, drawn with signals from a vehicle hurtling toward Saturn's orbit, moved, squatted in a powwow circle. The preferred Vahnaj conference ritual? They extended hands, representing the living beings behind the images. Touched fingers, five-fingered hands to four-fingered. The mechanical voice spoke as the figures' mouths appeared to open and close. "Kusta. Vahnaj."

Dian's voice cut over the machine's, explaining. "Kusta equals Talk. Vahnaj equals Earth. *Their* Earth."

Machine-voice: "Yes. Earth. Yes. Kusta. Talk. Signal equals

Talk. Bel equals Kusta. Sha." The figures were making gestures,
moving again. Demonstrating. Dian had sent signals such as
these, too, weeks ago. Apparently the alien machine had had to
think it over. And perhaps decided if it *wanted* to communicate
with such a species? In a way, humanity was on probation. As
Dian had said, most of the work would be done by the Vahnaj
machine. But Project Search had supplied its own share of the
key. Pidgin English. Baby talk.

But it was talk—with another species, from another world!

On the screen, the alien figures held something—a fruit or
vegetable shape, to human eyes. The human figure also held
something. The figures reached out to one another, trading what
they held. Again. Lines traced on the crude figures' faces, both
species'. Smiles.

"My God," Todd whispered, shaken by the discovery. Facial
muscles, only so many ways to stretch on a humanoid face. But
there were human cultures which didn't express friendliness and
pleasure with that expression. Not many, but a few. Another evolution, light-years away, had matched them, for all the peculiari-
ties of the Vahnaj physique.

Smile. Friend. We come in peace.

No guarantees. But it was one hell of a more convincing proof
of peaceful intentions than anything Todd had been able to show
anyone previously!

Dian froze the image on the scene of the four figures clasping
hands with one another, those smiles on their simplified faces.
"There's more. Kilotons of it. Pouring in now, faster than we can
absorb it. To us. To Goddard. To the science institutions' orbiting
telescopes, to ground stations. A flood. The machine's boosting its
gain now, Todd. It's finally understanding just how backward we
are. That is humiliating, but it's also wonderful. We have so much
to learn . . ."

"It'll revolutionize our communications systems, for a start,"
Todd said out of his own field of expertise, touching the tiniest
fragment of the significance of the new data.

"She's lying. It's a hoax." Jael. She didn't really believe what
she was saying. Todd detected the cornered-tigress defeat in her
tone.

"Keep saying that until the aliens get here, Mother. Eight

months, by our current vector calculations. Dian, give me the rest
of it. And you two, I can handle the alien. What I can't handle is
politics. In this case, murder."

The magnificent, enriching aspect of this four-way conversation
was over. Now Todd had to deal with the dark side, the mali-
ciousness, the cruelty. Dian gave her signal over fully, the screen
filling with a blizzard of data.

Facsimiles. Readouts. ComLink, calling in debts. Breaking
through the locks. Mikhail and Putnam, other loyal ComLink
staffers, going around when they couldn't get through the
scramblers. They had been digging everywhere. Just scraping the
surface, but there was, as Dian had described the alien signals, a
flood, even so. Not all the holes had been plugged. Not all the
conspirators had been paid enough to ensure their silence.

Stock transfers. Halmahera—Djailolo's conqueror—selling
stock cheap to Saunder Enterprises. Too cheap to be honest. !Ngai
—Elizabeth Gola's oppressor—stock sold to Saunder Enterprises.
Bloek—Van Eyck's enemy—stock to Saunder Enterprises. Energy. Transport. Syntha food. Fishing franchises.

Documents, with Patrick Saunder's recognizable, written signa-
ture. More stock changing hands. And property. A lot of valuable
property. Property in lands where slavery had been reinstituted to
serve tyrants. Property in countries ruled by oppressive governments and murderous warlords, countries which Protectors of
Earth was trying to reform. Saunder Enterprises, secretly profiting
off the blood of these millions.

"That's enough," Jael said tonelessly.

"There's more, Mrs. Saunder," Dian countered, rigidly correct.
"A very great deal more. Todd and I worked together on this—
him going to the Enclave, me putting ComLink's people on these
hidden stats. And this is just the surface."

Pat yelled, "Wait! Just wait! I didn't sign those!" He pointed at
the documents on the screen. "What the hell? Are you trying to
frame me, Todd? Do you know what this'll do to . . ."

"To the election? To the campaign? Face it, Pat, in a few
hours, if Galbraith and the others get what they deserve, Goddard
and the Moon are going to start lobbing missiles *back* at Earth.
You won't have a world to govern. No, I'm not trying to frame

you. These things are real. All we did was turn over the rocks and find out where they were hidden. *Some* of them."

Todd moved toward his brother and took him by the shoulders, holding Pat tightly, searching those eyes. "Tell me. Straight. Please. You didn't *know?*"

There was an endless moment of stillness. Then, together, like automatons, they turned toward Jael's image. A telltale dot was flashing on Dian's monitor. She was recording what was happening in the sealed room. Jael made no move to override her, contemptuous.

"Yes," Jael said. "He doesn't know. Why should he? There was no need." The voice was velvet, despite the years of bitterness in the words. "Patrick always let me handle the dirty details. He says I have a gift for it. And I do."

Pat staggered to the screen, looming over it, shouting at her impotently. "My God! Forged documents? You forged my name to those deeds and properties? You sold me out to those murdering bastards! Todd was right. My God. My God. I've been promising the world I'd free it from those chains. And behind my back you're putting more chains on! Don't you realize what you've done? You're fomenting rebellion, plunging those countries back into the Chaos. You can't buy lives this way. I believe in Earth First, in the party's principles—"

"So do I!" Jael declared with fierce pride. She smiled lovingly at him, amused by his outrage. "That's exactly why we needed these things, to give you power. That's the answer to Earth's misery, Patrick. You know it. You have to compromise along the way in order to get the power to do the just things in the future. Power. I've told you that a thousand times. It's the only way to make sure they'll never tear us down."

"And if you have to turn off cryo cubicles in the Enclave, killing people, that's a compromise, too, Mother?" Todd was in the Antarctic again, cold, cold clear through to that part of his being the new mysticism termed the soul.

Jael's round face tightened. "Do you know what the revival-rate potentials are for those silly cryo systems? Maybe you've forgotten. I haven't. There were ten volunteers in Protectors of Earth's experiment. *One* of them came out whole. Three others revived, then died within six months—healthy volunteers, not a thing wrong with them until they got in those cubicles. The others never revived at all. Anomalies. Diseases, the testers said. They had a live reviver, and half the governments and Third Millennium fanatics in the world clamored for them to go ahead. They waved money at them, and the P.O.E. was eager to take it. There's your wonderful cryogenic 'hope for the future.' But they paid well."

"And the dictators and generals are still paying, aren't they, Mother? Only now they're paying directly to Saunder Enterprises, with a few bribes along the way to a corrupt Human Rights Committee." Todd couldn't bring himself to approach the screen, shuddering, staring at her image. "They pay, and you arrange for certain people to die. I put my hand through what should have been Elizabeth Gola. I could have done the same with . . . what? A thousand people? Two thousand? Three? God knows how many you've condemned to death with a com call to the Enclave, a change in some tyrant's ledgers over to Saunder Enterprises. How many? Okay. Probably only the capital punishment opponents would howl about the criminals dying. You'd likely do that for free and consider it good riddance. I remember how you think on the subject. But Gola? Van Eyck? Bustamonte? Goddard supporters, Earth First opponents, Pat's business rivals—trumped-up trials, phony charges, ship 'em to the Enclave and pull the plug. Neat. They're never coming back. And you know damned well that a lot of them wouldn't have gone there without a fight if they hadn't believed they had a chance to come back to life someday. You and the dictators and P.O.E. tricked the dissidents and the rebels, and the people who loved them. We killed them. Saunder Enterprises killed them. And we covered it all up so that Pat can become Chairman of Protectors of Earth. My God, Pat. My God, indeed!"

Pat, his voice rising, that power to move worlds—or his own family? "You *did* kill them, Mother. The staffers have to get their orders from somewhere. What . . . what have you done?" Jael had convinced him, where Todd alone might have failed.

"I made sure the Saunders will survive." No remorse. Her head was held high. Jael Hartman Saunder, throwing away a fortune and an elitist family, and replacing what she had lost with her love for Ward Saunder and her children—and her unquenchable thirst for enough power to make them all invulnerable. "We're here. We're on top. And we're going to stay this way. We'll *always* be here, from now on. A Saunder, hand on the reins, taking Earth where it ought to go," Jael said. Serene, strong, the woman who had made kings and presidents grovel, and pay to have their enemies "eliminated" secretly.

"You tried to kill *me,* Mother. Twice," Todd reminded her.

For a fraction of a second, Jael's cool demeanor trembled. "I'm sorry I had to do that, Todd. But you just wouldn't listen. I *did* warn you. And I made sure you were out of the way. I thought that would teach you . . ."

"Scare me off? I don't scare off, Mother. I'm a Saunder, too. A man died in that firebombing. A good man, decent, intelligent. Other people suffered terribly, are still suffering. All the burn treatments and get-well wishes you send won't wipe that out. You hurt them, would have hurt me if you could have."

"I regret their being caught. I truly do. But it's your fault. You should have quashed this thing about the aliens, at least until Patrick—"

Pat hammered on the console. "Goddammit! There isn't going to *be* any election for me now, Mother! Can't you get that through your head? You killed all chance for me to reach the Chairmanship when you killed those people. It's over. Done!" He jerked around, suddenly seizing on something Todd had said earlier. "The Nairobi shuttle? What . . . ?"

"Yes. Gib Owens, a Goddard courier, was on board, in disguise. They sabotaged the plane to get him. A 'regrettable accident.' He'd delivered a message from Mari and Kevin, about the Enclave and a lot of missing funds. I dug a bit, and that's when those planes almost shot me out of the sky." Todd looked at Jael. "I had a scrambler lock with me on that wild ride. I listened in on their com. That's how I know they were part of your bunch of killers, part of the bunch that destroyed that plane." Jael frowned, disgusted at the ineptitude of her hirelings. "Who were the dead pilots, the dupes? More pests somebody wanted removed? Did you let CNAU find them, or is CNAU Enforcement in your pocket, too? How far does this conspiracy run? Galbraith, obviously. He's looked the other way for you on a lot of things, hasn't he? And now you're looking the other way while he kills your daughter . . ."

Jael tensed against that accusation. "If Mariette would just . . ."

"Mother, Galbraith's going to destroy Goddard if he can, he and the rest of Earth First's fanatics and what's-in-it-for-me specialists. And Pat helped them, blinding Earth's people, telling them Goddard was their enemy."

"We're not responsible for that stupid old man," Jael said harshly. "I told Galbraith it was quite unnecessary to fire those missiles. We could simply starve Goddard into seeing things our way."

"Or poison them? Like that contaminated-food shipment to Lunar Base?" Pat made a strangling sound when Todd mentioned that unknown plot, racked by new horror.

Jael shrugged. "It's done."

"No, it's not. It's just beginning. You bought off P.O.E.'s earlier investigation into the missile attacks, and Riccardi and the anti-Spacers kept it up. Well, Riccardi's dead. And Galbraith and his co-conspirators will make one final attempt. They're in so deep they can't get out any other way. They hope to be tyrants of what's left after the holocaust. If Goddard goes, though, it'll take us with it. You and Pat didn't learn anything from Dad. You should have come up to orbit more often when we were rebuilding the satellites after the wars. Found out what missiles can do. Full potential. It's years later, and the weapons are a great deal meaner. We'll all pay—you, me, Pat, Carissa, the baby . . ."

Todd had struck a nerve, a deep one. Jael come up out of her chair. "No one is going to harm that baby! They won't be able to reach her!"

Pat counterattacked. "No, they won't. I'll protect 'Rissa and our child with my dying breath. But they'll have me. That's the least I can give to all the people we've wronged. I've . . . I've got to speak to the world, before it's too late . . ."

Hope rose in Todd's heart.

"It can be suppressed," Jael said coldly.

"No, Mother." Todd closed his eyes a moment before speaking. "It can't be. I've given the evidence to a lot of people, too many for you to kill them all. And if Pat won't tell the world, I will— with his voice. I can do it, with the translator-splitter and the thousands of kilometers of footage my people have accumulated on my magnificent orator brother over the last few years."

Pat was eyeing Todd with admiration, not anger. Oddly, he didn't seem to resist the prospect of throwing himself on the world's mercy. A martyr. A sacrifice. Genuinely grief-stricken. And yet . . . Todd almost began to believe Pat would somehow emerge from this as noble and brave, turning hate and vengeful uproar into forgiveness and new glory.

"Of course," Jael said. "No, nothing will happen. You *would* go into telecom, Todd! And that little bitch is recording this, naturally. All right. Give *me* to the wolves. The media hate me, anyway. It'll work. Let me handle it."

Pat cut her off. "You forged my name, did all this to bring *me* to power. I *am* in power. And it's my responsibility. You're not in charge of me, never again. Whatever you did, you did out of mistaken family loyalty, Mother. But I'm *not* going to throw my own mother to the sharks. You're a genius at cutting throats, but the only side of human nature you know about is the ugly side." Pat gulped for air, looking over his shoulder at his brother. "My God," he repeated in a whisper, appalled, the horror of it still falling onto him. "She tried to kill *you*? And Mari? It was true. All of Mari's accusations were true."

"You're the only one who really counts, you and that baby." It hurt Todd to say that. Sibling rivalries and petty childhood jealousies. But it was the truth. And this time, the truth meant disgrace for the handsome, favored, older brother.

"I wanted to do all of this painlessly," Jael said with sweet reasonableness. "I tried to. The people in the Enclave never suffered. They were in a coma before they arrived. If you'd just taken my warning, Todd . . ."

He cocked his head, answering her in the same adult, ultracivilized tone. "Just out of curiosity, when did you figure out that I *wasn't* in orbit and *was* at the Enclave? I halfway expected you to sabotage one of my planes a lot earlier than you did."

There was an icy silence. Then Jael turned on him. "Your holo-message from orbit was very convincing. You and Ward were always good at those things. I did indeed think you were in space. By the time I realized you weren't . . ."

"So. It was just a matter of timing. Or I would be dead, and so would all the other passengers on the Antarctic shuttle or the Sur Atlantique flight. Just another regrettable accident. You've become addicted to killing, and to power."

Small lights were flashing in the corners of both monitor screens. Someone outside the scrambler lock was trying frantically to break through, paging for attention. Absently, still reeling emotionally, Pat opened a circuit. A third screen flared to life, one of his aides on the screen, talking fast. "P.O.E. Chairman Li Chu, sir—emergency session—missile attacks—something coming in from Goddard—"

"Put it on," Pat said, all the strength gone from his marvelous voice.

Kevin McKelvey's image formed. ". . . pro tem governor of Goddard Colony and Lunar City Copernicus . . ."

Todd stiffened, hearing the change in designation. "Governor of Goddard *and* Lunar *City* Copernicus." Desertion. The entire Lunar Base. Total union with Goddard's fortunes. All the last ties to Earth had been cut.

"You've done it, Pat," Todd said bitterly. "Secession. They're fully allied with the Moon."

"Shut up. I've got to hear this."

Jael said nothing. Neither did Dian. She and the entire Com-Link system must be receiving the same message simultaneously.

". . . Goddard Space Station Charter Authority is hereby voided. We will no longer acknowledge or honor any treaties or sanctions enacted under the previous Protectors of Earth franchise of 2036. By unanimous vote of the inhabitants of our combined governments . . ."

"Ten thousand raving fanatics," Jael said derisively. No one paid her any attention.

". . . severing diplomatic relations with the following Earth nations, quasi-nations, and political coalitions, effective immediately: Riccardi Incorporated Network . . ."

"Operating under new management," Todd put in with grisly humor.

". . . Central South American Union and President Galbraith's Social Traditionalists Party, President Halmahera's faction of Nippon-Malaysia, Premier Ybarra's faction of the Maui-Andean

Populist Democracies, Nakamura's Worldwide TeleCom, Patrick Saunder's division of Saunder Enterprises . . ."

Pat winced, taking the blow, acting like a man who felt he must pay and expiate his shame.

The list went on, ticking off those who hated Goddard, sabotaged its power sats, attacked it, convicted or killed its planetside allies. The Okhotsk Concord, some of the Rift Country dictators, the nasty little Asian ruler whose security chief Todd had seen on the tape Gib smuggled out of Goddard.

The missing names were just as significant. Those who had backed Goddard and bought its power output and extended credit. The Israeli branch of the Rift Federation was there; and Alamshah, one of SE's competitors and one of Ward Saunder's friendly rivals, but a Spacer just the same; Dian's Midwestern United Ghetto States; ComLink . . .

Todd was one of their allies, yet being reminded, along with the rest of Earth, just what that might mean.

". . . will no longer endure these assaults. We will retaliate. This is a step we do not wish to take, but we have armed ourselves. Recent events have left us no choice. Protectors of Earth has refused to act on our grievances. We must redress our wrongs ourselves . . ."

P.O.E.'s incumbent Chairman, Li Chu, the woman who had designated Patrick Saunder as her political heir—had Jael bought her off, too? Todd stared bleakly at Kevin McKelvey. The big man wasn't alone. He was broadcasting from Goddard's master com center, and the room was crowded with enthusiastic aides and members of the Planning Group. Mari was among them. She wore the pseudo uniform of Goddard's civilian fighter forces, proud, her wonderful eyes glaring out at her enemies on Earth. Kevin's huge hands were clenched into fists and resting heavily on the com panel before him. His face promised vengeance to anyone who didn't heed what he was saying.

"Don't do it, Kevin," Todd begged uselessly.

"Earth has declared war on us, and we hereby acknowledge that that state exists between us. We will lay down our arms if Earth does to the same degree, and agrees to full and binding arbitration by a court of all humanity—a legal hearing to be conducted openly, on Earth and in space, in all languages, for all peoples, via ComLink. No other truce terms will be considered."

Around Kevin McKelvey, whoops and shouts rose, yells of defiance. Mari threw her arms around him, momentarily destroying the fragile decorum of the terrible announcement. Her dark hair against his golden mane—just as they had looked in the candid holo-mode Todd had taken so long ago, in a happier time. Other habitat citizens leaned into the lenses, shaking their fists, grinning angrily, and vowing to give Earth as good as they got.

Todd knew billions of planetsiders were watching, most of Earth. What would they make of this? They had to take the threat seriously. Pat had to make them understand—as he hadn't made them understand the true significance of the alien messenger. Mari. The Saunder princess, sister of the world-famous Patrick Saunder. Earth remembered her as a hell-raiser, a celebrity noted for wild adventures. Yet she had changed. Now she was a Goddardite, ready to fight and die for the Colony, calling Pat her enemy, embracing that traitor to his planet and his service, Kevin McKelvey.

Finally, Mari backed away and the other habitat citizens calmed down, their expressions stern. Kevin resumed his speech. "Earth leaders have declared Goddard and Lunar City cannot survive without Earth. We *will* survive—alone. The future of humanity lies in the stars, with the race of Vahnaj . . ."

They had picked up the signals, just as Dian had said they would. They knew. And for all Mari's resentment at having been outraced, Goddard accepted the inevitable. A hand, from another intelligent species, reaching out, and they would take it.

". . . we will not be Earth's slaves!"

"They're cutting their own throats, seceding," Pat said, aghast.

Todd told him morosely, "No, they've had Earth First's knife at their throats for nearly five years, ever since they started the torus. They're just finally turning it around and using it on their attackers."

". . . of Earth, your leaders have lied to you," Kevin McKelvey said. The cameras zoomed in on him. It wasn't ComLink's good signal, but it was strong and bright, conveying McKelvey's determination. He didn't have Pat's stage presence or voice, but he epitomized Goddard's spirit. An equitable team. "We don't want to be your enemy. We want to be your friend. And we can offer you the future. On this date, February 15, 2041, we establish the full and irrevocable independence of Goddard Colony and Lunar City."

CHAPTER TWENTY

☆☆☆☆☆☆☆☆☆

SAUNDER = SURVIVAL

THE Chaos had been reborn in the subterranean apartments. Todd's contact with Dian fed to Ames and Fairchild and all the others in the Spacer underground. They had been waiting, hoping, and now, on Pat's orders, the security barriers were down. Strangers, people Todd didn't know, had been admitted to SE Mainland HQ and ushered into the command center. One by one, they were assuring Pat of their support and patience—*if* he did something to stop the madness looming over them all.

More orders going out. Aides and bodyguards running to and fro. A steady update from Carissa's doctors on her delicate state. Holding, so far. Just like the impossible tension between Earth and its first space station. People shouting at each other or whispering together. Former enemies and political opponents uniting in panic. Fairchild coming in, taking Pat's hand in her bony one, praising him for his courage.

She knew. The entire world didn't yet know. But Fairchild knew, was giving Pat a chance to repair the damage, rather than capitalizing on his tragedy to the benefit of her Third Millennium Movement. She acknowledged his superiority as an orator, as a favorite of humanity, and sacrificed.

They were all doing that, or trying to. Again and again, Jael came on the com, insisting that Pat make her the scapegoat. He kept brushing her aside impatiently, too busy to argue. Then, once, sharply, he said, "It'll probably come to that, Mother. I advise you to stay put at Saunderhome. I have more clout than Galbraith and the others, and I've got certain troops watching you right now. When I'm through at Protectors of Earth, we're going to talk about this and figure out just what you and I have to do to appease the world."

Abruptly, Jael broke the connection. Pat scowled, running his hands through his hair, looking around. Todd was standing in the corner, watching. The dreaded confrontation had taken place. He had caused it. Caused all this panic—just as he had caused, indirectly, the panic resulting from the Project Search announcement.

"Kid?" Todd came up out of his dazed shock. Pat was pointing at the screen where Jael's image had been. "Can you shut her off? Bottle her up? Pull the telecom plug on her? I've got so damned much to try to say—I can't afford to have Mother butting in now, of all times." More to it than that. He couldn't afford to have Jael, the dowager queen, reaching out from Saunderhome with telecom lines, calling on her assassins, on the hidden people who owed her, worsening the crisis with her meddling.

"I'm warning you, Todd . . ."

And her eyes had warned Pat, during that call. Obey Mother. Toe the line. Or . . .

Jael Hartman Saunder had her own warped plans for the future, still hoped to carry them out, with or without her children's cooperation.

"I'll try," Todd said breathlessly. "I can control ComLink, sure. The thing is, she's probably put in alternate sources. Do *you* know how much she's added on in that defensive wall around the island?" Morosely, Pat shook his head. "Convoluted. That's what this all is, what *she* is."

"Then I'll be that way, too, if I must. Like Mother, like son." Pat's chuckle was acid. The strangers and his aides were crowding in, all demanding his attention, each one with a political damage report, in effect. Pat attempted to handle a dozen conversations at once. "You contacted Li Chu? Okay. At least that much is straight. She's with us? Well, you make plain I've got to have the full assembly. Everybody. Todd will give me global and Goddard—"

"I don't know if I can get through to Goddard with ComLink,"

Todd warned. "Even with the military helping us." He saw the
look on Pat's face. "I'll do my damnedest. Just pray they listen."

"Mari will. She's never been vindictive. We'll need to—" Pat
suddenly was riveted by a report coming over a nearby monitor.
Readouts were rippling across it. Todd was too far away and at
the wrong angle, unable to see it. Pat's reaction was awesome. He
grabbed a chair and hurled it at the screen. Plasticene and circuitry showered the room and its occupants, sparks flying, as Pat
raged. "Those goddamned stupid . . . Todd? Galbraith's gone
underground, and Weng's executing half his country in the worst
purge since . . . they're hooking up with Riccardi's people to—"

He rushed toward Todd, gripping his biceps, shaking his
brother in his agitation. They faced each other across the years,
love and blood canceling the jealousies, the differences.

"Goddard. *And* Earth targets!" Todd said. "The last gamble.
To take out all their opponents. You're one, too, if you tell what's
been going on in the Enclave and with Saunder Enterprises . . ."
Todd was stricken for Pat's sake.

"But I'm going to. Nothing's going to stop me." Again Todd
saw that glint of martyrdom shining in those fathomless pale eyes.
"You know, something Dian said . . . she's right. We really *are*
primitives, aren't we, kid? Toddlers. Infants. Barely able to stand
on our feet, and we're trying to kill one another."

Around them, a dozen monitors chattered, whispered conversations went on. The broken terminal sizzled and popped, dying.
But for a moment, Todd and Pat were utterly alone. Pat took a
long breath. "I want my child to see that future you and Dian and
Mari have been talking about, Todd. I'm going to make it happen. And to do that, I need help. I hate to ask it of you, after all
I've done, all Mother's done . . ."

"Goddard," Todd said, nodding, understanding. He was afraid.
And yet pride filled him, thickened his throat with unshed tears.
His leg hurt. He still felt bruised from the rough handling the
P.O.E. enforcement troopers had dealt out rescuing him. He was
tired to the bone. But all that dropped into the background, like
the monitor chatter and the conversations. Unimportant, physical
white noise. Energy surged back into his exhausted limbs and
mind. He stood up very straight, looking Pat in the eye.

"Can you get through to them? Hell, you're probably the *only* one who can, now. The only one McKelvey might trust."

"Not on the com. He knows what can be done with a translator-splitter." Pat blinked. The idea had never occurred to him. Todd wished it hadn't occurred to *him*. No other way. "I'll go. I don't think they'll turn me back."

He didn't mention the other possibility—they might shoot him out of space before he could reach the Colony. Why should they trust anyone, after what had happened?

"Tell Mari . . . tell that blond maniac . . . tell them . . ." Pat bowed his head. "Tell them the truth, if they haven't heard it. And beg them to give me a chance. I'm going to stop Weng and Ybarra and the other anti-Spacers. It'll take time. I know that much about vectors and missile launchings. Ames and the other military who defected—no!—who stayed loyal to keep humanity alive, pinpointing the missiles the conspirators still have up there. Trying to disarm. Time. Beg for time, kid. Please. It's got to stop here, all the evil I've done."

"No, not you. Mother, loving too much and in the wrong way. And the tyrants who won't give up their power," Todd comforted him, hugging him, both of them tormented with the shame Jael had brought upon them.

"I let her. I knew it, subconsciously. None of this would have happened if I hadn't . . . people *trusted* me, Todd! I promised them! Promised *you* . . . one more promise. What do you need?"

Uniting. Together against the other kids in the crater towns.

We Saunders are the best.

"An escort that'll get me out into space in one piece." Todd saw one of the strangers, a woman in military garb, smiling cryptically, nodding, giving him an okay-and-ready sign. One of Ames's allies? Another Protector of Earth officer who hadn't swallowed the anti-Spacer propaganda? "SE Trans Co shares a heavy lifter with P.O.E. Enforcement. I'll need that. It's probably at New York-Philly Terminal. God knows I haven't got time to try to get to one of *my* shuttles in Orleans or Nairobi. After that . . ."

"Galbraith," Pat was muttering, distracted. "That power-hungry . . . all of them! And to think I let them, right under my nose. Under Saunder Enterprises' cover! God, kid, don't get yourself killed because of this!"

"That goes for us both." Todd forced his brother to look at him. "The backlash from your speech is bound to be terrible."

"I deserve it. I'll take it. But I'm not giving up. Not ever. Oh, Mari . . . !"

"Goddard's defense-capable, Pat. They'll make it. *She'll* make it."

"Ask her to forgive me. She was telling the truth and I wouldn't listen," Pat said. "I learn slow. But I learn forever."

Awkwardly, shaking with wildfire emotions, they embraced again, then exchanged one final look. Each was acutely aware of the abyss awaiting the other, and awaiting Earth. Then Todd ran out the door, the uniformed woman and other guards and P.O.E. troopers galloping along with him.

Forever, to get the elevator upstairs to the vehicle park, then up to the roof.

Forever, to get Pat's fastest flier airborne. One of his military-style craft. The woman, Ames's ally, piloted. She was good, as reckless and skilled as Mariette Saunder, better at handling the craft than Todd could ever be. He resented his amateur status and the advanced equipment encasing him. Supercargo. But he was the most important supercargo these troopers would ever transport.

He made the necessary calls from the air, en route to the space terminal. Dian. Mikhail. Relay. Shut off Jael. Button up Com-Link tight. It was Pat's package, to carry his words to all the world. The whole system in top gear. All translator-splitters full function. Make the world believe. Choke off the plunge toward disaster before it could carry through on its desperate plan.

Taking forever to get to the terminal. The ship was set, but they had to gear up, program. You couldn't operate a heavy orbital vehicle as you did a private flier.

The alien messenger, creeping across the astronomical units in a leisurely approach to Earth, on cosmic terms. Its electronic hand was out in greeting. Kusta. Talk, Earth. I am the Vahnaj messenger. I will talk to you.

For it, time was not of the essence. It had been traveling a very long while, in all probability. For Todd Saunder, straining to reach a space station at L5, time was a brutal enemy. He was racing the conspirators and the paranoia generated by Patrick Saunder's speeches.

Earth First must rule.

But Earth First Party *was* Pat Saunder. And Pat Saunder was, at this moment, on his way to a podium at Protectors of Earth assembly, to ComLink's visual and audial window to the world. And Pat Saunder was going to cancel every item on the Earth First Party platform, everything Jael Saunder had done in the campaign to make her son ruler of Earth.

Forever.

Ninety minutes to establish basic orbit. To link up with an IOTV. The suit systems couldn't keep Todd's sweat and shivering under control. He squirmed inside his protective gear and swam on his tether, in free fall once more, heading down a shining tunnel into another ship in parking orbit.

Not his ship. Military. Todd protested, saying Goddard would deem them hostiles. Their arguments overrode his. Faster than anything he owned. As fast as the Goddard Defense Units. The fastest ships humanity had yet flung into space. He had to concede.

Listen to me on the com, Mari. It's me. I'm on board, just as I was with Gib. This ship, these people with me—friends. We want to help you. Don't shoot!

The launch from parking orbit drove most of the breath from him, slamming him into the couch, reddening his vision near blackout. Had he sweated an expensive burn on his little IOTV shuttle? This ship had many times the power, and nobody was counting the fuel expenditure at all. They were a meteor *leaving* Earth. Climbing, climbing, across orbits, rising, velocity impossible. One-quarter gravity, up to one-half gravity, the screens yowling, warning of the stresses on the ship.

Above the point where the tyrants had built their missiles, now. Masking them with holo-modes, like the false cubicles and their occupants, like the trees outside the Spacer hangar.

Ward Saunder had shared his genius with the world. How he

would have alternately marveled at and raged against the uses to which they had put his work!

How many missiles had hit Goddard? How many were still hidden in orbit, ready for follow-up strikes? How soon could McKelvey's underground on Earth find them and disarm them? And if *more* were being built? It was a race. A long one. Distance, on Earth, could be reduced to a handspan by modern transport. In space, Todd Saunder still needed light-year boots to get where he was going fast.

Pat's speech, coming up on the com. Delayed basis. They were far enough out that the signal was starting to show an infinitesimal lag between the time it left Earth and the time it arrived on the ship's screens.

"Listeners, I have many things to tell you. I have made promises. I believed I could keep them. I still want to keep them. But I've learned that I have been lying to you. I didn't know I was, yet that is what has happened. Earth First Party members, acting in my name, out of good and evil motives, have done terrible things. I am here tonight to tell you about them. And perhaps the worst of all is the lie about Saunder Enterprises Antarctic Enclave. The heritage of Earth's tomorrow. The thousands sleeping there, awaiting the future. Many of them will never wake. I have killed them. People acting in my name have killed them, Listeners, and I must take full responsibility . . ."

Bleary-eyed, too anguished to weep, Todd watched him confess to the billions. And on another circuit, he continued to send out the call to Goddard, trying again and again to reach Mari. Blackout. If they were receiving—and they must be—they were refusing to answer him.

". . . payments made. Decisions to turn off the machines and kill the helpless people within the cubicles. I am sorry. I can never bring them back. I can only offer myself, my life, to atone. And I can bring to light the hideous mockery these people have committed in secret!"

Patrick Saunder. All the nuances of that voice, all the power of that presence. Thousands of kilometers away, yet beside Todd in the spaceship hurtling up toward Goddard.

The vain adolescent, posturing in front of a mirror, running his hand through his hair, turning his left profile—his best one—to his non-existent audience. He had learned to use those striking, hypnotic eyes, to hold his own gaze, as he now held the gaze of an entire planet.

Was there anybody down there who wasn't watching him, hearing him? Yes, there were probably those who were still working, scrabbling, even as he spoke, to commit still more crimes before Patrick Saunder might turn the tide of world opinion against them and drown them in the flood of revulsion.

He could do it, if anyone could.

Most important of all, was Goddard listening to him? Missiles poised to counterstrike, Mari *must* listen.

The speech went on. All of it. Everything Todd had relayed from Fairchild and Ames and his own digging into the dark, putrid underlayer of Saunder Enterprises and those who had paid them to kill. The power dealings to gain votes. The swaps of property and slaves to make the Saunders secure and fat. The quasi-nation that had become a world-gobbling monopoly in critical fields.

"Mari, please answer me," Todd pleaded into the com.

"Signal incoming, sir. Masked. I think it's Goddard," one of the crew said.

Todd woke out of frightened speculations. "I thought . . ."

"Breaking silence."

No picture. Either Goddard wouldn't send one, or the mask was so strong it wouldn't allow images to penetrate. Mari's disembodied voice, concerned, reaching out for Todd. "We hear him. Dian relayed us the tapes."

"Okay! He means it, Mari. He really means it. All of it. Give us a chance!"

"The missile strikes . . ."

He ignored the regs, talking over her com. "The Spacers are trying to disarm. You know that. Your agents, Fairchild's people —give them time. You've got to . . ."

A long pause, static-filled. "We read you, Earth ship." Mari, but sounding cold.

"I'm aboard, Mari. If you shoot us down, you take me out, too."

One of the crew interrupted. "Sir, tell your sister . . . tell McKelvey that we won't return fire if they hit us. Our armament won't be used against them. We're Spacers. We volunteered." Todd swiveled his head awkwardly, helmet still togged down, staring at them one by one. The Goddard isolation syndrome. Shuttle pilots and crewmen. They had known the risks when they took Todd aboard. Known his mission. Even if they survived to Goddard, there was still the chance the war would continue and they would be interned for months or years or the rest of their lives, people in limbo, citizens of Earth trapped on an independent Colony planning to go on out to Mars, not stay with Earth.

He did as they asked. Another long silence. This one wasn't broken. The signal was there, still heavily masked. But Mari didn't come back on the system to talk to him. There was no way of knowing if she believed Pat, believed him.

Pat's speech ended. It had been a long one, breaking all Pat Saunder's rules about leaving an audience before they got bored. Todd doubted anyone had been bored by this speech, despite its length. Pat had an awful lot to say, a whole lifetime of guilt to lay before them.

No adjournment to the V.I.P. lounge and the eyes of admiring colleagues and laudatory ComLink interviewers this time. The trial of Pat Saunder and Saunder Enterprises, accused of collusion in the murder of thousands in Antarctica, among other crimes, was beginning. The lenses stayed with Protectors of Earth assembly. Feedback—hostile, outraged, murderous—pouring in from ComLink's systems on day and night sides of the planet. The procedure was going to last for hours, it was plain. Night, where Pat was, and it would be day before this session ended, perhaps another night and day from now. Not until he was freed. He was never, really, going to be freed. He had clamped the guilty man's manacles on his own wrists.

Todd had to sleep. His systems refused to operate any longer. The screens glimmering, propulsion still coming on intermittently, pushing them to the acceleration limits, the soft, conducting-business murmur of the crew. Mari wouldn't come back on the

line. And Pat wouldn't be able to. The would-be Chairman of
P.O.E., his power still intact but his reputation in ruins, was en-
during hell, verbally, accepting it, his chosen martyr's role.
Lulled, helpless to do anything, suspended between Goddard and
Earth, Todd floated into dreams.

He awoke to monitors' excited jabbering.

Missiles. Launched. From Earth parking orbit. And Goddard?

"Still holding, sir," a crewman said. They were tracking the
deadly climbers below. "Masked. We just penetrated the screen.
Goddard's picking them up, too. They're about half an hour or
less below us. I make it about seven of them . . ."

Todd was past being scared. The whole arsenal. One last gamble. And he was riding ahead of it.

"We'll put you at Goddard if we can, Mr. Saunder. Then we'll
join their units and help them fight, if we can."

"Fight them from here," Todd said with sudden decisiveness.
"Look, you're maybe closer to them than the Defense Units . . ."

Their smiles were tolerant. "You're a civilian, sir. And what
you can do at Goddard is a hell of a lot more important than you
could do getting vaporized in orbit with us. Hang on . . ."

He didn't think it was possible for them to squeeze any more
power out of the systems. They did. Numbers spinning wildly.
Yet the ETA was a million kilometers away. He wanted to flog
them to still more speed, get himself off the ship, free them to
fight—free himself to convince Mari and Kevin.

Dian, safe planetside. Ames had promised.

Pat had promised, too, so much. And Pat hadn't been able to
fulfill those promises, thanks to Jael.

They rose ahead of the hostiles. Being shadowed. Again. Half
hours and hours ticking, even at full power. Todd made wistful
jokes about an improved ion drive and a Mars trip. The crew
winced. They wanted such a system *now*. They pushed their own
still more.

They barely made it.

Goddard fighters, Lunar City fighters—a lot of them coming
out, patrolling and heading down. Todd braced himself, seeing
the blips approaching. It looked very much like a collision
course. He waited for the red streaks to lace toward him, convert
him and the swift shuttle into molecules and tiny bits of debris.

The explosion didn't come.

They had heard! They accepted! At least this much! The shuttle was going to be allowed past. At speeds that Todd couldn't believe, they flashed inside the moving cordon of fighters, and another, larger blip began to form in the monitors. Goddard Colony, dead ahead. The shuttle decelerated, trying to bring all that tremendous velocity back under control, lest they become another form of missile.

Section Four had been hit again, Todd saw when they reached eyeball status. Not taken out completely, but hurt. And Section Three, too, was damaged. One of the orbiting attendant shacks was abandoned, a shattered hulk. Some missile had come in slightly off vector. It hadn't nailed Goddard, but had gotten one of its workshop suburbs.

Docking grabbed them, Traffic somehow coping with the shuttle's speed and nearly ramming it into the berth at the Hub. Todd was out of his safety webbing and clawing his way into the tunnel before the craft had fully engaged. Guards met him at the air lock, studying him a long minute, their weapons leveled.

Then Mari was there. Not closing with him. Not touching. Looking at him. "No weapons on me, Mari. The ship could have fired at you, coming in. The crew are with you. Give them a chance to help. They'll give you the ship if you demand it. But it's theirs. You know these people. They've carried Goddard Power Sats' products before. Spacers. Fuel them. Let them fight those missiles."

He was afraid his plea was in vain. Mari could order the guards to drag him and the crew off to Goddard's version of the brig. Would she? She was talking into her suit com, blocking him from hearing her. He read Kevin's name on her lips. Conferring? Telling Kevin what he had said? The guards were listening. Another exchange, again masked from Todd.

Then, behind him, he heard the noises of refueling apparatus connecting. Unexpectedly, the com mask was gone. ". . . turn around in six minutes. Give us your guidance key. We will direct. You are hereby deputized into the Goddard Defense Units."

They were accepting the offer of the crew! They couldn't afford to waste the ship. But it was a miraculous concession that they would trust this crew, even if they were fellow Spacers.

Mari swung her arm slowly, adapting to the null gravity. "Come on."

Command center was at the Hub, behind one of those doors Todd had been barred from entering the last time he had been to Goddard. The place was like the hangar, like Pat's subterranean control center, but even more concerned with survival and military efficiency. Goddard had had all too much experience with defense lately. And were they now going to get experience in offense as well?

Lunar Base's military capabilities. Correction: Lunar *City's*. Deserters. Revolutionaries. Kevin looked as if he had been on his feet for days. Leaning over his trackers' shoulders, coordinating, keeping them alive. The governor, but also the man at Goddard with the most training in exactly this sort of deadly game, and the people manning the systems looked to him for leadership. He couldn't afford to sleep, any more than Goddard could afford to let the shuttle sit idle.

"More incoming, Governor. They're going to try to get us good this time." Trackers picking out the distant blips amid a horde of defenders. Somewhere another monitor was showing a huge blip, the shuttle, moving out of docking and swinging around for a plunge back down from L5 toward the intruders.

"This is McKelvey," Kevin was saying to the Defense Units. "Don't take any chances. We don't need any pieces any more. Blow them to hell. We know who our enemies are now."

He glanced up, at Todd. No hatred in his rugged face. Trust. *We trust you. Or you wouldn't be here.*

"Mari . . ." Todd reached out, caught her hand. Gloves between them. But she was there, and she didn't pull away from him. They floated at the end of their tethers, looking at each other through their faceplates. "Pat did it. You heard it."

"He's lied before. Is this a campaign trick?"

"No! Mari, Kevin, believe him."

"Quadrant five . . . !"

Screens flashed. Impact, out there. A missile? Or one of Goddard's gallant Defense Units?

"One getting through, Commander—brace!"

The air seemed to boil. Concussion wave, Todd cataloged as he and Mari bobbed about helplessly, clinging to each other. Techs

struggling for handholds on their tethers and stanchions, screaming orders and calls for Damage Control into their monitors and
suit coms. "Rode him out!" McKelvey exulted. "Now get the next
bastard!"

"Secondary, incoming!"

Todd hung onto Mari and the guide rails. Another shock, the
command center's power flickering. Somewhere, transmitted
through the incredible immensity of the torus, a groaning, ripping
sound.

"Damn!" McKelvey shouted. He managed to drag himself back
toward the fire-control screens. "Hit them! Stop them! Everything! No reserve!" His breath rattled hoarsely in the com circuitry coming into Todd's helmet. No masking devices shutting
Todd out. He was part of it, like it or not. He had wanted to be
in. He was, and a target along with everyone else at Goddard.
Kevin shook his head, the helmet waggling. "Prepare to arm our
offensive orbiters . . ."

"No! You can't!" Todd yelled. He fought his way toward the
man. Security blocked him, then moved aside as Kevin jerked a
gloved hand. "This is the last wave, Kevin. Your agents have to
have told you. You got Riccardi. Protectors of Earth is finally
moving . . ." Todd pointed frantically at one monitor. ComLink.
P.O.E. assembly. Voting. Pulling the plug on a dozen tyrants and
generals and top-level payoff experts who had ruined the promise
of Saunder Enterprises Antarctic Enclave. It was daytime in that
hemisphere now. Hours had passed. A lot was being done—
finally. Months too late. Time gap. Acting against Todd. Com lag
into space. Missile launch time to reach target. If McKelvey acted
to strike back, the missiles could hit even after the criminals had
been caught and punished. And the war would start anew and engulf them all.

"Com!" a tech shouted. "Earth. Incoming through ComLink
Geosynch HQ, top priority. For you, Todd Saunder."

Todd dived toward the monitor the woman was indicating.
"Pat? Is that you?"

Static. Scramblers? Overrides? Clearing.

Carissa's face loomed out of the blizzard. Todd goggled in
amazement. She was the last person he expected to use that priority privilege. He hadn't realized she was even aware of the circuit

or of her right to use it. The time lapse figured in again, maddeningly. She took an eternity to respond to his stunned "Carissa? What the hell?"

"Just got off com . . . Jael . . ." Carissa was panting, excited. The baby, Todd thought, then flung the worry aside. A world to worry about.

"Where's Pat?"

"Heading . . . Saunderhome . . . P.O.E. arrest escort." Static as well as Carissa's excited manner interfered with the words. "Going to . . . custody of Jael. Agreed to . . . public hearing . . ."

Behind Todd, Mari was saying, "She'll buy her way out, even if Pat won't. You know she will. She'll get out of it. She holds credit on too many people. They'll never make her pay."

"Oh, Todd, they crucified him . . . terrible . . ." Carissa wailed.

Todd groaned. "I know. They had to. It's what Pat had to do, 'Rissa. He'll be okay."

"Jael . . ." Through the rotten signal. Todd felt the ominous note in Carissa's little-girl voice. "Jael called . . . with . . . instructions. Legal. Trust funds for me and the baby . . . mustn't depend on Pat . . . consult Eli firm regent clause in Pat's will . . . Jael said I must . . . guarantee . . . could be tangle if . . . happened to Pat."

The space station rocked from another concussive wave. Techs poised expectantly at their station, awaiting the orders to arm Goddard's own missiles. There could be a whole deadly ring of them in lower orbit, ready to fire. A chance to get even and continue the madness. They waited. The order didn't come. McKelvey was listening to Carissa.

Todd hung onto the com console so tightly he thought his fingers would break. "Pat? I've got to talk to him. Goddammit. 'Rissa, clear the line! Dian? Mikhail? Somebody! Put me through to Pat as fast as possible."

A strong, feminine voice, United Ghetto States accent, broke in. "Working. Got it. You're through, Todd."

"Love you, Dian."

Carissa was still with him, butting in. "I told you, Todd. That was the right thing to do, wasn't it? Todd, you promised you'd give him a chance to—"

Ruthlessly, Todd cut her off. "Pat? Cut out the override, Dian. Tap those military types. Tell them I've got to get past that arrest escort's com and talk to my brother. It's vital. Pat? *Answer me . . ."*

A picture! Terrible. Solarizing. Riddled with interference. Pat. Todd sagged with relief, as much as he could in free fall. He hastily read the military confirms with ERS and Navstar. Pat was in CNAU's Caribbean sector, off the Keys, heading east by southeast, closing fast with Saunderhome. Going to arrest his own mother, as acting officer of Protectors of Earth.

He looked awful. Carissa's words, "They crucified him," seemed no exaggeration. Pat Saunder was a man who had been flogged, cut down from a cross, and disemboweled emotionally.

Other screens flashed and flickered. Other defense tactics. Other missiles being triggered to self-destruct. Todd glanced at McKelvey. The techs were holding their breath. Missiles, trying to rip open the station's guts and kill its people. Strike-center screens jumped. Damage Control was pouring in reports of casualties. McKelvey said, "Hold. Use the fighters. Check for more hostile blips before we launch." Doubt and consternation on his techs' faces. But they obeyed.

Another hit. The room tumbled around Todd. Several screens gave way and a bulkhead seeped air. For a few minutes, there was wild confusion. Todd felt his suit ballooning. Puncture! Damage was beside him, scanning, slapping sealant on his shoulder. Somewhere, a tech was screaming in death agony. A call for medics was going out. Todd pulled himself back to the screen with Pat's face. Incredibly, Pat's staticky image was still there. "Kid? Mari? My God! Are you there?"

It was Todd's own heart-stopped plea of moments before, returned to him with frantic love. Mari was there. So was McKelvey. A monitor voice was reciting dispassionately, "Thirty-four dead, ninety-six casualties . . ."

On the blurry image, Pat's face drained of blood. "Todd, they can't hit back. Let them hit me, but not Earth. It's over. No more launches . . ."

Todd broke through. "Jael's making your will, Pat. She's not going to let you repair all the damage."

Technicolor streaks danced across the screen. Chatter. Military

talk. The arrest escort. Firing. Dogfight in progress. Pat's co-pilot
was a ghostly face, dimly seen behind Pat, the whites of the man's
eyes showing.

"You noticed, kid? She sabotaged my plane, too. How the hell
did . . . she always did pay for the best." He paused, apparently
listening to someone out of frame or to another communication
on his intercom. Then the already-erratic picture tore up completely for a moment as a near-miss rocked Pat's ship. When the
image steadied out once more, Pat was smiling, a smile that
terrified Todd. Very calmly, sounding amused, Pat said, "The
very best. We seem to be carrying the nastiest bomb Galbraith's
war suppliers make. Interesting, huh, kid? And it's rigged so well
we can't get rid of it, looks like." Pat's awful smile widened in
grim appreciation of his no-win situation. "My people have managed to disengage the timer. But that's the best we can do. When
they booby-trapped this baby, they made sure I'd never put her
down intact. Neat. Mother plans for me to go out in style, with a
glorious fireworks display."

Amid the bloody chaos in Goddard command center, people
heard him and stared at the screen in shock. On other screens,
the only blips were the surviving Goddard Defense Units. Losses
and hits totaled on the registers. No counterlaunch from the habitat yet, but trigger fingers poised over the switches. If McKelvey
would just continue to hold his fire . . . ! No more deaths!

And death was very much on Todd's mind. He tried to wish
Pat's words away. "She can't . . ."

"She has. Haven't you, Mother? Take a look, kid. She wants
me out of the setup entirely, so she can rule the roost the way she
used to. But it's not going to work out that way." Todd sensed the
steely resolve behind Pat's deceptively serene tone and shivered.

The screen, splitting, showing Jael in a frame beside her eldest.
Calm. As calm as Pat. She was still sitting at the desk. But outside the window the lovely land- and sea-scape was shattered by
red streaks and explosions. The dogfight, coming home to her.
Todd thought of the servants, of the innocent people living on the
island. More "regrettable accidents" in Jael's final grab for power.
Jael was going to take them, and Pat, with her. She peered out at
Todd, in the space station hundreds of thousands of kilometers
away, and at Pat, homing in on her at deadly speed. "I'm sorry

about this. You should have done it my way. I do love you. I love you all . . ."

"And if *you* can't take charge of my child, neither will I, is that it, Mother?" Pat shook his head. "You thought 'Rissa would be your little toady, safe under your thumb. My baby, too."

Todd heard the crackle of the energy bolts around them. Each contact with Pat or Jael was delayed by nearly a second. The rule of communications in space. He might as well have been at Saturn's orbit, listening to this as the alien messenger was.

"ETA three minutes, Mother." Pat turned, talking to someone in his ship. "I thought so. Can't eject. Sorry. I guess you'll ride it in with me. One last ride to earn your pay . . ."

"Patrick," Jael began.

"Roy's with Carissa. He's good with her. He'll take care of her. He and Todd. He died once for this family; no need for Roy to be hurt again."

But Roy *would* be hurt. So would they all, helplessly listening.

"I've got all the barriers up, Patrick," Jael said. "You won't get through."

"I'm a missile. You made me into one. And our fighters have knocked each other out. I'm all alone now, Mother, and your barrier fire teams are gone. You can't stop me and I can't land. So I suppose there's only one way to finish this off." He laughed. "Two minutes and closing. How's that, kid? Just like a vid drama. Or did they ever do that, even on those? I've got the ship now. I'll fly her in, just like we used to. Remember, brat? Are you there, Mari?"

Mariette touched her helmet com, connecting in. "I'm listening. Oh, Pat!"

"Don't cry. Mother knows best. I can see the island, kids. Shot to hell. It's not beautiful any more. The bridges are gone. The hurricane walls are broken, Jael. So much for all those fancy deterrents we installed." The strange smile slid off his handsome face. "My kid's not going to grow up in a world where Jael Hartman Saunder kills to gain power over the Earth."

"I'm sorry, Patrick," Jael said. Dry-eyed. No anger. A bit of regret.

"Fifteen seconds. Once-in-a-lifetime ride, Todd, Mari. Right in over the trees. Take care . . ."

"Patrick . . ." Jael was pursing her lips, chiding him, as she had when he was a boy and had been naughty.

The screen went blank.

They had been dead for several seconds when that happened. Gone. Both of them. And everyone else at Saunderhome. The mansion, the observation tower where Ward and Todd had played with inventions and gazed out at the tropical seas, the white beach where Todd and Dian had made love, the bubble-domed arena where Ward Saunder lived each year, for a while, on the anniversary of his birth—gone before the knowledge of the fact could reach Todd Saunder's eyes and brain.

Todd knew nothing. He had never been anywhere else. He had always been slumped over a monitor screen in Goddard's command center, his throat raw from suppressed screaming. He had no tears. He was empty.

After ages, he sensed a heavy, consoling touch on his shoulder. He turned and blinked. McKelvey. Kevin's gaze was agony. Mari was beside him, holding him, weeping behind her faceplate. "There aren't any more blips," Kevin said. "We'll hold our offensive launches. As long as necessary. We'll give the new people at Protectors of Earth a chance. Pat deserves that. Pat Saunder paid for it . . . the highest price anyone could ask."

CHAPTER TWENTY-ONE

☆☆☆☆☆☆☆☆☆

FULL INTERFACE: BEGIN

"Retro braking, two-second burn."

Todd gripped the safety hold, riding it out. Delicate adjustments on the ship's forward course. Good. They couldn't afford to overrun the vehicle waiting ahead in lunar parking orbit. McKelvey's pilots handled the big ship well. They were every bit as skilled as Kevin and Mari had bragged they were. Spacers. Pilots who had earned their experience moving craft between Earth, the Moon, Goddard, and mass driver nets. Now they brought the Earth-Goddard Science Council ship into line with a small messenger from beyond the Solar System.

Scientists shifted restlessly in their couches, eager to make contact. They had fought hard for berths on this ship, the first one to touch the alien machine. They had come from Earth and the Moon and the space station, proud of being selected. There were those who hadn't had to fight, who had received their tickets through unanimous acknowledgment of their achievements, efforts which had made all this possible. Dr. Dian Foix, Chief Tech Beth Isaacs, Tech Anaya, Todd Saunder . . .

Beth was seated to Dian's left. She was nodding, her eyes aglow. The scars were almost completely gone now, thanks to time and reconstructive surgery. Dian touched her colleague's hand, then smiled at Todd. "We're here. We made it."

He returned the smile, then looked at the ComLink view screen

before him. Signals from the vehicle ahead. And signals from
Earth, arriving simultaneously, even though the ones from Earth
had set forth minute seconds earlier than the alien's.

Global assembly of Protectors of Earth. The debate still went
on, though on a different plane. The paranoia hadn't completely
gone away. It couldn't, not until they knew a great deal more. A
million or more years of evolution built in the fear, the hesitation.
Another form of life, from another world. The child, looking
across a gulf of space, watching a messenger approach, excited
yet apprehensive.

A lot had happened in eight months. More changes, for a
planet bewildered by changes. Adjustments, learning, if not full
acceptance. And the woman on the podium had helped immeasur-
ably, astonishing those who had thought they knew what she was
like. Carissa Duryea Saunder. She didn't have her late husband's
wonderful voice, but she was beautiful, sweet-faced, an embodi-
ment of a new ideal—she and her tiny son. Roy Paige stood on the
podium beside her. He held a wide-eyed infant—Stuart Saunder,
who had never seen his father and never would, save via holo-
mode. General Ames was there, too. And many new, emergent
leaders who had come through the upheaval. Protectors of Earth
Chairman Fairchild was watching Carissa, approving. The Third
Millennium leader had provided just the calm, confident touch
Earth had needed during this crucial transition period. Carissa
had come under her wing, taking her own first steps into the public eye, as her baby would soon take his faltering initial strides
out into the world, and then into the universe.

". . . appreciate this honor you've given me. I will try to be
worthy of the trust. I know Patrick would have thanked you, too.
He wanted so to help you and make Earth a better place for us
all. In his memory, carrying forward the work he never had a
chance to finish, we will become part of a greater community, one
that reaches to the farthest stars."

A lot of humanity didn't want that yet. Shrank from the concept. But they were following, letting themselves be soothed and
persuaded. Trusting, once more. They had lived through the moment when Goddard held them in the palm of its hands, when the
tyrants nearly set loose extinction upon the planet and its Moon.
Now Carissa Duryea Saunder and the people on the stage prom-

ised they would take care of them, heal the lingering wounds, smooth the path to meeting the aliens. Belief, held in Carissa's husky, trembling, endearing voice. No powerful timbre, no mesmerizing stare. Softer, subtler, Pat's lovely widow. The newest assembly member of Protectors of Earth. It looked as if her climb to genuine rank and power would be as swift as Patrick's had been, but with a happier ending.

Todd looked at Dian again, exchanging confidences without a word. Carissa had to win. Jael had called her, and Carissa had called Todd to tip him off. If Jael had triumphed, Carissa knew she would have been safe, anyway. She could have blamed her disloyalty to Jael on hormonal upsets, the stresses of pregnancy. And if Pat had won, she would have tried to protect him. They had both perished, and Carissa had risen from their ashes. Saunder Enterprises had suffered. Stripped of much of its property and wealth, strict new laws set upon the power it could control in the future. The Antarctic Enclave was under new management, among most other divisions which Patrick and Jael Saunder had commanded. Yet Carissa wasn't a poverty case. The Duryeas were wealthy, too, and she had salvaged a great deal from the wreckage of Pat's fortune and Jael's. Stuart Saunder was going to be a very pampered little boy.

And his future was going to be complicated by the vehicle dead ahead.

Maneuvering gently, carefully. Todd and Dian and the others watching on the monitors. For once, even though he wasn't piloting, Todd had a ringside seat, could watch the fun. Mari and Kevin sitting nearby, equally enthralled at the procedure.

The alien vehicle, hanging in orbit. They had explained to it what they wanted to do. Even this close to Earth, it had thought over the requests for a while and analyzed them. Then . . . yes. It had agreed. They had passed its tests. And it had the technology to set them a humbling array of tests. It had slowed itself precisely, taking up lunar orbit, waiting for them to come to it. An instructor from beyond Pluto.

Immense bay doors opening. Waldos and grapnels extending, touching, guiding the vehicle into the bay with exquisite patience. Nothing must be disturbed or damaged. Man's servants, inviting the alien machine—the aliens' servant—into mankind's parlor.

The vehicle wasn't designed for planetary landing. Another test of
the intelligence and technology of whatever species it might contact. That species—in this case, *Homo sapiens*—would have to
have the ability to come out into space, at least a short distance,
or the vehicle's gifts would be lost. Entering atmosphere, it would
disintegrate. Only in space could its secrets be unlocked.

Todd suited up with the rest, wondering if he looked as shaky
and thrilled as some of them did. This was going to happen only
once in all the history of mankind. And the potentials!

The locks sighed open and they entered the bay. The suits were
a precaution the scientists advised. For now, the vehicle was
being kept in a vacuum, all pressure systems designed to prevent
contamination. So much to learn, including whether man was
compatible with whatever organisms the alien might have brought
across space with it from its masters.

Scanners were already running, greedy, capturing the close-up
image of the spindly, cylindrical, spider-shaped craft.

So much like some of our own early space explorers, Todd
thought, fascinated. *It might be one more evidence that they're
like us.*

"They could be lying to us." Surprisingly, it was Mari who
voiced that suspicion. She had gotten over the worst of her resentment at having Goddard's explorative thunder stolen by the aliens. But she was wise enough to touch the risks involved in this
first contact. "It could tell us whatever its makers wanted it to.
The truth, or an illusion to put us off guard."

"Yes, it could," Todd agreed. Dian and McKelvey and the scientists were glancing at them, momentarily tearing themselves
away from looking at the place where the waldos were gingerly inviting the vehicle to open its inner workings. "We won't know
until we meet them face to face. If they're still alive."

Science had attempted to educate humanity, these past months.
During the frenzy caused by Earth First's old campaign, the
planetsiders had believed almost without question that the aliens
were alive, waiting to strike and to enslave or kill everyone on
Earth. Now, after months in which to calm down and listen—
without the interference of campaign rhetoric—other possibilities
were being spelled out to them. There could be another situation,
a poignant and disappointing one. Maybe the vehicle was the relic

of a vanished species. A lonely little messenger, cruising forever in search of neighbors for its masters who were now dead.

They didn't know. They wouldn't know, for months, years, decades.

"Faster-than-light drive?" McKelvey speculated, his eyes bright. Dian was shaking her head. "I doubt it. A damned good drive, but there'd be no need, not for a robot messenger."

"If only . . ." Mari's gloved hand closed into a claw, possessive. The same lust Kevin McKelvey had expressed was in her voice and on her face. Goddard wanted the stars, and it wanted them now, not generations from now.

"We'll have to wait and see what we find," Todd said softly. Patience. He had a lot of that now. Once he had wanted things to happen in a hurry, too. Pat's death and Jael's seemed to have burned that out of his soul. He felt older, but not weary. Willing to bide his time. It no longer seemed so important that all the discoveries be made during his own life. There would be a future for mankind now. If not Todd Saunder—or Ward Saunder—maybe it would be a Saunder yet unborn who would find out what lay beyond the Sun's family.

The long view. Ward would have approved. Live and do the best you can. But Ward Saunder had never been greedy. And his surviving son didn't intend to be, either.

The alien machine. Opening. Communicating. On the close-up monitors Todd saw the microscopic inspection of the vehicle's com systems and started. Not identical to his own ComLink satellite equipment. Yet he recognized certain shapes and connections, despite the alien alloys and features. For an instant, he thought of holo-modes. The vehicle, capable of . . . what? Creating an illusion to make them think they were seeing these things?

No need, he repeated to himself. Distance was the alien species' protection. Humanity was an infant. Not yet a threat to them. If humanity grew up, maybe it would never be a threat, to the aliens or to itself, ever again.

One of the screens was continuing the relay from Earth. Carissa's speech, over. A swelling of applause within Protectors of Earth's assembly, a storm of approving feedback from the watching audience around the world. Carissa moving to Roy

Paige, taking baby Stuart Saunder from him, cradling the infant in her arms, smiling to the world.

Through the pain of memories, Todd smiled back at her image. Dian was moving toward the vehicle, wanting to see it up close. He followed, one among the distinguished scientists, loyal Beth Isaacs, his sister, McKelvey, the techs, and Dian. People who had helped along the way—Fairchild, Ed Lutz, Dr. Tedesco, General Ames, countless others—would read and see what they found here, their minds reaching out into space.

Todd didn't hurry, didn't crowd. He had sponsored the search. His team had found it. He could wait. He stood back, gazing at the vehicle that had come across time and space an unknown distance to say hello to mankind.

Time and space, and Earth. The answers weren't going to be simple. They rarely were. But mankind would get them. And someday, Todd Saunder was going to shake hands with a living being from another species, as well as observe the unlocking of that species' robot messenger. Smiling, the smile becoming an optimistic grin, he teetered on his boots, leaning forward, as the *real* communication process finally began.

ABOUT THE AUTHOR

Juanita Coulson began writing at age eleven and has been pursuing this career off and on ever since. Her first professional sale, to a science-fiction magazine, came in 1963. Since then she has sold fifteen novels, several short stories, and such odds and ends as an article on "Wonder Woman" and a pamphlet on how to appreciate art.

When she isn't writing, she may be singing and/or composing songs; painting (several of her works have been sold for excessively modest prices); reading biographies or books dealing with abnormal psychology, earthquakes and volcanoes, history, astronomy—or almost anything that has printing on it; gardening in the summer and shivering in the winter.

Juanita is married to Buck Coulson, who is also a writer. She and her husband spend much of their spare time actively participating in science-fiction fandom: attending conventions and publishing their Hugo-winning fanzine, *Yandro*. They live in a rented farmhouse in northeastern Indiana, miles from any town you ever heard of; the house is slowly sinking into the swampy ground under the weight of the accumulated books, magazines, records, typewriters, and other paraphernalia crammed into it.